A gout of black fluid washed the deck, darker than blood; the tentacles writhed like a nest of snakes. One caught me across the stomach, flinging me back. Dazed and gasping, I stared up as the arms fell slack against me. Was that a patch of night sky through the fog?

Relief came in a wave. If the mist was clearing, that meant we were nearly safe out of the Margins. As I lay there, the beast slid off the stern, limp and liquid, and sank into the deep, and the ship rose in the water. Pushing myself to my knees, I sucked in a breath. Then I staggered to the rail, ready to pull Kashmir up from the ladder.

He was gone.

For a moment I couldn't make sense of it. I stared, stupidly, at the empty ladder, at the churning wake, at the thinning fog.

No.

No, no, no, no, no no no—

THE

SHIP

BEYOND

TIME

HEIDI HEILIG

Greenwillow Books, *An Imprint of* **HarperCollins***Publishers*

The Ship Beyond Time
Copyright © 2017 by Heidi Heilig

First published in hardcover in 2017; first paperback edition, 2018.
All rights reserved. No part of this book may be used or reproduced in any manner whatsoever without written permission except in the case of brief quotations embodied in critical articles and reviews. Printed in the United States of America. For information address HarperCollins Children's Books, a division of HarperCollins Publishers, 195 Broadway, New York, NY 10007.
www.epicreads.com

Map illustrations copyright © 2017 by Maxime Plasse (pp. 16-17, 110) and Ryan O'Rourke (pp. 30, 388)

The text of this book is set in Simoncini Garamond.
Book design by Sylvie Le Floc'h

Library of Congress Control Number: 2016962542
ISBN 978-0-06-238078-4 (trade ed.)—ISBN 978-0-06-238079-1 (pbk.)

18 19 20 21 22 PC/LSCH 10 9 8 7 6 5 4 3 2 1

Greenwillow Books

To my father, from whom I learned to love to read,
and to my mother, from whom I learned to love to write

CHAPTER
ONE

On a warm December day in 1884, the *Temptation* was leaving Hawaii, as well as the nineteenth century, and her destination was entirely in my hands.

At least, it was in my hands *metaphorically* speaking. Although I'd spent the entire morning poring over the maps in the captain's extensive collection, I hadn't yet been able to decide on a time and place for us to visit next. I always plotted our routes, and it didn't usually take so long. But today was different—today was special. Today, my father had finally weighed anchor on the past, and the future unrolled before me, vast as the Pacific.

It was a heady thought, even for a time traveler. Just yesterday, I hadn't been certain I had a future. But when Slate had renounced his quest to undo my mother's death—and thus, my own birth—the burden of an uncertain fate had lifted away. An infinite freedom had flooded in to take its place. I might go anywhere from here. The horizon was bright and boundless; there was nothing to hold me back. It was a thrilling luxury, and strange—endless choices, and all of them mine to make.

"Is that our next map, amira?" Kashmir's voice pulled me back to the present—Kashmir, the one thing I was certain about. He'd been watching me work, perched backward on the captain's chair. The breeze through the deadlights stirred in his dark curls; for a moment, my hands itched to brush them out of his eyes.

Instead, I ran my fingers over the surface of the tattered map I held. The Fastitocalon, the giant, mythical sea turtle that ancient mariners often mistook for an island—that is, until the moment it woke and dove under the waves, dragging foolish sailors down with it. "It's intriguing," I said with some regret, refolding the leather along the creases. "But much too mythological."

"Too mythological?" Kashmir laughed. "I never thought I'd hear you say that!"

"Well." I couldn't help it—I glanced back over my shoulder. Kashmir followed my gaze to the bunk. Blake Hart was still sleeping there, his face paler than usual; that was the blood loss. The young aristocrat from Honolulu had nearly died last night, taking a bullet meant for me. Thank all the gods for the healing spring. Blake's presence aboard the ship was a reminder that my choices had consequences—I had to temper my excitement with caution. "It's not just about me."

Before Kash could respond, the captain's voice floated in through the open door. *"Nixie?"*

At the foot of the bed, Billie the beagle lifted her head at my father's call, but I ignored the both of them in favor of the rolled parchments in the cupboards. Someplace more historical might be less alien to Blake—after all, he'd never before left Hawaii, much less his own timeline. Here, Paris at the fin-de-siècle. But wasn't that rather glitzy after nineteenth-century Honolulu? Not to mention drowning in absinthe and opium, which presented a different sort of danger. It was only this morning that the captain had thrown his box of pills and potions overboard. Best not to steer us back to that port. I slid the map back onto the shelf.

"Are you looking for someplace perfect?" There was humor in Kashmir's voice—it was an old joke between us.

"You know there's no such place. But—"

"Nixie!"

"Just a minute, Dad!" Turning back to the maps, thoughts

collided in my mind—France and artists and islands—ah, yes. The South Pacific, 1901. "Some places come close."

Kash stood to look over my shoulder—near enough that I could feel the warmth of his skin. I swallowed, trying to keep the map from trembling. It was a lovely one, labeled in French and decorated with a fanciful drawing of a kraken. No . . . I squinted. Wasn't there a Tahitian octopus demon? Rogo-Tumu-Here . . . that was him, there, his many arms wrapped around the compass rose.

"Not another island paradise!" Kashmir rolled his eyes, and I bit my lip. Though I knew he was only teasing, our time in Hawaii hadn't been spent lounging on balmy beaches under sunny skies. We'd been coaxed into an act of piracy there—a plot against the crown in exchange for the map my father needed. And in the fallout, we'd nearly lost the ship, the map . . . and each other. But that was all behind us now. In Tahiti, we could rest. Recover. And make new plans.

"Hopefully this version of paradise has fewer metaphorical serpents," I said at last.

"I suppose I can work on my tan there," Kashmir said, flexing his golden arms. "I hear it's the custom to pearl dive nude."

"Are you considering a career change?"

"You have to admit, the uniform is attractive." He

winked outrageously and I blushed, grinning. "And who knows?" he added then. "If I pick enough pearls, maybe we can afford our own ship someday."

"A ship?" I blinked at him. That had been our plan—to set out on our own, to point our prow toward the far horizon, steered by the winds of fate. That was only yesterday, before my father had set me free, before I'd known that he still needed me near. But the thought was no less tempting now. "Someday."

He raised an eyebrow. "Someday soon?"

"I hope so." My hand crept to the pearl pendant at my throat—the necklace Kashmir had given me. Kashmir, my best friend, my crewmate. Kash, whose green eyes were a mystery and whose lips, I had discovered quite recently, tasted of oranges.

Gently, I laid the map of Tahiti down on the drafting table. Were there oranges there, in the high valleys? But maybe I didn't need a map to find paradise. I turned back to Kashmir. He cocked his head, and then those lips curved into a smile. He was so close. All I had to do was take a breath and lean in—

"Nix!"

Kash and I sprang apart. My father was standing in the doorway, silhouetted against the sunlight. "What do you want, Slate?" I said, half exasperated, half grinning, but my smile slid away when he stepped into the cabin.

At first I thought he'd been crying—his eyes were wet, gleaming—but when I recognized the other signs, my stomach sank. His blond hair was damp and lank with sweat, and there was the slouch that signaled the ache in his shoulders. His broad hands, usually so sure on the wheel, were palsied with tremors that occasionally traveled all the way up his arms. Usually, at times like these, he would make a beeline for the box of opium that used to be under his bed.

Nervously, I smoothed the curling edges of the map. We were sailing into uncharted territory.

Beside me, Kash stood at attention, his expression bland, though his eyes were troubled. "Aye, Captain?"

Slate didn't spare him a look. "Did you hear me, Nix?" His voice was shockingly loud in the cabin. I shot a meaningful glance back toward Blake, but he hadn't stirred, and the captain didn't seem to notice. "Why didn't you answer?"

"I—I didn't have an answer until just now."

"Okay." He swiped his lips with the back of his hand, as though the word had left a residue. "Is it far?"

"French Tahiti. Only fifteen years from this timeline. Should be easy passage." I frowned at him as he approached the map with uneven steps. He'd never asked that before. "Why?"

"It's just a question!" Slate gripped the corners of the desk as he peered at the map. Sweat shone on his brow despite the cool trade winds blowing through the deadlights, and his pupils—black moons—eclipsed the icy blue of his eyes. "What?" he said, and I jumped. The edge in his voice was sharp, serrated. "Why are you staring at me?"

I opened my mouth, but what could I say? He'd gotten rid of the box for me too, and his symptoms were to be expected. This was only a minor obstacle on our way to a bright future. We would get through this, and on the other side, everything would be better.

Wouldn't it?

"Nothing, Captain."

After a long silence, he turned back to the map. "Get on deck, the both of you," he muttered, tapping his fingers on the edge of the drafting table. "There's a ship after us."

"What?"

"A ship! *A ship*, following, gaining, do you understand?"

"Yes, but . . . why?"

Slate scoffed at my question. "Don't tell me you've forgotten robbing the Royal Hawaiian treasury!"

"No." I took a deep breath, trying to maintain my calm,

reminding myself it was the pain that made him cruel. "But how would they know it was us? We used a different ship."

"Do you want to tell them that, if they ask to search us?"

"They wouldn't find anything. We haven't got the gold."

"We have the son of a known conspirator," Slate said, his lip curling. "Which is far less valuable, but just as damning."

I took a breath to make a retort—to defend Blake—but Kashmir stopped me with a gentle hand on my wrist. "Come, amira. Let's go see about that ship." I pressed my lips together and followed him outside.

Once on deck, I shaded my eyes against the tropical sun as I peered off the stern. The island of Oahu floated in the distance, a blossom atop the blue mirror of the sea. Between us and the faraway shore, a coal steamer purled black smoke from her funnel. I watched her, the wind in my face. It blew in our favor over the quarters, and we had broad reach, but the steamship was traveling at speed, and yes, it was gaining. Another obstacle, this one slightly bigger. I ground my teeth. "We can't let them catch us."

"If we need more speed, we can always throw the dead weight overboard," Kash said as he strode toward the mizzenmast.

I frowned; our hold was nearly empty. "What dead weight?"

"Mr. Hart comes to mind."

I made a face, grabbing for the halyard. Kash had been born a thief, and Blake a gentleman; they hadn't had much in common, and that was before Blake had tried to stop the treasury raid. "He saved my life, you know."

The laughter in Kashmir's eyes faded. "For that, I'll always be grateful."

Together, we loosened the sail to take better advantage of the wind. The mast creaked as the sail billowed, straining against the ropes, and the *Temptation* surged ahead. She was a fast ship—a caravel, lateen rigged—and her black hull cleaved the white waves like a shark's fin. Still the steamer gained. I could make out the figures on her deck now—men in dark blue jackets and gleaming white pith helmets. The uniform of the Royal Hawaiian Guard. As we dipped on the waves, the sun flashed off their long rifles.

"Can the captain Navigate with them so close?" Kashmir asked. "They'll see us disappear."

"They'll see us sail into the fog," I corrected.

"A rather sudden fog!"

"We don't have many options," I said, staring at the guns. A flag was running up their slender mast, flapping blue and gold against the black coal smoke . . . a semaphore signal.

Rotgut, in the crow's nest, sang out its meaning. "Kilo!"

Beside me, Kash frowned. "What's that one again?"

"They wish to communicate with us," I said crisply. He scoffed.

"If wishes were fishes, aquariums would be much more terrifying."

On the quarterdeck, Bee drove her heel down hard, making the bell at her waist swing as she rapped—one, two, three—on the ceiling of the captain's cabin. But the door did not open, the captain did not appear, and still the ship behind us gained. The riflemen were formed up along her prow; they could not shoot accurately at this distance, but there were so many of them, they wouldn't really have to.

I scrubbed my palms on my trousers. Could we escape if I took the helm? I'd gotten a glimpse of the map of Tahiti. Maybe I could take us to the South Pacific.

Then again, I'd only Navigated twice before—I was by no means an expert, and the price of failure was high. The Margins were a strange place, difficult to find and even harder to leave: an ocean between worlds, inhabited by nameless creatures breaching in the waves, or far-off ships with tattered sails crewed by lost souls unable to escape the fog. Ancient sailors used to believe you would drop off the edge of the earth if you sailed beyond the borders of their maps, in the places where there be dragons.

I shuddered at the thought. They didn't know how right they were.

"Lima!" Rotgut called out as the steamer raised the next signal flag: *Stop your vessel immediately.*

Where was the captain? I ran to pound on the cabin door. "Slate!"

No answer—I tried the handle. The door swung open to reveal my father, vomiting into his laundry hamper.

I froze on the threshold. This was not the first time he'd been through the pain of withdrawal, but this was certainly the worst time. In more than one way. He blinked at me with red-rimmed eyes. "I'm sorry, Nixie, I—"

But a voice interrupted him, carried on the following wind. *"Ready!"*

And on the deck of the ship behind us, the men lowered their rifles.

We'd let them get too close. Swearing, I ran up the stairs to the helm. Bee raised one scarred eyebrow. "You can do it?"

"I'll have to." I spoke with more conviction than I felt, but she gave me a taut smile.

"That's my girl," she rasped. Then she went back to the

main deck, leaving me alone at the helm. Trying to ignore the crawling feeling of the target between my shoulder blades, I focused on the map of Tahiti, the lovely string of islands like scattered pearls.

Almost immediately, the fog drifted up like smoke on the horizon. My breath caught in my throat. It was easier than I'd expected; I hadn't spent more than a few minutes looking at the map. But it had always felt right to me—standing at the helm of the *Temptation*. My heart filled with pride; then it skipped a beat at the officer's shout.

"*Aim!*"

I gripped the wheel, my palms suddenly slick. Kash and Bee were on the main deck, shielded from fire by the height of the stern, but Rotgut was a sitting duck in the crow's nest, and I was standing with my back broadside to the riflemen. Trying to concentrate, I drew the fog closer. Through it, I watched for a glimpse of Tahiti, 1901: the craggy green mountains, the pale sand of the beaches, the crystalline water. Gauguin and pearl divers and—

"*Fire!*"

A rippling crack sounded behind us, and I ducked instinctively; white puffs of smoke popped above the steam ship. Rotgut shrieked and drew his legs up—just below him, the sails were peppered with holes. Kashmir had flattened himself on the deck as a round ripped through the sheet he was trying to shorten. In the cabin, Billie started howling: *"Roooooo! Rooooooo!"*

But off the prow, the fog thickened, and I kept the wheel steady as we raced for the cover the mist would afford. Then I frowned. What was that dark patch in the water ahead? "Rotgut!" I called up to the crow's nest. "What do you see?"

"I see the entire Hawaiian navy taking aim at my—"

"Ready!"

"I know! I meant—" I startled at a loud sound. A single round?

No. Slate had thrown his door open so hard it banged against the wall. Billie raced out with a howl; the captain followed, stumbling onto the deck and shading his bloodshot eyes. "Nixie? What are you doing?"

The officer's call came, loud and clear. *"Aim!"*

"I'm trying to get us out of here!"

Slate swore. "What if you get shot? Give me the wheel!"

"What if *you* get shot?"

He hauled himself up the stairs. "I'll be fine!" he shouted. Then he stopped to heave over the rail. "I'll be fine," he said again, wiping his mouth. "I don't die here, remember?"

"What?" The ship began to rock as the waves swelled, but I stared at my father. "What are you talking about?"

"My fate! My fortune." He staggered toward me as the deck rolled, a manic light in his eyes. "I die in Honolulu, in 1868. Joss saw it happen!"

"But Dad—"

"*Fire!*"

Another rifle volley came, lower this time. Bullets sang in my ears. But Slate shouldered me aside, gripping the handles with white knuckles. "Give me the wheel and get down on the deck. I won't die without seeing your mother again."

A mighty gust of wind whipped my hair across my cheeks as I hesitated on the quarterdeck. I didn't want to leave him, but I didn't want to wrestle him for the wheel, either. Besides, he was still the captain; it was my duty to obey. And we were nearly safe in the Margins—or were we?

The fog ahead had darkened, and lightning flickered in the lowering clouds. A wave burst over the port side in a white plume of foam. Tahiti shouldn't have been difficult, not like this. Over the crash of the water, I heard the officer's shout. *"Ready!"*

Slate only laughed. "Do your worst!" he shouted into the wind. "I dare you!"

"Aim!"

The fog curdled, darker still, and thunder grumbled a warning. What was worse, the storm ahead or the ship behind?

But then Billie scrambled toward starboard side, barking furiously. There, in the bank of fog, turbid tendrils of mist were twisting up from the surface like fingers—like tentacles. The water seemed to boil as something dark and heavy bodied rose from the deep.

A cry went up from the crew of the steamer, and I risked a glance back. Order broke down as men aimed at the shadows, firing at will. They were close enough that I could see the wide white panic in their eyes.

Bullets zipped in the air like bees; I crouched at my father's feet as the mist of the Margins swallowed us whole. Then Slate cried out—I blinked up at him in the sudden darkness. His face was pale in the gloom; he clutched his left side.

Blood was leaking through his fingers.

"Dad!" I sprang to my feet, reaching for him . . . as something fell to the quarterdeck beside me, thick and heavy as the mast.

But it glistened—and *moved*.

CHAPTER
TWO

Black flesh like wet leather—and underneath, rows of suckers the size of saucers. The tentacle writhed and coiled over the boards. Then it lashed around my ankle like a whip, and I screamed.

Billie raced across the deck to sink her teeth into the creature's flesh, but the tentacle only tightened; a dozen suckers ripped at my skin. I scrabbled at the stem of the wheel, but the creature dragged me across the deck.

"Amira!" Kashmir ran after me, his long knife shining in the gloam. With one slash, he severed the tip of the tentacle. In its dying throes, it curled around my leg, but I scooted backward, kicking, and it fell away. Billie dragged it off with a growl as the rest of it flopped and twisted, slithering back into the roiling sea.

Breathing hard, Kashmir reached for me. I let him

pull me to my feet, his hand so warm in mine. "Are you all right?" He murmured the words into my hair; I could smell the clove on his breath.

"Fine," I said, dizzy with fear and relief and the closeness of him. "But Slate—Slate's hurt."

Kash glanced at the captain, a furrow forming between his dark brows. In an instant, his expression changed to surprise as another tentacle slung over the rail to wind around his waist. Lightning flashed, and odd colors rippled over the creature's flesh. It *pulled*—and Kashmir's hand slipped from mine.

His knife clattered to the deck as he disappeared over the side.

"Kash!" Thunder rumbled, drowning out my scream. I rushed toward the rail, ready to leap into the dark water, but something grabbed me roughly by the arm and hauled me back.

My father.

With a cry, I shoved him away. He reeled, still reaching for me with bloody hands; the ship spun like a weathervane with no one at the wheel. "Nixie," he gasped. "He's gone!"

The words hit me like a slap, but Billie started howling again, and before I could respond, I was thrown to my knees. The *Temptation* bucked like a wild thing as another tentacle heaved onto the deck.

It wound like a vine around the foremast. With a crack, the boom snapped, and the wet sail dropped over the squirming limb. Rotgut shouted curses from his perch in the crow's nest as a second tentacle shook the main mast. A third wrapped itself around the captain's right arm. Slate snarled like a dog, sinking his teeth into the monster's slick flesh. The thing flinched, releasing him, and my father reached out for me. But I scrambled to my feet, swearing. "Just take the damn wheel!"

He stumbled back toward the helm as another wave hit us—this time over the bow—sending white spray high overhead as the tentacle undulated on the deck. Leaping over it, I pressed myself against the bulwark, ready to follow Kashmir over the side—but there he was, clinging to the rungs of the ladder embedded in the stern.

"Kashmir!" My voice was thick with relief, but he could not respond; the creature had a tentacle cinched around his chest, crushing the air from his lungs as waves crashed over his head. "Hold on!"

Fumbling on the deck, I grabbed his knife and wrapped my hands around the hilt. I leaned out over the bulwark, slashing downward, but the blade bounced off the monster's leathery skin; had I swung with the dull edge? I changed my grip, but the creature released him to reach for me. Screaming, I hacked at the thing, and it wriggled away. Gritting his teeth, Kash hooked one elbow over the rail. Before he could pull himself back to the deck, the beast yanked him down again.

The sound of gunfire split the air as Bee leveled her revolver. The creature flailed, slamming a tentacle down at her feet. Boards splintered, but she stood her ground to reload until another arm reared up and knocked her backward. Bee rolled across the deck, her gun tumbling overboard.

Another tentacle swung past me to grasp the stem of the wheel. Slate stomped on it, swearing, while Bee wrestled with the arm winding about her torso. Billie danced across the deck, ripping into a coiling limb. But the stern sank lower as the dark bulk of the thing rose up from the water, looming through the fog.

Eyes bigger than my head gleamed in a flash of electric blue as the creature poured over the bulwark. It was enormous—the body alone taller than I was. There was another crack of thunder, and Kash cried out as one hand slipped free; he swung by his fingers as the ship tilted on the rising sea.

Waves drenched the deck. Another minute and the monster would capsize us, dragging us all down to the ocean floor. But it was like a hydra—each time I swung the blade, another arm appeared. The knife felt like a toothpick in my hand as I stared into the creature's eyes, the pupils flat like a goat's.

The eyes . . . the eyes. A thought . . . a memory came to me, something I'd read once: Hawaiian fishermen killed octopus by biting them between the eyes. Why was I hacking at the limbs? With a grimace, I drew back the knife and plunged it hilt-deep into the bulbous head.

A gout of black fluid washed the deck, darker than blood; the tentacles writhed like a nest of snakes. One caught me across the stomach, flinging me back. Dazed and gasping, I stared up as the arms fell slack around me. Was that a patch of night sky through the fog?

Relief came in a wave. If the mist was clearing, that meant we were nearly safe out of the Margins. As I lay there, the beast slid off the stern, limp and liquid, and sank into the deep, and the ship rose in the water. Pushing myself to my knees, I sucked in a breath. Then I staggered to the rail, ready to pull Kashmir up from the ladder.

He was gone.

For a moment I couldn't make sense of it. I stared, stupidly, at the empty ladder, at the churning wake, at the thinning fog.

No.

No, no, no, no, no no no—

I didn't stop. I didn't think. I vaulted off the stern, hitting the dark waves like a hammer. The shattered sea collapsed over my head, but I fought the water, struggling upward, kicking frantically, finally bursting into the murky air.

"Kash!" I choked—my first call was drowned by the next wave. I spat. *"Kashmir!"*

Where was he? The ship had slowed in the storm. Still, it was sailing on faster than a man could swim. The fog swirled around me—I couldn't see farther than my fingertips—but that was good, that was good. We were both still in the Margins.

Salt stung in my wounds like the tail of a jellyfish; there must be blood in the water, and not only mine. Was there another monster lurking in the dark, drawn by the flesh and the fray?

Through the mist, someone was screaming my name—my father's voice. I swam in the opposite direction. Beside me, something large splashed on the surface. I shrieked, but it was only a buoy thrown from the ship. I slid my arm through the center and carried it with me as I swam. How long was the rope? Glancing back over my shoulder, there was nothing; the *Temptation* had vanished in the tattered fog . . . or out of it.

I had to find Kashmir before I followed.

"Kash!"

He had to be here. Or had the creature taken him under? I slammed my mind on the question, like the door to a tomb.

"Kashmir!"

Something brushed my leg and I bit back a cry. It was only the rope, wrapped around my ankle. All around me, the fog was clearing. I ducked under to loosen the loop from my leg, and when I resurfaced, I heard his voice.

"Amira!"

I whirled around, splashing. Kashmir's voice was faint over the shush and roar of the waves, but I kicked toward it with a single-minded purpose. I had to reach him, now or never. Throwing my shoulder forward, I cut through the water, dragging the buoy along. I dreaded a tug on the rope. What would I do if Kash had drifted beyond my reach?

The answer came to mind immediately; I would let go of the buoy. If the *Temptation* left the Margins without me, I might never see her again—nor Bee and Rotgut, nor my father. But I kept swimming, and at the top of the next wave, I saw him in the watery valley.

"Kash!"

"Amira?" In his wide eyes, relief chased away the panic.

The wave dropped and he was closer; he kicked toward me on the next swell and I toward him. I pushed the buoy into his hands and just like that, he was in my arms. "I've got you!"

"I thought I—" he sputtered, gasping. "I thought I'd never see you again."

"I'm here," I said, pulling him close just as the rope on the buoy stretched taut. "I'll always be here."

He stopped trying to speak, but I could feel his hot breath in the crook of my neck and the thunder of his heart against my chest. The dark sea had calmed, but I held him fiercely. We floated up the next wave and down its back. We might have drifted forever, storm tossed but safe in each other's arms. But the fog around us was melting into the night air, revealing the *Temptation*. My father was at the stern, hauling on the rope with all his might.

Bee threw down another rope for Kash; I looped it around his torso before sending him up the ladder. Water sluiced from his clothes, and there was a long strand of seaweed wrapped around one leg. His arms, usually so steady, shook as he climbed, so I stayed close behind him, murmuring encouragement.

Near the top, Bee and Slate lifted him the rest of the way. He tumbled over the bulwark and landed flat on the deck.

Billie bounded toward him, trying to lick his face, but Bee pushed her off to check Kashmir's breathing while Slate turned back and pulled me single-handedly over the rail. I started toward Kash, still needing him close, but the captain crushed me in an embrace so tight he squeezed water out of my clothes.

"I'm sorry, Nixie," he whispered fiercely. "I'm so sorry. I thought today was the day,"

I hugged him back, trying to comfort him; he must have been scared, too. "What day, Dad?"

"The day you lose Kashmir."

I stiffened, but he did not let go. "What are you talking about, Slate?"

"I told you from the start not to get too close to him." The words came in a whisper; I could smell his sour breath. "That he won't be around forever."

A flash of rage, like lightning. "How dare you say that?" I pushed him, hard, and he released me. "You, of all people?"

But as he stumbled back, my anger ebbed. His shirt was bloody and torn, his face waxy and pale in the dark. And in his eyes, an infinite sadness. "You think I'm just being cruel?" My father shook his head. "It wasn't only my fortune Joss told."

Though the storm had passed and the water was calm, I felt the world seesaw. "She told you about me?" Joss—Navigator, fortune-teller. My grandmother too, though I hadn't known it at first. I'd thought she was a charlatan, until the things she'd told me came true. But of course they had; everything she'd predicted, she'd already watched happen as she traveled back and forth across the years. "What did she say?"

Slate opened his mouth to reply, but then he bent double and vomited noisily over the rail.

I swore, rushing to his side as his shoulders shook. Away across the vast blackness of the waves, a glassy skyline glittered; he'd gotten us to his own timeline, twenty-first-century New York.

Not Tahiti, then. But maybe that was for the best.

"Dad . . ." I touched his side, my hands gentle, plucking at the blood-soaked fabric of his shirt; the bullet had dug a furrow through his flesh, skipping along his ribs like a stone. It wasn't life-threatening—but where would I have been shot, if I'd still been at the helm? Under my fingers, Slate's skin was clammy, and his whole body trembled. "We'll get you to the hospital."

"No!" Clumsily, he threw my hand off. "No hospitals."

I rounded on him. "What's wrong with you? You need stitches, you need medicine—"

"Oh, yeah?" He laughed coarsely as he struggled out of his shirt. Wadding it up, he wiped the blood from his tattooed flesh. Under the ink, it was pale as smoke. "Like painkillers?"

"You could still go to the hospital. Just tell them you don't want any drugs."

"You think so?" He smiled darkly, his voice bitter, and I realized how naive I must have sounded. He hadn't been clean for years—maybe not since my mother died. Who was he, without his opium? Had I ever known my own father?

Oblivious to my scrutiny, Slate leaned heavily against the bulwark and spat into the water, wiping his mouth with his arm. Then he closed his eyes and put his forehead down on the rail. "It's more blood than guts. I don't die today. I know my fate. I'll see her again."

He spoke the words like a dreadful incantation—a prayer, or a curse. My father loved my mother. I knew it like I knew the position of the stars, or the pitch of the deck. His search for her had defined the last sixteen years—the entirety of my existence, for her life had ended as mine began. She was his safe harbor . . . or, more accurately, his white whale.

Giving her up would be infinitely harder than giving up the drugs. His knuckles were pale as he gripped the brass. Was he trying to convince me, or himself?

After a long moment, he gritted his teeth and pushed himself upright. Then he turned from the rail and swore. "What are you looking at?"

I blinked, but he wasn't talking to me. Following his stare, my stomach sank like an anchor. There he was, standing in the open doorway of the captain's cabin: Blake Hart, the boy from 1884.

He still wore his nineteenth-century suit, very dapper once, though the hat he used to wear had gone missing somewhere back in Honolulu. Billie trotted up to him, wagging her tail slowly, but Blake ignored her, staring at the electric gleam of the glass fantasy of Manhattan. Over his shoulder, the green copper figure of Lady Liberty raised her spotlighted torch; back in his native time, Blake would not have even heard of her. "Send these, the homeless, tempest-tossed, to me," I said under my breath.

"What?" Blake's face was white, and his voice cracked when he spoke. "What is this place?"

I tried to smile. "Welcome to New York."

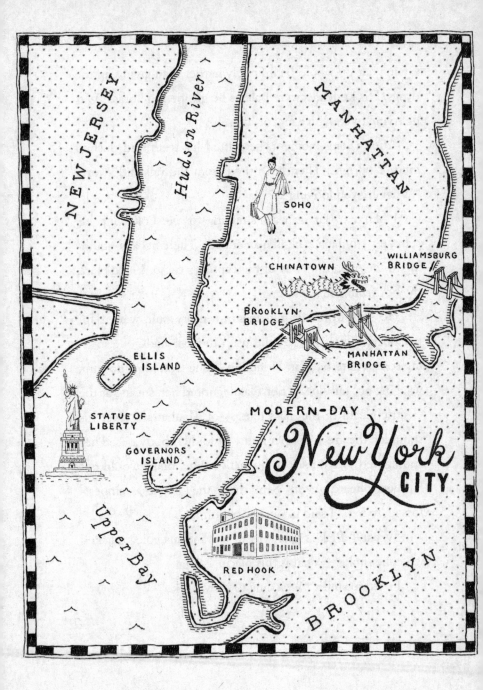

CHAPTER
THREE

Fifty years ago, Slate had been born during a blackout in this protean city; when he was a child, he had watched the Bronx burn. New York had changed a lot since then— so much so that some longtimers found it unrecognizable. But even they would have felt more at home in the city than a boy from a bygone kingdom.

A speedboat roared past us, the prow painted with leering teeth, the laughing shrieks of the passengers drowned out by the motor. A helicopter whuffed overhead, seeking the latest news. We passed a garbage barge heading south; the stench wafted to us along with the screams of the gulls. And Blake stood dazed on the main deck as the salt of the Atlantic curled his golden hair. "Where are we, Miss Song? And where are all the stars?"

I followed his eyes to the orangey-blue bruise of the

city night. A myth came to mind: a man cast out of paradise. But would any god be so cruel as to throw someone from Eden into New York City?

As I stood there, hesitating, it was Kashmir who took his arm. "Come, Mr. Hart. You should still be resting. Let's get you downstairs."

"He can have my cabin," I said suddenly, remembering a day, nearly three years ago, when I'd done the same thing for Kash. He too had come aboard with nothing but the clothes on his back; now he steered Blake toward the hatch with a surprisingly gentle hand. Perhaps they had more in common than I'd thought.

Slate disappeared into his room, leaving Bee to take the helm; as he flopped down on his bunk, I retrieved my cell phone from the secret cupboard where we kept the radio. When I powered it on, the date showed as August second.

The city slid by as the *Temptation* limped toward the dock at Red Hook; we only had two working sails, and the wind was sluggish. The summer humidity was as thick as the mist of the Margins, and the salt dried slowly on my skin. By the time we made fast to the wharf, it was near midnight. The rest of the crew went below to find their bunks, but I ducked back into the captain's cabin to check on my father. I found him sprawled on the bed, one arm flung over his eyes, Billie curled up beside him.

I wrinkled my nose; there was a sour smell in the room. It wafted up from the messy bucket at his bedside; at least he'd changed it out for the hamper. He'd tossed his bloody shirt to the floor. Beside it: a sewing kit, the first aid box, and a half-empty tube of antibacterial ointment curled next to its cap.

Using an excess of medical tape, Slate had secured a slapdash bandage on his left side, right beside the tattoo of the swallow over his heart. Swallows always returned to their nests; sailor superstition said to get one inked before you set out on your journey. The second one was for when you finally came home.

He only had one.

I watched his breathing for a while. It was slow and even—that was a relief. But the heat in the room was making my skin prickle, and Slate had the covers up to his chest. I approached his bedside on quiet feet; still, he stirred.

"Nixie?" Slate shifted his arm so he could peer at me through the gloom in the cabin. "Is that you?"

"I'm here." Reaching out, I touched his forehead with the back of my hand; it was warm. "You're going to get an infection, Dad."

He shook his head a little. "Kash went to get me some antibiotics."

"I have that mercury in my cabin," I offered. "The bottle I took from Qin's tomb. It's supposed to be a cure-all, if you want to give it a try."

Slate laughed—or was it a cough? "Save it for someone who needs it. I'll be fine, I told you."

"Okay." My hand fell back to my side, and I stared at him for a while. His eyes were closed again, and his breathing was slowing, but the question ate at me like a shipworm. "What did Joss say?"

Shifting, he murmured into the crook of his shoulder. "She promised I'll see your mother again before I die."

"No, I mean . . ." I made a face—I almost stopped myself there. Joss had offered to tell my fortune once, back in Honolulu. I'd declined, but that was before I knew her prediction concerned Kashmir. "What did she say will happen to me?"

"Oh. She . . . Nixie." Blinking, he peered at me with bleary eyes. "I tried so hard. But you didn't listen, did you? You're in love with him."

"Dad—"

"You are, I can tell." He tried to smile but coughed instead, a thick, phlegmy sound. "I know what love looks like."

My cheeks went pink; I clenched my jaw. I didn't want my love to look like his. "Just tell me, Slate."

"Fine. Here," he said, rolling onto his stomach, struggling free from the sheet, and looking over his right shoulder. There, high on his back, an old tattoo in a familiar handwriting, sharp and choppy—three columns of Chinese characters running down his shoulder blade, short, medium, long. "Joss got one of her goons to do it while I was . . . you know."

"Right." I'd seen it before, in passing, but my father was covered in tattoos, and I'd learned not to ask him their stories. "What does it say?"

"It was more than fifteen years ago. Just after I got back to Honolulu and found out your mother was . . ." His voice faltered; he cleared his throat. "I don't remember the exact words. But . . ." He tried to reach back over his shoulder with his left hand, then he swore, giving up. "That first line, that's where I die—down in Joss's opium den, back in 1868."

I shuddered at the words, spoken so casually, but Slate had never feared death. I'd always attributed it to a morbid twist in his mind, or maybe a manic optimism, but perhaps it was because he thought he'd die happy.

He went on, like it was nothing. "And next to that, it's

where she promised I'd see your mother before it's all over. The last part's about you."

I wet my lips. "What about me, exactly?"

"It's a warning." Slate sighed. "She said you'll end up just like me."

"But *how*?" My frustration was rising. "An addict? A captain? Covered in tattoos?"

"You'll lose the one you love!" he shot back, but his tone was not half so harsh as the words. He swallowed. "To the sea," he added softly. "It will break your heart."

"Lost at sea?" In the silence, my heart pounded. Behind my eyes, I could see the white wake, when Kash had gone over the side. I stared at the characters, stark in blue ink, but they were indecipherable to me. "When?"

"I didn't ask. I didn't believe her, back then."

"I don't believe her either," I said, as though saying it could make it true.

"Yeah?" Slate's eyes narrowed. "Good for you."

He closed his eyes and turned his face toward the wall. A pang of guilt hit me, but not as painful as the truth: Joss wasn't some showy mystic making fake predictions. And she had clearly taken measures to make sure I'd know the fate she'd seen for me. But why?

Surreptitiously, I slipped my cell phone out of my pocket and snapped a picture of the tattoo; this way I could go to Chinatown and get it translated. Maybe there was more to it than what my father remembered. Maybe he'd gotten the wording wrong. Joss was a hard woman, but not cruel—she would not have sent this fortune just to taunt me. But what good was a warning if she had already seen it happen? Did she expect me to simply brace myself for the inevitable?

Or did she want me to try to change it?

The thought surfaced like a bloated body; bile burned on the back of my tongue. For years, I had watched my father try to do that very thing, dragging me in his wake, unsure whether each journey would be my last. After all, not even science knew what would happen if the past were to be remade. Would I wink out of existence? Would the present bend to a new reality? Or would the tapestry of history unravel completely?

All my life, Slate had failed to find the answer to those questions, dashing himself against the rocks, as ceaseless and uncaring as the tide. It was only after this last trip—after Honolulu, after he'd almost killed us all—that he'd finally promised to stop trying.

Was I fated to take up where he'd left off?

My mind churned, turbulent. I shoved my phone back in my pocket and looked for distractions—in the captain's cabin, they were easy to find. Vigorously, I began to clean, clearing away the medical detritus, tossing Slate's bloody shirt into the bin, capping the tube of ointment, closing the first aid kit. What was I going to do?

My first instinct was to tell Kashmir, but could a warning avert his fate? Or would Joss's prediction only hang over his head like the sword of Damocles? And how would he view what amounted to an admission of star-crossed love, complete with an unhappy ending? How would we both have reacted today, had we known what Joss had predicted? Despair can drag a man down deeper than a kraken.

Swearing under my breath, I rolled the map of Tahiti, glaring at the flat-eyed demon decorating the compass rose. The beliefs of the mapmaker influenced what the Navigator would find on any map, I knew that. I should have paid more attention before choosing, instead of daydreaming about—about oranges. Any one of us could easily have died out there in the Margins.

But was the open ocean any safer? Kashmir could be swept overboard in a storm, or even slip on the pier and drown. Futures I'd never imagined played out in my head:

Kash and me, leaving the ship. Moving inland. Forging a life far from the sea, far from my home. The thought made my chest constrict, as though I were deep underwater—I couldn't imagine trading terra incognita for terra firma. But better to lose the sea than let it take Kashmir.

We'd never buy our own ship, then. So what would it be? A cottage? A flat? I could hardly build this strange life in my head; I had no firm foundation for it. And visions of global warming and massive tidal waves washed those plans away. If I'd learned anything from studying myths, it was that fate could not be cheated. I shook my head to clear it, wishing I'd never asked. What was the use of knowing? How could I ever protect Kashmir from all harm?

A soft knock at the door cut through my Gordian thoughts. I glanced at Slate, but he didn't move; his breathing had slowed and deepened into sleep. So I went to the door and found Kashmir standing just outside.

At the sight of him, my heart leaped, a fish on the line. He'd changed out of his wet clothes and into something typically dashing—a pair of artfully ragged jeans and a white linen shirt, open at the throat. In the fading light, the fabric glowed against his golden skin. He'd even tucked a sprig of seaweed behind one ear, as though to thumb his nose at the sea.

As for me, the salt had made my curls unruly, and my clothes were stained with blood and ink. But when he saw me, he drank me in with his eyes as though I'd come to the door wearing a full-length gown—or perhaps as though I were wearing nothing at all.

The thought made my blood rush. I looked down at my feet before he could read it in my expression. "What's going on, Kash?"

"I brought these up from the hold," he said, rattling a plastic bottle of pills. "Antibiotics," he added quickly, but I only nodded. "How is he?"

I shrugged. "Still alive."

"Was that ever in doubt?" Kashmir gave me a grin. "I thought Joss said he'd live till he got back to 1868."

I clenched my fists, and the map of Tahiti crumpled in my hands. "Joss said a lot of things."

Kashmir's brow furrowed; he cocked his head. "Is something wrong, amira?"

For a moment I wanted to shout a warning, like some weathered witch—the weird sisters standing over a cauldron, beware, beware. "Nothing." But I could see it in his eyes: he knew it was a lie. I reached for the pills, to cover. "I'll give him these. But how are *you* feeling?"

"Fine, thanks to you." He ran a casual hand through his hair; his fingers shook, ever so slightly. "But I'll admit it. I'd never been more terrified in my life."

"Really?" I kept my voice light. "I wouldn't have expected you to be scared of any old Tahitian octopus demon."

"That's not what I was afraid of."

His tone brought me up short. I knew his fear. I'd shared it: the threat of loss. Suddenly, I wanted to hold him again as I had held him out in the water—though I did not know which of us would be keeping the other afloat. And the older terror resurfaced like a leviathan in the depths: the fear of having something to lose in the first place. My father's lesson to me, and the one I'd learned best. How could I reach for Kashmir, knowing he'd be torn away? Or worse—what if by following my heart, I sealed his fate? I cast about for something else to say—a way to change the subject. "How's Blake?"

Kashmir's expression didn't change, but he shifted on his feet, the bells on his ankle chiming softly. "Settling in, I think. I gave him some clothes that should fit."

"You gave him your clothes?" I blinked at him, but Kash waved away my disbelief.

"I didn't say they were nice clothes." The ghost of a smile crossed his lips and faded. "I explained things as best

I could, but he still has questions that only you can answer."

"I'll go talk to him. Thank you, Kash."

"He'll need his vaccines soon, don't forget. I think there's a veterinarian just up the block."

"Right." I hid my smile and started to shut the door.

"One more thing, amira," he said, as the laughter in his eyes gave way to shy hope. "I know it's a beautiful night for sleeping under the stars. But I hope you know you're always welcome in my cabin."

"Oh?" My voice cracked; my mouth was dry. I tried again. "Oh. Thank you." My heart was pounding—could he hear it? A word echoed in my head: yes, yes. Instead I slammed the door and leaned against it; it was some time before I heard the sound of his ankle bells as he walked away.

More than anything, I wanted to go after him—to follow him to his cabin, to tell him what I felt, what I feared. But what a cruel thing, to lighten my burden by making him carry it!

Sighing, I pushed off the door, depositing the pill bottle at Slate's bedside. The map of Tahiti was still in my hand, crushed and sweaty; I smoothed it out against my thigh as best I could before sliding it back into its section: HISTORICAL MAPS OF THE PACIFIC. Beside it was one Blake had drawn for us—a map of Oahu, the only home he'd ever known.

Blake was an artist and an explorer. He and I had bonded over maps the day we'd met. He had showed me the healing spring that had saved his life, and sketches of hidden paths and secret places all over the island he knew so well—the island that would have been my home if my mother hadn't died. That had only been a few weeks ago, but in the time since, I had managed to betray his trust, to commit treason against his country, and to force him to choose between my life and his father's. Until Slate had given me Joss's fortune, I had thought that making peace with Blake would be my greatest challenge in the coming days. Could the two of us ever go back to before?

Perhaps it would be better to find a new route forward.

Opening a different cabinet, I rummaged through a set of charts until I found what I wanted. Then I slipped back out into the dusky night, taking a deep breath of the summer air: the diesel and the docks and the exhaust from the city, all of it so much fresher than the miasma in the captain's cabin.

It was very late and I was deeply tired, so I nearly didn't notice on my way toward the hatch—my hammock, already strung between the rail and the mast. A light quilt was folded neatly in the center, and on my pillow lay the sprig of seaweed that Kash had been wearing behind his ear. He must have known I wouldn't come to his cabin. Or maybe he'd wanted me to know that he hadn't confused hope with expectation. With a sigh, I slid down the ladder into the belly of the ship.

The *Temptation* hadn't been built for trade, but comfort. Space usually given to guns or cargo had been fitted out with spacious cabins on either side of a long hall lined with sky-herring lamps. My eyes adjusted to their shifting light as I lingered at the base of the ladder, close to the galley at the stern. At the far end of the corridor, toward the prow of the ship, there was a door that closed off the little triangle of space behind the forecastle.

It had been a storage space once, cramped and uncomfortable—the worst place on the ship, especially in high seas when the waves slammed the prow and the *Temptation* dipped like a duck on the water. But when Kash had come aboard, I'd moved my things there to give him a proper room. How many times had I walked this hall? Today, it seemed impossibly long.

I hesitated again outside the makeshift cabin. What would I say to Blake? What questions did he have? The little fish in the nearest lamp swam to the glass, hoping to be fed, but the bee pollen was in the hold. Soft light shimmered along her scales, illuminating the grain of the wood, the scarring on the finish; it was an odd feeling, to knock on my own door.

"Come."

Blake was sitting cross-legged on my tattered old quilt—the one my father had wrapped me in when he'd taken me from the islands. He had changed from his linen suit into an expensive pair of jeans and a vintage T-shirt with a mermaid on it; no matter how Kashmir teased, he hadn't been stingy. And across the knees of those nice jeans lay one of my history books, open to a black-and-white photograph . . . 1941, the explosions at Pearl Harbor, as seen from beneath the overhanging leaf of a palm.

Inside, I groaned. Why hadn't I taken my books before letting Blake into the room?

He looked up at me from under his thatch of blond hair. His cheeks, always pale, were now wan, and the skin under his blue eyes looked bruised. It startled me; for a moment, his face reminded me of my father's. "I wish you'd told me it was all for nothing," he said, his voice rusty.

"What was?"

"My hope that the kingdom of Hawaii could be saved." He closed the book and ran his hand over the cover. "It's in here, you know. The theft of the gold."

"Is it?" I blinked; my memory was usually faultless. "I don't remember that."

"A little footnote about an unconfirmed report in a California newspaper." He sighed. "It is a strange thing, reading the future written as the past. It feels like a fairy tale, where I've slept for a hundred years. You knew what would happen to the kingdom long before we met. But I can't help feeling I could have prevented it, had I made a different choice."

I toyed with the door handle. "What choice?"

"To stop you, rather than to save you." His eyes held mine, and I did not drop my gaze. "You must have known your actions would pave the way for the downfall of the kingdom. So why did you help my father rob the treasury?"

"The downfall was never in doubt, Blake. There were too many people, with too much power, all working against the monarchy. And we needed your father's map. The one of Honolulu in 1868." I sighed. "The captain would have done . . . almost anything to save my mother's life."

"Oh?" Something like compassion blunted the edge in his voice. "And has he saved her?"

I did look down then, at my bare feet, awkward on the threshold. "No."

"So it really was all for nothing."

Irritation stabbed through my guilt. "Don't you think I

would have changed things if I could? For you, and for Slate. But it wasn't up to me."

"Who do you blame it on, then?" His smile was as twisted as a noose. "Your father? Mine?"

I gestured to the book. "History."

"History?" He shut the book and tossed it aside. "What a pointless existence you must lead! How can you bear to see tragedy coming and not try to stop it?"

At his words, I went cold. "What would you have done instead?"

"Some Hawaiians fought for the monarchy. In 1893."

"If you read about them, you know they failed. Seven dead, and for what?"

"Your book says eight."

"Does it?" I half wanted to ask to see the book—but what did the difference matter? "Even worse."

"Why? A hundred years later, and everyone I knew is dead. But some were right, and some were wrong."

"So you prefer a pointless death to a pointless life?"

"Why shouldn't I set my sights higher, Miss Song? With a little luck, I could have both."

I bit my lip, trying to trim the sails on my anger; I'd wanted to help Blake, not bicker with him. I took a deep breath—then another. "May I come in?"

At his gesture, I stepped through the doorway. Blake's eyes darkened, taking in my bloody shirt, my wild hair, the blue rings of the bruises coiling up my right leg. "There was a storm," he said, leaving it up to me whether to answer the question implicit in the statement. But I only shook my head.

"It's over now."

The room, already small, felt crowded with the both of us in it. My trunk was open in the corner, and all my clothes and books were still scattered across the floor; I made a mental note to move everything into the hold in the morning. Folding my knees, I sat down by his side on the scrap of quilt. "Here. I brought you something."

"What are these?"

"They're all New York. This is from 1981," I said, smoothing out a hand-drawn map, shaded in watercolors, of the city's neighborhoods. "This one's a hundred years earlier. From 1880, around your time. Look how the coastline changed. And here's a subway map," I added, unfolding the colorful cartoon version from the modern day.

His brows dove together. "What's a subway?"

"I'll show you as soon as you're ready."

"Ready for what?"

I hesitated. "To face the future instead of looking to the past."

"Now is a convenient time to ask for a clean slate."

I threw my hands in the air. "Now is all I have, Blake. And if I recall correctly, you asked to come aboard."

That brought him up short. "I did, that's true." There was a long silence as he focused on the map in his hands. "Is New York to be home, then?"

"The ship is home," I said. "But we spend a lot of time docked here."

"I see." His eyes roamed over the page; behind them was a familiar look—curiosity. "Where is the colossus we passed on the way into the harbor?"

Blake was an explorer at heart, and once he started asking questions, he couldn't help but be drawn in. As we studied the charts of the city, he twirled a pen around his fingers; it was only when he opened a blank Stillman sketchbook that I realized both the book and the pen were very modern, though neither of them were mine. "Where did you get those?"

"Ah." He looked down at the pen. "Mr. Firas gave them to me. It seems I misjudged him too."

Too? I caught the subtle implication—he had misjudged

me, back in Hawaii—but I wasn't about to start arguing again. Pressing my lips together, I sat back on my heels, suddenly exhausted. "It's been a long day. I'll let you rest."

"Good night, then, Miss Song." But he watched me as I rummaged in my trunk for a change of clothes, and when I went to the door, he called me back. "Miss Song . . ."

"Yes?"

He hesitated then, his blue eyes soft as they searched mine. "I am sorry about your mother," he said at last. "I would have saved my own father, if I'd had the power to do so."

I raised an eyebrow, glancing at the bloody linen rag of his old suit, crumpled on the floor. "Even though he shot you?"

Blake sighed, running his hand through his hair. "I'd like to be more than what I inherited. Wouldn't you?"

I nodded and left him there, his sketchbook open to an unmarked page.

CHAPTER
FOUR

KASHMIR

I've always tried to resemble a brave man.

It didn't used to be so hard—and I've had so much practice pretending. After all, when you're a thief, you're always pretending not to be. The same is true when you're poor. And sometimes also when you're in love.

I still don't know just how it happened. Usually I'm better at guarding what little I have. But one day, I went looking for my heart and found it in Nix's hands.

I've never dared to tell her how I felt—at least, not in so many words. But then two weeks ago, we sat in the white sand as the sun melted into the sea, and . . . well.

Poets write often of love, but there is no poetry to match a kiss.

It was a promising start, but we hadn't spoken of it since. First there was the petty matter of piracy to keep us occupied. And I was still trying to find the words for what I wanted. Petite amie, doost dokhtoram, girlfriend . . . that word fell flat in any language I knew, and "wife" was too weighty for this effervescent feeling—like Coca-Cola, like champagne. But when I'd fallen, she had jumped, and inshallah, I had a chance now to say the things I should have said long ago. All I had to do was be brave.

Or at least, pretend I was, long enough to blurt something out.

It was more difficult than it sounded.

Part of the problem was time. She hadn't taken me up on my offer to share my cabin—but that had been a long shot, I knew. Still, it was hard to find a moment to talk; after we bound the *Temptation* to the docks, the whole crew bent their backs to making repairs under the fevered eye of the August sun. There were boards to sand, ropes to splice, supplies to stock—and the bilge to bail, which was a murky, mucky chore. I volunteered for the task—I knew Nix hated it, and it was a chance to sweat shirtless for her. But when I came up for meals, gleaming with saltwater and oil from repairing the pumps, she never spared me more than a glance.

At first I'd thought she was only brooding over the

captain's health, or the way his addiction dogged him. Despite knowing that Joss had seen his death, many years and miles from now, it hadn't been pretty watching him sweat and shiver in his cabin, wracked with pain and fever. That first night, he'd even called me in to beg me to go on one of his "errands," but when I finally agreed, he threw a mug at my head and cursed my name.

But as time passed and the captain improved, Nix's demeanor did not. If anything, she grew more troubled, chewing her nails to stubs, pulling so hard on the pendant I'd given her that the chain bit the back of her neck.

So after I finished my chores early on the third day, I joined her in hers. Nix was on deck, sewing up the bullet holes in the mainsail. I watched her for a while, but she didn't raise her eyes. "Your seams are crooked," I said at last, coming to sit beside her. I reached for the bundle of canvas she held. "Give it here."

She met my gaze then, and something in her look froze my smile. But she pursed her lips and handed me the needle. Under her scrutiny, I made doubly sure each row was perfect. "Slate should have had you do his ribs," she said at last, her mouth twisting in a wry smile.

"Oh, he did."

"Ugh."

She gave a dramatic shudder, and I laughed, tying off the thread. "I might be cocky too, if I knew it couldn't kill me."

I waited for her response—"Might be?" The joke was so easy to make. But instead of laughter, there was a small sound from her, like a word caught in her throat. I looked up to see her anguished face—and were those tears, standing in her eyes?

"Amira?" I threw aside the canvas to take her hand, which was precisely the moment Bee decided to climb through the hatch.

"My children!" Bee's voice was a rasp over the ropy scar at her throat, covered now by a stranded necklace. She glanced at our fingers, entwined, and winked. "Working hard, I see."

Nix pulled back her hand to dash it across her eyes. "Nearly done with the sails."

"Mmm." Bee took in Nix's expression. Then she turned to me, and the scars dotting her brow emphasized her frown.

I gave her an innocent look, and I wasn't even pretending. Whatever was bothering Nix was nothing I had done—at least, so I hoped. "Where are you off to?" I asked Bee, to remind her that she was leaving. "All dressed up."

Her frown melted away. "I finished my own repairs, so I'm taking my wife out to celebrate. It's a great day for us."

"Oh?"

"With young Blake aboard, we now have three children." Bee's chest filled with pride. "Our marriage is finally tied."

"Congratulations, Bee." Nix's smile was real, and I was glad to see it, even if it wasn't for me. "Are you taking her dancing?"

"Too early for that. Ayen wants ice cream—yes, yes," Bee added, but not to us. "A triple scoop with the rainbow sprinkles, I heard you. I told her she has no stomach, but she never listens to me."

"That's how you've stayed married so long," I said—another easy joke, but at least Nix laughed this time. Bee only swatted at me, still grinning even though she missed. Then she turned on her heel, walking down the gangplank by herself, but not alone.

Bee and Ayen were the only married people I knew—or instead I should say, the only married couple: Ayen was a ghost, slain by a jealous man soon after their wedding. But they were happy together, still in love after so many years. Too bad Nix could not take their example closer than her father's.

"We should do something nice for them," she said then.

"For who?"

"For Bee and Ayen. To celebrate."

"What's better than a triple scoop with rainbow sprinkles?"

Now Nix swatted at me, but instead of slipping away, I caught her fingers in mine. "She helped throw me a party for my theft day," she said. "It's important."

"I know, I know." I considered the plan, despite the distraction of her hand. Had I ever held such wealth in my palm? But a celebration would be welcome, after the last few weeks—it might lift everyone's mood, including Nix's. "I'll finish mending this last tear. You go below and tell Rotgut we're having a feast. Get him to pick up a roast. Maybe something from that barbecue place in Williamsburg?"

"Good idea."

"Of course it is. And you and I . . ." I trailed off, drawing my thumb over her knuckles. Courage, Kashmir! "You and I should . . . we should—"

"Go to Chinatown."

"What?"

"We should go to Chinatown," she repeated firmly, though her eyes flicked left, then right. "There are good bakeries there. I can pick up some cakes and the like. For the party."

"Ah yes," I said, nonplussed. Chinatown in summer was not the most romantic choice, the pavement slick with the melting ice of the open fish markets, and the smoggy haze of the bridge traffic hanging in the air, but I hadn't been quick enough on the draw. Still, SoHo was nearby, with little boutiques and cafés. I could work with that. "Chinatown it is."

Nix crossed the deck and slid down the ladder to find Rotgut while I finished up the last few stitches on the sail. Then I went below to my own cabin, changing into a new white shirt and smoothing my hair under my best Panama hat. A quick check of my teeth in my shard of mirror, and a few cloves in my pocket for my breath, and I was out the door, where I found Mr. Hart standing at the bottom of the hatch.

He glanced at me with hollow eyes, but he did not go up, nor did he stand aside; he only shifted in his borrowed shoes. "I overheard Miss Song saying she was on her way to Chinatown," he said at last.

"Ah." I kept my face still. But Honolulu's Chinatown was where the two of them had met. Did he hope New York's modern version would be something like home? I sighed; perhaps the fates were telling me that discretion was the better part of valor this day. I doffed my hat to them, and set it back down on Mr. Hart's head. He raised an eyebrow, surprised, but I clapped him on the shoulder. "A gentleman without a hat is like a thief without his lock picks. Viens, allez!"

We found Nix above, and she glanced from me to Mr. Hart, her eyes lingering on my hat. On her lips, was that a smile? They say generosity is its own reward, but her approval was even sweeter.

Together we walked down the sun-drenched sidewalks of Brooklyn. New Yorkers considered it rude to walk three abreast, so I let Nix lead, falling in stride with Mr. Hart. She was still distracted, so I kept an eye on him.

Though I'd spent the last three years sailing from unlikely scenario to improbable adventure, one of the strangest circumstances yet was becoming Mr. Hart's keeper. Still, I had to admire his composure in the busy streets. While he blushed at young people in deconstructed summer fashion—and in the hot fug underground, I could see the pulse under his jaw as the train roared into the station—by the time we reached Chinatown, awe had replaced the terror. Standing on the corner of Canal Street, he stared down the length of it, toward the water. "Is that the Brooklyn Bridge, there?"

"The Manhattan Bridge," Nix corrected. "The Brooklyn Bridge is maybe half a mile south."

"They say it's a marvel of engineering, and the longest suspension bridge in the world."

"It *was* the longest when it opened, back in 1883," Nix began. I elbowed her in the ribs before she named for him each successive bridge that had taken the title. It was bound to be an interesting side trip through history, but not, perhaps, for someone still reeling from a similar journey.

"Maybe we can walk back to Brooklyn," I suggested— not only for him. The walk over the bridge was reportedly a lovely one, very romantic. Less so, perhaps, with Mr. Hart along, but beggars couldn't always choose. "There's time."

Nix nodded, and Mr. Hart smiled. Then he took a deep breath through his nose, taking in the dock smell of fish and oil, and the warm scent of summer. "I could almost imagine being back in 1884, if I were to close my eyes." A car honked; he startled. "And my ears."

"If you close your mouth, I could imagine you back there too," I teased with a grin; his eyebrow went up, but so did the corners of his lips.

We meandered through the crowd to a bakery on Mott, where Nix filled two boxes with little confections—custards and cheesecakes and miniature pies. But, leaving the bakery, she turned north again, away from the bridge. "Amira? Where are we going?"

"One more errand," she threw back over her shoulder as she wove between a DVD seller and a passel of pale tourists. "It won't take long."

She moved quickly, as though she could escape the fact that she hadn't really answered my question, stopping a few doors up at a shop selling trinkets and baby turtles. The windows were plastered over with hand-lettered signs on neon paper, written in both English and Chinese: PHONE CASE, BELTS, T-SHIRTS THREE FOR TEN. What errand did she have?

"Wait here," she said, slipping her cell phone from her back pocket and touching the screen. I tried to get a glimpse over her shoulder, but all I saw was a picture of the captain's tattoos.

Mr. Hart watched her go, as did I. "Wait here," I told him after a moment.

"The hell I will," he replied, so we both walked into the shop.

She was standing before a counter at the end of a narrow aisle, her back to us; I could tell she was tense by the set of her shoulders. Behind the counter, an old man sat on a folding stool wearing a mint-green shirt—a terrible color under the fluorescent lights. "Your fortune?" he said, loud enough to be heard over the blare of the portable TV on a shelf beside him. "I'll tell you!"

"No, no." She stabbed the screen of her cell with one finger; she'd set it down on the counter. "I need you to read *this* fortune."

I chewed the clove on my tongue—a fortune? The pieces were starting to come together. But the old man had already taken a blue plastic basket from below the counter. When he tipped the contents onto the glass, I saw they were bones. "Hmm," he said to Nix, not even bothering to look at the vertebrae as they came to rest. "Your heart is pulling you in two directions!"

"No, it's not." She stiffened then—she must have followed his eyes—and when she turned and saw us, she scowled. "I told you to wait outside."

I cast about for an excuse, but it was Mr. Hart who responded. "But I wanted one of these." He plucked something at random from the shelf—a plush doll of a white cat in a red dress—and his expression turned from credible to puzzled. "What the devil?"

"Please, Blake. And that was clearly a sham reading,"

she said, glaring at the man behind the counter, who didn't even bother looking guilty.

"Okay, fine." He glanced down at the bones. "A stranger will ask for help. Say yes. Five dollars."

"I didn't want you to *tell* my fortune!" she said, raising her voice. "I wanted you to translate—" Nix pulled herself up short, glancing back at me, but the man had already taken up her phone.

"Ah, translation!" He squinted down at the screen for a moment, and his face fell. When he glanced up, he wasn't looking at her, but at Blake and me, and his eyes were full of pity. "Which one is it?"

Nix snatched back her phone. "Never mind," she said, digging in her bag and tossing a crumpled bill among the bones. Then she swept past us toward the door.

Mr. Hart shoved the doll back onto the shelf and we both scrambled after her. "What was that about?" I asked her; there was no point now in masking my curiosity.

"Something for Slate," she said, not meeting my eyes, and anger leaped like a flame in my chest.

"Why do you hide things from me?" I said, finally blurting something out. So much for discretion.

Out of the corner of my eye, I saw Mr. Hart take a hasty

step back. But I kept my focus on Nix. Her cheeks were pink, but her gaze was clear. She sighed, resigned. "I'll tell you on the way back. Brooklyn Bridge, right?"

We trudged south in silence, making our way along the summer streets, and this time it was Mr. Hart who trailed behind Nix and me. Although she did not speak, this was not the silence of still waters, but that of the gathering storm. In the pit of my stomach, the fire of my anger had burned out, leaving behind a lump like coal: did I truly want to know what she was hiding?

The bridge was crowded with joggers and bikers, tiny dogs fighting their leashes, and women with red wire carts selling mangoes carved in the shapes of roses. I bought one, to try to take the bitter taste of ash from my tongue. Nix finally stopped in the shade of the Manhattan tower, out of the way of the traffic. "You brought your sketchbook," she said to Mr. Hart—not a question, but a suggestion. "Give us a moment?"

"Certainly." He pulled his pen from behind his ear and sat in the shade of the pillar as Nix came to stand beside me at the rail. I offered her a bite of the mango. She accepted.

"God, that's good."

Side by side, almost touching, we traded bites and

watched the ships: the brunch yachts coming in, the sail-boats going out. I could smell the sun in her hair. Together we finished the mango; the nectar clung like perfume. Still she did not speak, and I did not prompt her—it seemed we were both summoning our courage.

My empty hands fluttered, useless; I longed to stroke her arm. Instead, I strummed my fingers along the row of locks fastened around a steel cable. They were brass and silver, old and new, pink and yellow and green—there must have been a dozen to a foot. They continued down the bridge, fastened to eyebolts and lampposts, rods and fences. Some had hearts drawn on them, others had names. I hefted one of them— an old iron thing, tarnished, antique—and slipped my picks from my pocket, for something to do. Nix snorted.

"What?" I glanced at her sideways. "It's not like some-one can steal the bridge."

"They're not for security, they're symbolic. Couples come to the bridge and attach a lock to signify their love. Then they throw the keys into the water."

"That's foolish."

"The authorities think so. Apparently a bridge railing collapsed under the excess weight. That was in Paris. City of love; it's ironic. At least no one was hurt."

"I wasn't talking about engineering." I probed the lock with hook and rake. There was a *click*, and it came free in my hand. "See? It's an imperfect metaphor."

"A weight too crushing to bear?" She shook my head. "It seems apt to me."

"Interesting." I lowered my gaze to the lock. But why was I hiding? I hooked the lock around a belt loop and clicked it shut. Then I raised my eyes to hers. "Love has only ever buoyed me up."

"Joss said I'm going to lose the one I love."

Misery stole her breath; she spoke no louder than a whisper, and it took a moment to understand. There was a long silence, the seconds measured in the beat of my heart at the base of my skull. "How?"

"The sea. Lost or drowned. She tattooed the fortune on Slate's back. I'd hoped he'd only misremembered the translation, but . . ." Nix shook her head.

I tried a disdainful laugh, though it came out like a croak. "Fortune-tellers! I knew a few, back in Almaas. Vague predictions, just like that one. They were a waste of good entrails."

"Kash—Joss was a Navigator. Whatever she knows, it's already happened in her past."

"Our lives are before us, not behind."

"That depends on where you're standing on the timeline."

"What of free will?"

"Some people don't believe free will exists."

"Some people don't believe in demon octopus, either. And did she mention when?"

Nix bit her lip. "No."

"Then it could be years!" I said.

"Or hours," she countered.

"Even if she's right, you know the poem." I looked into her face, hopeful. "'Tis better to have loved and lost than never to have loved at all.'"

"The only people who say that have never seen what loss looks like."

The implication took my breath away. I stared at the water again, glittering in the sun like a broken mirror—bad luck, bad luck. "You forget, amira. Before I came to the *Temptation*, loss was all I knew."

"How could you bear it?"

"Nothing lasts forever. Not even sorrow."

She only shook her head, and her eyes were faraway— she was back at the ship, back with her father—and I kept picking locks, tossing them, one by one, into the river.

CHAPTER
FIVE

The boys and I returned to the *Temptation* in the buzzy warmth of the afternoon. The black hull of the caravel shimmered in the heat off the asphalt, and the sun was like Hephaestus's hammer, striking sparks on the anvil of the water. A headache had wormed its way behind my eyes; I was certainly dehydrated, but it was easier to focus on the pounding at my temples than the ache in my heart.

The conversation with Kashmir could not have gone more poorly. I cringed at the memory of my thoughtless words. He had known more loss than I could imagine— but my father was a daily reality too stark for me to ignore. Slate had loved and lost, and it had ruined him. How could I follow in his footsteps?

Then again, how could I ignore the pull of my own heart? This, too, was a loss . . . only a slow torture instead of a sudden shock, stretched on the rack of longing.

I dragged myself down to the galley to stash the pastries in the icebox. Then I leaned against the counter and drank deep drafts of musty, lukewarm water from the barrel in the corner. The walk had left me exhausted. Or was it the nightmares I'd been having? The last three nights, I'd woken, drenched, from a dream where I'd followed Kashmir over the side and my father had thrown me an anchor rather than a buoy.

I should lie down, but where? I had given over my cabin, and with the sails furled, my hammock wasn't shaded. Rotgut hadn't returned yet, and neither had Bee; I couldn't just borrow one of their beds without asking first. Of course the captain wouldn't mind if I sprawled out on his floor— and though I didn't relish being in his cabin, it was my best option. I was halfway across the deck when I realized his door was ajar.

Had he left it that way to catch the breeze? I went inside to find his room empty.

And all the cupboards wide open.

Standing on the threshold, my eyes went to one of them as though pulled along on a current: HISTORICAL MAPS OF THE PACIFIC. The map of Tahiti was there, and a dozen other maps of Hawaii that the captain had collected over the years. There was only one missing—I knew it before I even started searching. I would have recognized it from across the room—the creases, the bloodstains. The map of Honolulu, 1868. The map we'd robbed a kingdom for. The one where my mother was still alive, and where my father was going to die.

Where had it gone?

Had Slate gone with it?

And I had thought he'd changed.

"What's wrong, amira?" Kash watched me from the doorway, his brow creasing as he scanned the open cupboards. "Thieves?"

"I think Slate might have . . ." It was hard for me to say the words. My stomach was roiling. What if I'd driven my father to his fate? Hadn't I told him I doubted Joss's prediction? He might have gone back only to prove me wrong. I hadn't even said good-bye. Tears threatened like a sudden storm—I wasn't ready. But would I ever have been? "I think—" But before I could finish the sentence, we both jumped at a sudden ruckus from the wharf.

A car horn was blaring, and over it—laughter? From belowdecks, Billie answered with a howl. *"Rooooo!"*

I rushed to the door. An old Honda was rolling slowly up to the pier. The man behind the wheel—a big man, stuffed into the little car—roared with laughter as the passenger opened the door and staggered out onto the hot pavement.

"Slate?" He couldn't hear me; I had spoken barely above a whisper. The tide of my fear had ebbed. Relief took its place. "Slate!"

Both men looked up—my father and Bruce, his old friend at the Coast Guard. At first I thought it was a trick of the glare on the curve of the windshield, but Bruce's face was florid, his eyes unfocused. Leaning over the passenger seat, he asked my father a question and reared back in mock surprise at the answer. He spoke with exaggerated care; I could read the words on his lips: "No shit!" Then he slapped the empty seat and rolled down his window. "Hey, kid! You're all grown up!"

"Thanks, Bruce," I said as Slate stumbled up the gangplank, swaying on his feet.

"You look just like your dad!"

I spoke through my teeth. "I hope not, Bruce."

"All right, all right. Hey, I'd love to catch up, but I'm gonna be late for work!" His voice was warm, and his words only a little slurred. "Take care of your old man! Don't be too pissed off!" Then he rolled up the window and drove away.

Slate stopped right in front of me, just a hair too close. He was still sweating, but his eyes were very bright; I grimaced. Through his white T-shirt, I could see blood seeping through the bandage over his ribs. Alcohol increased blood flow—I had read that somewhere. My anger was building in a wave. I'd been so hopeful when he'd tossed the box into the sea, but had opium ever been the problem, or only the treatment?

My father peered at me. "You're not going to, right?"

"Not going to what?"

"Be too pissed off."

I flung out my hands, exasperated. "Where are your shoes?"

"Don't remember." Slate looked down at his bare feet. The skin atop the right one was raised and red under a new tattoo—a simple design, one of his own, I could tell. The cross of a compass with an anchor's curve at the bottom. "You like it?" He raised his foot toward my face, then toppled to the left. I caught his arms; he smelled sweet and sharp, like an overripe peach. "I made it myself!"

"Did you drink an entire bottle of liquor?"

"Not the *whole* thing." He wiggled his foot. "I know I used some to sterilize my skin."

"I've never even seen you drink half a glass of weak beer!"

He shrugged loosely and headed toward his cabin. "You know what they say. When you can't be with the one you love— What the hell happened here?" Slate had stopped in the doorway.

"*You* did." I faltered, uncertain now. "Didn't you?"

"Didn't I what?"

"Didn't you take your map of Honolulu?"

"Take it where?" He walked toward his desk and stared at the surface—empty, but for a few coffee cups. "Where is it?"

I swallowed and glanced at Kashmir. Thieves, he'd said. Had someone come aboard while we'd been away? A crashing sound drew my attention back to the captain as he swept the shelves clear. "Slate, no!"

Scrolls scattered across the floor; he tossed heavy books atop delicate parchment. I leaped over a bronze tablet and barreled into him, shoving him away from the shelves. "*It was right there!*" he screamed, his eyes wild. "*Where did it go?*"

"You're not going to find it making a mess!"

His chest heaved; he gripped my arms. He looked so incredibly lost. "Nixie . . . Nixie . . ."

"It's okay, Dad. I'll find it. Just sit!" I pushed him back toward his bunk; his knees bent and he sank down. "Stay there." I took a deep breath. Both Kashmir and Blake were staring in through the doorway. "Blake, bring some water. Kash, can you . . . ?"

Kashmir came to the captain's side, putting his hand on Slate's shoulder to keep him in his bunk while I picked up the maps and set the room back in order. By the time Blake returned and put a cup into Slate's shaking hands, I hadn't discovered anything else missing—including maps that were far more valuable.

Had Slate only mislaid the map and forgotten? I shooed the boys out and knelt next to my father to ask, but he shook his head vehemently. "No. No, Nixie. How could I forget something like that? That map is everything to me."

The reminder stung more than it should have. I clenched my fists. "Everything?"

He bridled. "Don't take that tone. I'm still here, aren't I?"

"Barely. But why did you have the map out of the cupboard, Slate?" I made a face; he didn't answer, but of course

I already knew. "You tried to use it."

"Maybe I thought about it," he said, pugnacious. Then he grimaced. "But I was . . . afraid."

"Afraid?" I laughed a little, bitter. "Afraid to die?"

"No," he said scornfully, like the very question was a foolish one. "Afraid to lose you."

"Well, I'm not going back with you to 1868, to watch you overdose. I couldn't, even if I wanted to, but frankly—"

"That's not what I meant!" Slate clenched his jaw, scrubbing his hand through his blond hair. When he spoke again, his voice was soft. "That's not what I meant. I mean . . . Joss told me something else once."

I stared at him warily. "Do I want to know?"

"I don't know. Do you?"

Inside, I struggled—knowledge was power, ignorance bliss. "What was it?"

"She told me . . . she told me that it's possible. To change things."

I stared at him, unmoored; the world swirled around me and I felt like small craft tossed on a wild sea—lost, lost, but strangely free. "How?"

He gave me a half shrug. "With enormous effort and great sacrifice. Even then, nothing's for sure."

"Fine," I said, breathless. "But *how*? Does it take a special map? Or—or is it just a matter of finding the right time and making a different choice? How do you—"

"She never said more than that," he interrupted. "Maybe it's best I never figured it out."

The words made no sense at first, not from him. "But . . . why?"

"Someday, Nixie." My father peered at me, his blue eyes bleary, but on his lips—a dreamy smile. "Someday when I'm old and nearly gone, we'll sail together for the last time. We'll go together to the edge of the world. I'll give you the helm, and you'll give me the lifeboat. And I'll take the map of Honolulu and sail to Byzantium like an old man should. You'll be captain then. Captain of your own fate. And I'll be ready to let go. But if I went now . . ." He shook his head. "What would I give to have her back, Nixie? What would I have to sacrifice?"

Though he'd only asked a question, I knew the answer: me. He would have lost me, as I was, here and now, trading a daughter who loved the sea for one born and raised on a golden shore. But that understanding did not chill me, not today. I was already numb. The words echoed in my head: enormous effort. Great sacrifice.

But change was possible. And looking at Slate, his bent shoulders, his hollow eyes—I knew I could not let it happen to me. I would not end up like my father.

What must I do? What must I sacrifice? How would I stave off my fate? I needed answers—answers my father had never been able to discover, in all his years searching. But Slate was erratic, an addict, driven by demons, pulled along on his whims. I was more methodical. I had to be.

So where to start? Where did people go to seek knowledge?

Ideas bubbled up in my mind: all over the world and throughout history, every culture had a way of divination. Tarot cards and tasseography, dream interpreters . . . and fortune-tellers, of course. But those jobs were like chum for charlatans, as my trip to Chinatown had shown.

Maybe I should go back to the source of the prophecy— to Joss herself. I went to the cupboard, still open, and pulled out the maps of Honolulu that my father had collected over the years. Here, one from 1895. But it was useless; she was dead by then.

What about an older map? After all, Joss had known my fate by the time she'd tattooed it on my father's back. But how had she learned it? My stomach dropped at the next thought: what if by going back to see her in a past Honolulu, I would trigger Kashmir's loss? Could she learn my fortune from my own lips?

Better instead to meet her on my own timeline—after she'd already given my father the tattoo. I'd have to wait till the Royal Hawaiian Navy gave up the search for our ship, of course. Six months? A year? All I had to do was keep Kashmir safe until then. Maybe a stint in a landlocked country would be a good idea after all. Central Europe . . . perhaps Lichtenstein . . .

"God, my head hurts."

I turned back to look at Slate; he had scooted back into the shadows of the alcove, his knees pulled up to his chest. "It's called a hangover," I told him. Then I frowned—my own temples were still throbbing. "You're probably dehydrated."

"Do we have any aspirin?"

Tucking the maps back onto the shelves, I knelt to look in the cupboard under the desk. The first aid kit had been decimated in the last few days, and the little bottle of aspirin was empty. "I'll go get you some."

"I love you, Nixie."

The words made me stumble on the threshold. I licked my lips—I didn't know how to respond, so I hurried through the doorway, pretending I hadn't heard. Out on deck, the afternoon sunlight was like a knife through the eyes; my own headache had only worsened. When I looked west, I saw why. The horizon, so blue only half an hour ago, had curdled with clouds, and the air was as hot as steam. A summer storm was coming.

As I closed the door, Blake and Kashmir turned to me, faces expectant. "He's sleeping off the drink," I told them.

"And the map, amira? It wasn't in his pockets."

"It might be stolen—or it might only be misplaced." I bit my lip. "He took it out to—to look at it. Maybe it blew into the water. Or he left it at Bruce's. I don't know."

"Shouldn't we alert the authorities, Miss Song?" Blake's brow was furrowed. "Are there authorities here?"

"Oh, there are authorities," Kashmir said. "But they're not worth alerting. We could search his room again, just to be sure."

"Maybe later," I said, glancing up at the sun; there wasn't much time left before the party. "I need to run to the store for some aspirin first."

"Do you want some company, amira?" Kashmir's tone was casual, but the hope was back in his eyes, and it surprised me. How could he be so unconcerned? I hesitated, but only for a moment. After all, he was likely safer on land than on the ship, under my watchful eye.

"Sure." I took his hand as we went down the gangplank, to make sure he didn't slip. But when we reached the hot pavement of the wharf, I didn't let go. Our hands fit together perfectly; our palms two halves of a living shell, and something tender between them.

We matched steps in an easy rhythm. My shoulders dropped slowly as we walked, the tension in them easing; they'd been tighter than the halyard in a high wind. As we stood on the sidewalk, waiting for a bike to pass, Kashmir spoke. "I can't help but wonder . . . about what you said before."

"What part, exactly?"

"Joss said you're going to lose the one you love." His voice was quiet, as though the words were sneaking out; his fingers flexed around mine. "Is that me?"

I looked at him, startled. "Isn't it obvious?"

To my surprise, his face lit up, brighter than the noon sky. "It is when you put it that way."

I felt the color rising on my cheeks. Thankfully, the light changed; I started across the street. "Why do you look so happy about it?"

"Amira . . ." He faltered then. "I won't let fear of tomorrow steal joy from today."

"The joy of learning you'll be lost?"

"The joy of learning I'm loved."

"My love is a curse, Kashmir!"

"I'd rather be cursed with it than damned without it."

"Kash . . ." I turned to look at him; he gave me a crooked smile. "How can you talk about love at a time like this?"

His smile fell. "How much time do you think I have left?"

The next block was capped by a bodega with a red-and-yellow awning labeled GROCERY, the window lined with bottles of castile soap and bleach. Over the door, an ancient air conditioner dripped onto the sidewalk and did little to alleviate the stifling heat inside. The aspirin was behind the counter, between the condoms and the religious candles. "I won't let it happen," I said at last, as we waited for the proprietor to make change. "I'm not going to lose you, Kashmir."

He cocked his head. "How will you prevent it?"

I spoke through my teeth. "I'll find a way."

"Where your father never could?"

"I'm not my father," I said, but the words rang hollow.

To cover, I opened the bottle of pills and dry-swallowed two. Kash slid his hand up under my hair to rub the back of my neck; his fingers were cool on my skin. I took a deep breath, trying to relax, but the heat hit me like a fist as we stepped outside again.

Tossing the bottle of aspirin into my bag, I squinted up at the blackening sky. "We're about to get soaked."

Kash preened and plucked at his thin white shirt. "Glad I'm dressed for it."

I tried to laugh, and we hurried down the block so quickly I didn't register the first time the girl on the sidewalk called me by my name.

CHAPTER
SIX

There was something odd about her eyes.

They were the color of polished mahogany, almost doll-like, as though they were made of glass. Everything else about her seemed normal, or normal enough. She looked like she was my age, or maybe a bit younger. Her skin was rich brown, and her black hair, thick and glossy, was twisted into a bun. She wore a white bohemian top and carried a canvas tote bag, like a hundred other New Yorkers. I might never have looked at her if she hadn't said my name.

How did she know me? My scalp prickled and my heart started to race, the blood pounding in my aching head. I pressed my fingers to my temple. The last time a stranger had hailed me in port, he'd come with a deal we couldn't refuse—no matter how much I wished we had. So what did this girl want?

I bit my lip and glanced at Kashmir. He stood with his hip cocked and his free hand resting quite casually near his pocket. I knew he kept a knife there.

The girl had beckoned us to the meager slip of shade under the black awning of a retail shop that was selling, by all appearances, a single wooden chair, or perhaps the silk shirt draped over the chair's back. The store was empty but for a hopeful saleswoman. The woman kept casting glances toward us, but the door was closed against the heat; there was no way she could hear what we said. Still, I was not in the habit of speaking frankly to strangers.

"How do you know me?" I said at last.

"I don't think I do," the girl replied with a soft accent and a sideways look. "Not yet, anyway. But my father sent me to give you something." Her small hand dove into her tote bag. Kashmir tensed, but rather than a weapon, she lifted out a scroll.

A map.

A jolt went through me—but I could see immediately it wasn't the one my father was missing. The paper was too clean, too pale, and it was rolled instead of folded. It lay across her hands like an offering; beneath it, her palms were decorated with an intricate mehndi. What did the map depict? Part of me wanted to snatch it from her, and part of me was afraid to touch it until I knew where the strings were attached. "What's your name?" I said, stalling.

"I'm Dahut." The name was familiar, but I couldn't recall why, and she continued before it came to me. "Take the map. It's for you."

A distant grumble of thunder echoed her urgency—the storm was approaching, and if I stood here much longer, the paper would be damaged in the rain. I tugged on one end of the leather strip, and the map unrolled, crisp and white. My eyes skimmed over the curving lines of the brick-red ink, the same color as the design on her hands. They delineated an island city in the Iroise Sea, off the westernmost coast of France. I sucked in my breath. "Ys."

Kash peered over my shoulder. "Is what?"

"Ville D'Ys. Or Ker-Ys, if you're from Brittany rather than Bretagne. The city." I glanced up at Dahut. Then I took Kashmir's arm and pulled him closer. "The *mythical* city," I whispered. "A utopia. Supposedly the most beautiful city in Europe before it fell."

"Fell?" He cocked his head.

"Drowned."

"Like Atlantis?"

"Or Cantre'r Gwaelod, or Lyonesse. Or New Orleans, really. Much of Ker-Ys was built below sea level, and the Iroise is one of the roughest seas in the world. There was a wall protecting the city, you see?" I pointed at the map. "One day, at high tide, the king's daughter . . ." I looked back at Dahut, and now I remembered where I'd heard the name before. "Who's your father?"

She pressed her lips together—why did the question bother her? "His name is Donald. Donald Crowhurst."

I blinked at her. The mythical king of Ker-Ys had been Grandlon . . . but the name Crowhurst was still familiar. "An Englishman? Born in India?"

Her eyes narrowed then. "You know him."

"I know of him." I let the map roll shut. Kashmir was watching me closely, trying to piece it together, but I couldn't put it together myself. This was certainly not the myth I knew. "And he's the king?"

"In Ker-Ys? No," she said slowly. "Ys has no king. Not for many years. At least, that's what my father tells me."

"Really." I gave her a hard stare, but she didn't elaborate. Her hand went back into her bag; she drew out a letter.

"He wanted me to give you this, too."

A sudden wind rattled the envelope in her hand and kicked a newspaper down the street. "It's about to pour," Kash said.

I shook my head, frustrated; the heat was pressing down like a great hand, and I couldn't focus. I took the letter. It was sealed, but the mystery of the map was more compelling. It was clearly an invitation from Crowhurst. But why had he sent it to me? And was it safe to accept? Would we sail to Ker-Ys only to be caught in the flood? Joss's warnings echoed in my ears: lost at sea.

"So you've been here?" I said to the girl, gesturing with the scroll. "To Ker-Ys? What's it like?"

"What do you mean?"

"Is it as beautiful as the legend says?" A low roll of thunder thrummed in the air. "What happened to the king? And how did your father find Ker-Ys in the first place? I didn't think it had ever been mapped—"

"I don't know," she said, interrupting me. "I . . . I don't remember."

"What?" I stared at her. "Why not?"

Her jaw clenched, and a dark shadow dimmed the shine in her eyes. "I have a condition. With my memory."

"Oh." Another gust of wind pushed between us;

overhead, the clouds curdled in the heat. A memory condition? I wanted to ask, but I was sure it would be rude.

"So?" Dahut lifted her chin, making the word a challenge. "Will you help me?"

"Help you?" I tensed, remembering the words of the fortune-teller in Chinatown. "Help you do what?"

"I don't remember."

I swore under my breath. Then we both looked up as a crack of thunder split the sky. The rain began to hit the ground, distant, but coming closer, like the feet of an approaching army. Kash pulled me back under the shop's awning as the downpour swept over the sidewalk. Dahut only raised her ink-stained hand in farewell.

"Wait. Wait!"

But she walked off through the rain as steam rose from the hot concrete. I stared after her, still deeply curious—was she a Navigator too? Would she vanish as I watched? No, she only continued to the end of the block and turned the corner.

"I am torn," Kash murmured as we huddled under the canvas. "I'd like to see where she's going, but I don't want to leave you alone."

"You think she's dangerous?"

"You think she isn't?" He laughed. "What's that saying? About Trojans and horses?"

"Greeks bearing gifts."

"That's the one. But Doubt is not a Greek name."

"Dahut, I think," I corrected automatically, softening the T and giving the word a slight emphasis on the second syllable. I tucked the map into my bag. "It's the name of the princess from the fairy tale."

"The tale of Ker-Ys?" He raised an eyebrow. "And what did she do at high tide?"

I closed my eyes and pinched the bridge of my nose, trying to remember the story. "The sea gates were one of those utopian marvels. There were counterweights and springs and the like, so they opened when the tide went out, and closed when it came in. Of course, in any myth, there is always room for human error, so there was a key as well. The king kept it on a chain around his neck."

"He should have thrown it into the water. Why don't they ever do that?"

"I don't know. Maybe he did and a frog brought it back in exchange for a kiss." Kashmir cocked his head, and I waved my hand. "Different fairy tale. Never mind. Anyway, the story goes that one night, a red-bearded man—or a man dressed in red, the versions differ because of Celtic and Germanic influences on the—"

Kashmir interrupted me with an airy singsong. *"Anyway—"*

"Yes, sorry. *Anyway* . . ." I took a breath—where was I? "One night, he comes to the princess and asks her to run away with him. All she has to do is steal the key so they can lock the gates behind them and prevent the king from tracking them down. Of course, the strange man is the devil, and he uses the key to open the sea gates at high tide. Just as the city floods, a saint appears—"

"To save the town?"

"To denounce the princess for witchcraft. The town is doomed, I'm afraid."

"What kind of fairy tale is this?" Kash muttered.

I gave him a twisted smile. "Fairy tales can be pretty horrible, when you think about it. There were likely a few survivors who spread the story. But the myth only mentions the king escaping on his magical horse—a black steed that could run over the waves."

"And the princess?" Kash glanced down the sidewalk, but Dahut was long gone.

"She drowns," I said softly. "Or maybe turns into a

mermaid, depending again on the version."

Kashmir lifted his hand, catching raindrops in his palm. "I suppose in this weather, either could happen."

I laughed a little. "It does seem a little . . . far-fetched."

"It seems we've met her before her story ends."

"But even before the mermaid thing, the myth paints her as a . . ." I sorted words in my head, trying not to blush. "Well. You know how people talk about pretty women in power. They said she was . . . *sinful*."

"You mean sex."

The blush I'd been fighting won. "Yes. That's what the legends say—that she took a new lover every night, or that she was a witch and slept with the devil to get her powers. It was an allegory meant to focus on the wicked ways of the pagans. But she didn't seem . . ."

Kashmir grinned. "You can't tell just by looking."

My cheeks were hot. "She didn't seem like a princess, is what I was going to say."

"You can't always tell that, either."

"*And* the king's name in the myth was Grandlon, not Crowhurst. Crowhurst is definitely not a king."

"Then what is he?"

"Every sailor's heard the story." I dug my cell phone

out of my back pocket. Typing with a thumb, the name autocompleted once I hit C. "Donald Crowhurst," I read. "The Dark Horse of the Sea, they called him—very dramatic. Disappeared in 1969 while pretending to sail single-handedly around the world."

"Pretending?"

"He was trying to win a contest."

"Hmm. Money?"

"And fame. But he barely knew how to sail." I looked at the picture accompanying the article; a pale man in his thirties with deep-set eyes and a boyish grin. "Still, he was brilliant. He spent months alone, sending false calculations back to London that showed him in the lead. He tricked everyone—the judges, the newspapers. Even his family. They were planning a hero's welcome in England when his yacht was found abandoned in the Sargasso Sea, along with most of his logbooks. They were filled with wild ramblings and formulas for time travel. The last page showed a countdown to the end of some cosmic game. Everyone thought he'd gone mad from the strain and committed suicide, but . . ." A thrill kindled like a flame in my chest. "But he must have figured out how to Navigate instead."

How had he done it? I had learned my skills from the

captain, but Slate had discovered his abilities on a drug trip. Had months of solitude and uncertainty led Crowhurst down a similar path? But Kash was frowning. "His family? You mean aside from his daughter."

I scrolled down the screen. "He had a daughter, but her name wasn't Dahut."

Kash tapped his finger on his chin. "But Dahut is the name of the mythical princess."

"That's the weird thing."

He laughed. "Yes, *that's* the weird thing."

Tucking the phone back into my pocket, my hand went to my pearl pendant; I slid it back and forth on the chain. If there was no king, then Dahut was not a princess; if there was no princess, no one was fated to flood the city. Perhaps the map was safe to use. But was it worth it? I couldn't deny that I had questions—and more than that, I longed for this adventure. A journey to a strange utopian isle. But there were more pressing issues at hand than the mysterious fate of a mythical island.

Reluctantly, I dropped the pendant with a sigh. That was when I noticed Kash watching me, his eyes expectant. "If you're not going to read it, at least let me," he said.

"What?"

Quick as a wink, he snatched the envelope from my hand; I'd completely forgotten about it in my study of the map. He slid his finger under the flap and unfolded the paper. "'Dear Nixie,'" he began, and grimaced—even from the back, I could see the letter was written in nearly indecipherable cursive. "'Please accept my most . . . sincere apologies for . . . borrowing your father's map'?"

"What?" I snatched the letter back from him, rage pooling in my stomach. "The gall—"

"Keep reading!"

My voice was tight with anger, but I continued aloud. "'I had to ensure you would accept my invitation, as I have great need of your assistance in Ker-Ys. I have grand plans; already I have saved the island from its fate. I think it will be of particular interest to you and your father that, using the skills we share, I've conceived of a way to change—'"

I stopped then, the end of the sentence sticking to the back of my tongue.

"Change what, amira?"

My lips moved, but no sound came out. The rain drummed on the canvas overhead, falling so hard that the drops bounced from the concrete, wetting the toes of my shoes. The air was much cooler now, and smelled like minerals. Water flooded the gutters and ran in rivulets across the pavement.

"Amira? Change what?"

I cleared my throat and forced the words out. "The past."

CHAPTER
SEVEN

Kashmir shook his head. "This is the most obvious con I've ever seen."

I glanced up from the letter. "A con?"

"Step inside, I'll show you wonders!" He gave me a grand gesture and a huckster's smile. "Payment up front, of course."

Scanning Crowhurst's letter again, I shook my head. "He doesn't mention money at all."

"Your talents are more valuable. Remember, amira, this has happened before."

The air was cool now, but at his words, I went cold. "This isn't the same as Hawaii."

"No? Tell me. Utopia—isn't that another word for paradise?"

"Paradises are generally god-given. Utopias are man-made."

"I trust men even less than I trust gods. Come, amira. Doesn't this seem a little too convenient?"

In spite of his words, excitement kindled a flame in my chest. "But she said there was no king—that's very different from the myth. And if that was a new version of Dahut, he must have changed *something*."

"Version?" Kashmir stared at me, disgust thick in his voice. "What does that mean?"

"Well. You know. What I said before—how the myth talks about the princess being . . ." I made a vague, voluptuous gesture with my hands. "And she's still alive. I mean, if he's saved her, maybe I can—"

"What I mean is, how can a person have versions?"

"All myths have versions," I said with a shrug. "I mean, in some stories her name isn't even Dahut, it's Ahes. That's one of the things that makes it a myth. It's only once everyone agrees on one version of the past that it becomes history."

"But that's because people tell different stories, isn't it? Not because there are different *versions* walking about!"

"I don't know. Why does it bother you so much? I mean, you've been on the ship when we've visited mythological maps. You even came from a . . ." My voice trailed off at the look in his eyes. "Oh."

Kashmir turned his head, staring at the falling rain. I chewed my lip. For a long time, neither of us spoke.

"Some people say that everyone has a doppelgänger," I offered at last. "That's like a different version of you. Like a twin. But usually evil." I frowned as the next thought came. "Or sometimes just a harbinger of bad luck."

"That's not helpful."

"Right." I pressed my lips together to keep my foot out of my mouth. Kashmir did have a larger point. Crowhurst was infamous for his lies; moreover, his invitation did seem suspiciously well timed. And how had he found us in the first place? I wished Dahut had been more forthcoming—or that Crowhurst had come himself. Odd that he'd had sent her with a letter instead. Especially in light of her condition.

A memory disorder? It was hard to imagine; my own memory had always been encyclopedic. I made a new search on the cell phone. The link to the Mayo Clinic listed Alzheimer's, Huntington's, dementia—but the girl hadn't been older than sixteen. I kept scrolling. Traumatic head injury? No, she'd still be in the hospital if something like that had happened in the last few days. Retrograde amnesia was very rarely caused by brain tumors—I bit my lip; poor thing—but more often by alcohol, drugs . . . depression. I held my breath, my mind no longer on the girl.

My finger hovered over the blue hotlink on the word; at a touch, a new screen loaded. Causes: loss, death . . . genetics. I scrolled past them hurriedly; I'd read—and worried—about them before, when I'd first realized my father's peculiarities might have been heritable. My eyes fell on the risks: substance abuse. Family conflicts. Suicide.

I clicked the phone dark and dropped it into my bag. Then I scrubbed my palm on my shorts. "Slate will need his map back someday."

"Well." Kash folded his arms across his chest. "You and I are the only ones who know where it is."

"Kashmir." I gaped at him, and he threw his hands in the air.

"What? Amira! It's the same dans tous les cas! If the past cannot be changed, the captain will find a way back to Honolulu, no matter where that particular map is. And if it can be changed, then Joss's prediction for you and me is nothing to fear! Isn't that what this is really about?"

"What if Crowhurst is telling the truth?" I shot back. "What if he knows how to save us?"

"And what if this is how it happens? You said the sea was rough in Ker-Ys."

"You'd be roped in—" I started, but he shook his head.

"If it's fate, does it matter? There's a story about this—a man who fled his destiny only to meet it on the road. He blinded himself when he saw the truth of it."

"Oedipus?"

"That's the one. You taught me that."

The reproach in his face cut to the quick. "So I should do nothing? You want to be lost?"

"Of course I don't! But I don't want to lose you either."

"You won't."

"I already am." His voice was bitter; he kicked at a bottle cap. "There's a wall around you now, amira. You built it with your father. I don't know who holds the key."

I clenched my fists, crushing the letter. "There's got to be a way, Kashmir. There has to be a way for me to take my fate in my own hands."

"Khodaye man." Kash shook his head. "You sound just like him."

His words knocked the wind out of me. "Never say that again."

We waited in a prickly silence for the rain to ease before returning to the ship along sidewalks washed clean and fresh. Rotgut, Blake, and Bee were already sitting at the folding table on the deck, feasting under a makeshift sail-cloth awning. Overhead, the sky was clearing, and at their feet, Billie made Romeo eyes at the roast.

"Surprise," Bee said with a wry grin when she spotted us coming up the gangplank. I winced. I had completely forgotten the party. But she waved my shame away. "Come, sit! There is a brisket. What are children for if not to scold and feed?"

My appetite had deserted me, but I sat at the table, slipping bits of brisket to Billie as Bee regaled us with the story—her favorite—of how she and Ayen had married. I had heard it many times, but Blake had not, and he sat, rapt and a little bemused, at Bee's energetic retelling.

"We met at a dance, and she . . . hmm." Bee half closed her eyes at the memory. "Words fall so short. Her energy, her movement, her legs! I knew the moment I saw her that she was for me. She was being wooed already." She grinned toothily. "But I was a better man than him."

Blake cocked his head. "How so, exactly?"

"I had bigger cattle! More of them too." Bee's eyes went soft at the sight of her own memories. "It seems like yesterday we were betrothed. My family was proud, of course. My two brothers had died young, and my sister was married with many children. I alone kept our name, and our herd. We were very happy, Ayen and me. Not so much, her old suitor. But the joke is on him." Bee looked around the table and spread her arms. "For now we have three children, and his name is forgotten. I got revenge, you see." She drew one finger across the scar at her throat. "And he had no wife."

She hesitated then, glancing back toward the captain's cabin. Usually this was the part of the story where she mentioned how she and Slate had become friends—Bee seeking justice, her slit throat still healing, and Slate, heartbroken for her and happy to give over the gun he'd brought all the way from 1980s New York. But now she only smiled, her eyes touched with rare sorrow. "I am a lucky one, to know love."

"And to have lived to tell the tale," Blake said.

At that, Kashmir lifted his head and put down his fork; his eyes cut to me and then away. "The loving's more important than the living, Mr. Hart."

Blake only shrugged. "Love isn't much of a legacy, Mr. Firas."

"I think there's none better."

"It doesn't last."

"It doesn't have to."

"Maybe love is like life that way," Rotgut volunteered

through a mouthful of pastry. "Doesn't have to be forever to be worth it."

I gave him a weak smile. "Did you learn that back at the monastery?"

"Maybe. Or maybe it's from a pop song? Either way, it's top-notch wisdom, and don't forget it." He popped another bite of cheesecake into his mouth.

"I could have considered it a life well lived if I'd died in Ayen's arms." Bee gave us a wicked grin. "In fact, I did a little, and more than once, if you get my meaning. Ach! Ayen!" She ducked, her hand going to her ear as though it had been pinched—perhaps it had been.

"I was in love once," Rotgut said.

"With what?" Bee teased. "The pastry?"

"Oh!" He swatted at the air, dismissive. "That was just a fling!"

"A moment on the lips, eternally on the hips," Bee responded, elbowing him in the bony ribs. But I leaned forward across the table, curious. I'd never heard this story before.

"What was their name?"

"It's not respectful to say it." Rotgut shook his head, smiling a little. "He gave it up, you know. In the end. Like everything else. He was much more cut out for monking than I was. But I still try to live in the moment. To honor him."

Bee lifted her water glass; he clinked it with his bottle of lager. And across the table, Kashmir watched me, his eyes as green and turbulent as an ocean gyre. "That's all we can do," he said softly. "Live in the moment. Love in the moment."

In my chest, a pressure lifted, as though I had surfaced from deep water; looking at Kashmir, I wondered suddenly which one of us I had been trying to save. To the west, the sun reclined on a glorious pyre. A breeze from the ocean strummed the rigging, and the air was blissfully cool after the storm. Maybe they were right. Maybe love did not have to be forever. Maybe it could just be for *now*—after all, now was all we had.

Had Joss sent her warning not to protect me from loss, but to remind me not to follow my father's path in dealing with it? But in spite of all his foibles, Slate had chosen to stop. Maybe I could too.

Forget Ker-Ys. Forget the past and the future. I stood then, feeling the weight of my messenger bag in the strap across my shoulder, even though it only held the map. Bee cocked her head. "Where are you going, girl?"

"To check on the captain," I said—which was partially

true. I didn't want to say it in front of everyone else, but later tonight, when the moon was rising and the ship was quiet, I would find Kash in his cabin and tell him how I'd put the map of Ker-Ys in the cupboard with all the other improbable myths too dangerous to visit. For now, I only gave him a smile. "Be right back."

I strode across the deck, feeling energized—expansive. There was a silly grin forming on my face as I pushed open the door, peering into the dim. After a moment, it melted away.

The captain was sitting on the edge of the bed in his little alcove, shoving something under his pillow.

I saw two routes before me, then, like deep indigo rivers twisting between the azure threat of shallow reefs, both ways fraught with peril: say something, say nothing. The latter route was tempting, but I had floundered on those rocks before. I started toward him, propelled by a burst of sudden anger. "You swore you gave that up."

"Nixie, it's not what you think!" Slate held up his hands in a placating gesture, but I was already pulling back the pillow. Then I took another breath.

Instead of a syringe, it was a pistol.

"Well, you're right," I said at last. "It's not at all what I thought." I tossed the pillow aside and picked up the gun. It was a double-barreled derringer—small and complex and deadly as a cone snail. I shuddered; the last time I'd seen this weapon, it had been pointed at me. "This is Blake's."

"It was in his pocket when he came aboard. I found it in his jacket." Slate ran a hand through his blond hair; it was lank with sweat. "I haven't given it back yet. I will, but—"

"I don't know that he'd want it back." I shook my head. "Not just yet."

"No harm in me keeping it, then."

"I suppose. But not under your pillow. You could hurt yourself." I opened one of the cupboards—full of the maps we called dead enders—and put the gun on the shelf. Then I hesitated, considering. Light glinted off the stamped scrolling in the steel barrel. I turned back to my father, but he did not return my gaze. Substance abuse. Family conflicts. Suicide. "Slate."

"What, Nixie?" He did look then, his blue eyes wide, bloodshot. "What?"

My heart clenched in my chest; the pressure was back and I couldn't breathe. Still I hesitated: say something, say nothing. "Nothing," I said. But I snatched the gun from the shelf and shoved it into my back pocket. My palms were sweaty, my blood racing. But Slate only dropped his head to his hands. Why did he look so small? "Don't worry, Dad. I know where your map is. We're sailing tomorrow to get it back."

"No."

"No?" I stared at him, waiting for him to elaborate. "Why not?"

"Maybe it's better this way." He sighed, sinking lower still. "Easier, not to have to choose."

"Choose what? Between me and my mother? Or . . ." I didn't finish the sentence, and he didn't answer the question—he was bent, defeated, a broken thing. Was this my future? Was I staring my own fortune in the face? "Forget your map. We're still sailing."

"I'm not fit to take the helm."

"I'll do it, then."

"So eager now, to take my place?"

I swallowed, bracing myself, but he said nothing more. The only sound in the room was the rustling of the maps in the breeze through the deadlights, and the ragged sound of his breath, as though he was the one struggling to keep his head above the rising tide.

That night I lay in my hammock, studying the map of Ker-Ys as the moon climbed to the top of the sky and leaped.

The red lines had begun to blur and fade in my head when a sound made me blink awake.

"Mr. Firas said we'll be leaving soon. Is it true?"

So Kashmir had guessed—but of course he had. Perhaps there hadn't ever been any doubt. Rubbing the sleep from my eyes, I sat up, the hammock swaying beneath me. Blake was standing on deck facing the skyline, silhouetted against the glow of the city. "It is."

"We've barely scratched the surface here."

"We'll be back soon enough."

I heard the smile in his voice. "I thought we were supposed to live in the now."

"It's hard when what you need is in the past."

"I do know that." He turned from the rail to face me, although his eyes were shadowed and I could not read his expression. "Is that the map we'll be visiting?"

"Want to see?" I turned the paper toward him; he came closer and took it with gentle hands.

"Ker-Ys. From Souvestre's peasant tales from Brittany, isn't it?" I raised an eyebrow, impressed, but he only smiled. "I had a classical education, Miss Song. But how will we visit a place that exists only in myth?"

I wet my lips . . . how to put it? "As long as the mapmaker

believed what he drew, this map should work as well as any other."

Now it was his turn to look impressed. "Do mapmakers have so much power?"

"The Navigator has to believe too, of course."

"And do you?"

"Why shouldn't I? I grew up visiting places just like it."

"Fascinating." He squinted at the map. "I wonder how a utopia will compare to paradise? Though I suppose both are eventually lost."

"Well . . ." I turned toward the Atlantic, as though I could see all the way to the fabled vasty fields of France. "The myth may not play out as we've read it."

Blake looked at me sharply. "What do you mean?"

I took the map back from him and handed him the letter. "There's a man there who claims he knows how to . . . to alter history."

"What?" Blake's eyes gleamed as he scanned the page. "How?"

I traced the red lines of the map with one finger. "I hope to learn."

He caught his breath. "And what could you do with knowledge like that?"

I opened my mouth to answer, then closed it again when I saw the hope in his face. I had been so focused on rescuing Kashmir, but what else was possible? Could I save my mother, like Slate had dreamed he could? Could I save the island that Blake loved? Could I look through history with perfect hindsight and undo the injustices of the past? I took a deep breath, feeling giddy. "I . . . I suppose . . . if it works . . . I could do almost anything."

Island of Ker-Ys
- 17th Century -

1. Abbey
2. Cathedral
3. Palace
4. Square
5. Grand Rue
6. Tavern
7. Warehouse
8. Wharf
9. Harbor
10. Sea Gates
11. Sea Walls

CHAPTER
EIGHT

Late the next day, the *Temptation* pointed back toward the Atlantic. Her sails were full of the hot summer breeze, and I was at the helm, the wheel warm and firm in my hand.

The morning had seen a flurry of activity as the crew—my crew—made ready for the journey. Bee and Ayen had inspected the ship, double-checking our repairs in case we encountered rough weather in the Margins. Rotgut organized the supplies he'd ordered—toothpaste, vitamins, even a mattress for Blake's room. And Kashmir had taken Blake to get his vaccinations. When they returned, Bee clapped Blake on the shoulder.

"You make me proud!" Then she turned to Kashmir. "Did he flinch? You cannot flinch when you get your gaar," she said, pointing to the scars decorating her forehead.

"Or they cut you crooked and everyone will see you're a coward. Your *gaar* are different than mine, but I knew you'd be brave. You did not flinch the first time." She whacked Blake on the stomach, then, where the bullet had hit him. Then she hit him on the shoulder again, hard. "Why would you flinch the second?"

"Thank you for your faith in me. Though I should mention," Blake added, his smile deepening. "It was the other shoulder."

She laughed then, and hit him on the other side, and he did not flinch.

In preparation for our journey, I had spent some time cleaning the ship. Anything that wasn't bolted down had to be safely stowed, and physical work was always calming to me. Besides, now that I'd given over my room, most of the mess was made up of my scattered possessions.

I carted my books to the captain's cabin and shoved my clothes into my trunk, which Rotgut and Bee had moved to Kashmir's room with much winking and mugging. Crowhurst's letter, however, stayed with me. I didn't want to let it out of my hands. It felt like a talisman—a promise. Besides, what if Slate found it? I couldn't risk getting his hopes up, especially since I wasn't yet certain that Crowhurst was telling the truth. I didn't think my father could survive another disappointment.

I had not seen him since I'd told him I was taking the helm, in what might have been the least dramatic mutiny in history or myth. Even the crew had seemed unsurprised; Bee had only nodded at the news, and Rotgut had muttered that he'd known this day was coming. But as the wind breathed life into our sails and the sea unfurled before me, I couldn't help but think of Slate, lying in his cabin three yards under my feet.

I was not yet accustomed to taking the helm without my father at my side. I gripped the wheel tighter; it was fashioned of teak and bronze and inlaid with the words of the wheel of fortune in Latin: *regnabo, regno, regnavi, sum sine regno.* I shall reign, I reign, I have reigned, I have no kingdom.

Absently, I ran my thumb over a blue patch of verdigris. The first time I'd read those words, the *Temptation* had been at half sail in a mythical version of the Pileh Lagoon, where limestone cliffs cupped the calm jade waters like the fingers of a benevolent god. Earlier that day, Rotgut had bought a box of fruit off a peddler's colorful skiff; Slate had dumped out the produce and turned the box upside down, setting it before the wheel so I could reach the handles. Laughing, he'd stood behind me, adjusting my hands, showing me how to steer as lychee rolled this way and that across the deck. In the water, white hong swans with long flowing tails drifted around the ship, and their song was the sound of bells chiming.

But the Mer d'Iroise would be nothing like the still waters in Thailand. Would we be ready for the rough seas ahead? I swept my eyes across the deck to check the crew, but everyone was in place. Bee at the foremast, the cowbell clanging against her thigh. Rotgut up in the crow's nest, peering out with bright eyes at the shining water. And Kashmir, near the mizzenmast, his knees bent, his body moving with the ship as she skipped over the rippling bay.

I had insisted on checking his jack lines myself before we'd left the harbor. He'd watched me fuss, his expression serious. Kash had changed clothes in preparation for visiting an older era—a white tunic over dark, slim-fitting britches—but as I'd tugged the straps of his harness, I'd noticed the lock was still at his waist, hanging from his black leather belt. Would it be a weight, or a buoy? Swallowing, I'd started checking the straps a second time, but he caught my hand. "Aroom bash, amira. The lines are strong. The only way I'll be lost is if the ship goes down too."

"That won't happen," I said quickly—to him, or to myself? But Kashmir nodded.

"Not with you at the helm."

Now, I tightened my grip on the wheel, trying to focus again on the far horizon. But I was painfully aware of the distance between me and Kashmir. I wished he would trade places with Blake, who stood behind me on the quarterdeck. But Blake couldn't handle a sail. He'd only wanted to observe the Navigation and had promised to stay out of the way—a promise he kept for nearly fifteen minutes.

"I've been wondering—"

"Of course you have."

"Well, you can't present me a puzzle and expect me not to try to solve it!" Blake clasped his hands behind his back. His boots were freshly polished; already he looked more like the dapper young gentleman I'd met strolling through downtown Honolulu. "How does it work, Miss Song?"

"What, exactly?"

"The Navigation! Is it magic?"

"I suppose that's one theory."

"And the others?"

"Wormholes. Alternate universes. Mass energy causing closed timelike curves." At his look, I added, "I had a classical education, Mr. Hart." He laughed. The sails hummed overhead, waves whispered against the hull, and my father's words resurfaced from the day he'd taught me: know where you're going, let go of where you're from.

"We might be traveling between worlds," I added then. "Or just visiting a time before magic was replaced with science. But I've always just thought of it as . . . as Navigation."

"Typically, mariners restrict the seas they sail to the usual seven."

"Can you be sure?" I adjusted my hands on the wheel. "These maps, these stories—they reach us somehow. From somewhere."

"Are you saying Ker-Ys actually existed?"

"I'm saying it does exist, in some point in time. All stories come from somewhere—from a shared memory or a hope or a history now forgotten. And the peasants Souvestre spoke to definitely believed in it."

"Souvestre wrote about morgens and mermaids and man-eating wolves, as well. Do you believe in those too?"

"I do." Unbidden, the memory returned of the map of Tahiti and the creature in the water; I suppressed a shudder. Then I gave him a sidelong look. "But you're no stranger to the fantastical."

He rocked a little on his heels, and his hand went once more to his side. How much did he remember about that night in Honolulu, the healing spring, the Hu'akai Po? Blake's voice was faraway when he spoke again. "Sounds dangerous."

I glanced down at Kashmir once more, remembering his words: Trojans and horses. "It might be."

Why did Crowhurst need my assistance? His letter hadn't exactly been clear on the details. And on closer study, the map had raised questions of its own. The red lines charting Ker-Ys still swam behind my eyes. The paper itself was just that—paper, not parchment or vellum—and it was crisp and new. Crowhurst must have had an older version—the one he'd used to arrive in Ker-Ys in the first place. What had he found when he'd arrived? More importantly, how had he managed to change it?

Though early tales of a sunken city had begun circulating during the Age of Discovery, the map of Ker-Ys was marked 1637. The version of the myth describing the city's downfall had first been published that same year. By then, the story had included all the major elements: the princess, the devil, the king. At least—it should have. But Dahut had said there was no king. And of course there was Dahut herself, seeming more wayward than wicked. Was she still fated to open the sea gates and be cursed with a mermaid's tail? Was she a mythological princess, or just an ordinary girl like me?

Well. I raked the hair out of my eyes as I steered the black ship toward the edge of the world. Perhaps not so ordinary.

"What's changed, Miss Song?" Blake's voice was soft—only meant for me to hear.

"What?" I glanced over at him, but he was watching the horizon. "What do you mean?"

He sighed. "The other night, you were so willing to embrace the inevitable—to bend the knee to history as written. Today you're steering the ship to a mythic island to try to learn how to alter the past. What changed your mind?"

I squeezed the handles of the wheel. "You were right. About fighting back."

"Even if you'll fail?"

"I won't fail." The words came out low, fierce—and my eyes went back to Kashmir. Blake cocked his head; in the silence between us, I could practically hear his thoughts.

"I see."

Past the buoys at the mouth of the river, the fog crept up, floating, shimmering like a veil. The mist was cool, pleasant after the briny humidity of the city; it condensed on the warm bronze wheel and smelled faintly of honey.

Beside me, Blake took a deep breath of the foggy air. "Is this the Margins, Miss Song?"

I only nodded, putting all thoughts of New York behind me, shedding the heat, the horns, the crush of humanity. Ahead, the answers to my questions lay just beyond the horizon—all I had to do was get us there safely. The deck of the ship began to roll, but I'd roped in too—we all had. This was, after all, a fairy-tale map as well as the Mer d'Iroise; I'd expected the waves to rise. But the temperature was dropping as well. Even in the thick of the fog I could see my breath turn to crystal. Goose bumps flashed across my skin like a school of little fish. I shivered; I'd changed shorts for trousers, but my arms were still bare.

Blake rubbed his hands together. "Is Navigation always so cold?"

I shook my head. "It must be winter there."

"Winter." He shook his head, wondering. "I've only ever heard stories."

"Let's hope the weather is the most singular thing you see," I said. Then the ship surged forward with a current and the boom pulled at the rigging; I gave the wheel a quarter turn. The pale fog swirled around us, interminable and strange. As the wind rose, it carried notes of a song to my ears—distantly familiar—and snatched them away almost as quickly. I squinted up to see if it was Rotgut, but the crow's nest was lost in the mist. Besides, it didn't sound like his voice—it was too airy, too breathless. I bit my lip as it came again: above the roar and shush of the waves, a high voice, clear, singing a sad sea shanty.

"Go down and put on a coat, Blake."

"I'm quite hardy—"

"I need you out of the way."

His eyebrows went up at my tone, and for a moment, I wondered if he would disobey—and what I would do if he did. But the ship was under my command, and all souls aboard were too. I couldn't let him argue, not now. He must have seen it on my face, because he stepped down the stairs toward the hatch. I was briefly grateful for the silence, but alone on the quarterdeck, the white expanse of fog made me feel very small.

The crew moved on the deck like dark wraiths. The wind intensified, thrumming in the rat lines and snapping at the sails, and the ship groaned as the mast creaked. My heart hammered in my chest as the memory of our last journey crept into my head—the thick mists, the lightning, and the black tentacle dragging Kash overboard.

My hands were slick on the wheel. What had I been thinking, taking the helm without Slate to guide me? My anger at him had gotten the better of me—or perhaps it was my hubris. Was I a fool to try to cheat fate? I sought Kashmir through the fog. What if he'd been right? What if this was how I lost him?

Beneath my feet, the *Temptation* seesawed. The ship climbed a mountainous wave, then dipped down so sharply I was sure that, but for the mist, I'd be looking at the bottom of the sea. Kash was fairly dancing on the deck below—beside him, Bee was hauling in the lines on the foresail. She glanced back at me, her wide eyes bright in the dark. I could almost hear her voice in the look she gave me: you cannot flinch.

They'd done this before—and so had I. I tore my eyes away from the crew and pinned them to the uncertain horizon.

Squinting into the fog off the prow, I redrew the map in the space behind my eyes: the crescent of the island and the slip of a protected bay, all encircled by the thick seawalls. Ker-Ys, the most beautiful city in France—a kingdom without a king. I filled my mind with the myth I knew and the map I'd studied, and I did not search for a glimpse of our destination. Rather, I waited. I knew, without doubt, that the city was there.

This was the trick of Navigation—the most difficult part: the belief, the unflinching faith. And it was so clear in my head that I could not pinpoint the moment when it appeared through the shifting mist off the prow, but in the same way as dawn turns to day, there it was.

"Land!" Rotgut sang out from the crow's nest. The icy fog did not lift so much as thin in the golden light of morning. The sun was burning cold in the east, sparkling through the crystalline air and silhouetting the spires of Ker-Ys.

There, on the horizon: a sugarplum city, rising up from the silvery waves like a confection on a tray. The compact little town of slate roofs and Gothic steeples surrounded an elegant castle embroidered with stone carved like lace. The towers and turrets, cottages and cobbled streets—all were set inside the sun-gilded granite seawalls like a bezel of rough crystal, and around the wall, waves washed white as they broke on the stone.

Blake came back above, wearing a long coat of felted wool; when he glanced off the prow toward the city, I could hear his intake of breath.

"It looks like something out of a fairy tale," he said softly.

"Well." Pride bloomed in my chest; automatically, I glanced over my shoulder, looking for my father, before I realized he was not on deck. I took a deep breath and turned back toward the city on the horizon. "It is."

CHAPTER

NINE

We were out of the mist of the Margins, but the winter sun did little to warm us, and the wind purled in fitful gusts, pressing through my thin shirt as though it were made of gauze. Through chattering teeth, I called for the crew to spell off for warmer gear. Bee went below first, returning with an extra coat for Rotgut; Kash went next, bringing me my good red cloak.

"Here, Captain," he said, settling the heavy velvet around my shoulders as I held the wheel.

I blinked at the honorific. "Thank you, Kash."

He smiled, but only a little. Then he jogged back to the main deck as I turned the rudder to meet a current that drew us toward Ker-Ys on a path laced with creamy foam.

The city seemed to float on the white waves, stately: a castle in the clouds. Crowhurst was there, and so were the answers I needed. As we approached the island, my heart was beating like an oarsman's drum. But I kept a weather eye as Kash and Bee adjusted the sails to catch the capricious wind. It puffed in the sheets and scuffed the whitecaps, pushing us unsteadily east as the ship rocked on the rolling gray. The restless seas of the Margins had given way to the tumultuous Mer d'Iroise.

Here, locals claimed the tides rose at the speed of a galloping horse, the high water climbing fifty feet above the lurking rocks of low tide. Currents raced through the English Channel, harsh storms raked the coast, and patches of pale gray water hinted at rocky reefs under the shifting surface.

Tall menhir jutted out of the swirling water; we passed a pile of rock where the bones of old shipwrecks glittered under a crust of salt. The north side of the island was thick with twisted trees; nesting in them were creatures I mistook for cormorants until we came closer and I saw they were guivres. Souvestre had mentioned them too—a local sort of dragonlet that made a home near bodies of water.

The guivres circled out over the sea to fish, coasting on wings flung wide, until they folded like knives and tipped down into the sea. I smiled to see them emerging victorious, silver fish twisting in their jaws; they reminded me of Swag, the little sea dragon that had once belonged to both me and my mother.

The tide continued falling as we neared the island. The waves licked up the stones; pulling back, they revealed seaweed like glossy mounds of jade at the base of the wall. We came about to the south, where the bronze doors protected the little harbor. They were enormous, easily three feet thick and fifty feet tall, though the dark algal stain of the highwater mark was only a few feet from the top.

As we waited, the bells began to toll the changing tides— the fabled bells of Ker-Ys. A deep rumble vibrated through the deck of the ship, and little whirlpools formed in the foam at the base of the wall as the gates began to roll open.

Would Crowhurst meet us at the dock? It was only midmorning, and the island was small—even if I had to seek him out, I could certainly find him before evening. I leaned forward, eager to enter the harbor, but as the gates slid back, a little flotilla of fishing boats splashed out into the open water. They swarmed around us like goslings around a swan, slow and clumsy; in their bellies, red water sloshed from buckets of chum.

Rotgut called down from the crow's nest. "What do you catch in these waters?"

An oarsman squinted back with hard eyes in a weathered face. "Everything we can."

The fishing boats swept toward deeper water as we continued into the harbor. I searched the wharf for a glimpse of Crowhurst, but he was not there. Still, there was activity aboard a sleek corvette docked at the pier—the other tall ship in harbor.

Was this his vessel? I scanned her deck, but I did not see him at the helm or among the busy crew. They hopped and hefted, making ready to sail. The corvette was much bigger than the *Temptation*, maybe a hundred twenty feet at the waterline, but built with grace. Though it had been worn by the water and scraped by some sort of blade, the name *Santé* was barely visible in peeling paint along her prow, and her striped sails gave her a devil-may-care appearance, countered by the rotting head hanging in a net from the tip of her bowsprit.

I narrowed my eyes. This was the golden age of piracy, and corsairs schooled like sharks between San Malo and the Barbary Coasts. But the prim harbormaster directed us to a berth beside the corvette, and as we pulled up to the pier, her captain hailed us.

"Ho, *Temptation*!" She was a tall woman in her twenties, with freckled cheeks and wild curls barely contained by a

French cocked hat. Her crew swarmed around her, but she stood still, one hand up, the breeze toying with the ostrich feathers in her cap.

My own crew set to making fast—Kash showing Blake how to take in the sails, and Rotgut setting out the gangplank and tying us to the dock. I raised my hand in response, thinking it was only courtesy, but the woman sauntered to the rail.

"I know this ship!" Her hazel eyes glittered. "But not her captain."

My brows went up. I did not recognize her or her vessel—so when had she seen the *Temptation*? Bee came to the rail before I could ask. "Gwen." Bee's smile was guarded. "How long has it been?"

"Two years? Three?"

"Right." Bee gave me a significant look. "Ribat, in 1745."

I blinked. The map of Ker-Ys had been marked 1637.

Was the map I'd gotten from Dahut misdated? This wouldn't be the first time. But no—the harbormaster's tidy outfit had included a high wig and heels on his boots; by the eighteenth century, those fashions had gone by the wayside. I peered at Gwen. Could she be a Navigator as well? Slate had said he'd never met another. But if not, how had she gotten from her own time to a mythical island in seventeenth-century

France? I couldn't ask her—at least not directly. And she had noticed my scrutiny, meeting it with her own.

"Things have changed since last I saw the black ship." Gwen leaned over the rail to size me up. "Hullo, little chicken. Are you my replacement?"

"You were never captain of the *Temptation*," I said.

She smiled without humor. "Neither are you. Bee, tell me she lies," she cried then, pushing back from the rail, sweeping off her hat, and slapping it against her thigh. "Tell me he's not dead!"

The anguish in her voice shocked me, but before I could form the words to reassure her, Slate's rusty voice preceded him out of his cabin.

"Dead?" The door creaked open, and he stood, stooped, on the threshold, squinting at the light. He wore no shirt, though he didn't seem to feel the cold, and his tattoos looked like bruises on the pale skin of his arms. "Not yet."

"Slate!" Gwen's eyes went wide with glee. Leaping onto her ship's rail, she teetered on the edge for a moment, then hopped down, her hobnailed boots ringing on our deck as she pelted toward my father. But she faltered when she got close; one hand shot out, stopping inches from Slate's haggard face. "What happened to you?"

"Time." At his answer, her brow furrowed, but Slate turned his head, staring at our surroundings with incurious eyes. "Where the hell are we, Nixie?"

"I left the map on your desk," I told him, but Gwen interrupted.

"They call the place Ville d'Ys, but I'm marking it a vigia. I recommend you do the same."

Vigia—a term on maps that meant to keep close watch for danger. The sort of place marked HERE ARE DRAGONS BORN. I frowned. "Why's that?"

Gwen's eyes gleamed under the brim of her hat. "Strange fish in the water. You should turn back."

Slate half shrugged. "I'm not a fisherman."

"There's something weird about this place," she insisted. "Uncanny. We left the Port of London yesterday morning, and we were in harbor by first watch. My ship is fast, but not that fast. And this morning, my whole crew reported dreaming the same dream. I'll tell you this," she said, leaning closer, as though afraid to say the words too loud. "I've been on this route since I weren't no older than your new girl, and I never saw this place until last night."

I glanced at Slate, my eyes round. Was Gwen a Navigator after all? But my father didn't even seem curious. "Did you come through a fog?" I asked her.

"A fog? No. It was a storm." She laughed without joy and gave Slate a sidelong look. "Should have known better than to let a strange man handle my ship."

"Someone else took the helm?" My heart quickened. "Was his name Crowhurst, by any chance?"

"Couldn't tell you. His coin did most of his talking. Mark me, leave while the gate's open and the weather's clear. This place is cursed."

"You can't leave without him," I said quickly.

She turned back, incredulous. "Beg pardon?"

I bit my lip—but what could I tell her? That the Margins would rise up around her and trap her ship in a sailor's purgatory? "What if he needs passage back?"

"I'm not going back to London." Gwen spat on the deck as she strode starboard, toward her ship, but she stopped at the edge of the deck, both hands on the rail. "You haven't asked me where I'm bound," she said then, and I knew she wasn't talking to me.

She and I both turned to Slate, and I waited for him to tell her to stay—to tell her that she'd never make it past the mist without a Navigator at the helm. But would she listen, if he did? Slate only shook his head. "We risked our necks to free you from the *Santé*, Gwen. Why did you go back?"

"But she's not the *Santé* anymore. When I took over, I named her after her old captain. See?" Gwen nodded to the rotting head.

Slate frowned. "The *Jack*?"

"The *Fool*. I'm bound for Salé," she said, as though he had asked after all. "There's money there. I'll wait for you if you ask me to."

"Salé?" Slate's eyes narrowed, and my own shoulders tensed. The biggest slave markets in the Barbary trade could be found in Salé. Slate knew it too. "Are you carrying on Jack's trade, Gwen?"

"Why do you ask? It doesn't look like you're in the market for new crew."

Gwen leaped up then, catching hold of the anchor line and pulling herself aboard the *Fool*. The crew doubled their efforts under her watchful eye, and soon enough they were ready to cast off. I clamped all my warnings behind my teeth—I had little pity for a slaver. And Gwen didn't look back as she maneuvered the corvette out of the sea gates and into the open water. Slate watched after her—but when I caught his eye, he only turned and went back into his cabin.

CHAPTER

TEN

At least I knew Crowhurst was somewhere in the city. But where? He was not waiting at the dock, and when I asked the harbormaster, he told me he had never even heard of the man. Apparently he'd marked down the name of the Fool's captain as "Cook." Was it only a mistake, or was Crowhurst deliberately trying to hide his presence? I did not know, and I could not ask, at least not until he arrived. So I tried to conceal my disappointment as I handed over the port fee. It was higher than I'd expected, but the harbormaster's haughty look invited no bargaining.

Kashmir raised an eyebrow when he saw me counting out the coin. "I suppose that's how he affords such fancy dress," he murmured after the man had gone.

"What kind of utopia would it be without pretty shoes?" I asked.

"I might take a look around. Try to find out."

There was an invitation in Kashmir's voice; reluctantly, I shook my head. "I should stay with the ship in case Crowhurst comes. The harbor is the first place he'll look for me."

His eyes darkened, and he turned toward the gangplank. "Suit yourself."

I watched him go, unease growing in my chest—but he would be safe on land, wouldn't he? Unless there was a flood. "Come back before high tide," I told him.

"Aye, Captain."

"And be careful out there!"

He only laughed—a mocking sound. "It's a utopia, amira. What could go wrong?"

I made a face, watching him until he was out of sight. Then I settled in to wait, growing increasingly frustrated as the hours passed.

This far north, the winter days were short. By late afternoon, dusk had crept between the stone houses, the two-story malouinières and the low longères, nestling in corners and lying down in the streets. The tide rushed back home in time for sunset, and all before the church bells tolled six. The haunting sound of vespers drifted from the cathedral, and across the town, candlelight flickered like will-o' the-wisps as hearth smoke curled up to meet the clouds that scudded between the sea and the scattered stars.

But above the city, the craggy turrets of the château remained dark. Dahut had told the truth—I had confirmed it with the harbormaster. There was no king in Ker-Ys.

I'd tried to ask the man what had happened, but he'd made the sign of the fig—a fist, with his thumb trapped between his fore and middle fingers, meant to ward off evil—and gestured toward the castle. "Le château, il est abandonné," he'd said darkly, striding away over the cupped boards of the pier.

The temperature dropped even further as night fell, and after we'd eaten, the crew bundled up and disappeared into their cabins for some much-needed rest. Once they had, I strung my hammock—all by myself this time. Then I pulled socks over my hands and blankets over my head and tried to sleep.

I was doing all right too, until the sea gates opened again around eleven and the wind crowded into the embrace of the harbor. I gritted my teeth; now I knew why a key to open—or shut—the gates would be useful. But on the dark water, little fishing boats were rocking on the eddies, torches burning bright on their bows. Like all of us who served the sea, their lives were not ruled by the sun, but by the tides.

The wintery wind took me by the throat. I huddled back down, tucking the blankets tightly around me. How long had the gates been open this morning? Two hours? Three? Long enough for the fishermen to go out and check their trot lines. Shivering, I drew my knees to my chest.

Slate's room would be out of the cold, but the weather was not as bleak as my father's company. I had gone into his cabin to bring him dinner, hoping to ask about Gwen . . . not only for their history, although that had piqued my curiosity, but also about her arrival through the fog—and whether he thought she would be able to find her way back. Instead, I'd found my father crying into his sheets, great sobs that shook his frame. The sight had embarrassed me—I shifted in my hammock, uncomfortable still.

Should I knock instead on Kashmir's door? He would let me in . . . he would keep me warm. A thrill went through me, but in its wake, the fear—ever present. And Kash wasn't exactly happy I'd brought us here. Though he'd returned from his foray into the city with a glint in his eye and a weight in his pockets, he hadn't seemed in the mood for conversation over dinner. I curled up tighter and wrapped my own arms around my shoulders. It was very cold comfort.

I was reconsidering the captain's cabin when I heard someone opening the hatch. Not Kash, though—too noisy. I peeked out from under the pile of blankets. "Hello, Blake."

"Miss Song, please go back to your room." The zephyrs toyed with his hair and scattered the white mist of his breath. "You're humiliating me."

I pursed my lips, but another gust actually made the hammock sway. I clambered out, holding the blankets tight, and followed him down the ladder. But at the door of my old room, he wished me good night. I turned back to him. "Where are you going?"

"I'm going to bunk with Mr. Firas. If he'll have me."

I made a face. "Your nineteenth century is showing."

"Is it?" He raised an eyebrow. "Well, considering we're in the seventeenth, I'm ahead of the times."

"We'll share the room," I said firmly, and he made a small bow.

"Lady's choice. Never let it be said I'm not a modern man."

In spite of the new furnishings, the cabin felt bigger now my things were gone. It was bare except for the bed and the neat sea chest tucked into the corner. And it was so *warm*. I sank gratefully to the floor beside the mattress, my blankets still wrapped around me, and Blake barked a laugh. "For god's sake, Miss Song, take the bed!"

I only turned toward the wall, shoving a wad of quilt under my head. "I always used to sleep on the floor, when I slept in this room."

"Stubborn." He sighed and sat on the edge of the mattress; it creaked. "To be honest, I was surprised to find you in your hammock."

"Where else did you expect to find me?" The answering silence was delicate. I looked back over my shoulder to find a blush on his pale cheeks. "You're lucky I'm too cold to get up and punch you."

"Did something happen between you and Mr. Firas?"

All the possible answers to that question crowded into my head—yes, no, something, everything. "Nothing," I said at last. Nothing, nothing. I drew the blanket up closer to my chin.

"All right," he said evenly. For a while, there was only the soft sound of our breathing. In the lamp, the sky herring swam, making the light flicker. Slowly my toes began to thaw. I reached down and slipped my boots off my feet. Then he spoke again. "Did you ever really care for me, or was it only a ruse?"

I froze all over again—but in the back of my mind, I'd been wondering if he would ask. Back in Honolulu, there had been . . . something between us, though I'd thought we'd left it behind us in Nu'uanu Valley, along with a bag of stolen gold and the rest of the regrettable past. "What do you mean, a ruse?"

"To throw off my questions, of course. So you could rob the treasury."

My cheeks burned; I was glad I was facing the wall. "No. I . . . Blake. It wasn't a ruse."

"Then why do you feel responsible for me?"

"You're here because of what I did."

"But I asked to come aboard the ship, as you so kindly reminded me."

I sighed. "You couldn't stay in Hawaii after what happened."

"It certainly would have been very difficult," Blake said softly. "But perhaps not for the reasons you think."

The sadness in his voice gave me pause. "What reasons, then?"

There was another long silence, and I'd begun to think he would not answer when he did. "Hawaii is a small island, Miss Song. My father's debts, my mother's proclivities—they were no secret." The mattress settled as he shifted. "The day you and I met . . . it was the first conversation I'd had in years without anyone sneering at me. There were no implications. No knowing looks. Just you and me and a day in paradise. I might venture to say, Miss Song, that you were my first friend."

I stared steadily at the grain of the wood on the wall. I was his friend, and I had betrayed him. "And what am I now?"

"I'm not certain," he admitted. "But I'm glad we have time to find out. May I give you a gift?"

"I don't need any presents, Blake."

"I feel compelled. I want you to have it." I heard him sit up in bed; finally I turned toward him. He slid his sketchbook from under his pillow and tore out a page: a bold version of New York. Strong, clean lines, from the Narrows to the Harlem River. The southern neat line was made of silhouettes of buildings and water towers, bridges and trees, and the compass rose was the outline of Liberty's torch.

"This is beautiful."

"I did it the day we walked over the bridge," he said. "You gave me the city. Only fair I give it back."

I tucked the map into the pocket of my cloak and tried to smile. I'd taken paradise from him—but if Crowhurst was telling the truth, if the past could really be changed . . . could I return it?

Blake threw a cloth over the lamp and lay back down. Time passed, and his breathing grew even and deep. I might have dozed, but not deeply enough that the rumble of the gates didn't wake me as they slid shut. The ship rocked a little on the eddies. Moments later, my eyes sprang open at the sound of footsteps crossing the deck above.

My first thought was a thief. My second was Crowhurst—though perhaps it was fair to say they were one and the same. But whoever it was, was leaving. I sat up, the quilt slipping from my shoulders. Frost rimmed the small port window; I wiped it clear and peered outside. There was someone walking down the pier. I recognized his form easily, even in the sharp silver moonlight: my father, his shoulders hunched against the cold.

I struggled out of the tangle of blankets and pawed through them, searching for my boots in the dark. I'd laced them back on, with some difficulty, before I wondered why I was chasing after him. Why did I care where he was going or what he was doing? What did it matter if he wanted to go on a midnight stroll?

Pulling my cloak around my shoulders, I went

abovedecks, the answer ringing in my head: it was what I had always done. He'd always been my responsibility. He wandered off, I sought him out.

And right now, the way he'd been acting, it was too risky not to.

I opened the hatch; the cold stole my breath. Torchlight threw shadows across the stone docks where the fishermen were unloading their catch. Smoke mingled with the white plumes of hot breath and muttered curses as the men worked. I searched, but my father wasn't among them. Had he walked into the city? The Grand Rue curved up, away from the harbor, and I followed it.

Moonlight gave the town an ethereal grace, turning the stone to silver and the shadows to mysteries. Overhead, the buildings leaned in close as though telling secrets, and the sky shrank to a strip of stars. The windows at ground level were shuttered, and the ones above had curtains drawn; although the town was still and the hour was late, I couldn't shake the sensation of being watched through the gaps.

The dark intensified my hearing, or perhaps it was the sound carrying farther in the cold; I heard the *potch* of my boots against the rounded cobbles, the squeak of a hanging sign rocked by the wind, even the rise and fall of the ocean against the seawalls, like the breath of a sleeping giant. A small tabby ran ahead of me for half a block and then slipped under a cart, peering out at me with shining eyes.

Eventually the road spilled into a wide square. In the center, a fountain splashed over a beautifully crafted bronze mermaid. Icicles ran like tears down her cheeks. I walked all the way around, but there was no sign of Slate.

The south end of the plaza was bordered by the crenellated walls and turrets of the château. From this angle, high in one of the towers, light glimmered in a single window. Hadn't the harbormaster said it was abandoned? Was there a caretaker, waiting for the return of a long-lost king? Or a hermit wandering the otherwise empty halls?

I shivered; the drifting mist from the fountain was turning to frost in my hair. Aside from the *hish* of falling water, all was quiet. The west side of the square was lined with shuttered shops like closed jewel boxes; to the east stood a Gothic cathedral. The stained-glass arches glowed invitingly with colored light, but Slate had never been a religious man. Had I passed him somehow along the way? Or perhaps I had only missed him among the fishermen.

Another blast of wind scoured the square, scattering the arcing water in the fountain and blowing leaves across the cobbles—no, not leaves, but bits of paper. I frowned. This was not New York—paper wasn't trash, not in this era. Where had it come from?

Wrapping my velvet cloak tight around me, I followed the pieces like bread crumbs marking the invisible path of the southerly wind. Torn scraps gamboled at my feet as I approached the castle. There, before the gatehouse, lay a tattered book; I had knelt to pick it up when a movement caught my eye. Startled, I gasped, my heart leaping into my throat.

A man stood there, not two yards away, in the deep shadow under the stone archway of the castle gatehouse. He gripped the bars of the portcullis. The holes weren't big enough to fit a dog, but he pressed his head against the iron, as though he could pull himself into the keep by sheer force of will.

"Slate?" I spoke without thinking; as the man moved, I knew it was not the captain.

He turned slowly, unsteady on his feet, as though drunk or distracted, and tottered into the light of the unforgiving moon. Dirty blond hair lay in lank curls past his shoulders, and his robe and shoes were tattered, but he must have been a wealthy man, once. Under the grime was the dull shine of silk and velvet, and a gold chain gleamed on his neck.

"Do you know me?" His accent was quite thick—a rich brogue—but his voice was urgent. "Do you know who I am?"

"I . . . no," I said, taking a careful step back. "I'm only looking for my father."

"Your father?" He seemed to wilt, putting his face in his hands, and his voice throbbed with sudden grief. "I had a daughter once. The sea took her."

"The sea?" I tensed, recalling my own dire fortune—but this wasn't about Kash and me. "I'm sorry," I added hastily, the small words falling, worthless as pennies in a hat. But the man tilted his chin up; his eyes shone with tears—or was that rage? I took a step back. "I'll go. I just . . . Have you seen him? A tall man. He was—"

"Your father is the devil, witch! I can see it in your eyes."

My hand fluttered like a flag of surrender as I backed away across the square, but he followed with lurching steps. "A monster slavers in the castle!" he cried, his voice echoing from the stones and ringing in the bell tower. "A man wastes away in the pit!" He pulled the pendant of his necklace out of the folds of his robe, brandishing it at me. At first glance, it looked like a cross, but as he held it out, I saw it was a key.

"I was a king," he whispered. "I was a king, but I have no kingdom."

My jaw dropped; I stared at him. "What did you say?"

"Usurper! Witch!"

"Wait!" I raised my hand, but he slapped it away.

"Heed the warnings of the wayward saint! The flood will come! The dark horse will ride!" He lunged at me, and I stumbled back, tripping over the mangled book. "Witch! Witch!"

Panicked, I fled, my feet pelting on the granite cobbles. My breath came in short bursts as I skidded along the Grand Rue, speeding past the shuttered houses and the shadowy shops. Through the narrow gap between the buildings overhead, the night sky seemed to tilt as clouds blew past the moon. I neared the wharf—was he following? I risked a glance back over my shoulder and ran straight into a pair of outstretched arms.

For one wild, childish moment, I hoped it was my father, come to protect me. But though I recognized the man, it wasn't Slate. I knew him immediately from the picture I'd seen on my phone—only a little older. There, standing between me and the dock, was Donald Crowhurst.

CHAPTER
ELEVEN

I reeled, but he steadied me, his eyes bright in the dark. My chest was too hot, my fingers too cold; my heart rattled my ribs. I tried to speak, but I could not seem to catch my breath. The cold air burned like alcohol going down. "Mr. Crow—Mr. Crowhurst?"

The torches at the dock had been extinguished, the fishermen all gone to bed, and moonlight splashed across the wharf. But he was unmistakable, even in the dim light: a plain man, with a high forehead under a mop of curly hair and a long, sloping nose. There was wonder on his face—or was it fear? "You're here," he breathed.

"Yes. Yes!" I was giddy with relief. I held out my hand. "I came as soon as I could. It's so good to finally meet you!"

"It is." Crowhurst stared at me for a long time, but

he did not seem to share my joy. Still, he took my hand and shook it at last. "The pleasure is all mine, miss—but you have the advantage. Tell me, what's your name?"

My hand stilled. He released it, and my arm fell back to my side. "You . . . Don't you know me?"

He peered at me, his eyes guarded. "I've seen you before."

"Of course you have. You invited me here. By name." Did he have a memory condition as well? My heart sank.

Desperately, I dug my hand into my pocket and drew out his letter. Frowning, he scanned the page. "Nix . . . Nixie? You're Nixie?"

I furrowed my brow. The nickname sounded strange in his voice—too intimate. "Only my father calls me that."

"I was just speaking to him." Crowhurst looked up from the letter, concern on his face. "He's not a well man."

I followed his eyes to the wall, and there he was—the captain. I knew him not only by his silhouette, but by the fact that no one else would be up there, exposed to the cold sea air in the middle of the night—and standing perilously close to the edge. I swore. "Did you give him back his map?"

"His what?"

"The map of Honolulu." I glanced back at my father and swore again. "Tell me you haven't lost it!"

"I don't understand. What map?"

"The map you stole from his desk when you were in . . ." My voice trailed off as my mind raced toward realization. "When you *go*. To New York City."

"To New York?" he repeated. "How?"

Time coiled around me like a snake; on the water, the *Temptation* nodded knowingly. My fingers shook as I pulled the map out of my pocket—the map Blake had only just given me. I held it with an odd reluctance. But it had to happen, didn't it? It had already happened.

I'd seen this once before, with Joss in ancient China, and it had seemed something like fate then, too. What made it possible—these little loops in chronology, where time twisted like a Möbius strip? As I stared into Crowhurst's eyes, the answer came to me. "Two Navigators," I said softly. "Of course. Is that why you needed my help? Does changing the past require working together?"

"Changing the past." He breathed. "Yes. That's why you're here. That's why we're both here."

"Take this, then," I said, my hand just barely shaking as I held out the map of New York. "Take that letter too. And a map of Ker-Ys to give to me—a map drawn this morning. You must have one."

"I do," he said. Understanding crept across his face. "But of course I do."

"Dahut will find me in Brooklyn, near the docks." I bit my lip—I wanted to say more, but I had to go to my father. I started toward the edge of the wharf, where a set of stone stairs led to the top of the wall. "Hurry back!"

"I will!" he called after me. "I've been waiting for this for months!"

Months? I nearly turned back to ask what he meant, but now was not the time. Crossing the pier, I reached the wide stone stair that ran up to the rampart. It switched back once, and there was no balustrade; as I climbed higher, I glanced down toward the harbor and immediately regretted it. The only thing between me and the black water was twenty-five feet of chill air. Gulping, I pressed myself against the stone wall, continuing up on unsteady legs.

At the top, the cold made me gasp. The guard tower did nothing to slow the rushing wind, but I huddled in the curve of the turret to gather my courage. The top of the wall was slick with seawater, and there was no parapet here—nothing to prevent a person from losing her footing and tumbling headlong into the swirling blackness of the Mer d'Iroise.

Of course Slate was standing at the edge, his shoulders rounded, his face like a knot pulled tight. At least he was wearing a coat; the wind off the sea whipped it around his legs and scoured the stones underfoot.

It made me dizzy just to look at him. I steadied myself, one hand on the wall in the turret. The stone tower sheltered the bronze mechanisms that controlled the sea gates; from inside, it felt like standing in a gilded cage. My fingers trailed over an oval panel embedded in the stone. It was decorated in relief with two mermaids; between them, verdigris wept from an old keyhole.

With a start, I remembered the madman near the castle—and the key around his neck. Was that the key to the sea gates? Had he told the truth? Had he been a king? If so, what had happened? How had he fallen from power?

But I could not worry about another man's fall, not now. Pushing off the wall, I propelled myself toward my father.

He didn't turn when I approached. We stood side by side for a while in silence, watching the moonlight turn the spray to a scattering of diamonds. Minutes passed. Did he even know I was there? "So," I said, the wind tearing the word from my lips. I cleared my throat. "You met Donald Crowhurst."

Slate didn't respond for a long time, but when he did, I wished he hadn't. "There was a woman in the water."

I blinked at him. "Drowning?"

"Singing."

"Okay." I tried to keep my voice neutral, but my heart clenched. A woman in the water? Automatically, I searched for the sheen of sweat on my father's cheeks, the black hole eyes, but there was nothing in his face but sorrow. Could he be hallucinating even without the opium? I'd read about that somewhere—that one might see things, in the grip of mania or depression. And it couldn't have been real . . . could it? At our feet, an icy wave shattered against the stones. The wind rose and fell; it sounded like a song. "Since she's gone, can we go back to the ship?"

"I keep thinking about the bells," he said. "The ones that toll the tides. The myth of Ker-Ys says that on a quiet day, you can still hear them ringing under the water."

"I know, Slate." My hair lashed my cheeks; I hooked it with my finger and pulled it back. "I've read the same books you have."

He leaned out, looking down. "I wonder if anyone has ever fallen off the edge."

I made a face and took a fistful of the back of his coat. "Not tonight."

"Do the bells ring for them?"

"Slate . . ."

"I lied to her, Nixie."

"To who?"

"I told Gwen time had done this. It was love. I tried to warn you. Remember?" He glanced at me, his eyes full of regret, and then away, shaking his head, as though he couldn't bear to look. Instead, he stared down into the swirling blackness of the water. "I tried to help. I didn't want this to happen. I would have done anything to keep you from getting hurt—you know that, right? I still would. Anything."

"Dad." The word hung lonely in the air; I didn't know what else to say. But the wind gusted, and I slipped my arm into the crook of his elbow. He followed when I started walking, so I led him gently back to the ship.

CHAPTER
TWELVE

I spent the rest of the night in front of the door in the captain's cabin, sleeping only fitfully, worried he'd disappear again, this time for good. By the time dawn arrived, my entire body ached. The captain was still sleeping peacefully, damn him, so I beat Rotgut to the galley to start the coffee. He found me hunched over my second cup and recoiled in mock horror. "You look awful!"

I rolled my eyes. "You always know just what to say."

He fussed about, snatching ingredients and utensils off the shelves and dropping them on the scarred wooden counter. "What's the trouble?" In a puff of white, Rotgut popped open the tin of flour and dumped some into a bowl. "I'm going to guess it's a boy."

"What makes you think that?"

"Well, it traditionally *is* a boy. And there's that extra one now."

I made a face. "I'm not a girl who follows tradition."

"Me neither." He put a cast-iron pan on the stove and winked. "Fine. Tell me what the trouble really is."

"A man."

"Oh, dear." He cracked two eggs into the bowl, stirring vigorously.

I made a face. "I'm worried about Slate."

His hand stilled. "We're all worried about Slate."

"Right." Lowering my gaze, I traced my fingertip through a puddle of coffee. I'd been focusing so much on my own problem, I hadn't spent much time thinking about Bee and Rotgut. But they'd sailed with Slate for decades—they knew his history, they'd seen his ups and downs. If they were worried too, it wasn't a good sign. "He's been through worse, though, right?"

"At least once."

It was early and I was tired—I almost asked when. Then I sighed. Slate had survived my mother's loss once—he could do it again. Couldn't he? Frowning, I wiped the coffee off on my trousers. Speaking of the captain's past . . .

"Who was Gwen, anyway?"

"Ah. Gwen." As the pan started to smoke, Rotgut poured in a dollop of batter; it sizzled at the edges. "We met her in Ribat, must have been . . . nearly twenty years ago now. That was back when the *Fool* was the *Santé*—and the captain was named Skamber Jack. He was a Barbary slaver."

"And she was a pirate?"

"A captive."

"Oh." I bit my lip; overhead, smoke made the lantern light bleary. "Were she and Slate ever . . . ?"

"Ever what? Fishing buddies? Bingo partners?" Rotgut laughed a little as he shook the pan. "No. They were never. You should know, the captain's not like that."

I raised an eyebrow. "Like what?"

Rotgut flipped the pancake and gave me a look right back. "Likely to take advantage of someone who owed him."

I shifted on my feet, a little embarrassed; then again, my father's ethics had always been gray to me. "It seemed like she wished things were different."

"They do have that in common. Just not the same things. The captain said she could crew with us, but she refused. Too proud. Or maybe too painful."

I nodded. I could imagine both being true. "What will happen to her when she reaches the Margins?"

"That's probably a question for your father," he said. "But Gwen's a survivor."

"I believe that. What do you make of what she said? The dreams of her crew?"

"Who knows?" Rotgut shrugged. "I'm more interested in what she said about strange fish."

I smiled a little. "Are you going to try to get your line in the water?"

"If there's time. You can join me if you want. Good antidote to boy trouble."

"Is that why you like it so much?"

"Plenty of fish in the sea," he said, scraping at the pancake with a spatula. "Of course, there's always the one that got away. That's Gwenolé's problem."

I blinked. "Gwenolé?"

"Her full name. French or something"

"Celtic, actually. Very similar to the name of a saint from a local myth."

"Whatever." Rotgut gave the splotchy pancake a professional frown and flipped it onto the floor; Billie's head darted out from under the shelf to snatch it. Then Rotgut poured out a dollop of fresh batter. "The first one's always ugly."

I drained my coffee with a grimace—my stomach was sour with it—and started washing the mug in the basin. First the king, and now the saint—but neither were quite like the myth I knew. Was it coincidence or something more? The madman had mentioned the dark horse too. Then again, he'd also mentioned a man in the pit and a monster in the castle, and neither of those were part of the legend.

What did it all mean? Last night, I had fled before I could find out, but it was easier to be brave in the light of day. Perhaps I should go back and ask him. I put the mug upside down on the sideboard and started down the hall.

"You don't want a pancake?" Rotgut called after me. "This one is shaped kind of like a heart."

"Maybe later." I left the galley, but the smoke clung to my hair. I wrinkled my nose; if I was going to go back to the square, I'd need to change, and not just to get rid of the smell of breakfast. In this era, a woman wearing trousers in broad daylight would call attention I didn't need. I slowed as I approached Kashmir's door. My clothes were in there— but so was he.

What would I say to him? He wasn't happy we'd come to Ker-Ys in the first place—and the events of last night had scored points in his favor. Would it be an insult to ask him to accompany me to the square? Not for protection. Not *only* for protection, anyway. But because I wanted him to help me talk through the mystery of the madman's words.

And because I missed him.

But when I knocked, there was no answer, so I opened the door and found Kashmir's nest of pillows empty. The slight breeze stirred the poems tacked to his wall—Rumi and Hafiz, Frost and Angelou. Love and caged birds and roads diverging. Where had he gone? Disappointment warred with fear in my stomach as I went to my trunk.

Digging through the clothes was like archaeology. The top layer was modern—the tank tops, the denim shorts with the gun still in the back pocket. Beneath those, the clothes I'd worn in Honolulu: tropical Victoriana, pinafores and bustled dresses in light colors. What to wear in winter in seventeenth-century France? My hand hovered a moment before I found a bell-shaped wool skirt folded in the bottom of the trunk. And here, a white linen shirt with long puffed sleeves and tiny buttons. Over that, I laced up a bodice cut from black velvet.

It was a suitable outfit for the era, and not too showy— the last thing I wanted was to be singled out, a strange girl with foreign features in a small town. Hopefully no one else would call me a witch. But just in case . . . I dug back through the pile of discarded clothing and pulled out the gun. Tucking it into the lining of my cloak, I felt foolish, but less afraid.

Leaving Kashmir's room, I saw Blake coming from the galley, brushing crumbs from his lapel. He was wearing another of Kashmir's old jackets, this one a rich green wool trimmed in gold braid, and he raised an eyebrow when he saw me. "Good morning, Miss Song. When I woke, I worried you'd gone back to your hammock."

Rotgut tsked from the open doorway. "Boy trouble."

"I slept in the captain's cabin," I said loudly as I headed toward the hatch.

Blake climbed up after me. "Before that, you left the *Temptation*."

I made a face, though he couldn't see it. But he had always been observant. And nosy. "I'm surprised you didn't follow me."

"I considered it," he said, his voice mild, his eyes sharp. "But I noticed the captain had abandoned ship as well, and I didn't want to risk another lost map."

Sighing, I gripped the rail at the stern; the brass was cold as ice. So he had seen Slate leave; had he seen me lead him back from the edge of the wall? I did not know how to discuss it—the captain's condition. More than that, I didn't *want* to discuss it. "I went exploring."

"In the middle of the night?"

"I love a good adventure."

"So do I. Did you find one?"

"Blake . . ." I bit my lip—but maybe he could help sort this out. I tapped my fingers on the rail, considering my words. Overhead, the sky had lightened to a lovely shade of sapphire, and the thin light of dawn washed the deserted wharf. "I found a madman in the square last night," I said at last. "At least, I thought he was mad."

"That does sound like an adventure."

"More of a mystery. He claimed to be the king, and he wore a brass key on his neck. He mentioned the devil and the dark horse, and a daughter lost to the sea—"

"Like the myth?"

"Yes. He spoke like a prophet. Like he knew the ending of the story. But he also claimed there was a monster in the castle and a man in a pit, and that's not part of any legend I've read. Plus, he called me a witch."

"It's not exactly an unfair criticism, Miss Song." I whacked his shoulder with the back of my hand, but he laughed. "Well! Didn't you agree that Navigation is something like magic? The whole reason you're here is to learn to work wonders."

My smile fell away. "That's the other thing about last night. I—I met Crowhurst. Back on the dock."

Blake's eyes went wide. "And what did he say?"

"I . . . Nothing." It felt like an admission of guilt—as though Crowhurst and I were conspirators. "He—he didn't know anything yet. He hadn't even been to New York."

"But how—?"

"It seems as though we arrived here before he invited us."

Blake's brow furrowed, and then he guessed. "The map I drew—the map of New York City. You gave it to him? My god." Blake shook his head. "What would have happened if I hadn't given it to you?"

"I don't know." I laughed a little, but without humor. "I studied this for years, back when I first realized what might happen if Slate actually succeeded in saving my mother. Some people say that what's meant to happen will find a way, come hell or high water. And some people think that preventing history from happening would unmake the universe."

His eyebrows went up. "Are those the only two possibilities?"

"Oh, no, there are infinite possibilities. But very little hard science."

"Then how did Crowhurst learn?"

"What do you mean?"

"He has a way to change the past—or so his letter said. If he was telling the truth, he found a way, and all without ending the world."

"Blake . . ." I chewed my lip, staring at the harbor, the water, the boats gently bobbing. "That's the thing. I gave him the letter too."

"The letter he sent to you? Then . . . he doesn't have a way to change anything? It was all a lie?"

"Or it might have been what had to happen—"

"To keep the world from unraveling?" Blake searched my face for answers I did not have. "Do you think we're here for a reason, Miss Song?"

My mouth twisted like a rope—I knew the reason I'd brought us here, but Blake gave the word a shine beyond self-interest. "We have to wait for Crowhurst to return to find out for certain."

"It seems that way." Blake folded his arms. "But perhaps we can still track down the madman."

I looked at him, surprised. "We can?"

"Aren't you curious how he knows the ending of a story yet untold?"

"Of course I am," I said. "I just didn't realize you'd want to come with me."

"Well, I can't very well let you keep all the adventures to yourself, Miss Song." He offered me his arm then, and I took it. Together, we started out across the wharf, up the Grand Rue toward the castle.

It was the same route I'd taken last night, but the town was far more colorful in the light of day. The sun brought out the bright hues of the doors, enameled in rich blues and reds, and above the street swung the carved and painted signs for hat makers and haberdashers, porcelains and parfumeries—luxuries in this age, especially for a town so small. Where did this wealth come from? I saw no factories, no sign of industry. Then again, Ker-Ys was supposed to be a utopia.

The streets themselves were quiet, and most of the shops were still shuttered this early, but curtains were being drawn back from the windows in the living spaces above, and there was the feeling in the air—a murmur of voices, a scent of milk and smoke and rising bread—that people were stirring. As we turned into the square, bells in the cathedral began to ring.

The château was even lovelier under the sun than the moon: a profusion of slender towers, lacy with tracery and topped with conical slate roofs. My eye went to the upper window, but it was dark. Still, the entire atmosphere was halcyon, and the events of last night seemed far away, almost unreal, like a distant ship on the horizon.

"No madman," Blake murmured.

"Maybe he wandered off. But . . ." I scanned the square. Had it only been a strange nightmare? An odd dream? No— the old book was there, lying mangled on the cobbles in the shade of the gatehouse. As I knelt to pick up the cracked leather covers, Blake grasped the bars and rattled the port-cullis. It barely moved, although I could hear the faint clanking of chain in the mechanisms.

"This gate would keep all but the smallest monsters out," he said.

"Or in."

"Safest that way. What have you got there?"

I showed him the lettering on the book cover, stamped into the skin. L'HISTOIRE DE LA VILLE D'YS.

"A history book?" He raised an eyebrow. "The work of a revisionist, perhaps?"

"That's not funny. This book was priceless."

"I'm sorry, Miss Song. It's only that I can understand being enraged by history." He knelt to pluck up a handful of scraps; they had drifted like fallen petals into the corner of the gatehouse. "You're right, of course," he said softly, sorting through the pieces. Gold leaf shone in the morning sun; the book had been lovingly illuminated. "It was beautiful work."

"Don't bother." I opened my hand; the empty cover fell to the ground, a dead thing. "It's beyond repair."

"I know. But some of these are interesting. Look here." He smoothed a crumpled piece of vellum against his thigh and tilted it toward me. "Seems like a diagram of the island."

It was only a partial, but the design was still clear: the circular seawalls, the coil of the Grand Rue. But another path stretched across the city, leading to the sea wall and branching through the town. I traced the line with my finger. "Sewer system, maybe?"

"Perhaps. At the king's palace in Honolulu, there were rumors of secret underground passages. But look here." He tapped the paper; in the center of the castle, a dark circle was labeled LE TROU.

"Le trou . . ." I caught my breath when the meaning came to me. "The pit?"

Blake looked up at me through his lashes. "Maybe your madman . . . wasn't. And look, one of the tunnels passes right by it." He gave me a conspiratorial grin. "Shall we?"

"Shall we what?" I stared at him; there was a gleam in his eye. "Blake."

"Come, Miss Song! We've got to wait for Crowhurst anyway. What else have you got planned?"

"What if there actually is a monster in the castle?"

"What if there's actually a man in the pit?" His question brought me up short; he saw his victory in my hesitation. "I thought you loved adventure. But if you're frightened, I'll protect you."

My eyes narrowed—was he patronizing me? Then again, I did have the gun; I could protect us both. "Let me see that."

"Here." He handed me the slip of paper; it trembled in my hand. The path was a shadowy line running underneath the entire city; dark squares showed entrances at the cathedral, the castle, and near the docks. It made sense—castles and sanctuaries usually had exit routes in case of invasion.

"It's not very detailed," I said dubiously. "It might take a bit of searching."

"Then we'd best get started. Shall we try the cathedral

first?" He started across the square to the pile of towering granite. I jogged to catch up, and when I did, I was glad we'd taken a closer look.

From across the square, the cathedral had looked like a typical French Gothic house of God, but closer up, it seemed the god it housed might have been Poseidon. The high arches were graceful as anemones and studded with gargoyles— no, not gargoyles, but sea creatures. Stone mermaids made downspouts out of shells held in their outstretched hands; urchins encrusted the archivolts, and deep-sea fish with enormous teeth took the role of grotesques in the galleries. Above it all, the great bronze bells gleamed, tucked into the towers like great pearls in giant oysters. But the processional doors set in the arched portals were heavy oak and banded with iron, and all three were shut tight. Around the side of the building, a smaller entrance was no different.

Blake wasn't deterred. "Back to the docks, then."

We took last night's discarded torches from an empty fishing boat, and I stopped at the ship to slip a book of matches into my pocket. Then we crossed to the east side of the wharf. According to the map, the passage ran directly beneath a stone boathouse opposite the tavern. The building was decorated with old fishtails nailed over the doors, like trophies. They were huge, easily a yard across.

"Marlin?" Blake said with a quizzical glance.

"They don't live this far north." But what did? Sturgeon, of course, but the lobes of the caudal fin were each the same size. What was it Gwen had said? Strange fish in the water. "Whatever it was, it must have been huge."

"No wonder the fishermen look so rough."

We walked around the building; the side along the Grand Rue was devoted to a fish market, but it was still early, the gates closed, the fishermen abed. But there were bloody puddles of saltwater on the stones near the loading door, and we found it unbarred; the lucky trollers must have hauled their catch this way last night.

Stepping carefully on the slick stone, I followed Blake into the darkened market. The smell of sour brine tickled my nose, and my breath whitened in the gloom; it was even colder inside than out. I eased the door shut and lit the torches; orange firelight waltzed arm in arm with the shadows.

The room was cavernous, with barrels of salted herring lining the far wall, and swaybacked wooden tables holding fresh mackerel, their eyes like cloudy marbles. From inside a nearby barrel, I could hear the *click-clack* of crustaceans climbing over one another, claws scrabbling against the wood.

Meandering through the cool darkness, our shadows crept behind us. "We're looking for a tunnel of some sort," Blake said. "Perhaps a stairway leading down."

"Or a trapdoor." I watched my feet as we walked. The torchlight glittered off fish scales scattered across the stained flagstones. Lifting my skirt, I stepped over a curved gutter, icy with old blood; it ran toward a dark drain in the floor. Squinting, I tried to see inside, but the shadows were too deep and it wasn't wide enough to climb through, even if it hadn't been clotted with offal.

We passed bushel baskets piled high with the fruits of the sea: clams, mussels, sea lettuce, and here, something silvery and fibrous that I did not recognize. Lifting my torch, the flame shone on a mound of silky filament, the strands the color of spun moonlight.

Blake glanced over. "Too fine for linen."

"And the climate's wrong for silkworms." I drew a single thread from the basket; it was at least a yard long, and the thickness of a spiderweb. "It's sea silk," I said, breathless as the stories came to me. "Or sea wool, in ancient Rome. Apparently a glove woven from it could fit inside a thimble. The Egyptians called it byssus and used it to wrap the bodies of their god kings."

He reached out in wonder, running a finger along the strand. "But what is it?"

"The Chinese sometimes called it mermaid's hair."

We stared for a moment at the pile of silvery fiber. Now it made sense to me—the luxury of imported spices and fine fashion on the Grand Rue—and I could nearly hear Blake's thoughts as we both considered the meaning of the fishtails nailed to the boathouse wall.

"Right," he said briskly, wiping his hand on his jacket. "Let's keep looking for that passage."

Behind the fish market was the boathouse proper. The floor here was cracked; the flagstones rocked underfoot. Along the walls facing the dock, weak sunlight crept through the doorframes of the loading gates, hanging heavy on their hinges, but the light faded quickly into gloom. Haphazard crates made a dark maze out of the wide room; in corners, coils of rope and buckets of hardened tar gathered dust waiting for repairs. A rotting dinghy lay in the middle of the floor, its hull stove in by rocks. Had its crew been able to bail long enough to return to port? Or had the boat floated in, upside down and empty, on the tide?

We searched the walls, looking for a door, secret or

otherwise, but found nothing of interest until we reached the back corner. "Good god!"

At Blake's shout, I leapt back; by his feet was a child's skull. No . . .

"What on earth?"

At first I'd thought it was human, but the teeth were like an eel's: rows of slender needles. I picked it up and held it to the light. The bone was thin, almost translucent, like the nacreous scales of a fish.

My palms were slick with sweat, but Blake took it from me gently, turning it toward the light. "There are more things in heaven and earth," he breathed.

"That's definitely not Yorick." I shuddered—I couldn't help it. But Blake was staring in wonder. "You take very easily to such foreign waters."

His answering smile was a little ghoulish in the torch-light. "I wouldn't be much of an explorer if I found myself frightened by the unknown. What about you, Miss Song? Doesn't mystery tempt you?"

"I've always loved seeing what was just over the horizon. Still . . ." I considered the skull as he tucked it back into the corner. "I think I preferred the secret beaches and the hidden waterfalls."

"Perhaps you and I could go back to Hawaii someday." He straightened his jacket. "Do you still have a map that would work?"

"Honolulu is my native time. I can get there through the Margins. Of course, after . . . after what happened, I'd likely be recognized. I couldn't go back without—"

"Without changing the past?"

"Without a disguise, I was going to say."

"Ah." Blake was watching me again. The little pool of torchlight cupped us, drawing us close together, and the warmth of his body was comforting in the chill. Then it struck me—he'd said "you and I."

I blinked at him; he smiled. Abruptly, I took a step back onto the uneven flagstones; I had no warning at all before they cracked and crumbled away under my feet.

I fell right after, down into the dark.

CHAPTER
THIRTEEN

"**M**iss Song?"

"Hnnngh."

"Can you speak? Say something!"

As the sharp pain of my landing faded, I squinted up through sudden tears at the bright blur of the hole in the ceiling—which had recently been the floor. I had fallen straight down and landed in a heap.

"Miss Song!"

"Yes." The word hissed out of me; my ribs had hit something hard—a stone? No, a brick. I touched my side gingerly; it throbbed, but the pain wasn't acute. "I think . . ." Slowly I straightened out my legs, pushing aside bits of the broken flagstone; though I was shaken and sore, everything seemed to work. "I'm all right."

I clambered to my feet; as I did, my hip twanged. I

winced, putting my hand against my side. There was a hard lump there—the gun. Ugh. What a bruise that would make.

Brushing dirt from my clothes, I found something wet had wicked through the wool of my cloak. The sandy ground was quite damp here, so close to the harbor—and under the fish market. My torch had been snuffled out in the fall. Wrinkling my nose, I sniffed at the stain, but thankfully it was only saltwater, though it had wet my book of matches.

"Give me a moment." Blake's head was silhouetted against the light, perhaps ten feet overhead. "I'll be back with another torch."

He disappeared, taking the light with him, and the darkness wrapped around me like a shroud. I swallowed. Stretching out my arms, I could barely see as far as my fingertips. It seemed to take a very long time for him to return.

"Stand aside!"

I retreated to the edge of the circle of light. The shadows leaped back as Blake dropped a makeshift flambeau, a sailcloth wrapped around a scrap of board. I snatched it up from the silty floor and brandished it against the cowering dark.

The tunnel was tubelike, with a barrel ceiling and a ledge running along the wall at about the height of my shoulders.

High above, drains were dark pockets in the brick. It must have been a sewer, after all, although now the waterways were fairly dry. The stones here were rough, and sections of the wall were made of crumbling mortar. I peered upward—the ribs of the vault had weakened under the hole. More bricks were scattered on the floor around me; I was lucky I hadn't hit my head. "Well," I said, picking up the torch I'd dropped and lighting it from the flame dying on the canvas. "I've found the secret passage."

"Do you see a way up?" Blake's voice echoed down through the tunnel. I turned in a slow circle, looking for a door, a stair, anything.

"Not yet," I called up. But the ledge was clearly a walkway, made so workers could travel above the waterline; there must have been a way to reach it that didn't involve falling through a broken floor.

"There was a rope in the corner," Blake shouted. "I'll be right back."

Bits of rubble fell from the ceiling as he left. I stayed beneath the hole, in case anything else was going to come down. Then I frowned, lifting the torch; far down the tunnel, was that another path, branching off on the right? In spite of myself, the shadows called to me; I hadn't lied to

Blake when I'd told him I was tempted by mystery.

It wasn't long before a rope slithered down from the room above. Blake called down after it. "Can you climb, or shall I lift you?"

"What?" I tilted my head back to look at him—gingerly; I was still a bit dizzy. "Neither!"

He stared down at me. In the flickering light, his concern made sharp angles of his cheeks. "Are you well enough to go on?"

"Just come down!"

After a moment, he dropped his own torch at my feet. The dark pulled back farther as he slid down the rope. But when he reached the bottom, he picked up the torch and tipped his hat back on the crown of his head. Then he took my chin gently, peering closely into my eyes, first one, then the other. "What are you doing, Blake?"

"I'm making sure you're all right," he murmured softly; his breath stirred in my hair. I watched his lips curve into a half smile. "You don't look concussed. Most likely you'll live." I laughed, but in the dark it sounded nervous. Just as I was about to pull away, he released my chin and turned to stare into the dark. The glow from the fire made his eyes gleam. "This reminds me of the lava tunnels. Back in Hawaii.

You can get lost down there without a map."

"Good thing we have a cartographer," I said brusquely. "Which way toward the castle?"

Opening his sketchbook, he frowned at the scrap of paper, and then up toward the ceiling. After a moment spent consulting an internal compass, he pointed down the passage. "Down here."

Firelight played across the brick as we walked, flitting around corners, scampering along the ledge, and lunging into branching tunnels from the main. I paused to inspect one. "There's an archway along the edge. Are those stairs leading up?"

"I see them. But . . ." Blake looked back in the direction we'd come, though I'd lost sight of the rope in the darkness. Still, he shook his head, making a mark on the page. "We're only at three hundred paces."

Down here the air was still, though there was a rhythmic sound, a hollow metal drumming like the washing of the waves against a steel hull. It grew steadily louder as we traveled along the damp sand in the canal, walking slowly enough that he could add detail to his map. His shoulder brushed mine; was it an accident? Blake seemed completely focused on the sketchbook. But there was only one way to know. I licked my lips and summoned my courage. "Do you wish things had gone differently?" I said softly. "In Hawaii?"

"Of course I do." His answer was vague—as my question had been. I tried again.

"Between us, I mean?"

He lifted his head from his book. "Do you?"

I hesitated—for all my regrets, what would I have changed? "I wish I hadn't hurt you."

"That's a kindness." He looked back down to make another mark on the map. "But how, exactly?"

"What do you mean?"

"Well." Continuing forward, he tucked the pen behind his ear. "You might wish away our meeting, but that might have been the one good thing that came out of this—at least for me. You might wish away the robbery—but then you wish away the history as it was written. Would you risk ending the world to do the right thing?"

I made a face. "I wish I could say yes."

He turned his head, his face lost in shadow. "You might wish many things, but that doesn't mean they'll come true. This doesn't seem like that sort of fairy tale."

I bridled. "Would you do it? Would you really risk the end of the world just to keep your hands from getting dirty?"

"Depends on the dirt," he said pointedly. "Blood is harder to scrub clean. Would you kill an innocent if history dictated you must?"

"I'm not going to be drawn into a textbook ethics debate designed to . . ." My voice trailed off as a low rumble hummed in the air. We both stopped in our tracks. "What was that?"

Blake lifted his torch. Farther down the main path . . . was that the glimmer of bronze? I took a step closer, then another, as the rumbling sound came again. Squinting into the dark, I peered down the tunnel; it ended in a huge metal plate. No, not a plate. A door.

"It looks like the sea gates," Blake said, staring up at the wall of bronze. Then he knelt, dragging his fingers through the wet sand. "What time is it?"

Dread seized me as I took his meaning: this was a sewer, and the sand was damp. The tides changed every six and a quarter hours; low tide would come around eleven this morning. But the gate would open before low tide, so the water could fill the tunnel, then drain away.

How long had we been exploring?

I grabbed his hand and yanked him back up the passageway as another low rumble shook the earth.

"Up to the ledge!" We sped away from the doors as they began to roll open. Behind us, water burst through the widening gap and crashed onto the sand.

A gust of air made our torchlight flicker. The sea poured in faster than we could run; we splashed down the closest tunnel as the icy tide swept over our feet. Blake threw his torch onto the ledge and vaulted up; turning back, he reached for me, but I was already up beside him.

Still the water rose, rolling toward us and cresting in a wave. Together, we ran toward the archway; through it, stairs led up from the ledge. Blake took them two at a time; I was right behind him as the water roared through the tunnel, lapping at our heels. The stairway ended in a thick door. I pressed my back against it, but the water did not climb past the middle of the steps.

Breathing hard, we stared at the swirling black tide at our feet. Our torches licked the bricks at the top of the alcove, not much taller than the door. Blake leaned down to tug off one of his boots, pouring out the water. "Always an adventure with you, Miss Song."

I wrung saltwater out of the hem of my cloak. "I thought you loved adventure."

"Oh, I do." He shoved his foot back into his boot. "That

doesn't mean it isn't dangerous."

I swallowed, looking down at my feet. Inches away from my toes, the water glimmered darkly on the stair. "No argument there."

How long till the tide dropped and the water drained? It wouldn't be more than a few hours, but with the torches burning so high, we risked running out of oxygen before the water cleared the tunnel. Putting out the flames was an option, but I didn't relish waiting for hours in the pitch black. The door at my back was silvered with age and crusted with salt; there was no sign it had been opened in quite some time. When I tried the handle, the rusting iron crumbled in my hands, and the door wouldn't budge. I glared at the keyhole. "I wish Kash were here."

"Hmm." Blake frowned, inspecting the latch. "Iron? In sea air? Hold my torch."

I stepped back as far as I dared, the heat from both flames playing along my arms. "Do you pick locks too?" I asked, but he shook his head.

"No, Miss Song." Then he drove his shoulder into the door near the hinges—once, twice—and they disintegrated into flakes and powder. With a roar, Blake pushed, and the door scraped over the stones, giving us an opening large enough to slip through. Panting, he took his torch back from me. "I do not."

The echo of his shout still rang in the alcove. A thrill went through me as I thrust my own torch into the room—excitement or fear? Would there be monsters . . . witches . . . devils? But the light played over barrels and buckets and spades tumbled together in the dust, and my heart slowed. "Storage."

He shrugged, then he winced, rubbing his shoulder. "We might still be able to find the pit. It was somewhere near the tunnels."

"Do you think that's wise?"

Blake gave me a look. "I thought you loved adventure."

A smile flickered on my lips as I wound my way through crates and boxes and piles of bricks. The room opened into a series of vaulted galleries, a cellar with pillars and arches at regular intervals. Tucked into corners were stacks of casks and dusty bottles, and farther down, neat rows of bones.

Nothing moved; everything was quiet. The air was cold and still, and the dust was thick as carpet. And yet . . . I slowed and leaned down, peering more closely at the stones. "Look. Scuff marks."

"Footprints. Several pairs—or one person coming and going." He gave me a wry look. "Do monsters wear boots?"

"Some do." I lifted my eyes; the tracks led through the catacombs to a thick oak door. Who was wandering about in the abandoned castle? Was it the same person who had tended the light glowing in the tower window last night? As Blake tried the handle, I passed the torch into my left hand, slipping my right into the pocket that held the gun.

"Locked," he muttered. "And this time, the hardware has been well oiled."

The firelight gleamed on the intricate brass of the keyhole. It was made in the same design as the one on the sea gates: a pair of mermaids, their hands and tails touching. But there was no way now to see what the lock protected. Tracing the footprints backward across the room, I found a stairwell leading up. "Should we follow them?"

"I don't see another route. Is that daylight up there?"

At the top of the stairs, we came to a kitchen. Overhead, dingy gray light filtered through narrow windows, illuminating the huge work table that dominated the center of the room. There, a dozen bakers might knead dough or roll pastry for a feast. But instead of the smell of butter and yeast, there was only the scent of damp stone and mildewed plaster. Leaves stirred in the corners. Between a cold oven and an empty trough, a broken door opened onto a dying garden, the old herb beds and pathways a tangle of rotting weeds.

The dust was thinner here, blown about by the breeze through the doorway; I lost the trail of footprints. Had they come in from outside?

"Miss Song?"

I turned. Blake was kneeling by an arched doorway at the opposite end of the kitchen. He held up his fingers— they were red with blood.

I gasped, rushing to his side. "Are you hurt?"

"No." He stood, wiping his hand on the stone wall. "But someone is, rather seriously." At his feet, a black pool congealed, wider than his handspan, and marred by a footprint. Blake's boots were still clean—not his, then.

My heart pounded and my stomach turned. "Maybe . . . maybe an animal?" I whispered, but the thoughts swirled in my head—a witch, a monster, a man in the pit. I looked longingly toward the door that opened into the sunlit garden, but no—if someone was hurt, they might need help. In the gallery ahead, I could see the footprints fading into the shadows. Scarlet spattered the flagstones, shining in the light from the narrow windows lining the hall. Some of the leaded panes had broken. Glass shards glittered on the floor like diamonds, and some, red rubies. They rolled like gravel beneath my boots. I wrinkled my nose. "Do you smell something? Like . . . rotting meat."

"Maybe it *is* an animal."

"Maybe."

The gallery opened into a grand room—grand in size, though not in appointment. The smell was stronger here, though the light was very dim—the windows high, the panes clouded with years of filth. It was a dining hall with a long oak table, lined with chairs and piled with droppings. Above, birds nested in iron chandeliers, murmuring over our intrusion. The ceiling would have been beautiful under the grime, painted with faded angels—no. Mermaids. They swam in a murky gloom, their bellies as white as fish.

Then I saw movement out of the corner of my eye—a pair of legs behind the table. One foot jerked under the edge of a tattered silk robe. I grabbed Blake's arm and pointed, suddenly terrified. But the foot moved again and the motion was unnatural, and there came a liquid ripping sound, like damp sails tearing. I swallowed, raising the torch as I stepped closer. Was the madman the victor, or a victim?

Something crunched beneath my boot—the remains of a gull's broken wing. Small bones littered the flagstones, telling a dire fortune. In the shadows behind a broken chair, something pale gleamed: a cracked femur. My blood raced through my veins as I crept around the table, sweeping my torch in a circle.

On the floor, the madman lay, his dead eyes open and staring at the dirty ceiling. His belly was a red ruin. Above it, two green eyes glowed, and jagged teeth gleamed wetly as the wolf's lip curled back in a snarl.

CHAPTER
FOURTEEN

The beast was monstrous, a knotted mass of fur and muscle behind those yellow teeth, and larger than any wolf should be. Suddenly I was very aware of the other tales in Souvestre's little book of fables—mermaids, morgens, man-eating wolves—and the words of the madman: *a monster slavers in the castle.*

The animal stalked closer stiffy, first one step, then another; still I held my ground. I had never seen a wolf before, but I'd done a lot of reading. "Wolves fear fire," I said to Blake, my voice trembling. Then I thrust the torch boldly toward the creature. "Shoo!"

The low growl intensified as the wolf crouched.

The gun. I fumbled in my pocket; fabric ripped as I tore the derringer free. I leveled the barrel only moments before the wolf sprang, but as I squeezed the trigger, the gun jerked upward and the bullet went wide.

Overhead, the birds took wing in a flurry of feathers; before me, the creature was a blur of black fur and bright teeth. I had one more bullet, but my clumsy finger slipped on the catch. I threw the torch, and the animal twisted, landing on splayed paws the size of my hands. The wolf growled again, and I tried to level the shaking gun. But Blake dropped his own torch and grabbed the weapon from me. As the wolf leaped, he fired—and the beast went limp in midair, rolling toward us, blood trickling from the empty left eye.

I stared at Blake, breathing hard, my ears ringing with the sound of the gunshot. Then I glanced at the madman's body; my stomach roiled and I looked away quickly, breathing shallowly through my mouth.

Blake was turning the gun over and over in his hands. The silver barrel gleamed in the low flame of the dying torches. In the shadows, pigeons cooed, as though to comfort him. "Where did you find this?"

"I took it from . . ." I swallowed. "It was in your jacket. When you came aboard. I just . . . I thought you wouldn't want it back."

He held it out, between thumb and forefinger, as though it were filthy. "I don't."

I took it gingerly—the barrel was hot—and dropped it back in my pocket. Then I looked at the wolf, dead on the floor. Blood and gore clotted on the animal's muzzle. The single remaining eye was starting to glaze; the empty socket was a dark red hole. "Where did you learn to shoot like that?"

"My father." His voice was flat, and his hand crept to his side, where the bullet had hit him, back in Hawaii. "I was always the better shot. That night, I aimed to wound. He meant to kill."

I shifted my weight, the gun heavy against my side. "I'm sorry, Blake."

"It's not your fault."

"Really?" I looked for the truth in his eyes; they were like stars, far and cold. "You think that?"

"I made a choice that night too, Miss Song." His voice was soft. "I could have aimed differently."

At the look on his face, a current ran through my chest—was he talking about his father, or me? But then he straightened his jacket and stepped toward the body, kneeling down carefully to avoid the mess. I swallowed again; a sour scum coated the back of my tongue. "Leave him, Blake. He's dead."

"I know. But . . ."

"But what?" I approached slowly, at an angle, not wanting to look. I could see enough out of the corner of my eye: the crater of the abdomen, white and pink and purple, like a strange orchid. I had seen death before, but never in such vivid, violent color.

Blake stood then, slowly; his face was troubled, and he drummed his fingers against his thigh. "I don't think it was the wolf that killed him."

"What?" My eyes were wide, darting around the room. "What then?"

"You said he wore a key?"

I nodded. "Around his neck."

"It's gone. And someone slit his throat." He chewed his lip. "Quite a clean cut. A razor, perhaps. Or a very sharp knife."

"A knife?" A fresh burst of energy sped from my heart to my limbs to the tips of my fingers. I did look at the man then, at the red welted skin of his throat, obscenely parted, like hungry lips. The room seemed to tilt like the deck in rough weather. The smell in the room was nauseating—wet fur and cold flesh and the metallic tang of blood. The echo of the shot was rattling in my skull. "We should go."

"I think you're right." He took my arm. "Likely we can

find the winch by the gatehouse to open the portcullis."

"Yeah." I followed along toward the arched doorway at the far end of the great room. When we opened the door and stepped out into the wide cobbled courtyard, I drank great lungfuls of the cold, sweet air.

The sun sparkled on the frosty stones, and the sky was a cool, cloudless blue—the weather so incongruous with the tableau we'd just witnessed. Escape was close; by the time we reached the gatehouse, I was practically running, but I stopped just under the arch, staring at the open passage through the barbican. "Someone already raised the portcullis."

Blake stiffened. "Let's get out while the front door is open." He dropped my arm and stepped in front of me, into the dark tunnel. Just then, a figure strolled out of the shadows under the archway. "Who's there?" Blake demanded, but I pulled him back.

The man was silhouetted by the sunlight behind him; I couldn't see his face but I knew his cocky stance. "Is that a gun in your pocket, amira, or are you just happy to see me?"

A golden light appeared in his hand as Kashmir drew a small lamp from the breast pocket of his coat: one of the sky herring in a bottle. His white teeth gleamed as he grinned. Annoyed, I pushed him; he moved like water, twisting to the right and elbowing my tender shoulder. "Ow!"

Shock registered on his face. "Are you hurt?"

"No, I . . . no." I shrugged him off, still irritated; I wasn't about to admit to my bumps and bruises, not now. "Come on. Let's get out of here." We passed through the gatehouse and into the square. It was more crowded now, with people running errands, hurrying to and fro. In the bright sunlight, and surrounded by other living souls, I felt a weight lift; it made me light-headed. "Thanks for scaring me half to death."

"It wasn't my intention, amira. I hate half measures." His answer was glib, but I could see him eyeing me as he tucked the lamp back into his coat. "But I heard the shots. What were you two doing?"

Where to start? I licked my lips. "It's a long story. Where have *you* been?"

"Here and there." He patted his pocket; it jingled. Then he raised an eyebrow. "There's dirt on your back."

"What? Oh. Oh! Jesus, Kashmir. I fell." I put my hand on my temple; my head was starting to ache. "But we found a way into the castle and there's a man . . . there *was* a man . . . and now he's *dead*—"

"Likely murdered," Blake added. Then he glanced

down at Kashmir's belt, where the long dagger hung. "With a knife."

I turned to Blake, incredulous. "You can't honestly think Kash did that!"

"I'm only asking questions," Blake said mildly. "But tell us, Mr. Firas. Have you been out here all night long?"

"Ah, Mr. Hart. Despite the rumors, even I can't do anything all night long." But Kash didn't even smile at his joke. Instead, he took my arm. "Come, amira. Let's get back to the ship. I think we've been here long enough."

"At the castle?"

"In Ker-Ys."

I wanted to protest, but I thought back to the dead man, lying on the floor, and I shuddered. Who had killed him? Where was the key? And who was he, really? A king without a kingdom, or just a man who'd lost his mind?

We wound our way toward the dock. When would Crowhurst return from New York? Perhaps he'd already come in with this morning's tide—if so, I would be glad to get the captain's map back, ask my questions, and leave. I counted forward. The gates would open next sometime around midnight. Plenty of time to pick a new destination. I rubbed my temple—my headache was worsening.

Maybe I would rest a bit first.

"Amira, is something wrong?"

Blake frowned. "Rotgut mentioned she skipped breakfast," he said. "And that was some hours ago."

At the thought of food, my stomach turned again. But the dizziness was making it hard to walk; part of me felt as though I would float away into the wide blue sky if Kashmir let go. My skin felt strangely cool, even clammy; likely the adrenaline finally leaving. "Maybe food would be a good idea."

"Come." Kash steered us into a small shop near the bottom of the Grand Rue; baskets of pastry and bread lined the counters, and the smell of malt and sugar and butter warmed me far more than the bakery's ovens. The blond woman behind the counter frowned at Kashmir and me. Her eyes slid to Blake until Kash pulled a handful of coins out of his pocket; then she pasted on a smile for him. But glancing down at the baskets, I was suddenly too hot. I plucked at the collar of my shirt, fumbling at the button. The proprietor arched a brow and said something to me, but I couldn't hear her words.

"I'm sorry . . . can you . . ." I blinked and shook my head. "Sorry, I . . ."

"Amira?"

Suddenly the roar of the ocean was loud in my

ears—confusing. We were not on the water. But the bakery was spinning around me, and my vision narrowed to a small point. My chin dropped as my head grew incredibly heavy. A wave of darkness washed over me, so gently, and I floated on it, arms out, face to the sky, rocking on this strange sea.

When my eyes drifted open—why had I closed them?—I was looking up at a yellowed plaster ceiling and two concerned faces.

"Don't move," Kashmir said to me.

"What happened?" My tongue was thick; I reached back to touch my head—it was throbbing—and found a tender spot. I tried to roll to my side; had I fallen?

"You fainted, Miss Song." The words were distant, echoey.

A wave of dizziness hit me again, not as gentle this time. When it passed, I struggled to sit up. Kashmir put his hand behind my back to support me. "Slowly, slowly."

I shook my head—the roaring sound was still there, rising and falling. But it wasn't only in my ears. "Are people . . . cheering?"

There was music too; the sound of drums and some kind of wind instrument, a flute or a fife, distant but coming closer. Kashmir helped me to my feet, and I tottered over to the window; through it, I could see a press of backs as people lined the street outside. The shopkeeper was standing in the open doorway, her attention split between her strange customers and the excitement outside.

"Pardon," I said to her. "Qu'est-ce qu'il y a là bas? What is it, out there?"

"C'est Grand l'Un," she replied, giving me a once-over, her eyes suspicious.

"Grand l'Un? The Great One?"

"Oui," she said slowly, as though it should be obvious. "Le roi revient!"

"The king?" I asked, unsure that I'd heard her correctly. "What king?"

But Kashmir cocked his head. "The king of Ker-Ys, amira."

For a moment I thought he was joking, but he didn't laugh when I did. Then Blake nodded his agreement, and my knees went weak all over again.

CHAPTER
FIFTEEN

We stood outside the bakery in a thick scrum of people. Adults lifted toddlers onto their shoulders; children were ushered to the front where they could see. It was warmer now, or perhaps it only seemed so in the crowd. I swayed on my feet, still weak, but in the press of bodies, there was no way we could make it back to the ship.

Kashmir supported me on the left and Blake on my right, and they were pushed even closer as the crowd surged forward. The excitement rose around us and people started to chant. "Grand l'Un! Grand l'Un!"

My skin went cold, but the cheering reached its peak, ringing against the clear blue sky. Petals rained down in the crisp winter air—cherry, and gourdon, and lily of the valley; where had they come from, so early in the season? And then, there he was, waving from the wide window of a gilded carriage, the king of Ker-Ys: Donald Crowhurst.

His livery collar caught the afternoon sun, as did the golden crown on his head, and the red satin sash around his shoulders was very dashing. His eyes glimmered with joy as they swept across the faces of his people. He smiled down at the crowd, every inch a king; it struck me, then, that this was the welcome he would have had if he'd returned home triumphant from his race around the world. But this was a far greater feat. I willed him to look at me, but he did not glance my way, and my voice, shouting his real name, was lost in the roar of the crowd.

As the carriage passed us, I saw her—Dahut. She wore deep red velvet, her black hair bound with gold, and she sat beside Crowhurst like his shadow. But unlike the king, she did not wave at the crowd. Her eyes were fixed on a point above our heads, and there was something hard in them. I didn't blame her—as she passed, the cheering faltered, and a few in the crowd surreptitiously made the sign of the fig. Why?

"Kashmir," I said softly. "Do you recognize her?"

"The princess? We saw her in New York, yes."

I turned to him, incredulous. "Kash. She wasn't a princess then."

He tilted his head in confusion. "She's always been a princess."

"What makes you say that?"

Kashmir took in the parade, the crowd, the huzzah. "Everyone says that."

"Not everyone! Not me." The carriage passed from view on the way toward the castle, and the crowd flooded the narrow street behind them, turning from spectators to participants in the parade. People streamed by, pushing, jostling, and then they were gone. Petals stirred on the cobbles; it felt like a dream.

"I don't understand, amira."

"There is no king in Ker-Ys," I said. "I mean, there *was* no king. This morning." My voice faltered as I heard the echo of my own words then, reverberating in my head, along with the cheering of the crowd fading up the street. "You don't remember."

"Miss Song." Blake took my arm gently, leading me back toward the docks. "Perhaps you hit your head when you fell."

"We were just inside the castle, Blake! It was abandoned!" I put my fingers on my temples and pressed, trying to soothe my aching head. "There was a . . . a wolf in the great hall. You shot it dead, and it was eating the man's body—"

"A wolf?"

"This morning everything was different. I swear!" I tore away from them, crushing the petals under my heels to pace, trying to make sense of it all. "He did it. He changed the past. But the world hasn't been unmade—only the memories of it. But how on earth—" I staggered, and Kash caught me.

"Amira, please." In his eyes, a worried look—a look I recognized. I'd looked at my own father that way many times.

"I'm not crazy," I said. "I'm not." Only when he nodded did I let him take my arm.

They led me toward the docks, and my heartbeat drummed at the base of my skull. In my head, a litany: he'd done it, he'd done it, he'd actually done it.

By all the gods, how? My father had never gone so far. If he had, would he have erased memories of me as easily as Crowhurst had erased the memories of the townspeople? Was this the sacrifice Joss had mentioned? I leaned on Kashmir, drawing comfort like warmth from his closeness. When I squeezed my eyes shut, I saw the madman's pale face above the red ribbon at his throat.

When we reached the ship, Rotgut hailed us from the quarterdeck. He was on watch, lost inside a massive coat of mangy fur and oiled leather that made him look much fiercer than he actually was. His brows dove together as Kash helped me up the gangplank. "What's wrong with her?"

"I'm fine," I insisted. "I just feel a little dizzy."

"You should have had some pancakes," he said, tut-tutting.

I shrugged free of Kashmir's grip. "Rotgut . . . what do you remember about this morning?"

"Aside from your lack of appreciation for fine cooking?" He folded his arms, the fur coat bristling around his shoulders. "The motorboat sticks in my mind."

"The *what*?"

"Pretty flash." Rotgut pointed his chin toward the starboard side. There, docked beside the *Temptation*, a sleek black powerboat was moored where the *Fool* had been. "Definitely fit for a king."

"So you know he's the king?"

"Was it supposed to be a secret? Because the people chanting 'Hail to the king!' might have spilled the beans."

I rolled my eyes and went to look at the boat: a gorgeous thing of wood and fiberglass, completely out of place and time. "Wasn't there anything odd about that, to you?"

"No." Rotgut cocked his head. "Why?"

But I didn't answer; my focus was on the yacht. Her name was painted in gold on her stern: *Dark Horse*—the name the newspapers had given Crowhurst, back in the race. "The dark horse and the wayward saint. That's what the dead man said to me."

Out of the corner of my eye, I saw Blake and Kashmir glance at each other, and a flash of irritation shot through me. But Rotgut jerked his thumb over his shoulder. "I'll go make her some lunch."

He squeezed through the hatch as Kash took my arm, his hand very gentle. "You should rest."

Swallowing my annoyance, I let him lead me below, drifting behind him as though he was a tug. Rest was a good idea.

Kash ushered me into his cabin, his face a mask of concern. I curled up in his nest of pillows; he knelt at my side, arranging the cushions around me, tucking a blanket around my shoulders, brushing my hair back from my face. The silk smelled like clove and copper; I was warm and suddenly so tired, but I tried to connect one thought to the next. "It makes sense if you think about it," I murmured. "If

Navigation can actually change reality, the original memories of that old reality would have to change too."

"My memories." Kash sat back on his heels. "Mr. Hart's memories. The people's memories. But not yours."

"Perhaps the fainting is a reaction to that."

"You had a headache in New York," he said. "Just before we met the princess. Is that what happens when another Navigator arrives?"

"Maybe so. Slate had one too. I wonder if he remembers the same past I do. Are Navigators immune somehow?" I bit my lip; the thoughts were started to flow together, like clouds massing before a storm, but Kashmir did not seem to share my excitement. "What? What's wrong?"

"I don't know, amira. Or perhaps I just don't remember. But there are some things that should not be stolen." He stood then. "I'll go. You need your sleep, if you're going to get us out of here tonight."

"Tonight?" I sat back up. "No, Kash. We can't leave, not yet. Not till I know how he did it!"

"You think he'll tell you?"

"He has to—I have to know. And his letter said he would." The letter I had given him, I did not add.

But Kashmir laughed, low and rueful. "You're the

smartest person I know. Surely you can see this. People do not offer great things without a great cost."

"That's not always true, Kash. Sometimes . . . sometimes people give freely without asking anything in return. Like you and me."

He shook his head; he couldn't meet my eyes. "Amira. We may not ask. But there is still a cost. You pay it too."

I stared up at him—at his jaw as it clenched, at the memory of sorrow in the curve of his lips. But before I could respond, a knock came at the door. Kash opened it, and Rotgut handed over a little plate of cold pancakes, sandwiched around some raspberry jam.

Kash nodded his thanks and passed it over to me; I ate in silence. Kashmir's hand was still on the door, but he lingered on the threshold. Suddenly, more than anything, I wanted him to stay. The words bubbled in the back of my throat, like the start of a laugh, but he spoke first. "What was mine like?"

I swallowed the bite I was chewing. "Your what?"

"My map." Kashmir stole a glance at me, almost as if he couldn't bear to look. "You and the captain must have used a map to travel to Vaadi Al-Maas. I looked for my city once, in an atlas at the Brooklyn library, but I was never able to find it. Do you remember the one you used?"

"I do." It surprised me, how quickly it came back to mind. I'd last seen it nearly three years ago, as we'd sailed away through the briny waters of the Persian Gulf. Had I known somehow, even then, how much it would change my life? "It was from the early eighteenth century. Lamp black and walnut oil on vellum. A Frenchman made it."

"A Frenchman?"

"He'd read Scheherazade's tales—they'd just been translated from the Arabic—and went to visit. He was . . . inspired by reality, rather than constrained by it." I put the plate down on the wooden box beside his bed, nestled beside tiny treasures—a silver pillbox, a perfume bottle, a scattering of coins. "You won't find Vaadi Al-Maas on any modern maps."

"Because it was a myth."

I bit my lip. "Yes."

"Then what am I?"

"Kashmir—"

"If you can create a myth, why not a man? Am I merely a figment of some cartographer's imagination? Or did you make me up when you arrived?"

"No, Kash. I . . . No." I stood and reached for him,

taking his shoulders in my hands; they were warm and solid, as they always were. Could I have ever imagined anyone like Kashmir? "Don't say that. You are . . . you're very real to me."

But it wasn't what he needed to hear. He shook his head. "I need to be more than what is reflected in your eyes. Otherwise . . ." For a moment, he was at a loss for words, and the confusion of it made him look so young.

"Otherwise what?"

"Otherwise what am I without you?"

CHAPTER
SIXTEEN

KASHMIR

An old story had crept into my head. It was a story about a rogue, like me. But he was a marionette carved from crooked timber. He longed to be a real boy, and so he learned to be good—whatever that meant. He had been a myth: an Italian allegory only meant to scold the poor.

Nix had taught me that.

Out in the hall, I leaned against the door. Behind it, she slept. She'd been sapped, the coals of her eyes burning low; she needed to rest. And I needed to think. It was hard to do with her near.

I tried to clear my head. Still questions stole in. What was I made of? Who had carved me? All my life, I'd clung to the fact that my mind and body were my own—after all, I'd had nothing else to my name. But I'd never dreamed that someone else might be holding my strings.

And what of the memories Nix had claimed to have? The memories I was missing? Was my mind so malleable a stranger could change it? Were all of my thoughts now suspect? The wounds and the wonders I'd carried from my youth—the dreams and desires I'd fostered for my future . . . the love and longing for the girl who'd stolen my heart? My hand went to the lock at my belt, a comforting weight: solid, real. I'd worn it since the day on the bridge. At the memory, I sighed, catching the scent of her hair. It was sweet as water—fresh, not salt. Why did it make me weak in the knees?

No—no. Of all things, I would not doubt my love. I told myself that as I climbed abovedecks.

The angle of the sun surprised me—it felt later than midafternoon. The harbor gates had shut again. Petals spun on the still water, tumbled down from the street. The *Dark Horse* lay in the harbor, sleek as a seal; a suspicious group of townsfolk had gathered on the wharf to stare at the king's steed. I shook my head grudgingly. Crowhurst was bold, I'd grant him that.

Mr. Hart was waiting at the starboard rail, stiff-backed as any gentleman. "Is Miss Song . . . well?"

I knew what he meant, but I wasn't going to answer such a roundabout question. I pushed the clove I'd been chewing into my cheek and gave him a wide-eyed look. "Well, what?"

He grimaced, adjusting his grip on the brass; in the cold, his knuckles were white. "What do you make of her claims about the king?"

There it was. I considered my words. "Her memory is unquestionable, and she doesn't lie often."

"Oh?" Mr. Hart's face was bland but behind his eyes . . . was that pain?

"And when she does, she does it poorly. Many tells." I sighed. "You know this. You watch her nearly as closely as I do."

The corner of his mouth turned up, his expression rueful. "She's better at keeping secrets."

"Ah, yes." I spat the clove into the water and drew a fresh one from my pocket. "That, I can agree with."

"Hmm." His eyes flicked to me, then back to the harbor. "She really did fall, you know."

I threw back my head and laughed; did he think me jealous? "I know." For a long moment, we were quiet. I watched a young boy on the pier as he took a daring step toward the *Dark Horse*—and another. He got within spitting distance before he ran back to the safety of the crowd. A few of the men tittered, but not many—and no one else made a move toward the strange yacht. Out of the corner of my eye, I saw

Mr. Hart shift from foot to foot; the boy was troubled about this business with Crowhurst. Or was it about Nix? No matter which it was, I shared his concern. "Want a drink?"

"What?" He turned to me, his eyes incredulous. I nodded at the wharf.

"Well, I need one." I stepped down the gangplank without waiting for him to follow. I set a quick pace, making the lock swing, and soon enough I heard his footsteps behind me.

The tavern at the top of the wharf was a long building with a roof made of flaked stone. Small windows squinted suspiciously at the windy harbor. Inside, business was brisker than it had been last night; the red-faced fishermen had gathered for a late lunch after beating the tide home, and many were drinking to one another's health. "A la vôtre! A la vôtre!"

The benches were full, and the air was close with the smell of people and ale and the smoke from the fire. The decor might be convincingly called "charming" by only the greatest of liars: the walls were nailed with chipped shells and twisted driftwood, and the bar was built out of the yellowed jawbone of a great fish. I leaned against it and signaled the girl at the spigot. She looked hard at me with her washed-out eyes, but she took my coin and pulled two mugs of cider. I pretended not to notice her scrub the pennies on her apron before she put them in her pocket.

Still, as I took the cider back to the table, I let myself sigh. It was almost as bad in this little town as it was in modern New York City.

Mr. Hart and I sat across from each other at a wide wooden table. He watched me over his mug, his expression calculating. We drank for a while in a bubble of silence, and I did not fight it. Around us, conversation swirled. Men roared their toasts; others whispered in corners. They used an older dialect—different from the way I spoke it, but there were words that caught my ear: dangereux . . . magie noire . . .

Black magic—I traced a scar on the wood of the table. Did I speak French because of the man who drew my map? Was the suffering of my early years only some foreigner's fantasy?

Spinning the mug in his hands, Mr. Hart stared at the barkeep, but I do not think he was really watching the girl. At last he spoke. "If I hadn't seen the things I've seen on this journey, I'd question her sanity. Now I find myself questioning my own. The things Miss Song said, about the wolf. And the dead man. They seemed familiar, but like a dream does."

I gave him a half smile. "But you do remember her falling."

"Into a tunnel underground. Yes." He spoke slowly, as though he had to draw every word from the well of his memory. "We were passing time exploring the warehouse. . . . The floor fell away, and I threw down a rope to help her back up." He tapped his fingers on the pewter, making a dull ringing. "What do you remember from this morning?"

"Before the parade?" I downed a mouthful of cider. "Stealing our coin back from the harbormaster."

To Mr. Hart's credit, he laughed. "I should have expected something like that. But . . . was there anything else? Something you didn't do but somehow remember anyway?"

I held the clove between my back teeth, considering. "I . . . I dreamed last night about climbing over the abbey wall. It runs beside the castle, and I wanted to take a look inside—maybe find the treasury. I spent some time here listening, talking to the drunks. Apparently the king's treasure is kept in a pit below the castle."

He frowned. "A pit?"

"So they say. An ingenious design, so that if the walls were breached in war, the treasury would flood to hide the gold. I dreamed I went looking for it. But in my dream, the castle was empty. . . ." I glanced down at my palms; the calluses made bumps and ridges. That scrape there—had I actually roped down into the bailey and explored the grounds, rather than only dreaming I had?

Mr. Hart leaned closer. "Did your dream include frightening us in the gatehouse?"

With a crack like a wishbone, the clove broke between my teeth. I spat the pieces to the floor. "It did," I said, though he'd already seen the answer on my face.

Chewing his lip, he thrust his hand into his breast pocket, drawing out the sketchbook I'd given him. "You mentioned a pit," he murmured, paging through. Then he stopped, whistling low under his breath. "Look here."

I took the book and traced the drawing with one fingers. "A map?"

"Of the underground tunnels. See this?" He gestured at a colorful slip of paper tucked between the pages. "I dreamed we found it in the square—or I thought I dreamed it. But here it is. And it shows le trou, a pit. That's what we were searching for in my dream—or my memory. Miss Song thought there was a man trapped there." He sat back in his chair. "Tell me, in your travels aboard the *Temptation*, have you ever seen this happen?"

"Not that I know." Still studying the pages, I pulled another clove from my pocket. "Then again, I've always been on the ship when she's Navigated."

"Except once."

I shut the book and met his gaze head-on. "Yes."

Steepling his hands, he put his elbows on the table. "Do you have any . . . old memories from that time? Odd ones, that seem like dreams?"

The question was as pointed as a knife, and nearly as threatening, so I laughed. "I've only had half a cider, Mr. Hart. Far too little to tell you about my dreams."

He smiled, though his eyes were grim. "So you do have them, then."

Glancing at the fire, I watched it dance and crackle. Above, heat shimmered in the air, almost, but not quite, invisible. "I do."

"So do I."

I let the silence stretch—as did he. Farther down the table, a group of men broke into a ribald song; I waited till the end of the first chorus, but neither of us budged an inch. Finally I stood, sliding the sketchbook back across the table. "You're a hard lock to pick, Mr. Hart."

I drained my mug and held out my hand. He finished his too, and passed it over. Back to the bar, then. I smoothed my vest and prepared my best smile for the girl; my reward was a little blush on her pale cheeks, though she looked upset about it. "Have you got anything stronger?" I pushed an extra coin across the bar. "Mulled wine? Genièvre?"

She nodded, topping off the cider with a splash of what smelled like whiskey. As I waited, I pretended not to listen as one fisherman told another about the yacht. "It moves like nothing you've ever seen," he said. "Flies over the water."

"It's an enchantment," his companion hissed back. "They say the princess is a witch. She writes spells on her palms."

The words were like needles, pricking at my skin, but I let nothing show on my face as I picked up the mugs. Accusations like that were dangerous, not only for the accused, but for those who showed them sympathy.

Setting the cider down on our table, I slid back into my seat. Then I lifted my own drink and trotted out my native accent, just for fun—or maybe to spite the men at the bar. "Salamati."

"Hipahipa," Mr. Hart replied in Hawaiian, taking a deep draft and making a face.

I did the same; it had been whiskey, after all. For a moment, it burned like a coal under my ribs before settling into a pleasant warmth behind my navel. I rolled the clove over my tongue. "If . . . if these dreams are . . . are more like a memories . . . if we share them—does that make them real?"

Mr. Hart glanced at the cup. "What's in the drink, Mr. Firas?"

I laughed a little. "I mean to say, does this mean they happened? Somehow? Somewhere?"

"Miss Song mentioned alternate universes." He sighed, wistful. "Imagine if we could go back and forth between them, picking the best outcome each time."

I raised an eyebrow. "The best outcome for who?"

"Good point." He smiled wryly and saluted me with his cup. Outside, the light was fading. Near the hearth, a woman lit a rush and carried it to the lamps hanging on the wall, stopping briefly at each, like a pickpocket in a crowd. Mr. Hart sighed, rubbing his chin. "It is strange," he said. "How quickly fortune changes."

"How so?"

"Well!" He laughed, surprised. "Two weeks ago, I never would have imagined myself visiting a mythical city. Or commiserating with a confessed criminal."

"Is it so strange we find ourselves allies? After all, you're a confessed gentleman."

"What's wrong with being a gentleman?"

"In Hawaii? I've stolen much, Mr. Hart, but never an

island." At my words, his smile faded and fell away; a pang hit me. Was it guilt? I sighed. "But neither of us had a choice in our parents."

"Were you raised a thief?"

"For the brief time I was raised, yes." I smiled into my cup. "But even beyond that, you and I have much in common."

He raised an eyebrow. "Oh?"

"We both crew the same ship. We both left our homelands behind." I hesitated, but I couldn't resist. "We both dream of the same girl."

Mr. Hart snorted. "You were right, I'm not half drunk enough." He tipped his mug back and then wiped foam from his lips. Then he leaned forward over the table. "Something's changed since Hawaii. The two of you used to be as thick as thieves. Pardon the expression."

"Ah ah ah." I wagged my finger. "There's not enough beer in the world that I'll tell you what's between her and me."

"Fair enough," he said gamely. "Your other dreams, then."

I winked at him. "I'll tell you mine if you tell me yours."

His expression was wry. "I suppose that means I go first?"

"Bon courage, Mr. Hart." I lifted my cup.

Mr. Hart took another thoughtful sip. "That first day I came to the ship, I dreamed—or I think I dreamed—that I had stayed in Hawaii instead. Not so unexpected, really. And it might only be wishful thinking. But it was a strange dream. Vivid. And a week later, I can't shake it. What about you?"

I watched his right hand clench and loosen on the handle of the mug. There was something he was not telling me. No surprise there. But what to tell him, exactly? The words were hard to summon; odd, when the dream was so clear in my head. Draining my cup, I set it down firmly. "The night I came aboard, I dreamed I died instead."

Surprise flickered across his face, like the shadow of a sparrow flying by above. "How?"

My hand crept to my neck—thankfully, it still held my head to my shoulders. I shuddered; I couldn't stop it from happening. "Execution," I said at last.

The muscles in his throat jerked. He was nervous, but his voice was steady. Still, he toyed with the mug. "With a gun?"

"A sword." I could still feel it now, as soft as a whisper, as cold as the crescent moon. "Why do you ask?"

Mr. Hart's answer was a long time coming. "In my

dream, I . . . I killed someone, back in that cave above Nu'uanu Valley."

I ran my tongue over my teeth; the cider had left a sour aftertaste. "Your father?"

"No." He stared at me, a lost look in his eyes. "It was you."

CHAPTER
SEVENTEEN

Alone in Kashmir's bed, I slept too lightly to dream him there. My mind was still spinning; I tossed and turned as well. After a fitful hour, I gave up and opened my eyes. Before me was a poem; the page had been torn from a book and pinned to the wall with a silver tack. The edge of the paper fluttered with each breath. My eyes focused on the words . . . one of Rumi's about love and insanity.

The words stirred something in my chest as the events of the morning came back to me. The swirl of petals, the dead man gutted, the cheering crowd, the stench of the wolf. If I hadn't read Crowhurst's letter, if I hadn't known what to expect, I might think I was going mad. Or at least misremembering. After all, I *had* hit my head. I could still feel the bump—and the Mayo Clinic had listed head trauma as a factor in memory problems. Depression too.

And of course *that* was heritable.

No. No. I would not end up like my father—I would not lose Kashmir. Not if Crowhurst could help me avoid it.

I twisted around in the silk cushions, trying to get comfortable, but the pistol jabbed my hip. I slipped my hand into my pocket and pulled it out, running my fingers over the scrollwork. The silver barrel gleamed in the low light. How could Blake have forgotten shooting the wolf? I frowned, struggling to open the chamber to check. It took me a few tries—I had never studied guns—but no, the bullets were gone.

Then again . . . we'd fired both before coming aboard in Hawaii.

And how would Slate have gotten bullets for a derringer? In modern New York, the gun would have been an antique, the bullets custom.

For one very odd moment, the world seemed to twist in around me, like the tentacles of a sea monster. Was I actually going insane, or had the captain reloaded the gun?

Scattering the pillows, I hauled myself to my feet, holding on to the doorframe as a sudden dizzy feeling ebbed. Then I shoved the gun back into my cloak and made my way upstairs.

The captain was still curled in his little alcove; I whispered his name, but he did not stir. On the floor beside the bed, I saw a congealing stack of untouched pancakes—Rotgut's doing, certainly. I sighed, running my hand through the tangles of my hair. Had my father woken yet today? I had to remind myself that it wasn't unusual, during the dark times, for him to skip meals and spend many hours in his bed—and it was better than him wandering the city and climbing the walls.

Quietly I searched the cabin, checking his sea chest, the desk, and finally the cupboard beneath it: there it was at the bottom, a leather case stamped with Blake's initials. Inside, four bullets nestled in sleeves made for six.

I felt relieved—and silly, very silly—but why shouldn't I have doubted? What Crowhurst had done was incredible. Unbelievable. What a power to have, so vast . . . and so dangerous. When the evidence of your eyes contravenes the memories in your head, where can you put your trust?

Kash was right to warn me. Standing there with the leather case in my hand, I reloaded the gun.

From belowdecks, Billie started barking; automatically, I glanced to the captain, but his eyes stayed closed and his breathing did not change. A small, lost part of me wished he would wake. I wanted someone to talk to about Crowhurst, about Ker-Ys . . . about the past, and the future too. I wanted my father. I wanted his guidance. But I couldn't have it, even if he'd been awake. He would ask his own questions, and I had no answers for him. Besides, he wouldn't have the answers I needed, either. He never had.

Did Crowhurst? How had he done it? How had he changed the memories of the town—the very fabric of reality—to crown himself king? And out of all the possible things he might have done, why had he chosen this?

A soft knock at the cabin door interrupted my thoughts. Had Kashmir missed me downstairs? I stuffed the gun back into my pocket as I went to the door, but it wasn't him.

"Dahut!" I blinked at her in the low light. Dusk had settled across the harbor the way ash drifts down from a fire, soft and reverent, but the light from the ship's lanterns gleamed on the gold circlet in her hair, and the guarded, empty look in her eyes.

"You—you must be Nix."

"Yes." I faltered, suddenly off-balance; my heart sank.

"Yes," she repeated, her eyes narrowing. "I have something for you."

"Do you? Oh." In her hands, a folded piece of paper. I

recognized it immediately—my father's map of Honolulu. I took it from her, inspecting it briefly, but it was whole and undamaged. My mouth twisted, wry. "How fitting."

She watched me, suspicious. Her skirts whispered around my ankles as she shifted her weight. "We've met before."

The way she said it, I knew it was a question. "In New York."

"I'm sorry." Dahut curled her fingers into fists. "I have a problem with my memory."

"You told me." A sudden realization: perhaps her condition wouldn't have been listed in a medical dictionary. "You're not a Navigator."

"A what?"

"A Navigator. Someone who can use maps to travel through history? Through myths?"

"Am *I*? No. My father is."

"The king."

"Yes." She said it like it should be obvious—this, from the same girl who told me not three days ago that there was no king in Ker-Ys. My frustration was rising like steam through a stack . . . but it wasn't her fault. I tapped the map against my open palm. It seemed that whatever Crowhurst had done, it affected everyone around him, no matter if they were on his ship or no.

Or was that how Navigation always worked? Had Slate and I been imposing changes on the crew from place to place and era to era without even knowing it was happening? In the pit of my stomach, a whirlpool. Kashmir's words came back to me. *Some things should not be stolen.* Had I ever seen such a blank look in his eyes?

No . . . there was a difference between Dahut's missing memories and the way Blake and Kash remembered a whole new reality. But why? If Navigation caused memories to change, what could cause memories to vanish?

"Is something the matter?"

I took a breath, trying to compose myself. "You forget things often?"

"Usually I write things down in my diary so I don't forget. But sometimes . . ." Dahut's eyes flashed with sudden rage. "Sometimes my records are incomplete."

I blinked at her, but as quickly as the storm came, it had passed; had it only been a trick of the fading light? I took hold of the pearl at my throat, rubbing its smooth surface between my fingers. What could I say? How to begin? "What's the first thing you remember?"

"Coming into the harbor this morning."

I stared at her, shocked. "That's your first memory?" The thought of it took my breath away—automatically, my own mind riffled through the treasures of my past. My father teaching me to Navigate . . . a theft-day feast in Malta . . . kissing Kashmir on the beach. Now I knew why the idea of forgetting bothered him so much. "Ever?"

Dahut bit her lip; her eyes were faraway. "Before that? It's hazy, but . . .asking for help. Asking someone to help me."

I frowned. "You asked for my help in New York."

"Did I?"

"Come."

Tucking the Honolulu map into my pocket, I ushered her inside the cabin. Her dark eyes roamed the room, widening when she saw my father, sprawled on his bunk. "Is he all right?" she whispered.

I glanced at Slate. Was it so obvious? "He's fine," I lied.

"My own father barely sleeps."

Ignoring her naked curiosity, I went to the desk, pushing aside the coffee cups and picking up the map of Ker-Ys. "Do you remember this?"

She studied the map. "This is my handwriting."

"Is it?" A thin current of admiration trickled into my voice. "It's beautiful work."

"I've had a lot of practice."

I tilted my head. "How do you know that? I mean, how do you remember?"

"I wrote it down in my diary. It's one of my father's rules. He has me make a map every morning, for his records. He has a whole stack in his cabin."

"His records? To help him remember where you've been, or . . ." I furrowed my brow, but then I realized. "Or so you can return to a place if you Navigate away. God, that's clever." We'd done that once, in Hawaii with Blake. Why hadn't I thought of asking him to make maps wherever we went?

"My father is very clever," Dahut said then, but it didn't sound like a compliment. I bit my lip.

"How did . . . is Crowhurst . . ." I faltered, considering the question I had been about to ask: is he your real father? After all, as I'd mentioned to Kashmir, Crowhurst had a daughter on his timeline, but her name wasn't Dahut. But Slate and I did not immediately look alike, and I'd always hated how people looked at us, as though cataloging our differences. Maybe Crowhurst had had a second family—or maybe he'd adopted her. Either way, would she remember?

And what did it mean, anyway? *Real.* I let the question die unasked. "I'd like to talk to him, actually."

"He said you might. And I know he'd like to talk to you."

"Oh?"

She laughed a little. "I almost forgot to mention it. There's a dinner tonight. You and your father are both invited. He has something for you. A gift, and a request."

I almost asked her what they were, but she would have told me if she'd known. I sighed, running my hand through my hair. I knew the gift, at least. Crowhurst had already offered me knowledge in his letter—it was the reason I had brought us here. But what was the request? Kashmir's words came back to me: *people do not offer great things without great cost.*

And yet.

I had come so far, and the destination was so close. If I left now, without knowing for certain, would I regret it for the rest of my life? I glanced over at Slate—the gesture was almost automatic, but the sight of him made my jaw clench. I couldn't follow the same route as my father.

"Does it make him strange?" Dahut was staring at Slate too, peering into the darkened alcove. "The—the Navigating?"

"Strange how?"

"Intense. Like a fire with too much fuel."

"Sometimes. But I don't know if it's the Navigation or the . . . or something else."

"Something else?"

"He misses my mother," I said at last, which was only part of the truth, but the only part I felt comfortable admitting.

Dahut arched an eyebrow. "But you don't."

"I never knew her."

"I never knew mine," she said, her voice softening. "At least, I don't remember knowing her. But I miss her just the same." Then she sighed. "I know my father misses the rest of his family. Maybe that's what makes them odd—your father and mine. Something missing."

"Something missing, indeed." I made a face. "Though it does appear Navigation has some . . . unexpected side effects."

"Can *you* do it?"

"Do what?"

She made a vague gesture. *"Navigate."*

"Yes."

Her breath caught in her throat; her voice came out a whisper. "Then maybe you *can* help me."

"I might, if you could remember what you wanted."

"Can't you guess? My head. My memories!" Urgently, she took my hands. "There must be a way to help me get better!"

"I . . ." I was about to protest, but there *were* cures we could try: the panacea, the Aquae Sulis, the earth and spittle of Egyptian medicine, even the vial of mercury from Qin's tomb—any number of solutions on any number of maps. But would they work if the problem was born of Navigation itself? I licked my lips as the next thought came to me. "Has your father ever tried to help?"

She stiffened, and as the silence stretched, I felt my cheeks go pink. "Maybe you should ask him that," she said at last. "He never answers me."

"Maybe I will."

She took a deep breath, her slim shoulders rising and falling under the heavy velvet. "So you'll join us tonight?"

"Yes." I clenched my fists at my side, resolved. Was that excitement in my stomach, or trepidation? "But the captain will stay behind."

"Why?"

"He—he should rest," I said, which was not a lie. "And anyway, I'm the one with the questions."

"What do you want to know so badly?"

I led her to the door, though I hesitated on the threshold. Could I tell her? Perhaps she already knew—or wouldn't even remember. But more than anything, I wanted to share the thought. Excitement crept into my voice as I spoke. "I think . . . I think Crowhurst has found a way to change the past."

Her eyebrows went up, but she did not seem as thrilled as I was—she only pressed her lips together, and her large eyes dimmed. "So there's something missing for you too."

I stiffened, but she said nothing more as she went down the gangplank. Two guards waited for her on the pier; when one of them caught my stare, I turned back into the cabin. Then I startled. My father stood by his bed, swaying on his feet.

"Nixie," he growled, and his eyes were fever bright. "You're not the only one with questions."

CHAPTER
EIGHTEEN

In my father's voice, an accusation. But both Sun Tsu and Machiavelli knew the best defense was a good offense. I attacked. "Go back to sleep, Slate. I'm doing fine without you."

He took a breath to respond, then coughed into his fist—just standing had taken so much out of him. But he was fueled now by an inner fire—that old familiar drive—and he did not back down. "And what the hell are you doing, exactly, on this godforsaken rock?"

"Looking for answers."

"Don't play games! What did you mean about Crowhurst?"

I clenched my jaw—there was no use denying what he'd heard. "He told me he knows how to change things, Dad. I'm going to learn if that's true."

"And then what?"

Slate's expression was half disbelieving, half mocking, and I faltered—but of course he knew what I would change. I lifted my chin. "Then I'll be the master of my fate. Captain of my own damn soul."

"What happened to all your grand arguments about unmaking the world?"

"What happened to your quest to save the one you love?

His face paled, but his eyes caught fire. "You've fought me for years, but now that it's about Kashmir—"

"What did you really expect, Slate?" My voice shocked me—the anger in it. "After all this time watching you, what did you think I would do?"

"I don't know!" he shouted, flinging his arms into the air. "Maybe learn from my mistakes?"

"I did," I shot back. "Just not the lessons you thought. And now I have the chance to learn from experience."

"From *Donald Crowhurst*? Nixie." Slate shook his head in disbelief. "He's crazy."

I gave him a significant look. "Yeah, well, speaking of which . . ." I tossed his map on the table. "I got this back for you. And who knows? If I learn how to change the past, maybe we go find Lin next."

"Find . . . Lin?" He blinked at me, brought up short, and his voice was suddenly soft. His entire demeanor had changed at the sound of her name. "And what? Stay in Hawaii instead?"

"It depends, doesn't it?"

"On what?"

"On what's possible." I turned then, unable to watch his face, the hope growing in his eyes. "Stay here if you want. I'm going."

"Are you kidding me?" He went to the closet, picking a shirt from the floor and giving it a sniff. "I'll be ready in five."

Frustrated, I stormed out through the doorway and stomped down the ladder to find a change of clothes. I was halfway into a dress when I heard voices abovedecks—Kashmir's low comment, Blake's quick retort, and then . . . laughter? I poked my head out of Kashmir's door as the boys slid down the ladder, grinning. Clutching the frothy lace of the dress in front of my chest, I leaned into the hall. "Where have you two been?"

"Drinking, amira!"

I made a face. "I wish you'd brought me along."

Kashmir's lanky body stilled; he frowned at me. Behind

him, Blake's eyes flicked down to my bare shoulders, then quickly back up. "What's the occasion, Miss Song?"

"Dinner with the king."

"Really?" Blake's face was eager. But Kash raised an eyebrow, affecting a casual disdain.

"Isn't that just what you wanted, amira?"

I sighed and hiked my dress higher. "Slate's coming too."

"Ah." Kashmir tilted his head, his green eyes softening. It struck me then—he missed so little. He must have known how worried I'd been. "Well. It's a pretty dress, but of course you can't go to dinner at a palace without your best accessory."

"Which is?"

"A handsome man on your arm."

I raised my eyebrows, but a smile tugged at the corners of my lips. "And where could I find one of those?"

Kash gave a half shrug and turned to Blake. "Do you think Rotgut's free?"

"Maybe one of the fishermen at the bar," Blake suggested, grinning. "After all, a lady can't be expected to attend dinner with a strange man without an escort."

"My father will be there," I reminded them.

"Is there any man stranger?" Kash laughed as I smacked

him, almost losing hold of my gown. "All right, all right, amira! I'll come to dinner!"

"I will too, if you've got a free arm," Blake said. "I'm eager to meet Crowhurst. And I'll make sure Mr. Firas doesn't steal the silver."

Kashmir pretended to kick him, and Blake laughed as he dodged down the hall toward his room. I stared at Kash, half amused, half amazed. "How much did you two drink?"

He gave me a crooked smile. "Not enough to miss your wardrobe malfunction."

I passed a hand over my eyes. "It's all these damn buttons."

"Laisse moi." Kash shooed me away from the door.

I turned, pulling the embroidered sleeves up over my arms—they lay just off the shoulder, creating a wide, scooped neckline. Kashmir shut the door and stood behind me, his knuckles grazing my bare skin as he started on the buttons at the small of my back. I bit my lip, trying not to shiver, hoping he didn't notice my goose bumps. "What were you and Blake talking about at the tavern?"

"Killing each other."

"What?" I half turned, but he tugged at the row of button loops; I could hear the smile in his voice.

"I think a world exists where he and I could be great friends. Hopefully this is that world." He hesitated, just a moment. "He did notice something interesting. It seems we both remember the past—the real past. The one you remember."

"Really?" Relief welled up in my chest.

"Baleh. But only as one remembers a dream."

"But that's still good," I said, hopeful. "At least the memory isn't gone."

"For better or for worse," he said. Reaching my shoulder blades, he paused to brush my hair aside, his touch feather soft. "I wonder if there are some things I would rather forget."

My hand found the pendant at my throat. "Like what?"

"Perhaps that's a story best left for another day." He sighed then, and his breath was warm on my shoulders. Gently he adjusted the lie of the fabric against my skin, smoothing it down my back. "Turn around?"

I did, sweeping the waterfall bustle behind me; the skirt was a lacy dimity cotton the color of cream, more nineteenth century than seventeenth, but it was my best gown. And after seeing Crowhurst's yacht, it seemed pointless to stick to one era in clothing.

Kashmir's eyes swept down from my throat to my hips to the lace of the hem. "Lovely," he murmured.

"This is the one you helped design, remember? Back in Hawaii."

"Ah, yes. But I wasn't talking about the dress." He grinned, elbowing me, and I smiled back.

"Thank you," I said. "For coming with me tonight. I know you don't trust Crowhurst."

"Exactly why I would not let you go alone. We may not agree, but you are my captain," he said simply. "I will always follow you."

There was a feeling in my stomach—like being at the crest of a wave: ready to fly, frightened to fall. I fell. "You'd best get dressed, then."

"Right." He turned to rummage in his closet, but not before the light went out of his eyes. "We don't want to keep the king waiting."

Topside, my father was pacing the deck. He'd put on an old pair of dark breeches and a high-collared black jacket; they were good pieces, but they hung loose on his frame. When was the last time he'd eaten? But he'd brushed his hair and shined his shoes, and energy hummed through his body; he was alive once more. "Let's go!" he said, starting for the gangplank the moment he saw my head pop through the hatch.

"We're waiting on Blake and Kash," I said. He swore, though he did not protest. I watched him as he went back to pacing. The reddish-blond beard he'd been growing since Honolulu had gotten quite thick. Beards were practically a requirement for men of the era, but with the myth of Ker-Ys in the back of my mind, I half wanted to ask him to shave. And when Kash followed Blake through the hatch in a scarlet frock coat with gold-embroidered cuffs, a shiver skittered up my spine. "No. Not red."

Kash raised an eyebrow, but Slate had already surged forward, like a dog released from a leash. "We're going to be late!" he said, striding onto the wharf without looking back.

We hurried behind him, leaving Bee and Rotgut playing chess belowdecks, with Billie sleeping atop their feet. When I'd asked if they wanted to come, Bee had given me a dark look. "We'll stay with the ship, my girl."

"What's bothering you?"

"I don't like the way these people sneer," she'd said. "They whisper behind their hands. They won't meet my eyes. I don't want to walk about at night."

"I'm sorry, Bee."

She'd only waved her hand. "It's not the first time and place this has happened. But as a utopia, it could use some work."

Sure enough, as we made our way up the Grand Rue in our finery, people stared as we passed, their eyes dark pits in pale faces. As usual, Kashmir drew the most attention; he walked with his head high, striking in his red jacket and his black boots, seeming not to notice the glances—not even the ones I cast from under the hood of my cloak.

But as we neared the castle, the sound of music drifted to my ears, providing a welcome distraction, and when we reached the square, I gasped at the sight. The town had gathered under the velvet sky to hold a celebration in honor of the king. Bonfires roared on the corners, reaching to the sky to scatter embers like confetti. A giant pig turned on a spit in front of the cathedral, and tables groaned with pastries and cheeses, sausage and puddings, and platters of stewed fruit and nuts. Men in rich velvets danced with women gowned in shimmering sea silk, and musicians made their instruments sing: violins and pipes, lyres and flutes, tambourines and bells and a drum half the height of a very tall man.

And the château—so different tonight! Light glowed in each of the tall arched windows, and the portcullis was guarded by two men in blue-and-red uniforms. Torchlight glinted off the tips of their pikes. They saluted as we approached, striking the ground with the butts of their weapons. One escorted us across the bailey toward the great hall, though I could have guessed our destination; bright light and music spilled from the open archway. I hesitated outside, tangled in my memories of the morning. When I finally stepped through the doorway, I couldn't help but stare.

The smell of decay, the huge wolf, the dead man . . . all were gone. The enormous hearths bracketing the room were crackling, not with dry leaves but with merry flames, and rich tapestries undulated in the warm current of air. In the corner, a young man strummed a lute, while on the ceiling, the painted mermaids splashed in bright pools. A hundred candles dripped fire from each chandelier, and the long table was laid at one end with porcelain plates rimmed in gold.

How had it all changed so fast? Even the army of servants carrying platters to the sideboard couldn't have cleaned it up so quickly. The floor was polished, the broken chairs restored. It was like magic—it *was* magic, wrought by some trick of Navigation.

I stood, dizzy in the sudden warmth and the unexpected

luxury. Was this how myths originated? Was Navigation where rumors of magic began?

"Welcome! Welcome!" At the head of the table, Crowhurst stood to greet us. For all the pomp, he had changed out of the blue dress coat and into a twentieth-century jacket and tie—something from his own era, perhaps—though he still wore his crown and the livery collar. The thick chain gleamed in the low light, and as he approached, I noticed that, rather than a kingly pendant, the device hanging from the chain was an old copper flask stamped with a scrolling Greek key design. He thrust out his hand. "Captain Slate! Pleasure to see you again. And Nixie. Nixie, such a joy."

I tried to keep my face neutral. "Your Majesty."

"None of that, none of that!" The man wrinkled his nose and flapped his hands as though the word had left an odor in the air. "Call me Donald."

"I know who you are," Slate muttered.

I shot him a look, but Blake stepped in. "They call you Grand l'Un in the city," he said smoothly.

"I know! It gave me a bit of a shock to hear that name, but apparently it means Great One in the local dialect. I suppose King Donald doesn't sound quite right. And you know Dahut." She nodded at his gesture, and when her eyes met mine, I was glad to see a glint of familiarity. Then Crowhurst turned to Kashmir and extended his hand. "And . . . ?"

I made the introductions. Blake bowed at the waist like a gentleman, and Kashmir was all charm, bending low over the princess's wrist and coaxing out a smile. Crowhurst greeted them both warmly—if he was surprised I'd brought guests, he did not show it.

After the formalities, Crowhurst slid into his chair and picked up a bottle. "Come," he said, tipping it into the cut crystal glasses. Under his fingers, I read the label: CHÂTEAU D'YQUEM, 1811. "Let's have a toast!"

I took a glass, trying to keep my hand from shaking. In 2011, the papers had reported the sale of a two-hundred-year-old bottle of Château d'Yquem; it had gone for more than a hundred thousand dollars, making it one of the most expensive wines ever sold. It sparkled in the light from the candles. "What are we toasting?"

"New beginnings," Crowhurst said, setting down the bottle and raising his own glass. We all followed suit. "And new endings too."

My mouth was dry. I took a sip—the liquid was sweet and crisp. On all our travels to various eras, I'd never once considered trying the wine.

But Kashmir did not bring his glass to his lips. "New beginnings," he muttered as we drank. "Is that why you've crowned yourself king of a fairy tale?"

"Ah, that has more to do with new endings," Crowhurst said with a small smile. "You know how the story used to go—the town flooded, the people drowned. Becoming king was the best way to change the legend."

Blake stared at Crowhurst with deep fascination. "You're trying to save the town?"

"I have saved it."

"In point of fact, you only haven't yet destroyed it," Blake countered, but Slate's hand shot out and grabbed Blake by the shoulder, pushing him back in his chair.

"Who cares about the future?" my father said. "Tell us how you changed the past."

"All in good time." Crowhurst gave a signal, and the servants brought food around the table, many courses all at once in a service en confusion. There was a scalloped silver tureen filled with hot saffron soup, tiny china cups holding the pickled eggs of guivres, and a fat swan with gilded feet, roasted and sewn back into its own feathered skin. The centerpiece, set down with great ceremony, was a nest woven of willow twigs and filled with ortolans—whole broiled songbirds, blinded and drowned in Armagnac.

The sight of them gave me pause—they were banned in the modern era for the cruelty of their preparation—and when a man in livery offered me a second napkin, I declined. So did Slate. "I have one already," he said, but I leaned across the table.

"It's to cover your face while you eat the ortolan, Dad."

He looked at me askance. "Why?"

Crowhurst answered before I could. "They say it's to hide your greed from God, though I think it's because stuffing a whole bird in your mouth looks rather monstrous."

Slate threw his napkin on his plate. "There goes my appetite."

I felt queasy too—or was that only nerves? But I wasn't here to eat. "It's very impressive," I said to Crowhurst. "But I hope this isn't the gift you mentioned."

"Not at all!" His eyes twinkled; he took his glass and propped one elbow on the table. "The gift I have for you is much more rare than wine and songbirds."

"Knowledge," I guessed; in my lap, my fingers twisted in the lace of my dress. "That's what I came for."

"Alas, that's not the gift, but the request."

I froze in my chair, blinking—the request? But it was

Blake who spoke. "And what is it you want to know?"

"The same things you do." Crowhurst set down his glass and clasped his hands together. His face took on a grandiose expression as he looked around the table, taking us all in one by one. At last, his gaze settled on me. "Ever since my first revelation, when I was nearing the end of the race, I've wanted to discover the secrets of what you call Navigation. I've spent the last year exploring the limits of our abilities. So far, anything seems possible—"

"Anything, Father?" Dahut's question was pointed.

"Almost anything," Crowhurst amended without missing a beat. "But of course, there's a holy grail in this quest for knowledge. The question we all want to answer . . . all of us who chart courses through time—"

"Changing the past," Blake said.

"Yes. I've done it here, in Ker-Ys, it's true. But myths are strange things. Malleable. Uncertain. And what I really want to know is whether I can change history itself."

"What is history but a fable agreed upon?" I said softly— the words were Napoleon's. But Slate grimaced.

"No, no, no," he said, putting his hands on the table. "We didn't come here to help you discover gold in California or buy stock in Apple or whatever scheme you're dreaming up."

"Oh, come now, Captain!" Crowhurst tapped the heavy crown on his head. "Money is easy. My dreams are much grander than gold!"

Kashmir shifted in his chair. "What gives you the right to try to alter myth or history?"

"The right?" Crowhurst looked surprised; he glanced from me to Slate, as though we would understand. "The three of us . . . we're cosmic beings. We might even be gods."

His voice was pompous, grand. Was it only delusion? But the changes he had wrought were very real; I could still taste the wine on my tongue, and smell the oily scent of the ortolan.

"Christ." Slate picked up his glass and downed the contents. "You're even crazier than I am."

Crowhurst held on to his composure, though his eyes were stony. "Genius is often mistaken for madness, Captain, until the method's proven. That's why I need you."

"You're not convincing me." Slate refilled his glass. Wine sloshed onto the table, but Crowhurst waved his words away.

"I wasn't trying," he said, meeting my eyes.

I swallowed. "Me?"

"Haven't you ever wanted to shape the world, Nixie?"

"What the hell are you talking about?" Slate said, but I ignored him.

Across from me, Blake sat rapt, his eyes full of wonder; beneath the table, Kashmir took my hand. I squeezed his fingers. "Is that your request, then?" I said. "My help?"

Crowhurst nodded. "It is."

"Nixie . . ." My father had a warning in his voice, but I didn't even glance his way.

"Then what's the gift?"

Crowhurst watched me for a long moment. Then he smiled. "It's yours either way." At his gesture, a servant opened the side door. "But maybe I should have called it proof."

Kashmir seemed to coil in his chair, but Crowhurst was watching the captain, whose hand had stopped, the wine halfway to his lips.

In the doorway stood a strange woman dressed in a simple linen gown. She was clearly not local; her face was delicate and made pale by the black hair hanging loose, like a curtain, to her waist. She was Asian, Chinese most likely, like me.

Or rather . . . half of me.

Slate's glass shattered on the stone floor. I felt the wine splash my hem, but I didn't even glance down.

"What do you think, Captain?" Crowhurst's voice

seemed to echo in my ears, from very far away. "Genius or madness? Or does it matter either way?"

My father did not answer. He was white and weak as smoke; his hands shook, but not for opium, not this time. He stood stiffly, quietly, and then, suddenly, with a sob like a shout, he stumbled around the table, glass crunching under his feet.

The woman was smiling.

My mother was smiling.

CHAPTER
NINETEEN

I don't know how long they stood there—my mother and my father—compressed beyond fusion. I was on the perimeter, on the event horizon, where time seemed to stop. And then she looked at me, and all of the air was pulled from the room and the gravity was so strong it was nearly impossible to break away.

But I managed.

My chair fell over with a crash, but I didn't look back; I was already through the closest door and into an unfamiliar corridor. I took a turn at random, then another, then a left—perhaps it was a right. I stopped paying attention; my only goal was escape. I saw an open archway then, and burst out into the bailey, past guards who watched with impassive eyes. The cold air seized my lungs. Finally I slowed, coughing, panting. My legs shook. The world spun. The air tasted like torch fire and frost. I sank to my knees on the rough granite cobbles.

It was impossible.

But he'd done it.

But it was impossible.

But there she was.

Joss had told Slate he would see Lin again someday—and so he had. A laugh clawed its way up my throat. I hadn't known that I would too! We'd both thought it would be in Honolulu in 1868, on the map he'd sought all my life. The map he'd found and lost.

The map Crowhurst had taken.

My god.

And all this time, we had thought she was dead.

My gut twisted like a rag wrung out. What had I done, giving Crowhurst the map of New York?

I wrapped my arms around my shoulders—I was shaking; was I cold? And there was an odd feeling, or a lack of feeling, a numbness behind my ears and along my scalp and at the tips of my fingers. I was breathing much too fast. I closed my eyes and tried to slow down, watching colors like fireworks swirl and fade behind my lids.

"Nixie . . ."

I whirled around; Crowhurst put his palms up, placating. Though the bailey was wide, the walls were high, and I felt trapped with him so close. For a moment, I wanted to run again, all the way back to the ship.

Instead I pushed myself to my feet, thrumming like a mast under too much sail. "You did this," I growled, starting toward him, fists clenched. "You stole her."

"I saved her."

"You *what*?"

"I saved her life! Nixie—"

"Stop calling me that!" My shout echoed off the walls of the keep.

Crowhurst took a step back, concern on his face. "She needed help," he said softly. "Penicillin."

I shuddered to a stop. The words made no sense at first. The emotion was still coming in waves over my head; I took a deep breath, trying to keep an even keel. "You saved her. . . ."

"We did. You and I."

"Me?"

"You got the map into my hands, and I went back to help. Your own father couldn't do it," he went on. "He told me so the night we met. He said he didn't want to risk losing you."

"He said that?" My heart trembled in my chest—a bird against the cage. I had doubted him, but he had chosen me; in the end, he always had. "Did he . . . did Slate ask you to go to her?"

"He wasn't in any sort of condition to make requests, but I saw a need. I recognized his pain. You must understand," he said, his voice soft. "I lost my family too."

I stared at him, not comprehending. "But . . . they're still alive on your timeline," I stammered. Why did he look away? "I read that, in the articles. They waited for you—they're waiting. All you'd have to do is go back."

His face paled, and I saw his throat move as he swallowed. But before he could speak, I heard my father's voice. "Nixie?"

My heart leaped—my stomach churned. There they were, my mother and Slate, walking across the bailey hand in hand; it was as painful to look at them as it was to stare at the sun.

Still, I couldn't look away. I could see, now, the parts of me that were hers—the curve of her lips was the same as mine when I smiled. The tilt of her eyes—looking into them was like looking into a mirror. She couldn't have been more than a decade older than I; she'd been in her mid-twenties when I was born—when we'd thought she'd died, when I had saved her, or lost her, and all because I'd chosen to give Crowhurst a map.

An emptiness opened in my chest, like the tide pulling back the water before a tsunami, and my belly felt like a fish flopping on the wet sand. But my feet felt as though I'd grown roots. There were myths about that—girls turning into trees to escape some terrible fate. How long would I have to be still before I would never move again? But then my father reached for me, smiling. "Nixie. Nixie, come meet your mother."

I tottered toward him on wooden legs; he took my hand and squeezed my fingers, and I was human again.

She had looked so small, next to Slate, but when I got close, I realized we were the same height. Her hand went first to my cheek—her palm was calloused. Then her fingers alighted on my shoulder, then my chin, like a butterfly, fickle. Her eyes bored into mine, with a deep curiosity that was terribly familiar. "Are you really mine?" she said then.

My spine stiffened and I took a breath to tell her that I wasn't anybody's, but when I opened my mouth, what came out was a sob.

Tears filled my eyes; I tried to wipe them away, but they

flooded in, too fast to bail. My breath hitched in my throat, and I shuddered like the ship in a storm. A terrible weight crushed the air out of me, and sobs struggled up through my chest like bubbles from a rift in the floor of the sea. When she wrapped her arms around me, I clung to her as though she were a raft. The world spun inside my head, and fragmented thoughts popped up like flotsam from a wreck. She smelled like cream and incense. Her arms were cool. She was crying too.

Finally the tide of my own tears ebbed, and I blinked away the last of them. My face was hot and I felt strung together with loose twine; I lifted my chin and took deep, tremulous breaths. The others had followed them to the bailey, I realized—Blake and Kash, and Dahut too. Over my mother's shoulder, I caught her yearning stare before she turned away. Distantly, I realized I had told her an untruth, though not on purpose—I had missed my mother after all.

The rest of the world faded into the background—my father thanking Crowhurst over and over, his modest replies. An offer to stay the night; the ship would be crowded, he said, and the walk to the dock was dark and cold. In response, Slate wrapped the man in a bear hug.

Crowhurst sent a servant to the ship to fetch Bee and

Rotgut; they would be eager to see Lin. Another servant showed us to a suite of rooms surrounding a central parlor. There, my father swept my mother off her feet and carried her the rest of the way. She laid her head against his shoulder as he whispered into her hair, kicking the door shut behind them.

The rest of us stood in the parlor. It was well appointed, with soft chairs and a woven rug over the stone floor, but I had no eyes for luxury, not now. I floated across the room like a bubble, hollow, fragile, and lowered myself gently onto a velvet chaise. My whole body ached with the echo of my emotions—shock and guilt, but also a lightness, a relief, a tentative tendril of something strange. Joy?

Kash knelt beside me, close but not touching. I was the one to reach out, taking comfort from his steady presence as his hand folded around mine. It was so easy now—so natural. I stared down at his hand in wonder. What had I been waiting for?

"So?" Blake's question interrupted my thoughts; he was full of energy as he paced before the fire. "Which do you think it is?"

There was a long silence. Lifting my head took an enormous effort, but when I did, Blake was staring at me with those blue eyes. I cleared my throat; it was raw and rough. "Which what?"

"Genius or madness, Miss Song. Or does it matter?"

Kashmir gripped my hand more tightly. "What's that saying? Madness is doing the same thing over and over and expecting a different result."

"It's not madness if he gets the result he's after," Blake said.

"The man claimed to be a god, Mr. Hart!"

"Gods, witches, Navigators—different words for the same things."

"Hustler is the word that comes to my mind," Kash shot back. "We should leave the table while we're up."

"Leave? Miss Song." Blake turned to me, an appeal in his eyes, and the color was high in his cheeks. "Certainly you understand. We have to know more."

"Amira—"

"I have to go." I stood abruptly; I was completely drained, as empty as a sail on a windless day. "It's late. I have to go to bed."

Without waiting for an answer, I fled across the parlor to a room farthest from the captain's . . . from my parents' room. Shutting the door behind me, I sagged against it, but when I closed my eyes, I saw my mother's face.

Had I truly saved her by giving Crowhurst the map of New York? It was hard to imagine. All my life, I'd been the reason she was gone—though I supposed I still was. And what might have happened if Crowhurst had left her in Hawaii? I would never know. I would never have to worry.

It was a gift, indeed, and a rare one. A life I'd never thought possible—a future that included my mother without erasing my past. And what now, on the horizon? They'd had a flat in Honolulu. Slate had told me that once; he'd been quite willing to trade the sea for true love. Could I bring them back to Hawaii on my own timeline? Perhaps Kash and I could take the *Temptation* then, out and over the deep blue sea to make our fortune, and come back home for the holidays.

The thought made me giggle—it was almost unreal, mundane and extravagant all at once. And yet Crowhurst had made it possible.

Why? Had he truly seen a need, or was Kashmir right? Was Crowhurst only reeling me in?

I pushed myself off the door as though I were poling a barge. The room was cozy enough, the walls washed in white plaster and the high ceiling made of wooden beams. There was a banked fire on the hearth and a lantern on the side table, and when I sat on the edge of the bed I sank at least four inches. I stood again, struggling with my dress before giving up and flinging myself down among the pillows.

As I lay there, Blake's words echoed in my head—*we have to know more*. And it occurred to me that Crowhurst hadn't told me how, exactly, he wanted me to help.

CHAPTER
TWENTY

KASHMIR

After Nix went to bed, I too stood to leave. Mr. Hart was still afire with dreams of remaking reality, and the tension between us was so thick it left room for only the smallest of talk. Or so I thought.

He watched me stand, his expression cool. "Best to let her be, don't you think?"

It took me a moment to understand what he was getting at; when I did, an anger I'd never felt sprang up in me like a flame. "I'm not going after her," I said, articulating each word.

"Where, then?"

"To get some answers," I said. "Since Crowhurst isn't giving us any."

"I didn't know you were interested in changing the world."

"There are things I'd change, Mr. Hart, but not with a magic map."

He peered at me the way he had that last night in Honolulu, looking down the barrel of his gun. "What bothers you so much, Mr. Firas?" he said softly. "Is it that Miss Song might regret her choice in Hawaii?"

"No," I said, opening the door and slipping into the hall. "It bothers me that you might."

I shut the door in his face, softer than I felt like. Out in the hall, the candles flickered in their sconces. I leaned against the cool stone wall and took a moment to breathe. Then I rubbed the skin of my throat—behind my eyes, I could still see Mr. Hart taking aim. How many times had I cheated death? Would our next dance be my last? For the first time in my history, I was concerned about my future, and about my past as well.

Khodaye man. Did Navigation truly have the power to destroy—and to create? I shuddered at the memory of the look in Crowhurst's eyes as he'd claimed to be a god. Had Nix only made me in her image? Had I sprung fully formed from her head?

But this line of questioning was useless—the answers were not to be found within. And while Crowhurst might cloak his secrets in grandiose claims, Dahut seemed far more practical. There was a crack there, between them—one I hoped I could slip through. Her condition complicated matters, but Nix had mentioned a diary. I wrinkled my nose. A girl's diary wouldn't be the worst thing I'd ever stolen, though it would come close. But my honor was the least of my worries.

Gathering myself—the energy humming in my fingers, the anger simmering at the base of my skull, and the queasy bubbles in the pit of my stomach—I pulled them all tight into a knot in my chest and breathed in deep. It left me as I exhaled.

Then I threw back my shoulders and went boldly down the middle of the hall.

Although I would have preferred to be safe on the *Temptation*, being an invited guest in the castle did make my search easier. The servants I saw deferred, nodding to me, not meeting my eyes. I wandered as I walked; the castle sprawled, very large for such a small island. Finally, outside a wide door to the south wing, I was stopped by a guard with waxed blond mustaches. "Where do you think you're going?"

The smile I gave him was genuine; a guard was a sign

I was moving in the right direction. Besides, I'd come pre-pared. "I need to see the princess."

His jaw worked. "Pardon?"

"She dropped this," I said, pulling a silk handkerchief from my pocket, edged in lace, threaded with gold. "I want to return it."

The man rocked back on his heels, somewhat mollified. "I'll bring it to Her Highness."

"You don't understand," I said, cocking my hip just a little. "She dropped it in my lap."

Cold radiated from the man as from a frozen statue. It was a gamble. I would have preferred something from the king—after all, the princess was just a girl—but the only thing he'd had on him was that massive necklace and some-thing that jingled in his pocket, a set of keys, most likely. Nothing that could be construed as a token.

And I'd seen the way the servants looked at Dahut. I recognized the scorn, the suspicion, though it had a new spin—the ugliest type, that men reserved for women alone. It was there now, on the guard's face. After a moment, the man turned on his heel. "This way."

He led me through the royal wing and to the base of the southeast tower—a tower for a princess, how typical. But when he started up the stairs, I dismissed him. "I can find it from here."

"As you wish," he said with a barely concealed sneer. Out of the corner of my eye, I saw the man make the nah, with his thumb poking out between his fingers.

My back stiffened. It was a disgusting gesture, but I'd seen men do the same in the tavern when talking about sorcery. Did it mean the same thing here as it did where I was from? As I climbed the stairs, I withered inside. Stolen handkerchiefs were easily returned; not so stolen reputations.

But shame was a luxury I couldn't afford—the safety of my friends was at stake. Steeling myself, I continued up the stairs. At the top, a door, unguarded, unlocked . . . but there was more than one way to make a prisoner. Under the crack, dim light glowed and flickered. The fire in the hearth was dying. Surely she would be asleep by the time the flame went out.

I sat in the dark to wait. A chill seeped up from the stone; I did pushups on the landing to warm my blood. No sound came for an hour. Two. The light under the door was lower now, nearly gone. I stood, stretching my legs slowly. Then I opened the door just a crack, slow enough it did not squeak.

"Father?"

Inside, I cursed, but I painted embarrassment on my face as I poked my head into the room, waving the silk square like a white flag. "No. It's Kashmir. Please forgive me. I was trying to put your handkerchief under the door. I must have pushed it open." My eyes flicked around the room: a soft chair, leaded windows, and a table beside the bed holding a guttering candle and a pen—but no diary. "You dropped it earlier. In the excitement, I forgot I had it. I'm so sorry to intrude."

"It's all right." She was sitting up on her bed, her hair falling across her shoulders in black waves. The candle reflected in her eyes, as though there was nothing behind them. My body wanted to shudder; I stopped it. "Thank you," she added.

"A pleasure," I said, giving a little bow from the doorway. When I straightened up, I gave her an apologetic shrug. "I guess I couldn't sleep."

She cocked her head. "Me either."

"Oh?" I laughed a little, as though I hadn't already figured that out. "Why not?"

Dahut pursed her lips, and for a moment, I thought she wouldn't answer. "I had to write down everything that happened today," she said at last. "So I can remind myself later."

She tucked her hair behind her ear and then rested her hand on the stack of pillows behind her; her body language told me just where she'd hidden the diary when I'd opened the door. But how to get across the room without alarming her? And if I took it from under the pillow, how quickly would she realize?

"You do that every night?" I said, to draw her out. But the look of concern on my face was not hard to fake; the idea of forgetting terrified me.

"I can't sleep until I do."

"It must be frightening," I said. She tensed: too much. "I try to read every night, myself," I added, looking down at my feet as though embarrassed. "To practice. I'm still learning how. But all my books are on the ship, so here I am, wandering the halls." I lifted the handkerchief again, like I'd just remembered the reason for my visit. "May I?"

"Oh. Of course." She gestured. At last I stepped into the room, walking not toward her, huddled in her bed, but askew, to the table at her side. I folded the handkerchief and placed it down neatly, giving it a pat.

"There. Well. I'll let you sleep." I started to leave, trying to think of another excuse to stay, but when I was halfway across the room, she spoke.

"What keeps you up at night?"

I turned back—but slowly, so she didn't know how grateful I was for the opening. "That's quite a personal question."

She took a little breath. "I'm sorry."

"No, no, don't be." I put my hand on the back of my neck and sighed. "It's . . . Well. Sometimes I think about my own past. Where I came from. What my life was like before the ship."

"Do you miss it?"

"Never," I said. "Then again, I remember it. Or I think I do."

Silence from her.

In the hearth, the ashes settled. The room was drafty, despite the rug on the floor. "May I build up your fire, princess?"

"Please." She wrapped her arms around her knees as I knelt near the fireplace, snapping sticks and arranging them carefully. I blew on the coals, whispering the flame up from the embers. "Call me Dahut," she added.

"Of course. Dahut," I said. "Interesting name."

"So is Kashmir. Is that where you're from?"

"No." I faltered. "I . . . I've never seen the place I'm from on any map."

"Why not?"

"Well. I'm told it's because the place I'm from is a fairy tale. Much like this place."

She tilted her head. "Was it?"

"Not to me." I smiled a little. "You look disappointed."

"Well. Fairy tales aren't so bad," she said. "Quests and elixirs and finding your long-lost parents. I have no idea where I'm from." She cast the words out, too freely, to make me think she didn't care how they landed.

I couldn't keep the surprise from my face. "You weren't . . . born in Ker-Ys?"

"I'm not sure. My father says so, but . . ." Her lips twisted a little, half a smile, half a grimace. "I don't exactly fit in here."

I returned her look. "I know the feeling. They make it plain."

"And it's not just the . . ." Her vague gesture took in her dark skin, her black hair—different from my own dark skin, my own black hair, though not in the eyes of the people of Ker-Ys. "My accent is more like my father's than anyone else's. And no one else in Ker-Ys does this." She opened her hands, showing me the design on her palms. "I must have learned it somewhere, but I don't know where that would be."

"Doesn't your father know?"

"I think he does." Her fingers knotted in the coverlet; the fire, brighter now, limned her hair and blackened her eyes. "What was your own past like?" she said then, unabashedly changing the subject.

My smile faded, and my answer was not manipulation. "Lonely. But I have a friend now."

"You mean Nix."

"Yes." My answer was soft; it was too hard to mask the feeling there. But Dahut leaned forward, eager for the story.

"How did you meet?"

The memory rushed back as though it had been hiding close by—the guards with their shamshir, the girl with her ship. "I needed to escape," I said simply. "So I climbed aboard the *Temptation*, and there she was."

"And she helped you?"

"That's what friends do, right?"

"I wouldn't know."

I stood, coming closer, but still not too close. "We'll be here at least another day. Perhaps if you write me down in your book, when you wake up tomorrow, you'll remember I'm your friend."

She watched me to see if I was lying—and after a

moment, she smiled. Guilt twisted like a knife in my gut as she slipped her hand beneath the pillows and drew out her diary at last. "All right."

The book was a little thing with a hard cover and a cheap lock; as she paged through, I peered over her shoulder as if to help. "It starts with a K."

"I know." She stopped on a blank page, but I touched her wrist.

"Wait. Go back." She frowned up at me, but I flipped past pages covered in her delicate red script, stopping at one that had caught my eye: black ink, the letters crawling like ants across the paper. And there, the awkward space of something missing. "Who cut out these pages?"

"I don't remember," she said, but I could tell she had a guess.

I took the book from her hands, tilting it to the light. The story written there was the tale of Ker-Ys—the one Nix had told me. But Grandlon's name was replaced with Crowhurst's. "Dahut," I whispered to her. "This is your father's handwriting."

Her jaw clenched; she spoke through her teeth. "I know."

CHAPTER

TWENTY-ONE

I tossed on the thick mattress, wrestling with sleep. More than once I jolted out of a half dream; without the rocking of the waves, I felt as though I were falling. The bed smelled ever so slightly of lavender, so unlike the brine and the breeze on the wide sea. And the room was too quiet; I could hear nothing of the wind in the rigging or the breath of the ocean or the waves whispering secrets to the hull.

But the silence in the room was a sharp contrast to the thoughts racing around my head: my mother, here and now. The past, changed—though not the way I had imagined. Then again, wishes granted magically had a way of being twisted. There were so many stories about that—the magic fish, the monkey's paw, the treacherous genie. What would happen when it came time for me to rewrite my own past?

I threw back the covers and clawed out of the hollow formed by the down. Was Kashmir still awake too? In a shifting tide, he was my anchor. Smoothing my rumpled gown, I slipped out into the parlor, resolved to find him and tell him so. I peered at the doors; which room was his? The fire had burned low, and I didn't see Blake sitting on the chaise until he spoke.

"Hello, Miss Song." He lifted his face from his hands, and his eyes were dark as the midnight sea. "If you're looking for Mr. Firas, he's gone."

Had I been so obvious? Thankfully, the dim light hid my blush. "Where?"

"He wouldn't tell me."

"Oh." I shifted on my feet, awkward, and toyed with the lace on my skirt. "I couldn't sleep."

"I have the same problem of late. Vivid dreams." He sighed, running one hand through his hair. "Or perhaps they aren't dreams at all."

"Right." I wet my lips. "Kash told me you both remembered the time before Crowhurst was king."

"That, and other things." Blake gazed at the coals on the hearth. They lit his face in soft lines—the angle of his jaw, the downward curve of his mouth. "I recognized her."

"Who?"

"Your mother."

I swallowed—the word was so strange in my ears. "What do you mean, you recognized her?"

"I knew who she was the moment she came through the door. I . . . It seems . . . impossible, but weeks ago, the day you arrived in Honolulu, I had a dream I still remember. I was calling on the house next to mine. The one in Nuʻuanu Valley. I'd gone to see you there." His eyes were distant, as though he was watching the memory unfold. "You were my—my dear friend, my confidante. We'd grown up together. In the dream, I was only waiting in your parlor for you to come downstairs. Your mother brought me tea, and that's when I woke. Later that morning, I rode to town and heard there was a black ship sailing toward the harbor. And when I saw you standing on deck, I recognized you too."

"What are you saying?" I asked, even though I knew.

Still, he obliged me. "I think . . . Miss Song, I think there might be—in some lifetime, or timeline, in the range of infinite possibility . . ." Blake sighed again. "There may have been a place where your mother and the captain stayed. There may be a time where paradise still exists, the robbery never happened—and you and I never left."

My breath caught in my throat. I had always feared the price of having my mother back would be my own past, but the reality of the sacrifice was far more complicated. The worst part was: I could imagine it. He and I, best friends— we were so alike. It wouldn't have been such a bad life. Just not my life. But I had given Crowhurst the map. I had set this all in motion. "I'm sorry, Blake."

"Why?"

I stammered; I did not want to give words to my own complicity. "You sound . . . sad."

"Sad? No. Miss Song. Don't you see?" He smiled at me then—just like he used to. "If there are other possibilities out there, it means there must be a world where we're all very happy."

"If there is, I haven't got a map there."

"Maybe I could make one," he said, his voice whimsical. "Of course, I'd need someone to take me there."

Suddenly, more than anything, I wanted to be back on the ship—among the charts and the worlds where I felt at home. I strode to the door, my dress swishing around my ankles.

"Where are you going, Miss Song?"

"Back to the docks."

"You can't go alone." He stood, and I rounded on him.

"I damn well can."

He put his hands up, palms out. "Forgive me. I—what I meant to say was, I don't want to *be* alone."

My anger drained away, as quick as it had flooded in. "Come on then."

We stepped out into the hall side by side, and I picked a direction I only hoped was correct. I had been in a haze when I'd followed the servants to the suites, and now the rippled glass of the rare windows did not allow me clear sight of the stars.

Far away, the bells tolled the changing tide, followed by the low, grinding tremolo of the sea gates closing. I shivered; the halls were drafty, and my cloak was still on the floor in my room. As I considered going back for it, Blake shrugged off his jacket and draped it over my shoulders without a word. I was grateful, not only for the coat, but for the silence—rare for him. But perhaps it was my turn to speak.

"The idea of infinite worlds, infinite universes . . . it isn't new to me, but it's not the only theory." I sighed. "Some people think worlds are stacked thick as books in a library, and each choice you make creates a new story. But others think there's only one world. One book."

"And the arrival of a Navigator tears out whole pages?"

"Not on purpose. But even the smallest change might have unintended consequences." I bit my lip. "I don't know what your dream means—if it's a memory of a life that might have been, or one that was until I arrived. But my father told me, and my grandmother told him, whenever you try to change something, you sacrifice something else."

"Every choice has a cost, Miss Song. The real question is whether or not one is willing to pay it."

"No, Blake. The real question is whether it's worth the price."

"I wonder what Crowhurst sacrificed, to be king."

"We should ask him," I said. "Though that's not first on my list of questions."

"So you do want to know more," he said softly, and I could not deny it.

At the end of the hall, we found a tower. The stairs curled down inside it like the shell of a nautilus. Blake followed me down—one flight, two flights, three. At the bottom, I recognized the arched doorway. "Do you remember this, from our first visit?" I glanced back. Blake's brow was furrowed. "The bailey is just through the kitchens." But crossing through them, I stopped dead in my tracks. Blake bumped into my back.

"Speak of the devil," he whispered under his breath. There in the kitchen was Crowhurst.

He held a tray, and in the dim light of the banked hearth, he looked as surprised as I felt. But hadn't Dahut told me? Her father rarely slept. "Where are you both off to?" he said at last, glancing from me to Blake.

"I'm escorting Miss Song back to the docks. And you?"

Crowhurst hesitated, just a moment. "A midnight snack. With all the conversation over dinner, I forgot to eat."

Blake glanced at the tray he held. It was stacked with dirty plates, including a teapot and two cups. "You must love tea."

Crowhurst barked a laugh; the sound flitted through the dark like a bat. "I am an Englishman, of course I do! As does my daughter—I was with her." He turned back to me, concern etching a V on his brow. "But surely your own father wouldn't want you out in the middle of the night! Aren't your rooms comfortable?"

"They're fine," I said quickly. "Everything's fine, I'm just . . . I'm having trouble sleeping. I'm not used to being indoors."

"Well," he said, setting the tray down on the wide table. "There's a beautiful library on the second floor, and the ceiling is painted with stars. May I show you?"

Blake looked to me for the answer, but I could see the eagerness in his expression. It had nothing to do with paintings or books—I knew, for it must have mirrored my own. "I'd like that," I said.

"Excellent." Crowhurst clasped his hands and ushered us back toward the stairs. "Safer this way."

"Oh?" Blake cocked his head. "I thought Ker-Ys was supposed to be a utopia."

"Don't you think it is? A healthy population. Rare goods. Beautiful architecture."

And man-eating wolves, I did not add, nor did I mention the mermaid tails nailed above doorways, or the suspicious stares of the townspeople. "Yet you worry the town is dangerous at night."

"I don't want to risk it," he said, leading us into another long hall. "Not after I've spent so much time looking for you!"

Blake frowned. "Looking for . . . Miss Song?"

"Well. For others like her," he amended, glancing at me. "Like us."

The torches guttered in the drafts, and shadows played like dark sprites in the corners. I pulled Blake's coat more tightly around my shoulders. "When I was younger, I thought my father was the only one in the world who could do what he does."

He chuckled. "Daughters are like that with their fathers, aren't they?"

"I guess," I said, trying to keep my face neutral. If Crowhurst noticed my dubious tone, he didn't give any indication.

"It is a solitary endeavor, I suppose. I might have drawn the same conclusion myself," he added. "Except that I met another on one of my first journeys."

"Another Navigator?" I couldn't keep the surprise out of my voice. "Where?"

"Ancient Greece. Boeotia, to be specific."

"Boeotia? Near the oracle? Why was he there? And how did you know he was a Navigator?" The words tumbled out of me, one after the other; as they did, a smile spread down Crowhurst's face. "I'm sorry," I added then, breathless. "I just haven't met many others and I—I have a lot of questions."

He waved away my apology. "There were . . . certain signs. The clothing, for example. Wasn't from the era. But we didn't talk much. Still, after that, I knew I wasn't the only one. Here's the library," he added then, pushing open a heavy wooden door and ushering us inside.

The room was rectangular, with a barrel-shaped ceiling, and it was indeed painted with the constellations: the boreal hemisphere stitched with the signs of zodiac. The wall on the right was made of tall Gothic windows; an ornate desk sat beneath them, angled to catch the best daylight. On the left side of the room, just beneath the cove and all the way to the floor, the wall was lined with polished wooden shelves filled with books.

They were bound in leather and skin, thick with paint and ink and gold leaf. There must have been hundreds— truly a king's collection, every row full from end to end. But Crowhurst's revelation was much more impressive. How many other Navigators did history hide? Blake's own thoughts echoed my own. "Have you met many others?" he asked.

Slowly, Crowhurst lowered himself into a chair by the desk, as though trying to decide what to say. "It's not an everyday occurrence," he said finally. "It must have been fate that brought you here."

"I don't believe in fate," I said quickly. The answer was so automatic, I hardly noticed it was a lie.

"No? Well. When your ship appeared on the horizon, it was almost enough to convince me."

"When the ship appeared?" Blake frowned. "How did you know she was a Navigator then?"

"You both seem quite clever," Crowhurst said, his eyes still on me. "How do you think I knew?"

His scrutiny made me uncomfortable. I turned to the shelves, trailing my fingers along the spines of the books. How would Crowhurst know what I was? Had he seen us sail out of the fog? He'd spoken to Slate the night we arrived; the captain must have mentioned it then. Or had he?

I stopped before a gap between two quartos, the empty space where a book had once been, and suddenly I remembered torn pages drifting like snow in the wintery wind of the square. The answer came to me in a rising tide. "Something changed when we arrived."

There was a buttery feeling to the silence. I glanced over my shoulder, and sure enough, Crowhurst was smiling, smug. "I have a theory about Navigation and probability," he said. "Have you ever heard of Schrödinger's cat? It's a bit convoluted, but he developed a theory that possibility is infinite until the moment of observation. I think Navigators might be the great observers of the universe. Our arrival shapes the world according to our expectations."

"Expectations?" Blake glanced from him to me. "What changed, exactly?"

"When I first came to Ker-Ys, everything was very like the original myth." Crowhurst waved a hand. "There was a rather forward princess, and a king who wore a brass key around his neck. He seemed a good enough man, and he invited Dahut and I to stay here, at the castle, as his guests. Of course, his existence put me in a bit of a quandary. After all, I knew what he and the princess were going to do to the city. But when you appeared, they vanished, Nixie. As though they'd never been."

"Vanished?" My thoughts scattered like minnows, darting in all directions, then schooling again. "No. I met him."

"Who?"

"The king. The old one. He was outside the castle the night I met you. He was raving. I—I thought he was mad, but maybe he only remembered his past as a dream. Maybe . . ." I trailed off. The look on Crowhurst's face was less surprise than calculation.

"We found him the next day," Blake added then, his tone more certain. "Murdered."

"That's unfortunate," Crowhurst said smoothly. "But I wouldn't mourn long."

To my surprise, Blake laughed. "Of course you wouldn't! You were the one who stole his throne!"

Crowhurst stiffened in his chair. "I beg your pardon?"

"Navigators shape the world," Blake said. "But so do mapmakers. We arrived on a map you gave us. You used that map and Miss Song's arrival to overthrow the old king."

My eyes went wide at his bold accusation, but Crowhurst lifted his chin. "What's wrong with that? You know what he was going to do if he'd stayed in power. He was going to drown the city. He would have killed his own daughter."

"His daughter." I bit my lip. "What was her name?"

"Ahes. Why?"

My breath hitched in my throat. The myths mentioned them both—one drowned, one turned into a mermaid. Hadn't the madman said his daughter was taken by the sea? And Slate had seen a woman in the water, singing—perhaps it wasn't a hallucination after all. My thoughts churned as Crowhurst stroked his necklace—the flask with the Greek key design . . . the key . . . the key around his neck. My god. All the different versions now made sense—even the monster in the castle. That was the wolf the old king had mentioned. All except one thing . . . one missing piece. "Do you know anything about a man in a pit?"

Crowhurst froze in his chair, as though my words had turned him to stone. Was it a trick of the light, or did he blanch? "No."

"Nothing?" I watched him for a long time. There was something here, something he was not saying. Trying to piece it together, I raised my eyes toward the ceiling; above me, the painted stars shimmered in the firelight. There was Cetus, the sea monster, and Aquarius, Pisces, and Eridanus the River. "You say you've been able to change the past, but I'm not so sure anymore."

"What do you mean, Nixie?"

I ticked off the names on my fingers. "We have the saint, the dark horse, Dahut, and Grandlon. What's to guarantee there won't be a flood at the end of it all?"

"You think I would destroy my own city?"

I bit down on a glib response—but I'd read the articles. Rather than coming clean at the end of the race, Crowhurst had abandoned his family, his ship, his old life. The man was not known for his loyalty, but it wasn't the most diplomatic thing to point out. "If the past can't truly be changed, you might not have a choice," I said instead. My voice was bitter with the truth of it.

Crowhurst raised an eyebrow. "You don't think I can change things? What about your mother?"

I shook my head. "Slate never saw her dead and buried. He came back, and she was simply gone. In fact, this might be how it was always supposed to happen."

Crowhurst showed his teeth in a smile. "I thought you didn't believe in fate."

"No one does, until it catches up with them." Outside, the wind rose, sending a gust down the chimney and stirring the flames on the hearth. I folded my arms and watched the embers glow.

"You could take Dahut and go back to your timeline," Blake said then. "Burn the maps of Ker-Ys. That way the story can't end as written. If you do that—if you can—we'll all know whether a man can change the past as written."

"Yes." My heart leaped at the suggestion; hope returned. "And you'll see the rest of your family again. You said you missed them."

Crowhurst did not seem to share our excitement. Instead, he turned to stare out the windows—or at our murky reflections in the glass. "I saw my past in your future," he said at last. "I read what they said about me. The world thinks I'm a madman. A liar. A failure."

"So it's not about your family after all," Blake said. "You want fame. Fortune. You wish you'd won your race."

"Fame? No." He shook his head, still staring at the window. "You misunderstand."

"Then what?"

He sighed. "I want never to have set out on the journey."

Blake's eyes softened then, and he dropped his chin. But I shook my head. "That's a paradox," I said, though I don't know which of them I spoke to. "Your setting out is what brought you here."

Crowhurst was the one who replied. "And what brought you here, Nix? There must be something you want to change."

My mouth twisted; the words were bitter. "I still don't know if it's possible."

"Why don't you stay and help me find out? I'll have proof in two days' time."

"What happens in two days?"

The fire was fading on the hearth, but even in the dim light, he must have seen the look on my face. Curiosity. Desperation. The wind moaned again, and his eyes glittered. "You'll have to stay and see."

Blake pressed his lips together. "You're not doing this out of the goodness of your heart."

"Not only the goodness of my heart," Crowhurst allowed. "But Nix is a Navigator, and I need confirmation. After all, only a Navigator would remember how things had been. Nixie, I need you to tell me I'm not just . . . misremembering."

"Not crazy, you mean." At my words, he winced, but he did not protest. "Is this your request?"

"Not so onerous, is it? To help me learn? You'll know then too."

"It might not be safe to stay, if the flood is coming. And we could know in an hour if you take Dahut and leave."

"You might know," he countered. "But I'd be gone— having stepped into the paradox you mentioned without knowing what might happen to me. Please, Nixie. I need your help, and I hope I don't flatter myself to think you need mine."

There was silence; the fire popped. Crowhurst watched me as I weighed the balance. I did not trust him—but did I need him? Maybe. Maybe not. But I nodded anyway; best not to give him reason to distrust me. "All right."

"Excellent," Crowhurst said, but it was Blake's smile

that caught my eye—bright and unexpected. His words came back to me from earlier in the evening: *genius or madness?* I still had no answer.

Suppressing a shudder, I turned toward the door. "It's very late. I'm going to bed."

"Do you need me to show you the way back?"

"I remember it."

"Good night, then," he called after us. "Pleasant dreams."

CHAPTER
TWENTY-TWO

By the time we left the library, it was so late it was early. The candles had burned out in the halls, but Crowhurst had given us a taper to light our way back. In the soft light, Blake's expression was hard to discern, and he waited until we were back in the parlor to speak.

"I can't tell if you're brave or foolish," he said at last. "But I admire your choice to stay."

I met his eyes. "You don't trust him either."

"No," Blake said. "But I want to know what's possible."

"Me too." I sighed, handing back his jacket. "Good night, Blake."

He gave me a little bow. "Nix."

I blinked at him. He hadn't used my first name since Hawaii; it was good to hear. Smiling, I opened the door to my room and slipped inside, casting shadows before me.

On the far side of the room, one of them unfolded into flesh. "He cuts out her memories, amira."

"Christ, Kashmir!" Hot wax spilled over my knuckles as I jumped back; I swore and set the candle on the table beside the bed. Peeling back the wax, I shook my hand to ease the sting. "You scared me."

He was leaning against the mantel; at my words, he cocked his head. "*I* scared you? I seem to be the only thing that does."

Making a face, I sat on the bed. "I know, *I know*. Crowhurst is dangerous."

Concern flickered across Kashmir's face. "What happened?"

"Nothing! Nothing yet. But something will in two days, though he won't tell me what." The mattress sank as Kash sat beside me, and his shoulder brushed mine. He had taken off his red coat; I could feel the warmth of his skin through the thin cotton of his white shirt. My hands held each other in my lap, though I longed to hold his instead. "What do you mean, he cuts out her memories?"

"In her diary. He tears out pages and writes in his own stories. He altered the myth of Ker-Ys and named himself as king."

I swore under my breath, the curse a hollow susurration in the room. "So that's how he does it."

"You already knew?"

"Crowhurst admitted as much. Now I know why he hasn't helped her get better."

"Help her?" He raised an eyebrow. "Is that possible?"

"It should be. We have half a dozen maps that we could try."

"Then we should do it." His voice was urgent; he turned to me with new energy. "Take her away with us. Give her back her memories."

"Take her away?" I leaned back. "You mean kidnap her?"

"If we asked her to come, I think she'd say yes."

I frowned as something clicked in my mind. "You were with her tonight?"

"Earlier." He shifted, suddenly cautious. "It wasn't like that, amira—"

"I know." I held up my hand to forestall his explanation. "But when?"

"A few hours ago."

"Crowhurst told me they were having tea together."

"So?"

Squeezing my eyes shut, I rubbed my hand over my forehead. "So he's lying."

"We already knew that."

I sighed and let my hand drop, folding it around his. "Maybe you're right. Maybe we should take her somewhere else. He might never know, but I would."

"Know what?"

"Whether or not the past can be changed." Running my thumb over the white scars on his knuckles, I stared down at our fingers, entwined, remembering how Kashmir's hand had slipped from mine in the Margins—how I'd thought he might be gone. I tightened my grip. "If we take Dahut away from Ker-Ys, she can't open the sea gates. The city is safe and the myth is altered and I'll know for certain that fate isn't inevitable."

"Is that the only thing that matters to you?"

"Not the only thing. But it's close." I looked up at him, filling my eyes with the sight of his face. "I can't lose you, Kashmir. I can't."

"Why not?"

"What?" A cold feeling in my chest—unsettled. "Kashmir, you know how I feel—"

"Tell me then, so I can hear it from you."

"I . . . I . . ." I bit my lip, the words were there, in my

heart, but they stuck in my throat. As the moments passed, the hope in his face turned to sorrow.

"Do you regret it, amira?"

"Regret . . . what?"

"Meeting me. Knowing me." He searched my face. "Loving me."

Everything seemed to stop at the word; it hung in the air between us, tangible and real. "No," I said at last. *"No."*

"But you fear you will someday. That's why you hold back. That's why you want to know you can change things before you commit." He let go of my hand and stood. The distance between us ached like the cold of a winter sea. "You watched your father chase your mother for years, and you wished he didn't love her. What will you do to my memory when I'm gone? Will you chase it like a dragon? Or will you banish it like smoke?"

"I'm not going to lose you!"

"I know when you're lying, so tell me the truth. Why am I the only thing in your life not worth any risk?"

"No. Kash—" My voice broke. "Kashmir, that's why we're still here. I would risk anything for you."

"Anything but loss."

I felt the blood leave my face. Words deserted me.

Kashmir shook his head. "I'm going to the ship. I can't sleep under this roof."

"Wait—" But he had already opened the door, slipping out without even the decency to slam it behind him. "Come back!"

He did not.

Grabbing the candle, I yanked open the door just in time to see the one to the hall closing; Kashmir wasn't there in the parlor.

But my mother was.

She was kneeling at the hearth, pulling a copper pot off the coals of the fire. She rose and turned toward me, every movement graceful. "Only lovers fight like that."

"What can I say?" I shifted, fists clenched, on guard. "I'm a fighter, not a lover."

Her laugh was light, like chimes. "Your father used to say the opposite. Would you like some tea?"

Part of me wanted to flee back to my room; another part wanted to rush after Kashmir, though would I be able to say the words he needed to hear? Instead, I took one step, then another. The third came easier still. Finally I was close enough to set the candle down on the table near the chaise, where a tray held a fine porcelain tea service. "Okay."

Lin poured the water into the teapot and flipped two cups; their gold rims shone in the glow from the fire. She didn't bother with the saucers. As the tea steeped, she glanced up at me with her dark eyes, so like mine. There was a sharpness in them, as though she was trying to add me up. She dropped her gaze as she filled the cups; fragrant steam purled in the candlelight. Then she sat back, resting the other hand across her belly. "Sit?"

I sank into the chair opposite her; it was so soft, it made my body ache. I took my cup and held it close to my chest. "Thanks."

For a moment there was silence. She lowered her eyes again, giving me the courtesy of indirect scrutiny. "Are you up early?" she said delicately. "Or late?"

To my own surprise, I blushed. Had she thought Kash and I had been together all night? She'd been raised in the nineteenth century—but in an opium den, and despite Slate's commitment to her, I knew they'd never had a chance to marry. What would she think of the way my father had raised me? And should it matter? "It's hard to sleep with everything going on," I said, deliberately vague. "You?"

"I've missed too much already." She tilted her own cup

and took a delicate sip, watching me over the rim. "Tell me about Kashmir."

I bristled. "I don't want to talk about Kashmir." There was an edge in my voice. I thought she would push back, but she only nodded a little.

"That's all I need to know."

Still, I frowned. "Did Slate say something about him?"

"Only his name." She tilted her head. "But I saw the way he looked at you last night."

"And how was that?"

"Like nothing else is real." At her words, my heart ached, but her smile deepened, just a touch. "I thought you didn't want to talk about him."

"You're right," I said quickly. "I don't."

"Of course not. Let's talk about something else," she suggested. And then she waited, watching me.

Clutching the cup in my hand, I shifted in my chair. It was very difficult to look at her, and I did not know what else to say. Still, I wanted her to talk. I wanted to listen to her voice. "What happened?" I said finally, as though to the tea. "After you . . . after I was born?"

She was still for a long moment, but I couldn't lift my eyes to see her face, to try to see what she was thinking. "I held you as long as I could," she said at last. "When Joss told me a doctor had arrived, I knew something was wrong. Then for a while . . . nothing."

"Nothing?" I frowned. "Where did you meet Crowhurst?"

"He was the doctor."

I almost spilled my tea. "What?"

"He came in and gave me medicine."

"Penicillin?"

She only shrugged. "I drank it. It must have helped. But for a while . . . time disappeared. One moment there, the next, here. I lost so much and I didn't even know it, not until I woke." There was a quaver in her voice, a hitch in her breath; I was close enough to hear her swallow. "That was yesterday morning."

"Yesterday?" I looked at her then—really looked—taking in the slowness of her motions, the careful way she held herself. Still recovering, a new mother—and I, her daughter, already sixteen. As much as I'd lost, hadn't she lost the same things? Then I blinked. "What day was it, do you know? When you . . . when I—"

"Nineteenth of January, of course I do." Her dark brows swept down. "Why?"

A stinging sensation arced across the back of my mouth,

like I'd swallowed a jellyfish. I cleared my throat. "I just . . . never knew my birthday before."

Politely, she took another sip, waiting for me to collect myself. Then her eyes flicked toward the full cup in my hands. "You don't drink tea."

"I like coffee."

"Your father does too." She leaned back and sighed. "But tea reminds me of home."

"Of Hawaii?"

"Of the shop."

"You mean the opium den."

"Yes." No matter how I tried, she was unruffled; it was disconcerting—so different from the captain. "Joss always said tea tasted like truth. Bitter comfort. We would shape the tar and drink tea, always tea." She smiled at the memory. "Sometimes the patrons would ask me to read the leaves. and I would have to make something up. Only good fortunes for our customers."

A flicker of hope popped to life like a struck match. "Did Joss invent fortunes too?"

Her smile fell, and the spark guttered out. She sighed again, and the steam over her tea wavered. "On the rare occasions she told fortunes, it was always the truth. I never let her tell mine."

I nodded; I knew. Joss had told me that much. "Would you have done things differently? If you'd known what would happen?"

"Done what differently? Not fallen in love?" She laughed, a low, round sound. "Some people think life lasts longer when lived without joy, but I think it only feels that way. I have always tried to make the most of the time I have. Joss told me that, when I was very young."

I squinted, trying to imagine it. "That doesn't sound like her."

"She was a cautious person herself. But perhaps she wanted me to have a better life than she did. She hated everything about your father, except how he made me feel." She took another sip and sighed. "Love is a beautiful drug. Very addictive."

I nearly smiled. "Are you going to tell me to just say no?"

"Too late for that, don't you think? It's interesting." She inspected the bottom of her cup, then scraped the wet leaves out onto the tray. "The moment a new patron walked into the shop, I could always tell whether or not they'd be able to leave. I was never wrong. That's how I knew I could love your father."

I couldn't help it: my mouth twisted. "Because you knew he wouldn't leave?"

She looked up, surprised. "Because I knew he could—if he chose to."

"But he never did."

"When a captain goes down with his ship, it isn't because he doesn't know how to swim."

I made a face. "That's heartening."

"I think so. Because it's never up to you what happens. Your only choice is what to do when it does. What kind of person will you decide to be?"

"You saw the tattoo."

"Yes." She poured a fresh cup, her dark hair falling over one shoulder. We were quiet for a while. Coals glowed in the ashes as the fire died. I tried the tea. It was warm and mellow. "It must have been a hard life for you," she said then. "He kept a place for me. All these years."

An understatement. "He did."

"Maybe he shouldn't have."

"What? No." The response was immediate, and very different from what it might have been yesterday. Was Kashmir right? Had I ever wished Slate hadn't loved her? "No," I said again, more strongly. "Why would you say that?"

"I see on his face what these years did to him. I see in your eyes what they did to you. How different would your life have been if John had forgotten me?"

Tears threatened again at the thought; my throat closed, trying to shut them off. Different . . . yes, but not better, not now that I knew what he and I had missed. I couldn't say so, so I tried to laugh. "John?" The word was strange in my mouth: short, chipped. "I've never heard anyone call the captain that."

"Is that what you call him? Captain? Not Father?"

"Sometimes I call him Slate."

She hooked a finger behind the long fall of dark hair and tucked it behind her ear. "And what will you call me?"

In her black eyes, a guardedness like a bird with its head cocked, peering through the branches. I tried out the words in my head. . . . Mother. Mama. Mom. "I'd like to call you Lin. For now."

She nodded—on her face, relief mingled with disappointment. "Now is what we have," she said, and I blinked at her, surprised to hear my own words echoed in her voice. "Then again," she added, giving me a small smile. "Perhaps now is all we need."

Was it true? It felt that way. Something in my chest eased, and I dared to smile back. Then I downed my tea and stood.

"Where are you going?" she said to me as I went to the door.

"Back to my ship."

CHAPTER
TWENTY-THREE

KASHMIR

I had stormed out of Nix's room like a child, but the winter wind cooled my temper, and by the time I reached the wharf, I had almost put her words out of my head—almost.

Then I saw the *Temptation* gleaming like fool's gold on the black water, and my anger returned. The ship was hers too; everything was hers. The room where I slept, the life she had saved . . . had she created it in the first place? And even now, my heart. All hers.

I was not a jealous man—it wouldn't bother me at all if only I had something of my own. So what was mine? The coat I wore? Bought with stolen gold. The money in my pocket? Taken from the harbormaster. I pulled out the handful of tarnished silver; it gleamed dully in the moonlight. I cast the coins into the harbor like dice, like bones. They tumbled into the water and I watched the ripples disappear as though they'd never been.

What would Nix do if she learned how to change the past? The fact that I might not remember was not a comfort to me. But I was a man from nowhere, with nothing to offer her. Maybe I would be easy to forget. I stared at the *Temptation*, listening to the waves assault the walls of the city, but I couldn't bring myself to climb the gangplank. Instead, I continued down the pier to board the *Dark Horse*.

I did it just to spite her captain. Though the yacht was sleek and rich, I didn't want to keep anything Crowhurst had touched. But I hated the man—his smug face, the smokescreen of generosity that clouded his machinations, and most of all, the fact that he had brought us here.

Ready to do damage, I barged into his cabin, but I stopped just past the stair. The room was beautiful—teak and chrome, with wide windows, soft bunks, and a wooden desk. But the shelves were covered with ticking clocks.

There were dozens of them, of all makes and models. They hissed and whispered, cursed and hushed. The movement of their hands was like the scuttling of insects, and none were set to the same time. My skin crawled; it took all my willpower not to turn around and race back to the *Temptation*.

To steady my nerves, I started picking locks—cupboards,

drawers, and ah, the liquor cabinet. A sip of scotch settled me
further. I thumbed through his bookshelf: *The Odyssey*, *The
Voyage of Vasco de Gama*, *The Last Flight of Amelia Earhart*.
The Odyssey I knew—the myth of Odysseus—Nix spoke of
it often. The other names were only vaguely familiar—I was
sure she had mentioned them, but I couldn't remember why.
No matter. Calmer now, I pawed through Crowhurst's closet,
trying on his finest jacket—combed wool and black buttons,
too short in the arms.

I was not careful. I didn't bother watering the scotch,
and I tossed the jacket in a heap in the corner. I even spat a
clove onto the floor. It was reckless; it was freeing. I had left
my mark. I had been there—I existed.

Taking the bottle with me, I sat at Crowhurst's desk. I had
half a mind to scratch my name into its glossy surface. Instead,
I riffled through a stack of papers weighed down by a rough
chunk of stone: maps, all in red, just like the one Dahut had
given us back in New York. Boring. Next, I went through
his drawers for coins; in the top one, I found a gold watch—
mercifully wound down—a fancy pen . . . and his logbook.

Should I write a curse in the margins? Flipping through
the book, I glared at that ugly black writing. My hand slowed
when I recognized her name.

There was a lamp on the table. I flicked the switch and read.

Why name a child Nix? A cipher, nullity, oblivion. Portentous.

If life is a game, is she my opponent?

Mathematical calculations spattered the rest of the page, side by side with a snippet of terrible poetry.

Nix, the word, means nothing, or just no.
But there is something I must learn, or know—
Will my choices cause her soon to go . . . ?

My lip curled back. The man's mind was clearly diseased. Shuddering, I took another swig of scotch as I turned the page.

The game we call chess is a simplistic version of the Great Game which I shall call COSMIC CHESS the game that is played over and over with infinite patience and no malice. God against the devil, and humanity the pawn.

Each piece has a proscribed set of movements—fate? But the hand moving them—free will?

The rules are complex, but the ending is the same: the game ends when either side captures the king. When the king is threatened, the queen must move.

Queen: Nix.

King: Grandlon?

That was crossed out. Beneath he'd written:

King: James.

I hold the king in check.

I AM A COSMIC BEING.

That last sentence was written in letters two inches high and pressed so hard into the page that they marked the next three. But below, the handwriting changed again—precise and neat:

James has three days; on the fourth, the Friendship *sails without him and the game is over. Day One: My Arrival. Day Two: My Return.*

Day Three was left blank—but that was tomorrow. Or technically, today. Automatically, I glanced at the nearest clock, but it read just after eight, which was certainly wrong. Still, it was long past midnight.

Considering, I rubbed the paper between my fingers. What did it all mean? It would have been easiest to dismiss the whole thing as mad ranting. But there was something there, something compelling. I turned back in time, past more poetry and mathematics and some notes of the wind speeds and weather, and then—

It is a blessing and a curse to know too much. When

knowledge overflows the cup, there's no room left for faith.

I can see my machinations. Without him, I could not have found Ker-Ys.

Without him . . . without who? His god or someone else? But the rest of the page was blank. I flipped back farther and found more poetry—if you could call it that. A horrible ode to the sea.

Then another sound came—her voice, soft as perfume on a breeze. "Kashmir?"

I sat back in the chair, considering whether or not to answer—half a moment, then another. But why was I pretending I had a choice? I longed to see her face. Even now, the tension in my chest was easing, just knowing she was near. I couldn't fool anyone if I couldn't fool myself. "I'll be right there, amira."

I stood, hesitating. Then I locked the drawers. I hung the coat back in the closet, watered the scotch, closed the cabinets. I was looking for the clove I'd spat when I heard her footsteps on the stair.

"What in the world?" She ducked through the doorway, peering around the cabin, her expression part fear and part excitement. She shivered as her eyes swept over the clocks on the shelves.

I picked the clove off the floor and slipped it into my pocket. "You knew he was mad."

"It's one thing to say it, and another to see it." Her voice was distracted as she peered at one of the clocks. Then she cursed.

"Is this a bad time?" I said—a silly joke. But she shook her head.

"This one's not a clock, it's a barometer, see?" She pointed at the face of it. "The needle's dropped since yesterday."

"A storm coming?" I shook my head. "Poetic."

She only sighed. "What were you doing down here, Kash?"

I considered my answer. "Drinking, amira."

"Twice in one day?" Her jaw tightened. "Now who sounds like the captain?"

I barked a laugh. "Did you come all the way down here to fight with me?"

She opened her mouth and closed it again. "No."

"Good. Because I got you a present." I pointed my chin at the desk, and she followed my eyes. The frustration in her face gave way to delight as she reached not for the logbook, but the maps.

"Cantre'r Gwaelod?" She shuffled through the pages. "And Atlantis! Sunken cities . . . did Dahut draw these?"

"It seems that way," I said, nonplussed. "But look what else there is."

She blinked at me, then turned back to the desk. After a moment, she picked up the stone paperweight, holding it to the light. "Boeotia."

"What?"

"Ancient Greece," she breathed, running her fingertips over the flat surface of the chunk of marble, which I now realized was another map. "Crowhurst said he met another Navigator there. Look . . . the cave of the oracle, and the twin mythic pools of Mnemosyne and Lethe. This is second century if it's a day."

"Very valuable, then."

"Definitely!"

"Well. You're welcome. But look what *else* there is." I picked up the logbook and put it directly in her hands, lest she look next at the lamp.

"This is Crowhurst's?"

"You told me he once filled a logbook with wild rambling and formulas for time travel. I found the rambling parts. Perhaps you can find the formulas."

Nix scanned the pages, engrossed. "King James . . . like the Bible?"

"Possibly. The man is obsessed with playing god."

She heard it—the bitterness in my voice—and her hands stilled. After a moment, she sighed and shut the logbook, tucking it under her arm. "You think I'm scared," she said. "But you are too."

I only shrugged. "I won't bother lying, amira. Not to you."

Her hand went to the pearl pendant at her throat; in the silence, the ticking of the clocks. "Can we go back to the *Temptation*?"

"Aye, Captain."

I followed her off the *Dark Horse* and onto the pier, then up the gangplank to the deck of her ship. Nix dropped the logbook in the captain's cabin and met me at the rail. To the east, dawn was breaking red—a sailor's warning. Still, I was more at ease off the yacht. Together, we gazed into the mirror of the water, wreathed in the silvery mist of her breath. "What are you afraid of?" she said at last.

"Oblivion." The ghost of the word hung in the air.

"Dying?"

"Doubly dying." I grimaced. "Unwept, unhonored, and unsung. You know the poem."

She shifted on her feet and pulled her cloak tighter

around her shoulders. "You think I would forget you?"

"I . . . I don't know." I shook my head. "But it's not about you. Not truly."

"What then?"

"Amira . . ." How to explain? I took a deep breath. The night air filled me, cold as indifference. "All my life, I've never dared to call anything mine. It was too permanent an idea, in a world where nothing lasted. All I had were the thoughts in my head. The feelings in my heart. But now I don't know if those are mine either."

"What do you mean, Kash?"

I tapped my hands on the brass—would she ever understand? "Haven't you ever wondered why you love me?"

She looked at me, surprise on her face. "No."

The answer brought me up short. "Really?"

"There are a million things I wonder, but never that."

I opened my mouth . . . closed it. "Why not?"

"Because . . . well." She bit her lip. "Because it's so obvious. The answer always comes to me before I have the chance to ask myself the question. Why? Don't you know why you love me?"

"I know that I'm happiest at your side," I said fervently. "I know that when we're apart, my heart is with you, when we disagree I still want you near. It's like I was made for you, amira, but I don't know *why*."

"Kashmir . . ." She laughed a little in disbelief. "That's . . . that's what love looks like."

"But is it only a trick of Navigation?" I asked, nearly pleading. "And if so, what is truly mine?"

"I am."

Her words took me by surprise. She said it so simply— so quiet, so true. Only two words, three letters, one breath, but never had a promise held more meaning. She turned to me then, and in her eyes, I saw not oblivion, but infinity, and the stars were not as bright as her smile.

"Nix," I said, and her name was a poem. She tilted her face up to the dawn; my lips met hers. She pressed close to me, and then there was no past, no future—only now. No her, no me. Only us.

CHAPTER
TWENTY-FOUR

As I woke in Kashmir's arms, I was half afraid it had been a dream.

But the memories came back slowly, teasingly. Kissing on the deck—pulling him toward the ladder. Sliding down after him, into his arms, my back pressed against the rungs for another breathless kiss. Letting him lead me toward his cabin as though it were a dance—a two-step where he retreated and I advanced, our hands and eyes locked, and the music was the pounding of my heart.

He'd spun me through the door, stepping in behind me. His lips brushed my shoulders, my neck, the soft skin behind my ear. He murmured sweet words in half a dozen languages, and though I didn't know them, I understood them all. His fingers were deft on the pearl buttons of my dress; he undid them one by one, down to the small of my back. Then his hands on my skin, and tangled in my hair.

He had shrugged off his jacket. My hands slid up under his white shirt, along the rippled muscles of his stomach, and then—and then—

"Good morning, amira."

I froze at the sound of his voice, then melted again at the look in his eyes. His hair was tousled, his smile was warm and sleepy. Bright daylight streamed through the porthole and shone on his golden skin. "Barely," I said, my voice husky.

"Barely good?" His eyebrows shot up.

"Barely morning, I meant."

"Ah, that's a relief!" He propped himself up on one elbow among the silk pillows, and the blanket slipped dangerously low around his waist. I averted my eyes, then reverted them surreptitiously. I could hear the wicked grin in his voice. "It could get barer, if you like."

I slung a pillow at him. He batted it aside, then wrapped his arm around me, pulling me into a kiss that stopped time. I had seen countless worlds and boundless horizons, but nothing as wondrous as the space within the circle of his arms. It was only the ringing of the bells that brought me back to Ker-Ys.

Trying to catch my breath, I drank in the scent of his

skin, clove and copper, as the rumble of the gates reverberated through the hull. He kissed my cheek, my jaw, my throat. "If the tide's going out, it's nearly noon," I whispered as the ship rocked on the swells. "We should probably get back to the castle."

He brushed my hair back with a feather-light touch, and I never wanted to move again. "We probably should," he murmured in my ear, though I'd already forgotten what it was we should do. I kissed him again, deep and languid at first, but he slid one hand around my waist and the other around the back of my neck and pulled me close. A warm current flooded through me, and a feeling in my stomach like bubbles. I arched my back, pressing my body against his, like the sea reaching for the setting sun.

"Hello?"

Kash and I both blinked. The voice was familiar, and it came from outside the ship. For a long moment, neither he nor I responded, though I was certain the pounding of my heart was loud enough for anyone to hear. Then came the sound of footsteps on the gangplank, and Kashmir called out, "Just give us a minute, Dahut!"

"What do you think she wants?" I whispered.

"I have a guess," was all he said. He stood and went

to his closet, letting the coverlet fall away completely. I couldn't help but stare. Kash had always been shameless, and I was no prude; last night had not been the first time I'd seen him—what did he call it? Dishabille. But the way he stood now—his back to me, one hip cocked, his left hand on the back of his neck . . . it made my heart thunder and my fingertips tingle, as though my blood had turned to seafoam.

But from above came the sound of small feet pacing, so I turned toward my trunk and dug my hands through my clothes, and even the roughest material felt like silk against my skin. As I dressed, I stole glances at Kashmir out of the corner of my eye—the way his thigh flexed as he stepped into his trousers. The taut muscles of his back as he pulled his shirt over his head. The tilt of his head as he pinned his cuffs. And on his belt, the lock he'd taken from the Brooklyn Bridge that day. As he buckled it on, he looked up through his lashes. "If I had time and music, I could do it better in reverse."

My face went red, but he only grinned.

"Are you coming?" Dahut's voice drifted down the hatch.

"Patience!" Kashmir called, but I remembered then what she'd wanted, and I dug the vial of mercury out from the bottom of my trunk. "What is that?" he said, holding the door.

"A cure-all from Qin's tomb. It might help her memory."

Abovedecks, the wintery air cooled my cheeks. Dahut was waiting there in her enormous skirts, her expression half impatient and half afraid. As we climbed through the hatch, she held up her diary. "You told me we were friends," she said to Kashmir. "Was that true?"

He didn't even hesitate. "Yes."

"Good. I need to escape. Here I am."

Kash sighed and gave me a look that was almost apologetic. "I told you she'd want to come with us."

I considered it, tilting the bottle of mercury back and forth in my hands. At first blush, it seemed so wrong to take her from Crowhurst, to a place where he could not follow. After all, I'd had my own difficulties with my father, but I'd never actually cut him from my life. Then again, Slate and Crowhurst were not the same man. "Why?" I said at last. "Why do you want to go?"

"This place gives me nightmares," she said darkly. "I don't like it here."

"You're running away because you get bad dreams?" I gave her a dubious look, but Kash put his hand on my arm.

"What are your nightmares about, Dahut?"

"Drowning," she said, and something squirmed like an eel in my belly. Was it only coincidence that she dreamed of the way the myth ended? "Will you help me or not?"

Kash looked at me, a plea in his eyes, but I was already nodding. Hope broke like dawn on Dahut's face, and seeing it steeled something in me. "All right," I said firmly. "Bring whatever you need to the dock. We'll gather the crew and leave tonight."

"Tonight? No." Her smile fell away. "It has to be now, before my father wakes up."

I stared at her, at a loss. "Even if I wanted to leave them behind, this ship can't sail without a crew."

"If he finds out I took his keys, he'll stop me!"

A chill skittered up my spine as another piece of the legend fell into place. "You took his keys?"

"So he can't follow me on the yacht."

I swallowed, my mouth suddenly dry. "We will get you somewhere safe, Dahut, I promise. Just . . . just give me an hour."

"Crowhurst won't stop you," Kash added. "Even if he wakes up, trust me, we can sneak you out."

"You don't understand," she said, her mouth twisting. "If he finds me, he'll make me forget I wanted to leave."

I blinked at her. "What do you mean by that?"

But Dahut had run out of patience. "Never mind," she muttered, striding down the gangplank and toward the *Dark Horse*.

Kash rushed to the rail as she scrambled aboard the yacht. "What do you mean, he'll make you forget?"

Her only response was to fit the keys to the ignition.

"Dahut, wait!"

The motor purred as she pressed the throttle, and I had half a mind to let her go. After all, if she fled, she still couldn't open the sea gates. But that wouldn't guarantee *her* safety. And I needed to know what she meant about forgetting. Kashmir was one step ahead of me—as she pulled away from the pier, he vaulted over the rail of the *Temptation* and onto the deck of the *Dark Horse*.

Swearing, I followed. The yacht was accelerating, and I only barely made the leap. Instead of landing gracefully on my feet like Kash had, I stumbled forward and fell to my knees and one hand, clutching the bottle of mercury to my chest. He helped me up as we motored through the sea gates. Dahut set her jaw in a grim smile. "Change your mind?"

"No." I put the vial in my pocket and straightened my

shirt, raising my voice over the roar of the motor. "But you weren't born in this timeline, and you aren't a Navigator. If you go into the mist all alone, you'll never find your way out!"

"Good thing you're coming along," she said.

"So we can arrive in the past on a twenty-first-century powerboat? We'll run out of gas, or someone will accuse us of witchcraft—"

"They already do," she muttered. "And I'd rather burn than drown."

"They drown witches too," I shot back. "And hang them. Sometimes both. And sometimes they draw and quarter—"

"Amira."

"What?"

"Not helpful."

"Sorry."

Dahut only laughed, and the wind took her hair. The *Dark Horse* bounced on the chop when we hit the open water. Before us, fishing boats lay scattered across the surface of the Iroise, their oarsmen pulling hard against the current as harpooners crouched in the bows. Guivres were circling above as chummers scattered ropy chunks of offal from red-stained buckets. As Dahut wove between the boats, the men clenched their scarlet fists in the sign of the fig. "Benir la chassé!" one called in a jeering voice. "Bless the hunt, princess!"

But the *Dark Horse* was as sleek as a sea snake, and far faster than the *Temptation*. Soon enough, we were past them, skimming the surface of the dark rollers. How far could we go before we slipped into the Margins? If need be, Kash and I could take the helm by force—I still had the gun in my cloak—but mutiny didn't sit well with me. Better to try to convince her. Still, I wasn't the one she trusted. I gave Kashmir a pleading look and he nodded.

He made his way to stand beside Dahut at the helm, putting his hand over hers on the throttle. I clenched my jaw at an irrational stab of jealousy. Then I breathed it out; Kashmir wasn't like that.

"Dahut." He said her name so softly it was hard to hear—but perhaps that was his intention. "What does he do? How does he make you forget?"

Dahut's eyes cut to him, still suspicious, but then she opened her mouth, closed it. "I . . . think . . ." She eased back on the throttle, slipping the boat into neutral, and the sudden silence was startling. "I think there's something in the flask."

I felt my brow furrow. "What?"

"The copper flask! The one he wears on that chain." Her voice was urgent now; she clutched Kashmir's fingers. "Last night, I took a closer look at the page you noticed, the page my father wrote—"

"In your diary?"

"There are indentations on the paper, from what I'd written before. Something he tore out! Something about the flask—when you drink from it, you forget."

Kashmir turned to me, a question in his eyes. I held up one hand, trying to think. Lin had mentioned it too, hadn't she? Drinking something, and time disappearing. What sort of potion could erase memories? And where would Crowhurst have found such a thing?

The boat hummed beneath my feet; the guivres cried out as they dove toward the sea. I pulled the pearl pendant of my necklace back and forth on its chain. Then my hand stilled as a thought burst like a firework in my skull. "Boeotia."

"What?"

"One of his first trips, he told me." There was fear in my voice, and wonder too. "Come."

I led them both downstairs, into the cabin where the clocks whispered of the past. Heading straight to Crowhurst's desk, I flicked on the lamp and lifted the slab of marble to the light.

The map was the size of a half sheet of paper, and chipped around the edges, but the image was still clear. I ran a finger over the cuts and ridges of the pale stone. "The oracle of Trophonius. Here. And above the cave, the twin pools of Mnemosyne and Lethe. Memory, and oblivion."

"Oblivion?" Kashmir's voice was soft.

"It's an old myth. Greek." I held the stone in reverent hands. "The oracle is described in a guide by the geographer Pausanias. There's the Herkyna River—here, you see? The temple is built on her banks. At the mouth of the river, there's a hole in the ground where Trophonius lives. He was swallowed by the earth after he killed his brother. Petitioners looking for answers would be thrown into the cave and return with terrifying visions."

"And the pools?"

"They're fed directly from the rivers in Hades. One helps people remember what the god had told them, and one helps them forget." The slab of marble was colder than a tombstone. Crowhurst had clearly dipped from the waters of the Lethe—that was how he got Dahut to forget the old king, to change the myth with her maps. Had he also drunk from the Mnemosyne? Or had he learned the secrets of the universe at the feet of the oracle?

"So there is a cure?" Dahut's words brought me back to the present; she looked at me, her eyes full of hope.

"Yes," I said simply. "Come with us on the *Temptation*, and I will take you there."

She wrapped her arms around me, so tight I couldn't breathe; over her shoulder, Kashmir's smile was even more breathtaking. But then the sound of shouting came from outside—fairly close by. Had we been drifting?

Swearing, I ran back above, but once on deck, I didn't see any sign of rocks or reefs. Still, we'd gotten close to a cluster of fishing boats—the men in them were the ones I'd heard. By the time Dahut and Kashmir joined me, I saw the reason for the din.

In one of the boats, two fishermen hauled on a rope, struggling with a heavy weight on the other end. A third man crouched on the bow with his harpoon cocked. The line zig-zagged through the water, cutting right, then left, turning on a dime. Above, a guivre circled, waiting.

Kash came to my side. "What's happening, amira?"

"They caught something."

We watched, wordless, as white foam boiled on the

surface. A dark shape thrashed below the waves, then dove back down. But the hook was already set, and the fishermen dragged their catch ever closer while their fellows cheered them on from nearby skiffs. All eyes were fixed on the point where the rope met the water—all but Kashmir, who turned away.

Then the mermaid broke the surface, trailing spray.

Long silver hair whipped around in an arc; the muscular tail twisted and flailed. But she was smaller than I'd expected, about Dahut's size, and the fishermen were stronger. They whooped and hollered as they hauled her toward the boat: a creature only vaguely human, but for her cries. Her toothy mouth opened and closed around the rope; in the silvery skin of her throat, the steel hook gleamed.

The harpooner stood, taking aim, and the chummer caught sight of us. "La bénédiction!" he cried. "La bénédiction de la princesse!"

At his words, the harpoon flew, piercing the mermaid clean through the shoulder. As the fishermen hauled her into their boat, Dahut ran to the helm and dropped her hand to the throttle. The yacht roared to life; I stumbled back against the gunwale. "What the hell are you doing?"

"What the hell does it look like?"

The men left off their bloody work to stare with wide eyes as the *Dark Horse* bore down on their boat. Frantically, they took the oars, but I shouldered Dahut aside, grabbing the wheel and turning us hard to starboard. The yacht veered, throwing up a wall of icy water. It swamped the fishing boat—the men cried out, and the harpooner tumbled into the sea.

My hands shook on the wheel as my fortune played over in my head: lost, lost. But Kashmir was safe, thank all the gods. Not so the fishermen. Their boat listed, half in and half out of the water, and the mermaid thrashed on their boards, churning the water red in the belly of the boat. She lashed out with tooth and tail.

The oarsman screamed as she raked his leg with clawed hands; the chummer stumbled as the boat rocked. I swore, taking us back around to help, but the chummer finally got hold of the harpoon. He tore it from the mermaid's shoulder as we approached, and with a cry, he heaved it at my head. "The devil drag you down!"

Cursing, I swerved; the weapon glanced off the port side and disappeared into our wake.

"Let's go!" Dahut shouted, tugging at the wheel. "Come on!"

I held firm. "They're going to sink without our help!"

"They're going to kill us if we try to give it!"

"You tried to kill them first!"

"No! No!" Dahut's eyes were wild, pleading. "I was trying to save her."

"We can't do that either if we run!"

"Fine." She gritted her teeth, yanking open the cupboard in the cockpit; she pulled out a flare gun and hunkered down in the shelter of the stairwell.

I didn't bother protesting. Where was the harpooner? I eased up on the throttle, dreading the sound of a thud against the hull or the whine of a drag on the motor. Momentum carried us the rest of the way, but as we closed the distance, the oarsman abandoned ship. He was followed quickly by the chummer, and they both made for the nearest fishing boat. I didn't go after them—but I watched them swim to safety, shivering and swearing as their fellows hauled them out of the water.

Still no sign of the third man. Had he drowned, or worse? I cut the motor as the *Dark Horse* nosed up to the stricken boat. From the next boat, fifteen yards to port, the fishermen threw daggers with their eyes, and I couldn't help but notice that they still had their harpoons.

Kash noticed too. "We should go."

"We should," I said, but I hesitated. The mermaid still lay there, gasping over the oarsman's seat. She was such an odd beast—not half human and half fish, but a blend of the two. The skin of her face shone with tiny scales. Her spine was ridged, and fins flexed along the backs of her arms; like a ray, she had gills along her ribs. She was as alien as any creature from the depths. But suffering is universal. Drawing out the bottle of mercury in my pocket, I stepped down into the swamped fishing boat.

The water was freezing. The shock of it sent a jolt through me, but thankfully it only reached to my knees. I sent another worried glance across the water—the missing harpooner was at risk of hypothermia, on top of whatever lurked below the surface—but I saw no sign of him.

As I approached the mermaid, her tail twisted, but I could tell she had little fight left. Uncorking the bottle, I leaned out, keeping my distance as I dripped mercury over the pale, wet skin of her shoulder, where the harpoon had struck. Before my eyes, the skin knitted, sealing shut. It made my stomach turn.

"Amira?"

"Almost done!"

The fishhook posed a more complex problem, but I'd fished with Rotgut before. It was a simple contraption—no barb. Still, there was no way to pull it out backward without reaching down her throat and past her teeth.

The fisherman's blade was still in the bottom of the dinghy, gleaming through the murky red bilge; I used it to cut the rope short. Then, slowly, I inched close enough to take hold of the curve of the hook, my fingers brushing the glittering scales of her throat—so cold. In one quick motion, I yanked the assembly straight through.

The mermaid thrashed again as the rope passed through the hole. I fell back into the icy red water in the boat, though her scream was more chilling. Scrambling to my feet, I tossed the hook overboard; once she stopped writhing, I poured mercury over the wound.

Her mouth gaped as she healed, showing me her needle teeth. Was it a threat? I stepped back over the bench, picking up the abandoned blade, but she made no move toward me. Instead, she grasped the side of the boat and heaved herself back into the water.

The boat rocked underfoot. I watched, my heart pounding, as the ripples disappeared. What was I waiting for? Some sign of thanks or recognition? I shook my head at my childish hope—this was not that sort of fairy tale. Then Kashmir called to me again, a warning in his voice. "Amira."

I looked up, expecting to see the fishermen edging closer, but they were showing their sterns, the oarsmen pulling hard toward the safety of the city. Then a familiar voice drifted over from the other side of the yacht. "What in the devil's dark arse is this?"

Striped sails loomed as the *Fool* drew alongside. Gwen stood at the rail in all her wild glory, and there, beside her, the harpooner shivered under a rough woolen blanket. I was oddly relieved to see them both alive, but my relief knotted into irritation as Gwen tossed down a rope. She boarded the *Dark Horse* as easily as she'd boarded the *Temptation*—as though she owned whatever she saw. I scrambled back aboard too, leaving the swamped fishing boat to the mercy of the sea.

Gwen swore when she saw me. "Jumped ship, did you? Fickle thing."

"You're one to talk." I made a face as I wrung mermaid blood from the bottom of my cloak. "Go back to the *Fool*, where you belong."

She gave me a grim smile. "That's just what I'm doing. Where'd you leave him?"

It took me a moment to realize she was talking about my father. "He's at the castle," I replied primly. "With my mother. His wife."

"Well." Her smile froze on her face. "Well, well, well."

Gwen crossed her arms and gazed across the water, far and beyond the horizon. The wind ruffled her curls and played with the feather in her hat, and I almost felt sorry for her. Almost. "Is that why you turned around?" I said. "For him?"

"Half a mile out, we hit a bank of fog, thick as spoiled milk." She shook her head. "It only lifted when I turned round. It seemed to me a sign."

"Of what?"

"Don't know anymore. But he saved my life once. And when a life is saved, a debt's created."

"And this is how you repay it?" I jerked my chin toward the *Fool*. "By taking up a trade you knew he'd hate?"

"I only said that to pinch him, you stupid girl. My hold is full of Irish lace." She glared at me, as though daring me to say something. "The payment for a life is a life. I'm going to save his so there's nothing owed. And then maybe I can forget his name."

"Save him?" I watched as she took hold of the rope again. "From what?"

"I saw the way he looked," she said. "I know the face of despair."

"There's a lot that can change in a day."

"I know that too, believe me."

Gwen shimmied up the rope, shouting orders to raise the sails, and Dahut peeked out from the shelter of the stairs, still holding the flare gun. "Who was she?"

"Her name is Gwen. Gwenolé." I frowned as a thought began to form, but before it coalesced, Gwen called down to Dahut.

"You're mixed up in this too?" She spat on the deck. "I knew you were bad luck. Where are your masters, girl?"

Dahut adjusted her grip on the flare gun. "Who?"

"The two men who sailed with you. The ones who brought you here."

I blinked. "Two?"

"Did you curse me for leaving them?" Gwen called to Dahut. "Did you bring the fog?"

"What do you mean, two?" I called back.

"Ask her!"

"I don't remember!" Dahut said, exasperated, but the next question died on my lips as the wind carried the distant sound of bells to my ears.

Spinning around, I swore. Back at the city, the fishing boats were pouring through the gates and into the safety of the harbor. Outside, I could see the tide rising along the wall in a wave. I ran to the helm. "Hold on!"

We left the *Fool* in our white wake as Gwen cursed our names. I cursed right back. Ahead, eddies were forming near the base of the wall. As the gates began to move, I gave it all she had. The *Dark Horse* rose, her prow cutting through the water, running over the waves just like the legend promised. The motor roared, the wind whipped my hair—and I held a grin between my teeth; my own ship was not half so fast. Streaming away from our stern, a wake like the tail of a comet, and the *Dark Horse* burst into the harbor as the doors slammed shut behind us.

Easing up quickly, I whooped like a maniac as the wave of our entry rolled up toward the wharf, making the boats bob—and sloshing water right at Crowhurst's feet.

CHAPTER
TWENTY-FIVE

My giddy thrill twisted into dread; beside me, Dahut stiffened. Her father was practically hopping with anger. He'd brought four guards to the wharf, and sunlight gleamed on the hilts of their swords.

As if that was not enough, the fishermen had clustered in groups on the pier, muttering and casting dark glances our way. News of the scrum on the water had clearly spread—and they might not know their harpooner had been rescued.

Maybe Crowhurst's guards were not such a bad thing.

Then I saw Blake, hailing us from the deck of the *Temptation*, and the tension between my shoulders eased a little further. Though his presence only brought us up to four against five, he was an excellent shot, if it came to that.

But the gun was still in my pocket. Could I use it bluff

our way out of this? I bit my lip, considering. As though reading my thoughts, Kashmir turned to me. "What are we going to do, amira?"

I glanced over my shoulder—the gates were firmly shut. There was no escape, not until the next low tide. But we couldn't have left anyway—not without my family, not without my ship. "Same plan," I said softly, slipping my hand into my pocket. "We're gathering the crew and taking Dahut to Boeotia."

She narrowed her eyes. "You swear you'll try to help me?"

I was almost offended. "Of course."

"Then I'll go with him, for now." To my surprise, she tossed the flare gun into the cupboard. I met her eyes, a question in my own, but she was resolved, and I couldn't deny I was relieved.

"All right." Swallowing the lump in my throat, I released the gun and motored toward the pier. Then, hidden from view by the helm, she pulled the diary from her pocket and pressed it against my leg.

"Keep this for me," she whispered. "Don't let me forget."

I let the throttle slip into neutral; we glided up to the dock as my hand closed around the book.

"What are you doing?" Crowhurst shouted from the pier. "What on earth was going through your head?"

Her response was blithe. "I can't remember."

"This isn't a game! You could have killed yourselves out there!"

"Sorry, Father." Dahut's voice was unusually contrite, and she tossed him the rope to belay to the bollard. While his eyes were on her, I slipped the book into the pocket of my cloak. Then I went to turn the ignition, but I froze with the keys on my palm. I recognized one of them: an ornate brass thing that looked a bit like a cross. The long gold chain still dangled from it.

"Give me those!" Crowhurst snatched the keys out of my hand. Standing there at the helm, he loomed over me, but Kash was right by my side.

"We're all safe," he said, his tone soothing. "No need to shout."

"All's well that ends well," Blake added with forced cheer as he trotted down the pier. Billie followed close at his heels, wagging her tail.

Crowhurst took a deep breath then, glancing from Billie and Blake to Kashmir and me—but I was staring at the keys that dangled from his fist. There it was, the brass key. Had he taken it from a dead man's neck? He looked down at the set for a moment, then back up. "What's wrong, Nix?"

"Nothing." I shook my head, but I'd spoken too quickly; he narrowed his eyes. Tucking the keys into his pocket, he pulled himself together, glancing from me to Dahut and back.

"I shouldn't have yelled," he said. "I'm sorry. But I have to keep her safe. You understand?"

"Of course," I said. "I'm sorry."

"You can't always listen to what she says," he added. "She forgets things."

Out of the corner of my eye, I could see anger flash across Dahut's face; I only nodded. "Sure."

Crowhurst took a deep breath, straightening his crown, regaining his composure. He even forced a smile. "Shall we all go back to the castle?"

"I . . . uh. I have to . . . uh." My whole body was stiff. My mind was blank. All I could think was that I didn't want to go anywhere with Crowhurst and his guards.

"Chores," Blake said then, nodding toward the *Temptation*.

"We have to feed the dog," Kashmir added smoothly. At the mention of food, Billie licked her chops.

"I see." Crowhurst searched my face; was that doubt in his own? "Well. I suppose I'll see you all later."

I only nodded. Crowhurst led Dahut away, the guards falling in before and behind. The fishermen parted ranks around them, but the tension was still thick, and a small part of me wondered if we should have taken Crowhurst up on his offer of escort. I slid my hand into my pocket; the gun was still there, but it was useless in my hands. "Blake?"

"Miss Song?"

"Can you take this? Just in case?" I slipped the derringer out of my pocket; the silver barrel gleamed in the sunlight.

Reluctantly, he tucked it into his jacket. "What's going on, Miss Song?"

"Let's go to the ship," I murmured, ushering the boys up the gangplank. As we ducked into the cabin, I cast one more glance toward Crowhurst as he crossed the wharf, only to find he was looking back over his shoulder at me.

Shuddering, I shut and locked the door behind us. Billie trotted up to the captain's bunk, and Kashmir took a position near the port window to keep an eye on the fishermen. Blake stood in the center of the room. "Your mother told me I could find you on the ship," he said with a frown. "She didn't mention it would be *Crowhurst's* ship."

"It was a bit of a last-minute thing," I said. "Dahut was trying to escape."

"So you two stopped her?"

"Not exactly—well, yes," I said. "But we actually have to help her."

"Help her escape?" Blake's look was incredulous. "I thought you wanted to stay. I thought you wanted to learn if it was possible to change the past."

"I do—I did. But . . ." I bit my lip. "Not like this. Not from him."

"Crowhurst steals her memories!" Kashmir abandoned his post at the porthole. "Makes her forget things. He's not a good man!"

"What on earth do you mean, Mr. Firas?"

"Dahut told us she read something about it in her diary. Here." I pulled the book from my pocket, flipping through. It was easy to find the page she had mentioned—the page where Crowhurst had written his version of the myth. The book folded oddly around the missing pages. I ran my finger down the cut edges. They were sliced very close to the spine, as though with a razor.

Or a very sharp knife.

My breath came faster as I remembered the king's cut

throat. No wonder Crowhurst had not seemed shocked to hear of the man's death. But after Dahut's revelation, it didn't surprise me either. I ran my fingers over the page, trying to look past his version of the story to see what was underneath. Squinting, I tilted the diary toward the porthole, letting the wintery sunlight illuminate the indentations on the paper. "'Father brought James to . . . the treasury?" I furrowed my brow. "Made him drink from . . . from the flask. . . . And now he . . . remembers nothing.'"

Blake shook his head, disbelieving. "You're saying Crowhurst has some sort of elixir that takes away memories?"

"Lethe water," I murmured, only half listening. "But who is James?"

Kash peered over my shoulder. "Wasn't that the name in Crowhurst's logbook, amira?"

"It was, wasn't it?" Chewing my cheek, I handed him the diary and went to the desk. I'd put the logbook there, beside my father's empty coffee cups. I found the page Kash had showed me last night. "King: James," I read quietly. "I hold the king in check."

Blake was frowning. "Mr. Firas, didn't you mention that the treasury was a pit beneath the castle?"

"Baleh," Kash said, but I ignored them, paging back.

James has three days; on the fourth, the Friendship *sails without him.* A thought was forming in my head, a question bothering me. I studied the line, trying to listen to my softest thoughts past the sound of the waves on the seawall and the breeze in the lines. The words fell from my lips on a breath. "Gwen said there was a second man. And they left from the Port of London, in 1748."

"A second man, Miss Song?"

"Crowhurst told me he was looking for other Navigators." I swore. "The harbormaster even told me his name the first day I was here!"

"Whose name, amira?"

"Cook," I said, stabbing the page with a finger. "James Cook. The man in the pit."

"James Cook?" Blake's eyes were round. "Captain James Cook?"

Kashmir frowned. "Was he the first European in America?"

"No, Hawaii," I said softly. "That is, unless he ends up trapped in a dungeon on a mythical island."

For a moment, all of us were quiet, but there was a sound in my ears, as though I was listening to the ocean in a seashell. The world seemed to crystallize—and was this feeling horror or awe? Cosmic chess indeed. If this was a game to him, Crowhurst was many moves ahead. Damn the man. I could not tell if I despised him more or less than I admired him.

"So Cook is a Navigator too, Miss Song?"

"I should have guessed. Crowhurst *did* guess." The words were bitter in my mouth. Glaring at my father's bookshelves, I found Cook's biography and slammed it down on the desk. "Look at the history! He found the route to Australia and Hawaii when no one in Europe knew those places existed! He set out knowing they'd be there, and there they were. That's what Navigation is!"

"But why would Crowhurst keep him here in Ker-Ys?"

"He wants to change the past, Kashmir! He wants to know whether or not he can prevent himself from setting out on his own journey."

"How does stopping Cook teach him that?"

"By watching what happens to me." I shook my head. "My mother too, and Blake, while he's at it. We were all born in Hawaii, though none of us are native."

"So he's going to keep Cook trapped in the treasury for the rest of his life?"

"Just till he misses his ship." I scanned the page,

breathless. "The *Friendship*—that was Cook's commission, back when he was a journeyman in 1748. That's how he earned his captaincy. Three days . . ." I counted back on my fingers. "Tomorrow. His ship leaves tomorrow."

"More than enough time." Kashmir clapped his hands together. "You had a map to the pit, yes? We'll go find Cook first, then gather the crew, get Dahut, and go."

"But . . ." There was a strange look in Blake's eyes—was it loss or hope? "Cook's arrival in Hawaii led to the deaths of tens of thousands of people."

Kashmir cocked his head. "And the birth of many more, Mr. Hart. You among them."

"But didn't you tell me, Miss Song? Some people think that choices create new worlds. What if both worlds could coexist?"

"It's just as likely we'll have neither," I said. "And there's no proof, either way."

He met my gaze. "Not yet."

"Blake." Words deserted me, but Blake was bubbling over with them.

"You suggested it yourself! You want to take Dahut aboard and stop her story from playing out. But how do you dare, if you really think the past can't safely be changed? Mr.

Firas." He appealed to Kashmir. "You and I both have memories of another life. I know you wonder what they mean!"

"I'm happy to keep wondering," Kash said grimly. "Mystery is the spice of life."

"Then you, Miss Song." Blake's eyes were pleading. "You told me you wanted to be more than what you inherited. I'm not asking you to risk anything I'm not risking."

I opened my mouth to reply—but was he right? Was I being selfish? But then I met Kashmir's eyes, and in them, everything I stood to lose. "It's not just me. It's Kashmir too. It's my mother, my grandmother. People I love."

"What about the country I love?"

"Let's start by saving ourselves and Dahut. If we do, we'll save Ker-Ys too. Maybe . . . maybe if this works, we can find a way to help Hawaii. But when the gates open next, we're sailing, and Cook is coming with us. Are you?"

Blake met my eyes, and for a long moment I did not know what his answer would be. But then he looked away and pulled the sketchbook from his pocket. "We'd best try to find the pit, then."

CHAPTER
TWENTY-SIX

KASHMIR

Nix pondered our next move, there in the captain's cabin. There were many pieces to consider—the ship, the crew, the princess, the pit. And the Mnemosyne water too—we would need it for Cook, according to Dahut's diary. Once the fishermen dispersed, I slipped back over to the *Dark Horse* for the map of Boeotia; by the time I came back with it, she had the plan outlined.

She would go to the castle and gather the crew to send them to the ship. Mr. Hart and I would find the pit and rescue Cook. From there, Blake would lead James back to the docks while I went on to look for Dahut. At first, Nix had insisted she would come with me; I declined. "I prefer to sneak alone, amira."

"But Kashmir—"

"Remember, you're to lose me at sea. Not in a castle."

I gave her my best smile, but her face paled.

"I've been wondering about that."

Her tone of voice left me cold. "What do you mean?"

Nix folded her arms and glanced out the deadlights, toward the sea. "Gwenolé is on her way back to the city," she said softly. "Dahut stole the keys from the king. The end of the myth might be coming. And if Dahut opens the gate at high tide—"

"She wouldn't," I said firmly. "She won't. Besides, high tide is at sunset. I'll be back at the ship by then, with Dahut in tow."

Nix bit her lip—I saw her wrestle with the decision. Would she order me to bring her along? If she did, I would obey, but it was not the wise choice, and she knew it. "Fine," she said, but her voice was fierce. She took my shoulders, and her eyes were dark as ink. "But if you don't come to the ship, I'm coming back for you," she said. "Come hell or high water."

Out of the corner of my eye, I saw Mr. Hart turn his head; I had never been more grateful for his gentleman's discretion. Pulling Nix into my arms, I kissed her to make my own promises. "Don't worry," I whispered as my hand went to the lock on my belt. It was the matter of a moment to open it and place it in her palm. "Love has always buoyed me up."

She smiled at me and closed her fingers around the iron. I gave her a wink. Then I turned and breezed out the door.

"Allez, Mr. Hart!"

We headed toward the warehouse as he drew his sketchbook from his pocket. The map inside showed the route we'd take through the sewers; Nix herself would take the Grand Rue toward the castle.

It wasn't easy to walk away, not with the scent of her skin still lingering on mine. The part of me that was always watching finally understood how the captain spent so much time in the past. I followed Mr. Hart through the cold boathouse, lost in a warm memory.

But when I climbed down the rope into the tunnels, something chilled me. Maybe it was the darkness, almost tangible; maybe it was the weight of the city crouching there above my head. Or maybe it was the distance between me and Nix, growing by the moment. Still, I had made my choice, and so I crept through the shadows toward the castle.

Mr. Hart and I traveled along the sandy waterway by the light of my little glass lamp, following the path he'd marked in his book. Passing beneath the city, I caught a whiff of manure—was there a stable somewhere above? And when we neared the cathedral, the droning song of the monks drifted to my ears. Far down a side tunnel, the wind moaned; closer, water dripped and dropped. Mr. Hart himself was very quiet, and I was almost glad I could not see his face to read his troubled thoughts. I knew he was disappointed, but I did not understand it. Perhaps I did not want to.

I could not fathom a man who would flirt with destruction. What had he lost in Hawaii that was worth risking his life for? I did not ask, and he did not volunteer it. We only traveled silently, side by side in the dark.

Soon enough, we found the stair. At the top, the door stood ajar on crumbling hinges. It opened into a vaulted cellar, the walls of which were lost in the shadows. Curved stone pillars stretched before me like tree trunks in an old forest, away into the gloom.

Here, the wine was stored alongside the dusty dead. In the glow of the sky herring, the empty skulls watched us as we passed. I nodded to them like old friends. I liked to see them—these remains, these reminders of lives lived long ago. Men lived and died every day—how many could say they'd be remembered well?

A glow came again to my chest, and it had nothing to do with the lamp I held.

"This way," Mr. Hart said, leading me through the cellar to a door of heavy oak. The room behind it was protected by an elaborate lock—a masterwork, at least for the era, though the one I'd taken from my belt might have been a greater challenge.

"Hold this?" I took my picks from my pockets and handed him the lantern.

He raised it high, sharpening the shadows. "Can you see?"

"Yes," I lied, because I didn't need to; I could feel the tumblers moving as I worked, quick and sure.

Mr. Hart stood by. "I wonder why Crowhurst didn't kill him," he mused, his voice only a whisper in the gloom.

"Cook?" I held my hands steady, though I chewed my lip—it was a very good question. I let my mind wander as I sought the pins. What had the logbook said? "I think he needs him," I said at last.

"For what?"

"Navigation takes belief, right? But the man has lost his faith—displaced by knowledge or so he said. Maybe he needed someone else to steer him to Ker-Ys. Ah." The last pin moved. I turned the hook, and the door opened. "Après vous."

We stepped through the door and into a room so wide that the sound of our footsteps didn't echo; they merely faded before they reached the walls. The lantern threw shadows up into the ceiling—and down into the pit on the floor, wide as the eye of a giant. Mr. Hart saw it at the same time I did; startled, he drew back, so I took the lead.

It was a circular hole lined with stone, very regular, like an enormous well, though there was no water in it. A stairwell had been built into the side, spiraling down into the gloom. At the bottom of the oubliette, something gleamed, like the toothy fish of the deep sea.

Mr. Hart followed me down. The stone steps were wet with condensation, the air cool and damp on my skin; I could still taste the tang of the sea. As we descended, the glow from the lamp illuminated the riches in the pit: crowns and goblets, coins and platters, bracelets and rings. Any other day I would have lined my pockets with the best of it and returned above, triumphant, but it wasn't gold that Crowhurst was trying to keep here.

The light was gilded now, brighter. Still, it took me a moment to find what I was looking for—in fact, Mr. Hart noticed him first.

"My god," he whispered, raising the lantern. On a pile of

quilts and furs, a tall man slept. He was young—perhaps only a few years older than me—and unshaven, though he appeared in good health. His clothes were well made: a fine jacket with horn buttons, dark woolen britches . . . and manacles, fastened around both ankles, the chain passing through a ring in the floor. "Is this him?" Mr. Hart said, leaning close. "Is this the man who touched off the theft of Hawaii?"

At his words, Cook stirred, then startled. With a rattle of chains, he scrambled to his feet, holding up one hand against my light. "Who are you?"

"Your saviors," I replied. "We've come to take you back to London."

"London." He blinked. "Was I ever in London?"

I froze then, unsure—had Nix been wrong in her guess, or was this only the effect of the Lethe water? But Mr. Hart spoke. "Are you Captain James Cook?"

The man looked at him askance. "That is my name, but I am no captain." His eyes grew distant then. "Though I've always dreamed of going to sea."

"It's your lucky day." Crouching, I took hold of one of the manacles. "There's a ship waiting for us at the dock. We'll get you out of here. Mr. Hart, bring the light closer." Focused as I was on unlocking the irons, I didn't notice that he hadn't obeyed until the first manacle fell away. "Mr. Hart?"

His response was a long time coming, but once he spoke, I wished he hadn't. "Maybe we should reconsider."

My hands froze, as did my blood. Not now, not here, not alone with a man who'd lost his past and another willing to risk his future. "Let me remind you, Mr. Hart, that if Cook is not allowed to find Hawaii, you will never be standing there, able to ask me not to let him do so."

"Did you know he pretends to be a god, too? On his last voyage."

Cook started at him. "Do I?"

"It brings you to ruin," Mr. Hart whispered in the dark.

"Be that as it may." I took hold of the second manacle, trying to keep my fingers steady. "On this particular voyage, you'll go upstairs, out the door, and to the docks via the sewer." I spoke as though by telling the story, I could make it come true. "Mr. Hart has a map. He'll show you the way."

"Mr. Firas—"

The manacle opened. Cook stepped free. I stood, turning slowly to face Mr. Hart. "You'll show him the way to the *Temptation*," I told him, but he shook his head. There was anguish on his face.

"I can't."

"Then I will. Where's that map?" I reached for Mr. Hart, but he batted my hand aside, so I punched him in the nose.

It was only a left hook, but he stumbled back against the slick wall of the oubliette; I pressed the advantage, taking him by the shoulder and plucking the sketchbook from his pocket. "*She* is not philosophy," I growled. "*I* am not an ethical question. I will not risk my existence to satisfy your curiosity."

"You think that's all it is?" He wrenched out of my grip, wiping blood from his face, but I wasn't in the mood for questions.

Taking Cook by the arm, I flipped through the book to the map of the sewers—could he use it to reach the ship if I went on to find Dahut? "Come, James." I shoved him in front of me, up the stairs. "We have to hurry."

"I'm sorry," Mr. Hart said, but that's not what stopped me in my tracks. Rather, it was a sound—a little click, like the second hand of a clock, slicing time.

My throat went dry. Very slowly, I passed Cook the sketchbook. He stared at me, bewildered, but he took it. "Go to the ship," I whispered to him. "Nix will meet you there."

"Don't move," Mr. Hart warned, his voice echoing up the hollow well.

Slowly, I turned to face him. His chin was high, his arm raised, and the barrel of the gun a silver iris around a deep black pupil. It was a familiar sight, but not exactly the same as it was in Hawaii—his pale face was paler still, and his hand actually shook as it held the pistol.

And of course this time I had no Kevlar vest.

What did I have? Words, nothing else. At least I stood between him and Cook; he might not have hesitated if he was aiming at the erstwhile captain. "Make the other choice, Mr. Hart."

"I'm trying to," he replied. "I can't make the same mistake twice."

I kept my eyes on his face, and I found regret, but no mercy. So I made a little prayer to the god I hadn't spoken to in years: *just get James to safety and no more drinking, as long as I live.*

Which might be the case, either way.

I took a deep breath. "Cook?"

"Yes?"

I sprang toward Mr. Hart. "Run!"

CHAPTER
TWENTY-SEVEN

As soon as Blake and Kash were out of sight, I regretted letting them go without me. Parting was neither sweet nor sorrow, but a deep unease riven with fear. But it was the only rational choice—I knew that. And I had my own job to do.

I raced from the ship to the castle. Overhead, the sky was a faultless blue, but inside me . . . a storm. My feet pounded, my heart raced, my thoughts churned. Breathless, agitated, I slowed only when I reached the suites and heard my father's hearty laughter behind the door. It was so incongruous that it gave me pause. I entered the parlor as it faded, and all eyes turned to me.

Then I stopped on the threshold. The crew was sitting there by the fire, and Crowhurst and Dahut were with them.

"Ah, Nix!" Crowhurst stood; I took a step back involuntarily. "Seems like the dog ate quickly."

"The dog?" I tried to catch my breath, to slow my heart, all while a little voice screamed in the back of my head. Here before me, my unmaking. I stared into the abyss of his eyes. "The dog. Right. Yes."

Crowhurst cocked his head. "I came to apologize," he said then. "I shouldn't have yelled at you on the docks. Please forgive me."

"Sure. Of course." I took a deep breath and reminded myself to blink. "I shouldn't have taken your yacht."

"It's quite all right, really. I borrowed a car or two when I was young." There was a twinkle in his eye, and he glanced at Slate then. "Your father was just telling us a story about your last time on a powerboat."

"Remember, Nixie?" Slate still had tears in his eyes, and his face was split in an easy grin. He was sprawled back on the chaise like a great cat, his head in my mother's lap; I had never seen him so relaxed. "You were, like, ten, and so small the Coast Guard cap was slipping down over your forehead. I still don't know why I agreed to let you drive."

"Because you knew she'd be good at it," Bee said.

"And I was right!" Slate laughed again. "Too bad about that buoy, though!"

Crowhurst chuckled along with him, and my nerves

jangled like a broken bell. But I tried to return their smiles, to slow my heart, to keep my fists from clenching. Thinking back to that day helped; the memory was calming. That had been just before Bruce was bumped to dispatch for drinking on the job. "I didn't run anything over this time," I said, which was only barely true. I glanced at Dahut, but she wouldn't meet my eyes.

"Just a little joyride, I'm sure. But you seemed troubled at the docks," Crowhurst added. "It was only on the walk back that I realized why. I know you're worried about the myth playing out."

Rotgut raised an eyebrow. "The myth?"

"It's nothing to worry about," Crowhurst said. "But I'll keep a closer eye on Dahut in the future. I'm wearing the key to the gates now." He reached up and tapped his chest; beside the flask, the key hung around his neck. "She won't get hold of it again. Will you, Dahut?"

She looked up from her hands then, and my heart sank. Her eyes were glassy—all recognition gone. "No, Father."

"Right." The word barely made it past my lips; I cleared my throat. "Are you okay, Dahut?"

Her brows furrowed. She looked to Crowhurst for an answer, which he gave. "Unfortunately, she's had another of her spells. I think the exertion aboard the boat did her in."

"I see." I tried to school my expression, but he was still watching me. So was Lin, I realized with a start; when I met her gaze, she raised an eyebrow very slightly and sipped her tea.

"One more thing," Crowhurst added then. "This may be an odd question, but you wouldn't have seen a little book with a red cover, would you? It might help her remember things."

I opened my mouth, but I couldn't think of a lie. Crowhurst narrowed his eyes. "I . . . I saw it on the yacht," I blurted out. "On the bench. She left it there."

"Strange. I didn't see it."

"Maybe in the cockpit? I can't remember. But I did see it on the yacht."

"Well. I'll send down to the harbor. She hates being without it." He rocked a little on his heels, his gaze steady, piercing. Inside my boots, my toes curled. Then he and I both looked over at Lin's sharp intake of breath. She curled her arms around her belly and bent her head, wincing.

Slate sat bolt upright. "Lin, baby, you okay?"

"Apologies," she said then, her voice breathless. "I think I need to rest," she said, turning to Crowhurst. "Do you mind?"

"No, certainly not." Now he was the one who looked flustered. He took Dahut's arm and went to the door.

"Shall I have the servants bring anything?"

Lin only shook her head, her expression pained. But when Crowhurst left the room, her brow smoothed. She straightened up and brushed back her hair.

My eyes widened, admiring. "You could tell?"

Bee rolled her eyes. "Everyone could tell, my girl."

Slate frowned. "Tell what?"

"There's something wrong," Lin said, setting down her tea. "What happened, Nix?"

I took a breath. Where to start? "Crowhurst kidnapped James Cook to try to change the past."

My words were met with a fragile silence. Slate was the first to break it. "Who?"

"The first European to map Hawaii! Crowhurst is trying to stop him from doing it. He has him locked up in the pit below the castle."

Slate leaped to his feet. "What the hell?"

"That's why Crowhurst wanted us to stay." My face felt hot, flushed. "He wanted to see what would happen to me. Or to Lin."

"I'll kill him," Slate said, rolling up his sleeves, the tattoos writhing as he flexed his arms. "I'll choke him with that ugly chain he wears."

Bee grunted her approval as she sat back on the chaise, stroking the scar at her throat. "Best not to leave enemies at your back."

Rotgut waved a hand. "Excuse me, but wouldn't it be best to focus on rescuing Cook?"

"Blake should be bringing him to the ship right now.

Lin frowned. "And Kashmir?"

I closed my hand around the pearl pendant of my necklace. "Kashmir was going to try to rescue Dahut."

Rotgut nodded. "If anyone can rescue a princess, it's Kashmir."

"On a normal day," I said. "But I don't think Crowhurst will let her out of his sight."

"And we have to get Cook out of here," my father said, his voice urgent.

"There's something else—" I began, but Slate swore again. I bit my lip, glancing toward the rippled window, to gauge the height of the sun. "It's like Crowhurst said. I think the myth is ending."

"What the hell does that mean?"

"The myth of Ker-Ys, Dad. The flood." I swallowed—the thought was chilling, especially with Kashmir still wandering around the castle. "Gwenolé couldn't get past the edge of the map, so she's on her way back to the city. And there's a storm coming—if the story ends as written, Dahut will open the gate at high tide."

"I thought Crowhurst changed all that," Slate said.

"He thought he could, but there's no evidence it's even possible."

"Evidence?" Lin cocked her head. "Look around. Everyone here will tell you a story about the time their fortunes changed."

I followed her gesture—to Rotgut, who'd come aboard to escape the expectations of his former life; to Bee, who'd avenged her wife with Slate's gun; to my father, who'd lost my mother and found her again. "But it's not a fortune," I said, still unsure. "It's myth. It's history."

"Yeah?" Slate stood. "And who writes history, Nixie?"

"The victors," I said. I knew the quote.

"Damn right," Slate said. "Who cares what history says, or fate or fortune or whatever? We're going to fight it, and we're going to win."

"Right," I said softly, trying to believe it the way my father did. I had to, didn't I? That was the most important part. "Right."

"So what's the plan, then?" Bee said.

I straightened my shoulders, galvanized. "We've got to get back to the ship and make ready to sail. Kash and Blake will meet us there with Cook and Dahut. Then we'll make a brief stop in Boeotia before bringing Cook back to London."

"Why Boeotia?"

"Crowhurst erased Cook's memory," I said. "The cure is there."

"Fine," Slate said, waving away my explanation; he'd never been one for complexity. "Do you have a map of Cook's era?"

"It's his native time. He'll take the helm through the Margins, and we should arrive right back in London."

"Right. Okay." Slate grinned at me. "Good plan."

"Thanks, Dad."

He stood then, clapping his hands together. "Are we ready?" Without waiting for an answer, he strode across the parlor and yanked the door open. But in the hall, two guards turned to face him with stony stares and crossed pikes.

They had not been there before.

Slate looked them up and down. "Get out of the way, dammit."

"No one leaves," said the one on the left. "Order of the king."

My stomach turned to ice. Why had Crowhurst sent guards? What had happened to Cook, to Blake, to Kashmir? But Slate cursed again and slammed the door. "Where is Kash when you need him? Anyone else have a knife?"

Lin gave Slate a stony look. "You're not going to brawl to the front gate."

"Fine," he muttered, crossing the parlor. "Plan B?"

I folded my arms, trying to tamp down on my fears. But I had to think—two guards at the door—and how many more between the suite and the front gate? If only I'd kept the gun. Was there a solution from the myths I knew? My mind threw me ideas like a dealer throws cards. Sleeping powders or potions . . . even the Tarnkappe, the Welsh cloak of concealment. But all of my maps were on the ship. I had no way to Navigate to the Isle of Britain, much less back again. How could I—

The crash of glass shattered my reflections. Slate was standing by the broken window, glaring down. Standing by his shoulder, I peeked into the bailey, thirty feet below. Guards were gathering around a battered chair, shards of glass glittering in the light of their torches.

Slate gave them the finger and stalked away from the window. "Plan C then," he said to me. "You can do this one."

Outside, the sky was thick with massing clouds, nearly obscuring the sun. Cold wind from the open window whipped my hair around my face, and I could hear the distant sound of the waves rising against the walls. A selfish thought—maybe it was best that Crowhurst was keeping an eye on Dahut and the key to the sea gates.

Disgusted with myself, I turned from the window. What did we have to work with? I could Navigate away, as could Slate, but that didn't help the rest of the crew—nor would I be willing to leave Cook and the boys behind.

But perhaps they were already back at the ship—or at least out of the castle, in the sewers. . . .

"There's a way through the sewers if we can just get everyone to the cellar."

Rotgut cocked his head. "What, like a tunnel?"

"It leads down to the dock."

He grimaced, half amused. "Well. There's a much closer entrance than the cellar."

"What do you mean?" I followed his eyes to the door of the little room off the parlor that concealed the water closet. "Oh. Oh god, gross."

Still, it was the best option we had. I went to the door to look inside. The room was small and square, furnished only with the primitive toilet—a polished board with a cut-out in the center—and a set of wooden hooks for robes. It was medieval custom to hang one's best dresses in the water closet—the garderobe, they called it—in the hopes the smell would keep moths away. Here, the twice-daily tides prevented much smell, thankfully. I peered down through the seat into the dank circular hole that was, indeed, an entrance to the sewers. Below that, the light faded; it was a long way down.

Slate stove in the seat, the boards falling away into the dark, and Bee, Rotgut, and I stripped the bedding from each room, ripping it to long shreds and weaving the pieces into a thick rope. We worked as quickly as we could—we had to get out before the sea gates opened and the tide filled the tunnels—but it was equally important to make sure the rope was sturdy.

I listened for the bells that tracked the tide as it rose and began to fall again, and I breathed a little easier when high tide passed without incident. The sun was far below the horizon by the time we finished the rope, but after that things went fast. The crew was used to clambering over the rigging. Lin was the only one who needed help, so Slate went down first, boldly into the dark. Once he shouted the all clear, we pulled up the rope, made a harness for her, and lowered my mother down into his waiting arms.

The rest of us followed, trying our best to avoid touching the dank scum on the stone walls. It wasn't hard to recall the map that Blake had drawn, and I led the crew quickly, safely through the tunnels. I could hear the washing of the waves on the gates, and I envisioned a wall of water sweeping us away any moment. When we emerged at last from the warehouse, relief flooded through me.

Overhead, the clouds were dark and lowering; the wind was knotting them into a storm. The harbor was dark, the fishermen nowhere to be seen—only a fool would brave this sea in a skiff. But the wharf was not entirely deserted. As we approached the *Temptation*, my heart stuttered at the sight of the man standing on the stern. I recognized his face from paintings—the hooked nose, the piercing eyes.

I realized then that I'd held out a slip of hope that I'd been wrong about Crowhurst's plot, that the responsibility of rescuing Cook would not fall to me. One of the greatest navigators to have lived—a man who found worlds only to help destroy them. Had Blake been right? Should we have left him in the pit? I could not risk it—but I was not proud of that fact.

As we reached the gangplank, Slate recognized him too,

and his feelings were much less mixed. "Good goddamn," he said as came down the pier. "Captain Cook!"

Cook regarded Slate, confusion on his face. "Why does everyone call me captain?"

"Aren't you?" Slate turned to me. "Isn't he?"

Before I could explain, the tidal bells began to ring. A deep rumble juddered up through the belly of the ship as the gates ground open, and the wind barged into the harbor. On the horizon, the sky was a threat the sea would make good on. Even at low tide, the swells were strong. But as I scanned the black water, squinting, I saw them: the *Fool's* ghostly lights.

She'd held back, away from the walls—a safe choice in the gathering storm, with the currents and the tides driving at the rocks. Would Gwenolé come into port now that the gates were open? But this was not a time to wait and wonder. I turned to Cook, who stood on the deck beside me, watching the sea with awe. "Where are the boys?" I asked him.

"Who?"

"Blake and Kashmir. The boys who rescued you. Where are they?"

Cook turned to me, his eyes hollow. "Last I saw, one had shot the other."

CHAPTER
TWENTY-EIGHT

KASHMIR

The pain was deeper than a blade—raw and shocking, and it did not fade, even when my arm went numb. And there was a strange feeling in my chest, a heaviness, as though I couldn't catch my breath. But the bullet had only hit my shoulder—nothing vital, or so I hoped. I clung to that as I gritted my teeth, curled on a bed of gold.

I could still hear the roar of the gun echoing in my ear, and strangely, Mr. Hart's voice.

"My god," he had whispered. "My god."

But he was gone now. Wasn't he? Run off after Cook—but not right away. He'd waited long enough to take my picks and close the manacle around my ankle. At least he'd bound my shoulder, staunching the flow of blood. Still, I was dizzy . . . light-headed . . . cold . . .

I wished I could get his voice out of my head.

But wishing did little good. I gathered my strength and struggled up to one elbow, gasping as fresh blood soaked the binding. After the dizziness passed, I searched for something I could use on the manacles. Pawing through the pile of treasure, I tossed aside diamond-crusted rings and opals like eggs; I would have traded it all for a bent pin. I was so focused on the search that I didn't notice Mr. Hart's return until he spoke.

"Looking for something, Mr. Firas?" His voice drifted down from the stairs.

"A key." I didn't bother looking up. "I can't let your smug face be the last one I see."

Mr. Hart didn't laugh—but behind him, Crowhurst did. "What about mine?"

I sprang to my feet, and immediately regretted it. Bending double, I tried to catch my breath. Out of the corner of my eye, I could see them both, and Dahut too. Hopeful, I lifted my face, but her own was blank, and a little afraid. It was then that I recognized the strange, heavy feeling I'd had. It was despair.

"It won't be either of us," Mr. Hart said softly. "Miss Song will come back for you."

"I know it," I said. "But she's smarter than the two of you together. She'll find a way to get Cook to safety first."

Crowhurst only smiled. "She's a worthy opponent. A true queen." He took the crown from his own head and put it down on mine. "But now I have her king."

Painfully, I straightened my back, so I wasn't bowing before him. For good measure, I spat at Crowhurst's feet. He only made a face.

"One more thing," he said calmly, pulling a handkerchief from his pocket and using it to wipe his shoe. As he did, his keys jingled in his pocket. "Mr. Hart told me you have my daughter's diary. She'd like it back."

"I don't know what you're talking about," I said, angling my body slightly, as though trying to hide the location of the book.

"Where is it?"

I spat again, and he lost his temper, bulling into me. The pain rattled my teeth, but I pretended to flail as he searched my pockets. Finally he found the diary, pulling it free and shoving me away. I fell, not entirely by accident, but I was breathing hard now. That was not a trick.

Mr. Hart crouched beside me, his hand soft on my shoulder as he adjusted the binding—the tenderness of his touch offended me. "Why are you doing this?" I asked through gritted teeth.

Crowhurst laughed. "You couldn't understand, even if I explained."

"I wasn't asking you." I looked up into Mr. Hart's face, but he wouldn't meet my eyes. "How can you risk sacrificing the ones you love for a cause?"

"I don't love her," he said, and even though the light was low, I saw the shame on his face.

"I don't believe that."

"Then you should understand why I have to try, Mr. Firas."

"Why don't you tell me?"

I saw his jaw clench, then he sighed. "If this works I'll know if . . . I'll know what's possible. And maybe . . . just maybe I can make my own version of paradise."

"A heavy price, for a shot in the dark." I tried to smile.

"What is? Death?"

"Betrayal. There's a poet with your name who said something wise. It's easier to forgive an enemy than to forgive a friend."

He stiffened, standing. "I didn't ask for your forgiveness."

"Then I don't fear disappointing you." I watched as he

followed Crowhurst and Dahut toward the stairs, the light fading away like an ember flying up from a fire. I called after him, wanting to sound brave, but my voice rose like a ghost, soft and insubstantial. "Let's hope you live long enough to regret this."

CHAPTER
TWENTY-NINE

Inside me, rage exploded, and a wild despair—then it sucked back inward, shrinking, collapsing under its weight into a cold black hole where my heart used to be. "Where is he?" I whispered. "Did he fall, or did he run?"

"I didn't stay to watch," Cook said, shifting on his feet. "He bade me come to the ship. The last I saw him, he was in the treasury."

I turned with the mercury in my pocket and murder in my heart, ready to run all the way to the castle, but my father collared me on the gangplank. Struggling, I nearly fell into the harbor. "Let go of me!"

"Where are you going?"

"To Kashmir!" I lunged again, but Slate lifted me off my feet and hauled me back aboard the ship.

"No, Nixie. Look!" He jerked his chin toward the

plaza. Three figures stood there, wreathed in torchlight, at the mouth of the Grand Rue: Blake, Dahut, and Crowhurst.

Seeing them standing together chilled me; a part of me had hoped Cook was lying, or mistaken—that the gun had gone off accidentally or that whatever argument they'd had, it was over. The alternative was too terrible to consider; I had seen Blake shoot.

"Cast off the lines!" my father called.

"No!" I renewed my struggles, but he only held me tighter as the crew pushed off from the dock.

"Crowhurst has a key to the gates, Nixie. I'm not waiting for him to shut us in."

"I'm not leaving without Kashmir! You said I should fight, let me fight!"

"Not with your fists!" he said, swinging me around. But then my mother came to stand beside me, and her voice was soothing.

"Make a plan, Nix. Think it through."

It was nigh impossible to think about anything but Kashmir, but the *Temptation* passed through the gates and into the choppy water before my father relaxed his grip. I threw off his arms and pressed against the rail, as close as I could get to Kash without diving off the side. Slate still hovered, as though worried I would consider doing just that.

With only Bee and Rotgut at their posts, the ship was unsteady and moving slow. But of course Crowhurst was in no rush—he knew I wouldn't leave. He ambled across the wharf as though taking in the sea air, Dahut and Blake at his side. Once we reached the open water, the three of them were obscured from view by the wall. Was he heading to his yacht? No. I caught sight of him again as they reappeared near the lookout tower.

Did he hope to parlay? The wind herded dark clouds overhead, and the waves smashed themselves against the stones; we were too far away to be heard over the rush and the roar. "We have to get closer, Slate."

The captain gave me a dubious look: the tide was low enough that the rocks at the base of the wall were exposed, shining black and slick with algae, and jagged as broken teeth. "Dangerous bit of sailing," he said.

"Good thing you're such a skilled sailor."

"Promise me you're not going to jump."

"Just bring us around!"

Slate chewed his cheek, looking for a moment like he was going to refuse, but at last he took the helm and brought the ship in toward the tower. We hove to about ten feet out.

Bee was the one to drop the anchor; she threw it over the side like a body. Her eyes were stony as she stared at Crowhurst, and though her voice was soft, I heard what she said. "He better hope there's no need for revenge."

But Crowhurst didn't seem to notice the promise in her eyes—or perhaps he was always brave in the face of danger. He had strolled up to the edge of the wall, and he didn't even look down. "Hello again, Nix!" He gave a cheery wave. "It seems you have something of mine, and I have something of yours! Fancy a trade?"

I bit off a curse. Behind him, Blake and Dahut huddled close in the lee of the tower, trying to avoid the wind. I narrowed my eyes; Blake was not carrying a torch, but Kashmir's little glass lamp, and at his belt hung the knife Kashmir had been carrying. And there was something dark on his sleeve—a stain. Ink? Or blood?

It was only with great difficulty that I stopped myself from launching across the water to strangle him. My own blood pounded in my veins, and I slammed my open palm down on the railing. "What did you do?" My voice seemed high in my ears, too delicate to contain my anger. "What did you do to Kashmir?"

"Nothing permanent—yet." Crowhurst pitched his

voice to carry over the hush of the swirling waves. "We made him comfortable in the treasury. Aside from the manacles, of course. Just bring Cook back and I'll set Kashmir free."

Relief eased the pain in my chest. Kash was alive, at least for now. "That's not much of a bargain," I called back to Crowhurst. "Considering that back in Al-Maas, Kash would have died without me!"

He only shrugged. "He still might."

I clenched my fists, trying to keep a grip on my anger. But I couldn't let Crowhurst get to me. Manacles? There was no lock that could hold Kashmir, not if he didn't want to be held. A grim smile touched my lips. "I very much doubt that," I said, but my bravado evaporated when he drew something familiar out of his pocket.

"Here, then. Blake gave me these, but I'm sure Kash would prefer you have them." Crowhurst tossed the bundle toward me, underhand; it landed near my feet with a clink. Kashmir's pick set. My heart sank. "Something to remember him by."

A hole opened up in my chest, like a burn through a page. Beside me, Bee slapped the rail. "How could you betray your brother?" she cried, but her voice was lost in the wind.

Still, Blake understood. In the light of the lamp, I saw his jaw clench, but his shame wasn't enough. I wished I had a basilisk's gaze, to strike them all down dead. My blood boiled like venom in my veins; I spat my words like poison. "After all that about the blood of innocents, Blake? This won't scrub clean so easily!"

There was misery in his voice. "Are any of us truly innocent, Miss Song?"

Crowhurst laughed. "Don't be angry, Nixie. You've been a worthy opponent. But it seems I've won the game."

"A game?" I stared at him—but that's what he'd written in his logbook. Moves and countermoves. If this was a game to him, I had to be smart. Lin was right. I had to think it through. Cure Cook. Save Dahut. And Kashmir too, of course.

But how? Every move I made, Crowhurst was already ahead of me. How could I play against him if he held all the cards? He'd been planning for months, he'd said. At least since New York.

No . . . not New York. Boeotia.

Damn the man. He'd given me the hint last night. He'd told me himself: he'd met another Navigator there.

I spun on my heel, striding back across the deck. "New plan."

"Good," Slate muttered. "This one wasn't going so great."

"Thanks, Dad," I said drily. "Can you give Bee the wheel? I'm going to need your help."

"With what?"

I knew what I had to do, but it was hard to say aloud. "I have to go to Boeotia."

He stared at me, shocked. "You'd leave without Kashmir?"

The pain at his words was physical—like a punch to the gut: it took my breath away. "I'm coming back. And I'll need you to stay here. I'll have to Navigate to the ship when I'm done."

"To the ship! You haven't got a map, Nixie."

"Not yet. But I'm guessing you still have some needles?" I watched as understanding dawned on his face. My father wasn't a cartographer, but he'd done dozens of tattoos.

"Yeah. Okay." He scrubbed one hand through his hair and sighed. "Come to the cabin."

"I'll meet you there."

He called to Bee and handed off the wheel while I went down to the galley to get a canteen for the Mnemosyne water. Then I climbed back above to find Slate, but I stopped dead when I ducked inside the cabin. Lin was there too. The sight of her still brought me up short, especially here on the ship.

Had she ever stood on these boards? Lin had never

sailed with Slate—I knew that much. Joss had forbidden it. But though she looked out of place in my eyes, she seemed completely at ease. I went to the desk, to try to study the map of Boeotia, while Slate rummaged in the bottom of his sea chest, handing her materials. But I could feel her eyes on me, and finally I turned. "What is it?"

She smiled a little. "I think you're a fighter and a lover."

"Come, Nixie." Slate folded his long legs and sat on the floor, arranging his tools beside him—a bottle of India ink, a pen, a pencil, and a needle and thread. I shrugged off my cloak and sat cross-legged before him. Rolling up the sleeve of my shirt, I exposed the soft flesh of my inner arm.

"Do it here," I said. "Where I can see it."

"Are you sure you don't want me to just draw?" He pushed the back of the needle into the eraser and started to wind it with thread.

"You don't just draw, Dad." I glanced at his hands, at the ink peeking out from under his sleeves. "This is my way home. It has to be right."

"Okay." He wet his lips. I could tell he was nervous, but he uncapped the pen and laid my arm across his lap. "Top down? How big?"

I held my thumb and forefinger about three inches apart.

He nodded and bent his head over my arm. The pen tickled my skin as the outline took form: an almond shape, graceful, with circles for the masts and a square for the hatch. The *Temptation*, in simple lines, clean and clear. My father's hands were surprisingly steady. I grunted, pleased. "This is good."

"Good. That was the easy part."

Slate popped a match to life, heating the needle till it gleamed. As the smoke danced snakelike in the air, Lin took a bottle from her pocket. "Here," she said, uncorking it. "I took it from Rotgut."

"What is it?" I said, wrinkling my nose.

"He said it was like gin."

"Good," Slate said, reaching for the bottle, but Lin yanked it back. "For my hands, baby," he said, wounded. "Christ." She narrowed her eyes, but she gave over the bottle.

He poured it over his hands, and then splashed some over my arm. Finally he handed it to me and I took a swallow. Whatever it was burned like fire. "That is *not* gin," I wheezed, looking at Lin. She only shrugged.

"He said it was *like* gin," she reminded me, but already the fire in my throat had faded into a warmth in my stomach. I lay on the floor with my arm across Slate's lap; my other hand found Lin's. My father uncapped the ink, placing it down beside him, fussing with the position of the bottle. His preparations seemed to take forever, and as I waited, a fear crept in. What if this didn't work? What if the map wouldn't bring me back to the ship, and I never saw any of them again? Not Slate, not Lin . . . not Kashmir . . .

I had been dreading the pain, but when the first spark of it lit up my arm, I was grateful for the distraction. In the silence of the cabin, I could almost hear the skin—my skin— breaking with a little *pock*. Tears squeezed out the corners of my eyes; the motion of the needle was sharp and snappy. The gin didn't seem to be helping much at first, although after a few minutes, the pain ebbed a little. I sighed, and Slate barked a laugh.

"What?"

"Endorphins? The natural high. Nothing. Sorry."

"It's fine." There was shame on his face, behind the humor. I squeezed his hand; it was so warm. The fear was creeping back, nestling against me like a cat. "Dad . . . if this doesn't work . . ."

"It will."

"How do you know?"

"It has to." He spoke with the surety that always used to infuriate me; why was it comforting now? "You love him," he said then, and I did not deny it. "And he loves you. I can tell. I know what love looks like."

I grimaced at his old refrain, but he didn't see my expression—his eyes were on Lin. He gave her a crooked smile, and she leaned into his shoulder. I saw it then. The look of love.

Kash had looked at me like that. Had I watched him with the same longing on my face? It was beautiful, it was terrible—and I knew now, how Slate had done what he'd done, and why. And in that moment, all was forgiven.

I couldn't watch them too long, so I averted my eyes. Then I caught a glimpse of the flesh of my arm, dotted with ink and blood where he'd gone too deep. My stomach roiled. "Right," I gulped. "Keep going."

He did, but now the fear had wrapped itself around me in coils that tightened with each breath, like the serpent Dahn, corseting the world. What would I do if I could not return to the ship with the cure?

We had Cook. If time ran out, Slate could always help him steer the ship through the Margins. At the very least, he could get back to his native time. Perhaps once James was aboard the *Friendship*, he'd prove a quick learner. And if we all somehow survived, I could meet the *Temptation* back in my own native time—Honolulu, 1884. Surely my father could find a map to bring the ship there; all I'd have to do to meet him was walk through the Margins at the edge of the map of Boeotia.

But what of Kashmir? His face swam before me, his careless grin at contrast with the intensity of his eyes. If I lost him . . . if I lost him . . .

I could not follow that thought to its conclusion—it was a golden thread through a winding maze, at the center of which lurked something more terrifying than any minotaur. How had it come to this? I had spent so much time trying to escape the monster, but I was already trapped in the labyrinth. Like Theseus, I had claimed my birthright, and the route ahead was fraught with peril.

"It's done."

Slate's words woke me, as though from a dream. My breath hitched in my throat as I sat up and looked at my arm. The skin was raised, but the line was thick and dark, red and black—the ship a part of me, like it always had been. And suddenly, I was certain, at least, about this map. No matter where I was, it would bring me home. "Thanks, Dad."

"Don't worry about it." Wiping his hands on his shirt, he gave me a half smile, but his eyes were troubled as he helped me to my feet. Then, suddenly, he wrapped his arms around me. "I told you the other night I'd do anything to help you," he whispered into my hair. "I meant it, Nixie. I hope you know that. I hope you know how much I love you."

The fierceness in his words gave me pause—but though my arm was throbbing, I hugged him back tightly. "I love you too," I told him, and I could feel him smile.

Finally he released me, and stood alone on unsteady legs. I clenched my fist a few times; my skin tingled, but the sharp pain had already faded to a dull ache. Then Lin pulled the bottle of mercury from the pocket of my cloak and anointed my arm with a few drops of quicksilver; soon enough, even the ache had faded. When we opened the door, the crew turned to look at me. Bee smiled tightly. "Did you flinch?"

Slate put his hand on my shoulder. "She didn't."

I took a deep breath of the fresh cold air. It cleared my head. I felt galvanized, strong—but the greatest challenge was still ahead. Morning was not far off. Twilight struggled through dark clouds. The tide had risen; the water licked up the wall. Farther out to sea, the storm was building; the *Fool* had closed in on Ker-Ys. Could the flood be far behind?

I made my way toward the bow, as far as I could get from Crowhurst, from the city—from Kashmir. But I would be going farther still. I'd studied the marble map closely. Still,

I'd never Navigated without the ship propelling me through the Margins, and I did not want to have the time to hesitate, to think of what I might be leaving behind. So I stood on the beak of the prow. Below me, the red-haired figurehead gazed with wooden eyes over the foam-flecked surface of the Iroise: a starry midnight, endlessly deep. The wind cut through my thin shirt, and the sea swirled like a galaxy between the ship and the wall, dashing itself into spray. But I did not look back, and the mist began to glitter in the air like frost.

"Where are you going?" Crowhurst called as the fog rolled in. "You can't leave! You can't!"

Ignoring his frantic cries, I faced the wilderness of the sea. Nothing could hold me here. Not even Kashmir. I had to leave everything behind. Everything, everyone. I stared at the dark horizon until my eyes watered; I took a deep breath, and another. The mist was thick enough to choke me; I drew it close as a shawl—or a noose—until I could no longer feel the cold of the northern sea.

On Parnassus, the white lime was shining in the heat of the Mediterranean sun. On the breeze, was that the iron tang of the sirocco? The shush of the waves had faded to the sound of wind in the laurel leaves.

I closed my eyes and dove off the edge of the ship.

CHAPTER
THIRTY

I fell.

And kept falling, much farther than the distance from the deck to the water.

I had half a moment to worry that I'd fall forever, but then, in a burst of bright white light, I hit the ground.

My shoulder connected first, with a clumsy crunch. I tried to roll forward, like Kash would have, but something in my neck twanged and I would have screamed if I had the air. Instead, I grunted as I flopped onto my back. But I was still falling—sliding in a shower of pebbles down a hillside. I scrabbled at the soil, tearing a nail on a rough stone, digging my fingers into the gravel, and finally grinding to a stop with my hip against a shrub made almost entirely of thorns.

I lay there, panting in the sudden warmth, my eyes

turned to the faultless blue sky. Stones still rattled down the slope below me. Finally they found their rest, and there was silence. I coughed as the dust settled at the back of my throat. The heavy air was herbal and syrupy on my tongue, from the plants I'd crushed, and something dead nearby. Far above me, a pale buzzard floated on the updraft. To my right, a tiny amphisbaena encircled an anthill, two tongues flicking out of both heads.

I sat up slowly. My shoulder throbbed and my palms were bloody; good thing Slate hadn't drawn the ship on my hands.

The ship. With a start that sent another trickle of stones skittering, I pushed back my torn and filthy sleeve, but the tattoo was intact. Next I patted my pocket—the canteen I'd brought was still there. I rolled the shirt back down, letting my hand linger over the ink as I tried to get my bearings.

The slope was dry and steep; bees hummed in pockets of dusty thyme, and where there was grass, it was short and sparse. Behind me, the ground rose toward towering cliffs the color of chalk, shining in the relentless sun. Down below, the slope ended in a copse of green trees from which flowed a silver ribbon of water. In the valley, the Herkyna unspooled through a town where the priests of the oracle presided at

the temple and over the pits, where the bones of the sacrifi-
cial animals were cast down.

But the pools were in the woods, somewhere near
Trophonius's cave. Gingerly, I pushed myself to unsteady
feet and started down the slope.

It was hard not to hurry, even though I knew that time
was not passing in Ker-Ys. I took careful steps on a meandering path around scree and scrub, my eyes half on the
shifting ground, and half on my surroundings. Where was
Crowhurst? If he was nearby, he must have seen the dust
and the gravel of my dramatic arrival, but although there
was no cover on the mountainside, I could not see him
anywhere.

Perhaps I would not see him. Perhaps he'd only seen me
and run. Part of me hoped so as I made my way down the
rocky slope.

But why was I afraid of him? When had he begun to
loom so large in my thoughts? Here and now, at the beginning of our story, I might finally know more than he did.

The sun rode heavy on my shoulders; I bent under the
weight of it, like Atlas under the pillar of the sky. Sweat
trickled down my neck and burned in the raw skin on my
palms as I slid and stumbled to the bottom, dust still rising

around me. Finally I reached the shade of the trees, and the cool air felt like forgiveness.

I slipped between the twisted silver trunks, blinking as my eyes adjusted to the dim. The thin light shivered in the leaves above my head, and the earth here was sewn with roots and studded with acorns. My feet fell softly on the loam, and I could smell the water, clean as mint.

I heard it too, now, the bubbling of a spring. My steps quickened as I flitted from tree to tree, searching the shadows, but I saw nothing until the trees thinned. There, in a sunny clearing scattered with poppies, the pools gleamed in tiered basins of natural limestone. Between them, the dark maw of the cave gaped black. Crowhurst knelt beside it, dipping his flask into the pool on the right.

Dahut was on the ground beside him.

I hadn't expected to see her, and certainly not like this. She was trussed hand and foot, her cheek against the grass, and as I stared, her own eyes widened. "Help!" she cried. "Help me!"

"Quiet!" Crowhurst whirled, and I pressed myself against the rough bark of a bent oak. Had he seen me? No—I heard his footsteps, hesitant, searching, a few steps one way, and then the other.

"There's someone there," Dahut said, her voice ragged. "A girl."

"Where?"

"She's coming," Dahut said, like a threat. "Help me!"

"No one's bloody coming!"

"She's right there!"

I shuddered like a fish on a line. Would she give me away? I risked a glance, but Dahut was staring into the woods in the opposite direction. Following her gaze, Crowhurst plunged into the trees on the other side of the clearing, crushing leaves beneath his feet. His footsteps grew fainter by the moment, but my heartbeat was so loud that I very nearly didn't hear Dahut whispering. "Please help."

Could I save her now? If I took her from him, she'd never make his maps. Would it prevent my fate or unmake my reality? I still didn't know the answer, but I couldn't just leave her there. Trying to move quietly, I rushed to her side. Beside me, the pools shone like crystal in the sun; cool air flowed from the dark grotto. "I've got you," I said softly, and she started crying.

I plucked at the ropes. They were clearly tied by a sailor, tight and secure—I wished for a knife as I dug my raw fingers into the knots at her ankles. "Are you going to take me home?" she whispered then.

I froze. Had she sipped yet from the Lethe? "Where is home, to you?"

"Raispur. Please keep working," she added. I redoubled my efforts on the knots, my heart beating faster.

"That's in Ghaziabad," I said, my mind racing. "In India?"

"You've been there?"

"It's where Crowhurst was born."

She shuddered. "What's wrong with him?"

"He's mad," I said, but was it true? If he was, so was my father—and so was I. But it didn't matter. I tugged on the last knot; it was loose now. "Almost done. Tell me more about your family."

"My father works for the railroad. My mother—" Her voice broke on the word. "She does mehndi for brides."

"What are their names?" I said urgently. "Give me an address!"

But she did not answer. Her eyes went wide, and I knew what I'd find when I whirled around. "Crowhurst."

He was breathing hard from his run through the woods, and his suit was stained at the knees. Other than that, he looked very nearly the same as he did in his future, in my past. His hair was just a touch shorter, but that was the only difference—or was it? Something in his eyes was different too, something hollow and lonely—a brokenness he had not yet mended or hidden.

Poppies swayed at our feet, and bees zipped in lazy circles around us. Behind me, Dahut kicked against her bindings, the knots growing looser still. Could she get free? Could we stop him now, before it all began? Crowhurst watched me; I could almost hear his own thoughts churning. "How do you know my name?"

How much to tell him? I clenched my fists, my hands still smarting. "We've met. Or we will. I've come to warn you—to tell you not to go to Ker-Ys."

"Ker-Ys?" He frowned. "Where's that?"

"A drowned city, from a French myth . . ." My voice trailed off—had I just planted the idea in his head? I bit down on a curse. What could I say to stop him? If Lin could make up fortunes, so could I. "If you go there, you'll die."

Crowhurst blinked at me. "How can you know that?"

"I've seen the future."

"Have you?" He stepped closer, still peering at me with those empty eyes—but in them now, a spark. "So have I."

Behind him, Dahut leaped to her feet, finally free of the ropes . . . but at the same moment, Crowhurst turned, as if he'd known. Had he? Grabbing her by the shoulders, he threw her face-first into the sparkling pool.

"No!" I dove for her as she thrashed in the water, but Crowhurst dragged me back.

"Didn't see that coming, did you?"

I threw him off. Dahut had pushed herself to the edge of the water, but that blank look was back in her eyes. I backed away, grinding my teeth. Had Crowhurst truly seem the future? More questions—but I only wanted answers.

Before me, Crowhurst grinned. Behind me, the pit of the oracle.

I stepped backward into the dark.

This time the drop was short, and something soft cushioned my fall—a lamb, freshly killed. I swore, scrambling away. The eye still shone, the blood still dripped—a sacrifice. Crowhurst had come for knowledge after all.

Above my head, the circle of light was eclipsed by his figure—a colossus, a dark angel above the tomb. "You think you can learn the secrets of the universe?" he shouted down to me, his voice echoing in the cavern, mingled with the buzzing of bees. "You think you know how the game will end?"

I did not answer, and finally the light returned. I could

see the hive now, humming at the lip of the cavern; bees flew back and forth through the cleft, in and out of the sun, and the ground around me was littered with insects, dead and dying. I had leaped without looking; there was no ladder back to the world above. I wasn't trapped—I could see the map of the ship in the light streaming down—but how would I collect the Mnemosyne water?

My heart was pounding; the tattoo on my arm throbbed with each beat. I took a deep breath. The air was deathly cold and smelled of honey. Perhaps there was a way out through the dark. Peering into the shadows, I could see nothing beyond the circle of sunlight. But this was the cave of the oracle himself. And Trophonius was no wispy seer with a white rag over his eyes. He had murdered his own brother. How would he react to my arrival, and without a sacrifice to offer?

Maybe that would be the only question he answered.

I swore again, softly. Then I froze as a laugh returned, like an echo, from the dark. I swallowed. "Hello?" What else to say? "Ave?" Then I cursed again; that was Latin, not Greek.

The laugh came once more, and a voice, harsh and sibilant. *"Such language."*

My response was immediate. "You speak English?" Irritation overcame awe. "Stop laughing."

Silence from the dark.

"Who are you?"

Silence, again, and the hum of the bees.

So I guessed. "Trophonius."

"Nix."

"How do you know my name?" I waited for an answer, growing impatient. "You're not much of an oracle if you don't answer questions."

"Knowledge takes sacrifice." The voice was almost a hiss.

"What kind of sacrifice?"

Silence in response.

"You won't answer questions without one." No answer. Of course. I bit my lip. "But I have nothing!"

A sigh. Or was it the wind rushing out of the cavern?

I glared into the dark. A sacrifice . . . I crouched, searching for movement on the floor. There. A honeybee, too old to fly, crawling painfully on the earth. The sphinx's riddle came to mind: what has four legs in the morning . . . ?

But I was not here to answer questions. I was here to ask them. I plucked up the bee between my fingers; air hissed between my teeth when the sting came. The creature tore itself apart as the hot pain bloomed at the base of my thumb.

Laughter again. "Was that your sacrifice or the bee's?"

"His death, my pain. Sacrifice is always shared." Wincing, I scraped the stinger out of my flesh. "But I shouldn't answer your question without a sacrifice of your own."

I heard the smile in his voice. "Come closer."

I hesitated only a moment, and then stepped out of the circle of light.

Beyond, the darkness was absolute. Slowly, blindly, I slid my feet forward along the floor of the cavern. It was smooth, polished by water or by hands, but the bodies of insects crunched and crumbled beneath my shoes. The scent of honey coated the roof of my mouth, as thick as though I'd eaten it. The drone of the hive seemed louder in the dark. At my next step, my toe hit something—something rounded and hollow. I froze as it rolled away into the dark, rattling. "What was that?"

When the answer came, I was not surprised. "My brother."

I swallowed. "You kept his head?"

"It seemed only fair. I'm the one who took it."

His voice echoed, seeming to come from nowhere and

everywhere. My eyes skittered side to side, but I could see nothing, nothing but the heavy black. "But why?"

"A sacrifice."

I frowned—that was not part of his legend. "For what?"

"To hide the truth." There was a long silence. Then he sighed. "We were stealing from the king, and my brother was caught in a trap, his leg crushed between two stones. I couldn't save him, but I couldn't leave him—not all of him. We were inseparable. If the king saw his face, he'd know I'd been there too. I remember it so well. The smell of the blood. The sound of his sobbing. He died calling for our mother. I had to saw at the tendons. Stomp on the bones of his neck. The blood on my face felt like tears. His death, my pain. I sacrificed, but to keep secrets, and now I remember . . . everything."

My face twisted in disgust, in pity. "Can't you drink from the Lethe?"

"And forget him? Never. I love my brother." He sighed again, and his voice echoed in the dark. "Seeing the skull reminds me of him."

"You can see in this?"

"It's easier if you close your eyes."

"What is?"

When the answer came, I felt his hot breath in my ear. *"Remembering."*

A hand grabbed my wrist; I screamed and flailed at him, but I didn't connect. Still, he released me, and I stumbled back with a splash. Cold water seeped into my boots as I panted, searching the blackness with unseeing eyes. His laughter echoed through the cavern, shaking my core.

"I didn't come here to amuse you," I shouted, louder than I had to, but my voice was high and scared in the dark.

"A happy coincidence, then," he replied.

I gritted my teeth, trying to slow my racing heart. I'd been wasting time with these questions about Trophonius. What did I really need to know? "Is Crowhurst waiting for me by the pools?"

"He's already fled."

A stab of disappointment—but perhaps it had been impossible, undoing the very circumstances that had brought me here. "How do I get back to the Mnemosyne?"

"You're already there."

I blinked, suddenly very aware of the icy coldness climbing the leg of my trousers. "It's not above?"

"The pools above are Lethe. It is always easier to forget than to remember."

He said it simply, and I believed him. I knelt and dipped the canteen into the pool. Full, it was cold and heavy. I slid it back into my pocket, where it matched the weight of the lock. I paused, turning the next question over in my mind, considering whether or not to ask. "Will I save Kashmir?"

"No."

Everything fell away then, and the air of the cave was not half as cold as the pit of my despair. "Why not?"

"It's not up to you."

"Then who?"

"It's not your fate," he said. "I cannot tell you."

"I don't believe you."

"It doesn't matter."

"I don't believe you!"

"I don't care. Though perhaps it's not the Mnemosyne you want, but the Lethe."

"I will never forget Kashmir."

"I know."

I swore at him. Trophonius was wrong, he had to be. I had not come so far to be foiled—I would find a way, if I had to go down to the treasury and carry Kashmir out myself. Plowing through the water, I returned to dry ground. Where was the mouth of the cave? I could no longer see the light. "How do I get out of here?"

"But . . ." The oracle's tone changed, and a note of uncertainty vibrated in the cavern. "Won't you drink?"

"Why should I?"

"Because if you do, you'll know what will happen."

"With Kashmir?"

"With everything," he said, and his voice low and tempting. "You will know what is possible, what is probable, and what only has a passing chance. What might happen, and what should never. If you drink, your eyes will become open. You will emerge from the dark cave, and all that came before will be like shadows on the wall. You will finally see, and you will know everything."

"Everything?" For a moment, my mind reeled with the prospect of knowledge—of truth, bitter and beautiful. I had chased it for so long. But then I frowned. "Why are you asking whether I'll drink? Don't you know the answer?"

"I know the most likely answer, and the least. But I don't know which you'll actually give."

"So Joss was right. There is a chance to change things." There came no answer—but then again, I had not asked a question. "Did Crowhurst drink?"

When the oracle spoke, I heard the smile in his voice. "What do you think?"

"I think . . ." I swallowed. "I think knowledge takes sacrifice. I already know what I need to."

He laughed again. "And what is that, little girl?"

"Enough to know better. How do I get out?"

He was silent then, for a long time. "The map."

I touched my arm; the sleeve still covered the ink. "But I can't see like you can."

"I told you. Close your eyes."

I did, and there she was, my ship, my home, the memory clear in my mind's eye. My arm itched; the lines of ink seemed to prickle, and then I felt it: moisture on my skin, and the taste of the sea mist over the flavor of honey. The fog was coming.

It was easy to cast aside the cave, for there was nothing there to hold me. The pull of the ship was almost physical; would this be my last time aboard? Once I returned to the *Temptation*, I wouldn't have much time—if I was going to go after Kashmir, I'd have to send Cook on to London without me and trust that Slate could find me later in Honolulu.

But either way, I wouldn't leave Kashmir behind. We had been apart too long already. I was almost eager to face

Crowhurst as the mist curdled around me, condensing on my cheeks, curling in my hair, clinging to my clothes. The temperature dropped in the cave, and gooseflesh rose along my arms. I started shivering as the hum of the bees turned into the roar of the ocean, but something was wrong. The fog continued to thicken until it was impossible to breathe, and at first I thought I was falling again, no, tumbling—*so cold*—not through the air, but through the icy currents of the Iroise.

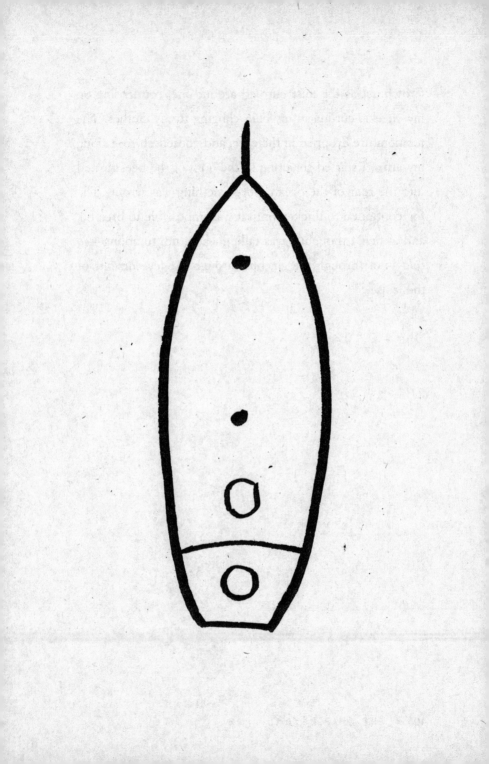

CHAPTER
THIRTY-ONE

I screamed, or tried to, and water filled my throat. I coughed, convulsing, tossed like a fishing boat in a hurricane. The waves pushed, the current pulled. I struggled toward the surface—or toward the ocean floor? I could not tell up from down, I could no more sense gravity than I could breathe, and any moment I dreaded being dashed against the rocks, if I did not drown first.

And then I did hit something—but not stone. The current was sweeping me along the smooth belly of the ship. I scrabbled for purchase with my raw fingers, but the hull was slick—copper clad. Still, I'd felt the curve of her and knew where the surface lay. I fought the current, kicking upward, but the sea was stronger than I was.

Could I take hold of the safety line as I passed the stern? My limbs were already numb with cold. I fought for air, my fingers frozen, lungs aflame, sliding along the back of the ship—then past. My hands swept through icy emptiness; I had never felt more alone.

Was this what Kash had felt, out in the Margins? What he would feel, if the sea took him from me? Despair flooded in, colder than the water.

But then something took my arm.

Claws bit my skin. The hand was scaled—I opened my mouth in shock, and the tide poured in. Yanked against the current, I rose toward the surface, where my grasping fingers tangled in a rope. The strange hand released me as I hauled myself along the line with strength I didn't know I'd had. When I broke into the air, my first breath was more primal than a scream. Shaking water out of my face, I searched for a glimpse of my savior, but the foamy sea gave nothing away.

Then I heard shouting over the sound of the waves. Blinking away the salt, I saw I was holding fast to the *Fool*'s anchor line; she'd hove to beside the *Temptation*. I never thought I'd be happy to see Gwenolé's face.

Oddly, she looked happy to see me too—or at least, satisfied. "She's here!"

At her shout, my father rushed to the rail of the caravel. He grinned, giddy with relief, and hung over the side, calling out encouragement as Gwen herself reeled me in like a fish. As soon as I was close enough to the corvette, I slid my arm through the rung of the ladder that ran down the *Fool's* stern. I was bleeding from five deep scratches in my forearm, but the air was colder than the water and I could hardly feel the wound.

I was coughing now and shivering, too weak to climb up. But Gwen threw down another rope, tied in a loop; I slipped it over my head and under my other arm. With her taking my waterlogged weight, I managed to guide myself up the ladder. At the top, she pulled me over the rail and onto the deck.

I lay like a landed fish, gasping at the grim sky. Clouds boiled overhead as water pooled beneath me. Gwen rubbed some life into my limbs; as blood returned to my extremities, my skin burned. Now my arm began to sting.

"I saw you go over the side," she said to me, and though her voice was brusque, there was concern in her face. "What the hell were you thinking?"

With numb hands, I felt for the bottle of Mnemosyne water, safe in my pocket. "I'm t-t-trying to lift a c-c-curse," I said through chattering teeth.

"By drowning yourself? Hmm." She gave me a twisted

smile. "Maybe I should throw you back into the sea."

I rolled my eyes and tried to sit up. "Throw me b-back to the *Temptation* instead."

"Probably best that way." Gwen helped me to my feet; standing was an excruciating pain. My feet felt swollen but hollow, as though they'd gone to sleep. "You're no kind of captain if you keep jumping ship."

Together, we staggered to the rail; already, her crew was rigging a rope from the *Fool* to the *Temptation*. I took it in my hands, but I hesitated as a realization came. "I can get you past the f-f-fog," I said then. "Back to the Port of London."

Beside me, Gwen stiffened. "How, exactly?"

"All you have to do is let J-James take the helm."

"Who?"

"James Cook. The man who brought you here."

She raised an eyebrow. "That's a tall order."

"It's your only way out," I told her; but that was the wrong tactic. "And I know Slate would consider it a great favor."

"Oh, yeah? Why's that?"

I hesitated—could I tell her? "A life for a life, you said."

"You're telling me Captain Slate's life depends on this?"

"Not his," I said. "Mine. And my mother's."

Gwen folded her arms and glared at me; behind the anger, pain shifted to regret. What kind of person was she, really? For a long time I thought she'd refuse, but then she waved me away toward my ship. "Get off my ship and send him over."

I climbed down to the *Temptation*; my father met me at the rail. "Let's get you out of the cold," he said, trying to steer me toward the cabin, but I shrugged out of his grip.

"No time," I told him, digging my fingers into the stiff pocket of my trousers. With difficulty, I slid the canteen free and handed it to Slate. "For James. Only a little at a time. Stop when he remembers arriving in Ker-Ys. Then send him over to the *Fool*."

Slate took the bottle, but he hovered until Lin shooed him away. She held out my red cloak, settling it around my shoulders—I'd left it in the captain's cabin for my trip to Greece. She'd brought the flask of mercury too. Lin inspected the claw marks on my arm and gently daubed them with the elixir. "What is that?" she said then. "In your pocket?"

I sighed; the throbbing pain in my arm was fading fast. "Kashmir gave it to me."

"A strange gift," she said, turning her attention to my bee sting.

"It's what he had to give at the time."

"You'll have more time with him."

She said it with such certainty—but was it only a made-up fortune? I looked up into her eyes; her expression was serious. "I know," I said softly, hoping that could make it true.

Lin corked the flask of mercury and held it out to me. "You should take this with you too," she said. "If he's hurt, he'll need it."

I blinked at her. How had she guessed I might go to him? Then again, how could she imagine I wouldn't? I gave her a wan smile and slipped the bottle into my pocket. Then I went to the rail to face Crowhurst.

He smiled when he saw me, but there was something behind it, an edge I hadn't seen before. "How was Boeotia?"

"Enlightening." A gust made my wet hair crackle; the wind was so cold, I was crowned in frost. "But you know that. You drank from the Mnemosyne."

"Didn't you?"

I looked at him then—at the glint in his eyes. "The price was too high for me. What did you sacrifice, Crowhurst? What have you lost?"

"Nothing!" he called back, a touch too loud. "I've won, Nixie."

"You knew I could bring the water for Cook."

"I knew you might," he countered. "I also know you won't leave."

"I don't have to. Gwen is taking James back to London. Your gambit failed, Crowhurst. You've lost."

"I still have Kashmir!"

"I don't think Blake will let you keep him just to spite me. Would you?" I turned to Blake, and I saw the answer in his face. I smiled grimly. "In fact, there's only one move left for the both of you, if you want to know if you can change the past."

Blake glanced from me to Crowhurst—he had always had so many questions. "What is it, Miss Song?"

"Let us take Dahut. Now, before the storm. Before the myth has a chance to end."

Dahut shifted on her feet. "What does she mean, Father?"

Crowhurst ignored her. "Why would I do that?"

"Because you can go back to your native time and read the myths about Ker-Ys. You'll know if the legend is altered. You'll know what's possible."

"Go back?" Crowhurst's jaw worked. Was he considering it? His hand went to the flask at his throat—no . . . to the brass key. "I told you. I can't go back, not yet. But I have another move."

"What is it?" I asked, but I had my answer when he pulled the chain over his neck.

"Call Cook back," he said; there was a threat in his voice.

My heart pounded, but I could not do as he asked. "No."

"Kashmir's in the pit, Nixie." Crowhurst gave me a thin smile. "If the town floods, he'll drown first. Are you sure you won't reconsider?"

Blake turned to him, eyes wide. "You would flood the town?"

"Not if she brings me Cook." Crowhurst fitted the key to the lock.

"You can't do this!" I called, but he rounded on me.

"Prove it!" Crowhurst roared. "Prove we can change things, Nixie!"

There was a challenge in his eyes; did he actually want me to stop him? But he was not the one I was trying to save. "You can prove it to all of us!" I cried. "Throw the key into the water!"

But Crowhurst only shook his head.

"Stop him!" I shouted to Blake, to Dahut, to the gods— but my cry was lost in the squeal of the gears.

Underfoot, the mechanism rumbled. Metal groaned as the gates slid open. The pressure from the high tide warped them in their tracks; they ground to a halt a foot apart. But a green waterfall poured through, spilling into the harbor.

The flood was coming.

On the wall, Blake grabbed for the key, but Crowhurst belted him across the jaw. He reeled, sliding down into the lee of the tower. I had to help—I had to close the gate. "Slate!" I screamed over the wind. "Bring us closer!"

"This is as close as I can get!"

Swearing, I ran to the mast, pulling myself up the ratlines, the halyard in my hand.

"What are you doing, Nixie?"

I didn't bother answering—my father knew what love looked like. Stepping quickly to keep my momentum, I teetered out to the edge of the boom; without stopping to think, I leaped, swinging across the gap. There was a moment of terrifying freedom between ship and shore. Then I landed on the wall and stumbled into a run, my bare feet slapping the slick stone.

Spray soaked my legs as I ran. The sea was whipped to a frenzy, the water swirling in spouts and vortices. The harbor was filling quickly. I careened toward the tower. But Dahut was already there.

She put her hand on Crowhurst's arm. "Close the gate!"

He only threw her off. "Bring the yacht to the wall! Quick, before the wharf is covered." Then he frowned, patting his pockets. "Where the hell are my other keys?"

"I won't let you do this," she said, shaking her head. "I won't let them all drown!"

She lunged for the key again, but Crowhurst grabbed her. She twisted in his arms, struggling as he yanked her away from the mechanism. Her eyes flashed and she pushed him, hard—Crowhurst stumbled, catching himself on the very lip of the wall. She dove at him again, but she was so small. They struggled . . . she screamed—

He swung her around and let her go.

She tumbled off the wall and into the harbor.

"Dahut!" I skidded to a stop at the edge, breathless, disbelieving. Below, the green water swirled to white where she'd gone down. At my feet, Blake groaned, but I couldn't tear my eyes from the harbor. Crowhurst stood beside me, panting, both of us watching for a sign of Dahut. Would she surface? I did not see it happen.

But something else splashed in the harbor then, a flash

of silver in the light of the moon. I was watching when the next mermaid slipped through the open gates, her clawed hands gouging the brass as she propelled toward the wharf. She was followed by another, and another. Over the city, the bells of Ker-Ys began jangling an alarm. Then Crowhurst turned to me, and I realized just how alone I was on the wall.

The metal squealed again, the gates sliding open another foot, and the earth itself seemed to shudder as a fresh tide rolled across the harbor. The rising water twisted the fishing boats on their moorings, turning them stern up, like dipping ducks. The docks were already swamped, and silver shapes circled hungrily in the water. Even now the tide would be rising through the sewers and pouring into the room where Cook had been—where Kash was now, without his lock picks, without me.

I couldn't get there in time to free him, even if I could swim through the icy waves. I had to shut the gate. But Crowhurst stood between me and the key, clenching his empty hands. "Maybe you were right," he said then, and his voice was strange and faraway. "Maybe the past can never be changed."

"I didn't say that." I slipped my hand into my pocket. "I just said *you* couldn't do it."

Crowhurst's eyes glittered and in his voice, a warning. "I am a cosmic being."

"You're a madman." I slid my finger through the loop of the lock as my heel wavered on the edge. From the *Temptation*, Slate was shouting over the wind, trying to push the ship closer, but I didn't turn my head. "And you've lost."

"I know I have," Crowhurst said, his voice almost sad.

"So let me close the gate," I said to him, almost pleading. "Let me save Kashmir."

But he only reached for me, and I swung the lock. It connected with a meaty sound. He clutched his jaw and swore, the curse thick on his tongue. I tried to dart around him, scrambling along the lip of the wall, but he grabbed a fistful of my cloak and shook me—my god, he was strong! My toes brushed the stone as he hauled me close to his face; it was twisted with rage. A fleeting thought struck me then: *here* was the monster in the castle. "Just because I lose," he growled, "doesn't mean you'll win."

Out of the corner of my eye, I saw someone leaping the gap from the ship—could they reach me in time? I hit Crowhurst again, but he didn't even seem to feel it. He stepped back, and I clutched desperately at his sleeve, his shoulder. My hand tangled in the chain at his neck as he heaved me toward the sea.

I dragged him to his knees as I fell, one hand on the flask and one scrabbling at the edge of the wall. I let go of the chain and grasped the slick stone with both hands. The high tide pulled at my ankles as I struggled to haul myself up. Crowhurst scrambled to his feet above me. The chain had snapped; the flask slid to the wall and clanged on the stone beside his right foot. As I watched, he lifted his boot above my fingertips.

But then—over the wind, the sound of running feet, and a small shaped barreled into him.

My mother.

They grappled on the wall, he with new fury, and she, fierce but overmatched. Gasping, I dragged myself back up to the wall as he wrapped his hand around her throat. She beat at his chest with her fists, but he did not let go. But then a sound like the crack of a whip, and Crowhurst staggered, eyes wide. Above the red sash he wore, a darker crimson started to spread.

There, in the lee of the tower, Blake was propped up on his elbow, the silver derringer smoking in his hand.

Crowhurst met my eyes—in his own, the shock of loss. He took one step, then another. The third took him over the wall, and my mother went with him.

CHAPTER
THIRTY-TWO

The wind was screaming, and so was I. Out on the water, my father shouted Lin's name as waves rammed the *Temptation*. The ship tilted on the tide, the stern swinging toward the wall; Slate had abandoned the helm to stare down at the clouds of spray, drifting up like smoke.

Bee scrambled for the wheel as it spun freely. But the captain only looked up at me, and the air between us seemed to dim and thicken before my eyes. His words were drowned out by the sound of the waves, but I knew what he said.

Then he leaped over the rail and vanished into the mist.

"Captain!"

I crawled to the edge of the wall. The water eddied and swirled in the fog below. On the wind, was that a siren song?

"Dad!"

There was no sign of him.

"Mom!"

No sign of either of them, as the waves splintered into fog and obscured the furious sea.

My ears rang, echoing with my father's voice. Or was it the cries of the crew? Or Gwen's own grief? Or the distant screams that rang from the town? I did not know, I did not care. This wasn't right, it wasn't happening. He had to surface, and soon—he couldn't hold his breath much longer. Where were they? Where were they?

I rolled to my side and curled like a nautilus. The cold had numbed me, but not enough. Beside me, Crowhurst's broken chain, and the copper flask; it was like a chip of ice in my palm. Starlight glittered on its surface. How much of the Lethe water remained?

A scream brought me back to my senses as the ship loomed out of the mist. The storm was too high, the wall was too close, and with a sound like snapping bones, the *Temptation* drove into the wall.

The rising waves ground her ribs against the rocks. Rotgut had left the sails, using a pole to try to fend off the stones, and Bee was frantically signaling the *Fool*, but there were not enough hands, not with Slate gone, not with Kashmir . . . Kashmir—

In a flash I was on my feet; spinning, I nearly ran into Blake. He grabbed my arms, steadying me—or perhaps himself. "Miss Song!" He squinted at me; his eye was swollen where Crowhurst had hit him. "We must get to the ship."

I stared at him—in his face there was such sorrow, and I rejected it. "No!" Something snapped in me. "Let go of me! Let go!" I shoved him; he staggered back, slipping on the ice on the wall.

"Where are you going, then?" Blake said.

"To save Kashmir!" Out on the water, Rotgut called to me—there was desperation in his voice. But Gwen would help them, wouldn't she? I started toward the stairs.

"Nix!" Blake grabbed my wrist and spun me around. "He's gone!" I followed his stare to the city, the water swirling around the slate roofs of the houses. "He was locked in the pit. He had no picks. The water is ice cold, and you would drown in it too. He's gone, Miss Song."

With a roar, I flung him away and sprinted toward the stairs, but I didn't get far. Blake tackled me to the stones, wrapping me up in his arms and crushing the breath out of my lungs. Kicking, I tried to regain my footing, but he swung me over his shoulder.

"No!" I pounded on his back. "I won't lose him too!"

But Blake did not listen, or if he did, he did not stop, not until we reached the ship. He tossed me to the deck and leaped aboard after me. I landed in a heap.

Scrambling to my hands and knees, I felt the snapping of timbers through my palms—belowdecks, water would be pouring into the hold. The *Fool* had belayed a line to the *Temptation*, and she was ready to haul against the tide. We could not stay longer, or the storm would smash the hull to pieces. But Gwen had Cook; they did not need me to travel. Could I jump back to the wall?

"Let me go!" I struggled upward, pulling myself to my feet against the bulwark. Why was my ankle buckling? "Take Cook to London and let—me—go!"

I put both hands on the rail as another wave lifted the ship from the stones, but Blake yanked me back to the deck. Furious, I wrenched Kashmir's knife from his belt—only then did he back away, hands up, face pale. But the wave withdrew, and the *Fool* swung her sails to catch the gusting wind. With a groan, the *Temptation* shuddered out to sea.

"No!" I rushed back to the rail as the wall retreated. "No!"

"I'm sorry, Miss Song." Blake's voice broke, and he could not meet my eyes. He turned to help Bee and Rotgut with the ship. But I stayed at the rail, screaming wordless rage as Ker-Ys receded. It wasn't right. It wasn't fair. This was not how the story ended.

The wayward saint had returned with her warnings. The devil had opened the gates and cast Dahut into the sea. But the king was dead—who would ride away on the *Dark Horse*?

Crowhurst's question had stayed with me; he had taken Kashmir's lock picks, but where had his keys gone? The key to the treasury, the key to the manacles, the key to the yacht . . .

Kash had them. He must have. I believed it with all my heart. I watched for him, and waited. I knew he was coming. Beneath my feet, the *Temptation* trembled as the *Fool* towed us toward the gathering fog, but I kept my eyes on the sea gates as the city receded. Then Bee took my arm; I spun in shock at the touch.

"Come away, my girl." Her voice was soft with anguish. "The ship is lost."

"What?" Finally I tore my eyes from the flooding city, only to realize the *Temptation* was sinking.

The deck tilted. The sails sagged as if defeated. The ship

sighed and shuddered in her grief. Her prow was already submerged, the carved mermaid figurehead greeting the sea at last. Repair would be impossible; her ribs had been snapped. She was gutted; water poured into the broken heart of her. The ship was going down with her captain.

On deck, Gwen and her crew were helping to salvage our belongings. Sailors scrambled back and forth from the *Fool*, hauling armloads of maps and medicine, books and baubles, crates and clothing. As I watched, Blake abandoned ship, carrying Billie in his arms. Rotgut followed, clutching his old mahjong set. And now Bee was tugging at my hand.

Still holding Kashmir's knife, I let her lead me to starboard side, where the crew of the *Fool* had made fast to the *Temptation*. A ladder hung from Gwen's ship; Bee pushed me toward it, but I shook my head. "Go on, Bee. I'll be right behind you."

She searched my face, and I could tell I hadn't fooled her. "Nix . . ."

"Go," I said again, my voice harsh with grief. "Captain's orders."

Tears shone in her eyes as she pulled me into a fierce hug, but then she released me. Taking hold of the ladder, she climbed free of the wreck, and she did not look back.

So I raised Kashmir's knife and swung it down on the rope binding the *Fool* to the *Temptation*.

The corvette sprang free, leaving the caravel behind, with me aboard.

The captain was going down with her ship.

Off the *Fool*'s prow, I could see the bank of fog beginning to form. I didn't waste my time watching her meet it; instead, I clambered toward the stern, uphill against the slant of the deck. I had to use the rails to climb the stairs. When I reached the helm, I clung to the wheel.

Water crept up toward my feet. Waves broke over the bulwark, turning to a million sparkling stars. On the horizon, the city was nearly lost in the white mist, but I could still hear, very faintly, the ringing of the bells. I ran numb fingers over the bronze: regnabo, regno, regnavi, sum sine regno. I was drenched by the time the waves wrapped themselves around my ankles, and shivering as they rose around my hips.

Still, I didn't let go of the helm, not even as the *Temptation* slipped at last beneath the surface, pulling me down with her. And for a moment, as the icy water closed over my head, I wondered if I could ever let go. But all around me, bubbles rose from the sinking ship, carrying me to the surface. The

Temptation herself still buoyed me up.

I struggled for air even after I broke free of the water; the cold had taken my breath away. Blinking the salt out of my eyes, I scanned the horizon, but saw neither ship nor shore. Panic played tug-of-war with despair, my heart fraying like a rope: the sea was wide and deep, and I was alone.

Like a coward, I longed to escape, to call up the mist and Navigate away. But I had not left Bee and Rotgut only to leave Kashmir as well. Being lost at sea was not the worst fate had to offer.

And Kashmir was coming. I knew it, like I knew the positions of the stars or the pitch of the deck. I did not search for a glimpse of him, rather, I waited—I believed, without doubt, with faith unshakable.

Where was he?

Around me, the waves were flecked with lines of foam, like the starry band of the Milky Way. Treading water, I kept my head above the surface, but the air was even colder than the sea. It wasn't long before I was shivering uncontrollably; it made it harder to fight the waves. I let the next one roll over my head—just to rest for a moment—but when it passed, I was disoriented; it was only when my lungs started burning that I realized I'd been swimming down. I rolled in the water and struggled back toward the steely sky, taking a quick breath, and another—I had to keep my head above the surface.

I closed my eyes. They stung with the salt, an ocean of tears. I was so tired. Then something big brushed my leg, and my eyes snapped open. Was it flotsam from the wreck, or something worse? I panted as a rush of adrenaline hit, and I scanned the waves frantically for a flash of silver, but the Iroise kept her secrets.

Another swarm of bubbles fizzed up from below. I had read about wrecks; I knew what was happening to my ship. As she sank, the water pressure was crushing the cabin walls, releasing pockets of air. My heart squeezed too, and I saw it in my mind's eye—the sea riffling through my books, sweeping through the maps, scattering Kashmir's poems across the blackness of the ocean floor. Lost at sea, lost at sea.

The adrenaline faded. I kept swallowing water, my head sinking beneath the waves. The sea filled my eyes, my ears. Maybe I should have sipped from the Mnemosyne. Joss's voice came back to me: *who you'll marry—how you'll die.* Why hadn't I let her tell me? I couldn't remember now. But perhaps she had been wrong after all. Perhaps I was the one to be lost.

It was a fitting end, to follow the *Temptation* down. After all, I was my father's daughter. The ocean roared; my mother hummed a song—or was that the sound of a motor?

"Kash." My throat was raw with salt and screaming—my voice was a whisper even I couldn't hear. But the hum was louder now; I turned my head this way and that, trying to see the yacht, but the waves were too high. "Kashmir."

Just the one word left me breathless. He would never hear me, and he would pass right by in the twilight. Still, I smiled—or I thought I did. He had escaped. I'd been right. He was alive. I only wished I could have kissed him one more time.

In the water, bubbles rose once more from the wreck below. It pained me to see them, for what destruction was there left to do? But would Kash see the effervescence—a white flag, a beacon? No . . . the wind was high and the waves were skimmed with foam as far as I could see. But then something in the water flashed—not silver, but gold.

At first I didn't understand. I thought it was a star, reflected. But it grew brighter and brighter until it broke the surface: a sky herring, glimmering in the gloom.

She twisted in the air above my head; a slip of light, a slice of the aurora. Another followed, and another; free of the ship, they returned to the celestial sphere, gleaming brightly as they schooled, floating upward like the embers of the pyre of the *Temptation*. The roar of the motor crescendoed in my ears. Then it cut out, and I heard his voice.

"Amira?"

Kashmir hauled me into the yacht, and his hands scorched my skin. I lay shivering on the deck, looking up at his pale face, his wan smile—and the last stars were like a crown in his hair.

"Stay with me," he said, trying to help me downstairs, awkward with only one arm.

"Always," I murmured, still struggling against the dark.

With difficulty, we stumbled below to huddle in the warmth of the cabin, where the clocks swept the future into the past. Kash plugged in the kettle and helped strip my wet clothes. I forced out the words to indicate the bottle in my pocket. He wrapped me in blankets first, and I drifted in and out as he applied the mercury to his shoulder. I could tell by the way he sighed that it was working.

Kashmir brought me a cup of hot water then, and propped me up to drink. "Did they get away, amira? Did they get James Cook to London?"

"I think so."

"But you stayed."

"I'm not going to lose you too." My voice caught in my throat.

Pain flashed across his face. "The crew?"

"Bee and Rotgut are safe aboard the *Fool*. Blake too." It was all I could bring myself to say—but he heard what I had omitted.

"The captain? Your mother? Oh, amira." He wrapped his arms around me. "I'm so sorry."

I buried my face in his chest as the tears came. But Trophonius had told me the truth—saving Kashmir hadn't been up to me. But he was safe. We had each other. And a ship of our own, just like we'd planned.

I sobbed in his arms.

Eventually I ran out of tears, but we lay together on the bunk a long time. I was warmer now, though I had never been so tired. All I wanted to do was sleep, but I couldn't, not with the clocks ticking, ticking, ticking. "I wish you'd stolen one of the fishing boats instead," I murmured.

The joke felt flat in my mouth; still, I heard his smile. "Hard to handle those shorthanded." He sighed then, his chest rising and falling against my back. "What will Bee and Rotgut do after Cook is safe in London?"

"I'm not sure."

"And Blake?" At the name, I stiffened.

"Why do you ask?"

For a while, Kashmir stroked my hair. When he spoke again, I could hear the sorrow in his voice. "Do you think he had to do it?"

"What do you mean?"

"Do you think he was meant to—to betray us? That it's all a part of the way things have to be?" Kashmir propped himself up on an elbow to gaze down at me. "I was supposed to be lost—or . . . or maybe the captain was. One of us, anyway. Joss told you so."

I bit my lip. "She did."

"And if it's all fate, is anyone really at fault?"

"He still made his choices, Kash. He could have tried."

"And what about us?" he murmured into my hair. "Can we choose to forgive?"

"You can do what you like," I said, though my voice was bitter. But his gunshot had healed, leaving not even a scar. My own wounds were fresh and raw. I'd lost everything because of Blake—or nearly everything. My ship, my family, my crew.

Kashmir pulled me close again. But under the blankets,

my hand crept to my arm—the raised flesh of the tattoo of the ship—and I pushed myself up on one elbow. There, on the desk: Crowhurst's maps. I swung my legs out of bed.

"Amira, you need to rest."

I only shook my head. Keeping the blankets wrapped around me, I sank down into the chair at Crowhurst's desk. "He found Cook," I said, searching for our next map. "So can I."

CHAPTER
THIRTY-THREE

Three days later, Kash and I stood on the dock at the Port of London and watched the *Fool* glide into the harbor. Dawn was still struggling through the shroud of gray, gleaming on the oily banks of the River Thames. But the wharf was already bustling, and the gritty air echoed with the shouts and raucous laughter of the dockhands.

The night we abandoned the *Dark Horse* in the Margins, Crowhurst had also arrived in the smoggy Port of London. Kash and I had stripped the yacht of valuables—including a stash of gold he'd grabbed from the treasury—and used some of the odd coins to take a room in a run-down sailor's inn overlooking the dock. From the grimy window, I'd seen Crowhurst approach Cook at the wharf, deploying the full force of his charm. It had been difficult to stand by as my past unfolded, but I didn't want to risk making the other choice; I wasn't sure what sacrifice it might entail.

And now Cook stepped off the *Fool* and onto the muddy wharf. His face was troubled as he took his bearings. I knew why. Passage between France and England was fairly quick through the channel, but not half as quick as passage through the Margins. As he approached, I pulled my shawl up over my face to make sure he didn't recognize me. How would I explain my appearance in London when my last known location was floundering in the Iroise?

But as he passed by, I couldn't help it—I darted after him, reaching out to take his arm. "Your first two voyages," I whispered to him, my voice urgent, my heart racing. "They'll bring you fame and fortune. But if you sent out on your third, you'll die."

Cook wrenched his arm away, reeling, and he met my eyes. For a long time we stood there, and I wondered—had I changed his fate and my own? Had I saved Hawaii and sacrificed myself? Had I fought Crowhurst only to become my own unmaking? But who was I if I didn't try? Finally Cook turned and vanished into the crowd—but I was still whole, and the world unchanged.

Kash caught up with me then, a question on his face,

but I only shook my head and let him lead me back toward the *Fool*. And when he hailed her, I had never before seen nor shed as many tears. Bee howled her joy, as did Billie, and Rotgut started dancing on the deck. Even Gwen clapped me on the back. But Blake stood apart from us, pale as a ghost. "Thank god," he whispered. "Thank god."

It took everything in me not to make his black eye a matched set.

I blamed him still. I could not help it. Was it fair? I didn't know—but in the days that followed, I avoided him. It wasn't hard. There was a lot of work to do. We had to sort our salvage—there were maps and clothes and books thrown together, all grabbed in the mad dash from the sinking ship. But there were valuables too, jewels and baubles, and the crown Crowhurst had set down on Kashmir's head. Kash took the pile to the jeweler's district and came back with a small fortune in coin. "For you, Captain."

The wind rang hollow in my ears, and I spent a while staring at the wealth at my feet. How could I ever replace the *Temptation*? But a captain without a ship was no better than a king without a kingdom, so I gathered the gold with my courage and made some inquiries. It didn't take long to find what I was looking for: a caravel for sale in port. She was light and fast, cleverly made, and her lateen rigged sails reminded me of home. I named her the *Fortune*.

We tried to settle in aboard, with Bee, Rotgut, and Blake in bunks below, and Kash and I in the captain's cabin, where I began to sort through my jumbled belongings. A few books, a paltry collection of maps—less than half of what had been. The Mnemosyne water was there too, wrapped in one of my father's sweaters. I pressed the cloth to my face, but it only smelled of laundry soap, so I used it to wipe away the tears that had started to form. Then I took the flask, turning it over and over in my hands.

Even now, having made my choice, I felt the temptation of boundless knowledge. The bottle wasn't safe to keep, not aboard the ship. I stood for a long time at the dock, considering whether or not to pour it into the sea, but I couldn't bring myself to do it. Instead, I went to the maps.

There wasn't much left, but it was enough. After some searching, I found a map of Hawaii in 1858. When we reached the balmy waters of the Pacific, it felt like coming home. Not in the way of returning to a place of comfort, but rather like seeing a familiar place anew, and gone was the gilded glow of childhood.

We sailed into Honolulu harbor alongside a mail ship as

locals cast flowers into the sea. The soft breeze carried their scent to me—and to Blake, who came up from belowdecks like the mirror image of Persephone: he did not bring life back to the world above, but instead life was brought back into him. The sun gilded his hair and kissed his cheeks, and was that a smile on his lips? I turned away before I could see it bloom, though Kashmir's words echoed faintly in my head. Something about forgiveness.

Whose fault was it, really? If Blake had not betrayed us, we would have gotten away clean. Then again, if I'd never brought us to Ker-Ys, Kash wouldn't have been trapped in the first place—though Cook might have been, and perhaps then the world really would have been unmade. What would I have lost, had I chosen differently? I shook my head. It was dizzying—cause and effect, round and round, stretching back to the source.

I found Joss at her shop in Chinatown, and when I stepped through the door, I was surprised by the tinkling chime of tiny bells. Of course that wasn't the only thing that was different—the last time I'd been here was thirty years in the future. In those days, the shop was a faded apothecary crouched over a hidden opium den, the air redolent with the sickly sweet smell of pipe smoke, the wooden shelves sagging with boxes and jars of pills and powders, and all of it covered in a thin layer of dust.

But here and now, everything was still new. The shop was lovingly kept, swept and dusted. The windows were thrown open to catch the warm trade winds. The red counter shone, freshly lacquered, and the woman behind it was startlingly young, though the gleam in her pebble-black eyes was the same as it always would be.

If I hadn't already known who she was, I would have been able to guess. She stood there holding a cup of tea, looking so much like Lin that tears burned in the corners of my eyes. And the look on her face made it clear she recognized me too—though not for the same reason. In her expression, I saw the memories fall into place like stones into a deep well. The last time she'd seen me was in Emperor Qin's tomb, where she'd been buried alive.

But here and now, I was the one who felt trapped—the knowledge of what had happened, or had yet to happen, was a crushing weight. She saw it. She missed nothing. "You look like you could use some tea."

I nodded as she prepared the cup, taking leaves from a jar on the shelf behind her and pouring water from a pot resting on a stone on the counter. The fragrant, bitter scent filled the air. I took the cup, and she refilled her own, watching me with those bird-bright eyes. "I didn't think I would see you again," she said at last.

How much did she already know? And how much could I tell her? I tested the tea—it was hot, but not scalding—and chose my answer carefully, an echo of her own future words to me. "You will, though this is probably the last time I'll see you."

"Then let me thank you now, while I can. After all," she added, her eyes twinkling. "Who can know what the future holds?"

The words were like a knife in the gut. I looked down, blinking hard, watching the tea leaves settle in my cup. "You seem to," I said at last.

"I know some things," she answered, and I heard the smile in her voice.

My throat was dry. I drained the tea and set the cup down on the counter. Then I drew the flask from my pocket. "I have something for you."

"What is it?"

"Knowledge. I can't keep it, but I think you might be able to."

She lifted the flask to the light. "You trust me with this?"

"I know you—and I know myself."

"Ah." Her smile dazzled me. "Then you're wise already."

I laughed—I couldn't help it—and I realized then, to my surprise, that I liked her. I was still turning over that thought when she spoke.

"You lost someone."

I blinked at her—but Joss was looking down at the tea leaves at the bottom of my cup. She turned the cup around in her hands. "Someone you loved," she added then, looking up through her lashes. "Lost at sea."

Tears welled up in my eyes. "Yes."

She lowered her own eyes and set the cup back down on the counter. "Do you think you'll find him again?"

"I . . . I don't know."

"Will you try?"

I hesitated—not because I did not know the answer, but because I did not want to say it aloud. A smile crept across her lips. "Have another cup, if you like, and maybe I can tell you."

"No," I said then, straightening up. "But thank you." The chimes rang as I passed through the door; as I walked through the streets of old Honolulu, the sound of the bells stayed with me all the way back to the ship.

Blake was still there, standing at the rail; I passed him right by on the way to the captain's . . . to my cabin. Inside, Kash slept on the bunk, a copy of *The Little Prince* held loosely in his hand.

Quietly I went to the table, where our next map already lay—one I'd taken from Crowhurst's yacht: New York, 2016, the lines inked in red. Dahut's version of the map Blake had made. I was studying it when a soft knock came at the door. "Yes?"

The door opened; there was Blake, standing on the threshold, holding Kashmir's Panama hat in his hands. My entire body tensed; I wasn't ready. Still, here he was, at my door, and he did not speak, so I did. "What do you want, Blake?"

He spun the hat as I waited for an answer. "I want to go," he said at last.

"Go where?"

"Home."

"Home?" My mouth twisted. "Where's that?"

"I have no place aboard your ship."

"My ship." My voice broke on the words like waves on a shore. "You want to go back to your own timeline? They'll recognize you from the theft."

"Not if we give it a few years. Say, 1892."

Something about the way he said it—his tone, too casual—made me take another look. In his eyes, the regret echoed my own, reverberating in my chest until I felt like I might crack in two. To cover, I went to rummage through the remaining maps of Hawaii. "That's a dangerous year, with the revolution. And here, look . . . 1895."

Blake came to stand beside me, and when he spoke, his voice was soft. "It has to be before 1892."

"We don't have a map of 1892. You'll have to wait until we reach it on my native timeline—that's nearly six years."

"I can be patient."

Gritting my teeth, I rounded on him. "Why would you join the Wilcox rebellion? Don't you remember? They failed. Seven men died."

"Your book said eight, Miss Song."

I stared at him; he did not flinch. "You think I'll help you martyr yourself?" I said at last. "Now? When I've lost so much?"

"Lost so much because of me."

"Because of you?" Hearing him say it shook something loose in me. "He—he made a choice too, Blake. Don't take that from him."

"And don't take mine from me, Miss Song." For a long time we stood there, eyes locked, but I was the first to turn away. Gently, I slid the map of 1895 back into the cupboard. Then I swallowed, blinking rapidly, focusing on the porthole, the desk—and Crowhurst's flask full of Lethe water, glowing in the golden light of afternoon.

I had not thought to give it to Joss, for it was not half so tempting as the Mnemosyne. Or at least, it hadn't been. I took it up, rubbing my thumb over the warm copper. Then I shook my head and threw it into the cupboard below the desk. "I have time to change your mind."

"You may try, Miss Song."

I shut the cupboard and dashed away my tears with the back of my hand. "Maybe a visit to New York will help. I know how much you liked the city."

"New York?"

"Slate will need his map. The one of 1868. He left it behind when he . . . he left it behind."

"Slate?" Blake stepped closer, hesitant. "You think he survived?"

My heart squeezed like a fist; his words choked me. I closed my eyes and saw my father's face—the smile as he said his last words to me: *I love you, Nixie.* "He dies in 1868, in

Joss's opium den. Not at sea. He was lost, but he survived."

"So we'll wait for him there? In New York?"

"We will. But not forever." I sighed. "There's still something to be said for letting go."

"I agree with you there." Blake smiled a little and put his hat back on his head. He made a little bow on his way out. I shut the door behind him and leaned my head against it.

"Must we lose him too, amira?" Kash had propped himself up on one elbow, and he watched me with sorrow in his green eyes.

Pushing off the door, I sank down beside him on the edge of the bed, gathering one of his hands in mine. "We all have to make our own choices."

Kashmir sighed, brushing my hand against his lips. "Then what's next? After New York?"

"I don't know," I said softly. "But we have time to figure it out."

AUTHOR'S
NOTE

The border between myth and history is less like a line drawn on a map and more like the Margins themselves—uncertain gray areas that shift over time. History is indeed written by the victors—or more accurately, the dominant culture—and even primary documents can be influenced by the worldview of their authors. So in this book, what do we consider myth and what do we agree is history?

MYTHS

KER-YS

When I was looking for a setting for Book Two, I wondered where to go after Paradise. Two choices presented themselves: a utopia or a hell. Ker-Ys is a bit of both.

Ker-Ys itself is a myth, but I based my description of

it loosely on Mont Saint-Michel, an island commune off the coast of France, accessible by a strip of land only exposed by low tide. As noted in the novel, the legend gives different names given for Dahut (or Ahes). In addition, the king's name is alternately given as Gralon, Granlon, or Gradlon (the version "Grand L'Un" is my own invention). Gradlon the Great was a popular hero of many Celtic myths from the fifth century; Saint Guinole (aka Saint Winwaloe) also lived during that time. But the story of Ker-Ys likely originated much later, near the end of the fifteenth century, after which it was told and retold in various different versions, including Emile Souvestre's 1844 *Foyer breton*.

Ker-Ys is not the only lost land in Celtic lore: Lyonesse and Cantr'er Gwaelod are similar legends. Interestingly, during both the fifth and the fifteenth centuries, two geological events took place that might have inspired these stories. Between 400 and 500 A.D., rising sea levels flooded a great island off the Cornish Peninsula, turning it into an archipelago now called the Isles of Scilly. And in the fifteenth century, Europe was under the frozen spell of the Little Ice Age, where glacial expansion lowered sea levels again. These real-life events may have given rise to tales of sunken cities.

THE ORACLE AT BOEOTIA

The story of Trophonius also has several versions. Some say he was a hero, others that he was a demon, still others than he was a god. In one origin story, he and his brother built Apollo's temple at Delphi—in another, the two siblings robbed a king's treasury. The second version is the one I used. Either way, Trophonius disappeared into a cavern at Lebadea to become a chthonic being.

His cavern and his cult were described in detail by Pausanias, the great second-century geographer. Unfortunately, the primary documents were lost, and his words survive only through a fifteenth-century copy filled with errors. Still, the ritual by which petitioners would seek knowledge seems terrifying—so much so that "to descend into the cave of Trophonius" was another way of saying "to be frightened out of one's wits."

After making sacrifices and drinking the sacred waters, one would enter into a narrow hole in the ground, with a feeling akin to being buried alive. There, afraid and alone, the petitioner would be given a glimpse of the future, after which they would be spit out of the earth. The priests would then carry the gibbering victim to the temple and seat him on the Mnemosyne Throne, where his ramblings would be recorded and shaped into prophecy before they were forgotten.

Pausanias also mentioned the two mythic rivers—the Lethe and the Mnemosyne—that bubbled up in springs beside the cavern. Here geography shades to myth; though the Herkyna River is fed by springs in the area, the Lethe and the Mnemosyne are most commonly found in Hades, as in Plato's Myth of Er.

HISTORY

DONALD CROWHURST'S LAST VOYAGE

In 1968, Donald Crowhurst set out from England on a trimaran called *Teignmouth Electron*, in the hopes of winning a single-handed race around the world. At first, he seemed a long shot: his boat was untested, he was competing against much more experienced sailors, and he'd had a string of personal and business failures to date. Still, he was certain he could win—in fact, he *had* to win. His debts left no other option.

Surprisingly, he reported record speeds sailing south toward the Horn and soon became a media darling; after six months, as competitors dropped out of the race through choice or circumstance, he became a sure thing. Welcome parties were planned, grand ceremonies and parades—and an inspection of his logbooks, of course, just to make sure everything was on the level. All of that was set aside when the *Teignmouth Electron* was found drifting in the Sargasso Sea, abandoned without sign of a storm or struggle.

The ship's clock was missing, along with one of his logbooks—likely, the one in which he'd recorded the fake version of his journey: the version where he raced around the world at record-breaking speeds. Review of the books left behind pointed to Crowhurst's probable fate—suicide after eight months of solitude and pressure—though as in any mysterious disappearance, some people are certain he survived.

Either way, his logbooks show a descent into madness and despair, countered by an odd certainty that he had unlocked the secrets of the universe. References to "the game" and becoming a "cosmic being" are taken from those passages. For readers interested in further information, *The Strange Last Voyage of Donald Crowhurst,* by Tomalin and Hall, was invaluable to me.

THE THIRD VOYAGE OF CAPTAIN JAMES COOK

Nearly two hundred years before Crowhurst, another famous mariner set out on his own final voyage. By 1776, Captain James Cook had circumnavigated the globe twice. Hailed as a hero, he'd been made a fellow of the Royal Society and was given an honorary retirement by the royal navy as well as the Copley Gold medal.

Certainly he'd come a long way from his apprenticeship days, and no one would have blamed him for taking his retirement. But something drove him back to sea. Perhaps it was his ambition, which he said led him "not only farther than any man has been before me, but as far as I think it is possible for a man to go." On this voyage, though, Cook went too far.

By all accounts, he'd been a fair and beloved leader, but something changed between his second and third voyages. Though he was greeted warmly upon his arrival in Hawaii, he wore out his welcome rather quickly with his irrational behavior and demands. When a group of frustrated Hawaiians stole one of Cook's small boats, Cook himself marched up to the king of Hawaii and attempted to hold him as ransom for the return of the cutter. The Hawaiians fought back, and Cook was struck and killed in the fray.

What caused the bizarre behavior that led to his death in Kealakekua Bay? One may speculate, though there is no record of a prophecy made by a mysterious woman in the Port of London.

ACKNOWLEDGMENTS

All ships need a good crew—this past year, I've sailed with the best.

My great thanks to Martha Mihalick, for making sure this book is shipshape, stem to stern, through her patience both at the helm and at the holystone. Thanks also to Molly Ker Hawn, without whom the *Temptation* would not have left port.

To the librarians and booksellers, thank you for being real-life Navigators, carrying us magically to places out of myth and history.

Fair winds brought me to the Sweet Sixteens—more real than two pieces of eight (pardon the puns) and worth their weight in gold. Special thanks to Alwyn Hamilton, who, when asked for an emergency critique, swung to the rescue with guns blazing.

I salute the assorted tars, salts, and scalawags who inspire me: here are dragons born. Cristina Das, Elspeth Morris, and Michelle Veazie on art history; Matt Holohan and Tommaso Sciortino on gods and devils; Paul Bruno on fate and free will; Nelson Lugo with all the cards up his sleeves; Fyodor Pavlov for the cut of his jib; Mike Pettry and Allison Posner for their siren song; London Shah for last-minute help, heaven sent.

I'm ever grateful for Jennifer Baker, Bean River Haskell, Brittany of *Brittany's Book Rambles,* Kris of *My Friends are Fiction,* and Rachel of *A Perfection Called Books.* Thank you for ringing the ship's bell for Book One (or were you sounding the alarm?).

To the old salts and sea dogs—Becky Albertalli, Rae Carson, Jodi Meadows, Danielle Paige, Adam Silvera, and Anne Ursu—thank you for sharing your charts of the seas through which I'm now sailing.

My boundless appreciation for the team at Greenwillow, particularly Tim Smith for his weather eye on first watch, Gina Rizzo for flying our flag, and Sylvie Le Floc'h for designing it.

Love and gratitude to my family—Thekla and Duncan, Matt and Lisa, Ken and Cindy, Mom and Dad—for being there under red skies, at night or in the morning.

And always, to Bret and Felix, who buoy me up.

READ ON FOR:

Alternate endings to
The Ship Beyond Time

An excerpt from *For a Muse of Fire*,
the first book in a new trilogy by Heidi Heilig

THE SHIP BEYOND TIME

ALTERNATE ENDINGS

Scene: Author Heidi Heilig's and editor Martha Mihalick's respective desks and computers.

Heidi: Okay. Deep breath. One-two-three SEND. [clicks.]

Martha: Hooray! I can't wait to read it!

ALTERNATE ENDING NUMBER ONE

As dawn struggled through the shroud of gray, it gleamed on the oily banks of the River Thames. Ships were already loading in the busy Port of London, and the gritty air echoed with the shouts and raucous laughter of dockhands.

Cook had left the ship nearly a week ago, his face troubled; though he never said why, I could have guessed. Even the fastest modern ships took more than an hour to make the crossing. He had muttered something about the powerful winds, the strength of the storm, the unnatural fog. I'd nodded and responded with some dull nonsense about the speed of the ship.

Blake had said not a word to the man the whole journey, but

when James reached the gangplank, his hand shot out to grab Cook's wrist. "Your first two voyages will earn you fame and fortune. You'll be hailed as a champion, greeted like a god. But your third voyage will curse an entire race, and you with them."

James shook him off and pushed past him with an odd look. Then he vanished into the crowd on the wharf without looking back. I did not see him again, although later that day, I watched the *Friendship* sail.

He must have made it aboard. After all, I was still here. For better or for worse.

The repairs to the hull had taken us four days, but that wasn't all that had been broken. I'd spent the entire week poring not over maps, but over Crowhurst's logbooks. The notes were a mess in that ugly handwriting, jumping from topic to topic mid-sentence. He'd done so much research, and so much speculation, and all of it was jumbled together, interspersed with mundane observations about the wind or the currents, and some truly awful poetry about life at sea and melancholy. But there must be something. There had to be *something*.

A knock at the door interrupted my study. I slammed the book shut and blinked, light-headed. When had I last eaten?

I glanced at the scattered coffee cups on the desk, all of them cold, none of them more than half full. They couldn't have been from today.

I rubbed my hand on my forehead and took a deep breath; the smell of smoke and dung—the scent of a city before the Industrial Revolution—had permeated everything aboard. Then the knock came again. "What?"

The door opened; there was Blake, standing on the threshold. My entire body tensed; I hadn't talked to him since we'd left Ker-Ys. I didn't know what to say. The only words that came to mind were vile things, but it was only the ugly scum over a deep well of despair. Still, here he was, at my door, and he did not speak, so I did. "What do you want?"

He spun the hat as I waited for an answer. "I want to go," he said at last.

"Go where?"

"Home."

"Home?" I snorted. "Where's that?"

"Not here, Miss Song. I have no place aboard your ship."

"My ship." The words were bitter. I couldn't look at him any longer; I smoothed my hand over the blue cover of the logbook. My fingers were smudged with ink and oil and god knows what; under my thumbnail, was that blood? "You want to go back to Hawaii? They'll recognize you from the theft."

"Not if we give it a decade or so. Your—you have a map from 1892."

Something about the way he said it—his tone, too casual—made me take another look. In his eyes, the guilt echoed my own. In his hands, the hat—Kashmir's hat. My heart squeezed like a fist, choking me; I could barely force out the words. "That's a dangerous year, with the revolution. I have another map of Hawaii from 1895."

His jaw tightened. "It has to be 1892."

"Why would you join the Wilcox rebellion?" I stood, throwing my pen on the table; it rattled off a coffee cup and rolled onto a map. "Don't you remember? They failed. Seven men died."

"Your book said eight."

I stared at him; he did not flinch. For a long time we stood there, eyes locked; I turned away first. "No."

"No?"

"No." I went back to my desk. "You think I'll help you martyr yourself? Now? When I've lost so much?"

"Lost so much because of me."

"Because of you," I echoed, digging my words into his guilt and feeling the wound in me. It was not his fault—not all his fault—but I could not lose him, too. "You owe me."

"And what is the payment?" he asked softly.

"You're a cartographer, Blake. I need you." I picked up the map on my desk: New York, 2016, the lines inked in red, finished only a day after we'd left. "Tell the crew to make ready. We're leaving."

His brows dove together. "Where are we bound?"

"New York. Dahut's version." I went to the cupboards to pull another map—my father's, and Blake's father's—Honolulu, 1868. "I need to leave something there for Slate if he . . . when he comes back."

"Leave something?"

"With Bruce."

"But . . . that's your father's native time." He stepped closer, hesitant. "Why not wait for him? If he survived the storm, won't he appear there?"

If.

It seemed Joss has been right after all. If she was, I had to close the loop. Slate would need the map of 1868 someday. Hopefully after a long life with Lin—the life he deserved to share with her. The life Crowhurst had stolen.

But if not—if Joss had only made some lucky guesses—if he'd gone over the wall and that was the end . . . .

I didn't want to know.

I swallowed, blinking rapidly, focusing on the desk, the coffee cups. Composure returned, as slow as an ebb tide. I'd have to tidy up before we sailed. And we did need to sail soon. New York was only a pit stop. "I don't have time to wait around."

Blake's jaw worked, and he spun that hat; I wanted to rip it out of his hands. Instead, I turned back to the desk, trying without much success to organize the mess. I stacked the cups carefully, making sure they didn't spill on the books on the desk—the logbook, and the slender volume that held the myth of Ker-Ys.

The story hadn't ended correctly. Crowhurst was dead—so someone had to ride away on the dark horse. His question had stayed with me; he had taken Kashmir's lock picks, but where had his keys gone? The key to the treasury, the key to the manacles, the key to the yacht. Kashmir had to be alive.

And in my mind's eye, I saw the crabbed script unrolling, crawling across the page like ants after crumbs—Crowhurst's plans, not to find a place, but to find a person. *Find him, find him, find him. . . .*

His plans, and my father's—now mine. How to explain it to Blake? When I'd taken my father's place, I'd claimed my birthright?

Then my eyes fell on the flask, glowing in the yellow light. It was still a third full; I'd checked every day for the past week.

"Miss Song—"

"And take those cups to the galley when you go."

He put the hat back on his head and gathered the mugs in silence, but even with his hands full, he lingered, watching me. "How long will you be needing my services?"

I rubbed my thumb over the warm copper. Then I dropped the flask back on the desk. "Until he's home."

Martha: HEIDI. HEIDI, WHAT HAVE YOU DONE TO KASH.

Heidi [getting more and more animated]: See it's metaphorical, she has to lose him like her father lost his wife! She'll go on searching forever, having learned NOTHING from her trials, because all of us are actually doomed to repeat the sins of our fathers in one big endless time loop!

Martha: But . . . but it's the final book and you ended it on a cliffhanger! Is Nix going to find Kash? I AM WORRIED ABOUT KASH ALL ALONE OUT THERE.

Heidi: As the reader should be! See? It works on so many levels!

Martha:: But . . . could it be a happier ending, maybe? You can't leave your readers like this.

One week later . . .

Heidi: Yeah, I think maybe I needed to eat something. How about this one?

ALTERNATE ENDING NUMBER TWO

Honolulu, 1855

Stepping through the door of Joss's shop, I was surprised by the tinkling chime of tiny bells.

That wasn't the only thing that was different. The last time I'd been here was thirty years in the future. In 1885, the shop had been a faded apothecary crouched over a hidden opium den. In those days, the air had been redolent with the sickly sweet smell of pipe smoke, and the wooden shelves lining the walls were sagging, heavy with boxes and jars of pills and powders, all covered in a thin layer of dust.

But here and now, everything was still new. The shop was lovingly kept—swept and dusted. The windows were thrown open to catch the warm trade winds. The red counter shone—freshly lacquered—and the woman behind it was startlingly young, though the gleam in her pebble-black eyes was the same as it always would be.

If I hadn't already known who she was, I would have been able to guess; she stood there holding a cup of tea, looking so much like Lin. And the look on her face made it clear she recognized me, too—though not for the same reason. The last time she'd seen me was at the helm of the ship, when I'd Navigated to the tomb where she'd been buried alive and left a map for her there: a map of Honolulu.

That was a few months ago for me; perhaps six years ago for her. I watched her piece together the memories—they fell into place behind her eyes like stones into a deep well. But after the shock wore off, her smile dazzled me. "Welcome." Her voice was like music, softly accented. "How to pay for a life saved?"

I smiled back. "I'd love some tea."

Joss bowed deeply, folding herself like a fan. Then she ducked down under the counter and drew out another cup. She took leaves from a jar on the shelf behind her, and poured the water from a pot resting on a stone on the counter. The fragrant, bitter scent filled the air. I took the cup, and she refilled her own, watching me with those bird bright eyes. "I didn't know if I would ever see you again," she said at last.

How much did she already know? And how much could I tell her? I tested the tea—it was hot, but not scalding—and chose my answer carefully: an echo of her own future words to me. "You will, though this is the last time I'll see you."

"Then let me thank you now, while I can. After all," she added, her eyes twinkling. "Who can know what the future holds?"

I laughed—I couldn't help it—and I realized then, to my

surprise, that I liked her. I was still turning over that thought when a small girl ran giggling through the open door.

She skidded to a stop in front of me, schooling her expression, but her eyes still twinkled. Under her long black hair, was that the glint of golden scales? My heart thundered in my chest as she gave me a once-over. "Hello."

"Hi." The word barely made it past my lips. I tried again. "Hello."

She made a little bow. Then she turned carefully to slip past me, pelting again toward the back of the shop and clattering down the stairs.

When she was gone, I turned back to Joss. She was watching me closely, measuring my every move. "Why have you come?" she said softly.

My throat was dry; I drained the tea. Could I tell her the truth? "I had to," I said at last. "You told me I would."

"Is that the only reason?"

"No." My palms felt slick; I set the cup down on the counter, lest I drop it. "I . . . I . . . recently, I . . . ." The words stuck in my throat—I could not get them past my lips. But if I could not say them, how would she know? I tried to gather the words, but then she spoke.

"You lost someone." I blinked at her—but Joss was

looking down at the tea leaves at the bottom of my cup. She turned the cup around in her hands. "Someone you loved," she added then, looking up through her lashes. "Lost at sea."

I couldn't help it—tears welled up in my eyes. All I could do was nod. She lowered her own eyes and set the cup back down on the counter. The silence stretched. "I have a gift," I said at last, slipping my hand into my pocket and drawing out a little satchel.

Joss took the bag and plucked at the drawstrings. "For me?"

"For Lin—well. For Swag, actually."

Joss tipped the bag out; pearls spilled into her palm. "Swag?"

"The dragon on her shoulders. That's . . . that's his name."

"I see." She poured the pearls back into the pouch. "I'll tell her so."

"Tell her something else for me, would you?" The words came out in a rush—I couldn't have stopped them if I tried.

"What is it?"

"Tell her to make the most of the time she has." I straightened up, adjusting my hat, and went to the door. "Thank you for the tea."

As I walked through the streets of old Honolulu, the sound of the bells stayed with me all the way back to the ship.

Martha: Well, that's happier, but maybe still not quite right?

Heidi: Too long? It's too long, isn't it. It kind of drags. But I like how it references the fortune-telling and the tea and the sense of family and ancestry. But it drags. How about this one?

ALTERNATE ENDING NUMBER THREE

Honolulu, 1886

I wait in the smoldering rubble of what was once Chinatown. The air is thick with smoke; it writhes and dances above the charred earth like the souls of the damned. It's been nearly two years since I was last here—I did not have a map of the time and place. Instead I had waited, and traveled, counting the hours that had passed on my timeline.

I hadn't been far off. We'd made anchor ten days ago on the north side of the island, just in case anyone was still looking for the black caravel that had escaped into the mist all those months ago. The crew had enjoyed the rest as I'd watched the mountains, waiting for the thick gout of black smoke that signaled the start of the fire.

The hike over the mountains had taken me only a day and a half. I could have pushed myself, but there was no reason to arrive before the fire was out. And Kashmir had admonished me to be careful—very careful.

He'd become even more attentive in the last few months. He'd wanted to come along, of course, but I'd asked him to stay with Blake. In the time since we'd left Ker-Ys, I had forgiven him, too, and I had hoped he'd forgiven himself. After all, it had to happen. But when we had returned to Hawaii after so long away, he drank in the island like a parched man, and I didn't want him jumping ship to slake his thirst by drowning in it.

And so I wait alone in the rubble. Adjusting the shawl over my face, I breathe through the fabric. The acrid smell nauseates me, and it can't be good for my health. Still, I wait—I have to—and soon enough, she steps out of the bleary air.

A young woman—only a few years older than me. In her slender hands, she holds a map, and she looks around with sharp eyes, black as pebbles, as though she's never seen the place before.

She hasn't.

She is far too pale to be a local, and she wears a very traditional silk cheongsam. Under the wide belt, her belly curves, soft and ripe as a peach. My hand goes to my own belly—an unconscious gesture. At the motion, she sees me through the mist. I clear my throat to speak. "Joss?"

She stares at me for a long moment, and then she smiles, and I am surprised by how much it means, to know she recognizes me.

But she only speaks Chinese, and I do not—not the way she does, liquid and steeped in years. I only lift my hand—in it, a slip of paper. Chinese characters dance across the page. I had it copied from the picture I'd taken of the captain's tattoo.

She takes it and tucks it into her belt, still watching me. I surprise us both by throwing my arms around her neck, hugging her tight.

And then I turn and stride away through the smoke, and I do not look back.

Martha: Almost . . .
Heidi: You know what, let's just go back to the first one and make it happier. Wait, isn't that what you said initially?
Martha: Do you think Kash should be in the ending?
Heidi: Yes. YES. Brilliant. That's what I was thinking all along, really. It's genius. I'M genius.

END SCENE

FOR A MUSE of FIRE

A young woman with a dangerous power she barely understands. A smuggler with secrets of his own. A country torn between a merciless colonial army, a terrifying tyrant, and a feared rebel leader. The first book in a new trilogy from the acclaimed Heidi Heilig is an engrossing journey that weaves magic, simmering romance, and the deep bonds of family with the high stakes of epic adventure.

The most thrilling moments in life are when everything comes together.

The delicious chords when harmony joins melody. The way a scrap of leather, a shaft of light, and a clever player can make a shadow come alive. Or the roar of an audience after a show—when they become a creature with many heads and one heart.

Sefondre, the Aquitans call it—to coalesce. I love that word. Madame Audrinne once used it to describe our performance as she toasted us in the parlor of her plantation. I've remembered it ever since.

Will it happen tonight at La Fête des Ombres? The signs are promising. The weather is holding clear—just right for the outdoor stages. Papa's voice is rich and steady as it floats through our roulotte's carved scrollwork; he is singing a story song as he drives. Beside him on the bench, maman keeps perfect time on the thom. Inside, I direct the little shadow play that flickers on the silken scrim that makes up one side of our roulotte. A thick stack of flyers lays beside me, ready to tout tonight's show. And I'm wearing my best costume—a scarlet wrap with ruffled edges, a red silk shawl draped artfully over the rippled scar on my shoulder, and a striped corset in a nod to Aquitan fashion. My dark hair is swept into a twist, the stray ends patted down with a touch of oil, my eyes smudged with bone black and my lips with lucky red. A perfect picture for the Aquitans in the audience: local color, foreign polish.

Everything is nearly perfect. All except for the ghost of a kitten who won't stop pouncing on my fantouches.

I don't know where she came from, or where her body is. The little uhane must have crept into our roulotte after we stopped for a quick meal on the edge of town— tempted by our food, no doubt. Then again, does it matter why or where? There is no shortage of spirits in Chakrana. The more pressing question is, how can I get her to leave?

Being easily distracted is one of the tamest parts of my malheur, and I can't afford any distractions tonight. Not at La Fête des Ombres.